Praise for the Novels of Lorraine López

The Realm of Hungry Spirits

"A humorous, often raucous story...THE REALM OF HUNGRY SPIRITS is, first and foremost, a spiritual journey; one that leads a good soul toward a life-changing discovery."

—Judith Ortiz Cofer, author of *Call Me Maria*

"This warm comic novel is trademark Lorraine López: gritty, true, hilarious, wise, moving—all the good things."

—Joy Castro, author of *The Truth Book*

"With her deft and pitch-perfect prose, López has created a wickedly funny and warmly empathetic tale of life in contemporary America. THE REALM OF HUNGRY SPIRITS is the work of one of our finest literary artists."

—Lynn Pruett, author *Ruby River*

"Brilliantly written...at once profound, intelligent, deeply spiritual, and laugh-out-loud funny. It gives a unique look into the varied and complex spiritual life of the Latino community."

—Daniel Chacón, award-winning author of
Unending Rooms

The Gifted Gabaldón Sisters

"A beautifully written, zesty family chronicle, *The Gifted Gabaldón Sisters* covers over a century of women's lives, pieced together like a Southwest quilt."

—Teresa de la Caridad Doval, author of
A Girl Like Che Guevara

"Reminiscent of the novels of Cristina Garcia and Sandra Cisneros, López's book presents a lively, loving Latino family. Highly recommended."

—*Library Journal*

"López establishes herself as an excellent storyteller with this multilayered tale of sisterhood, growing up, self-awareness, and honoring history."

—*Publishers Weekly*

"It has been a long time since I have cared for the characters of a novel as much as I care for the Gabaldón sisters. Their individual perspectives and personalities are woven together to create a three-dimensional world full of promise in spite of the daily obstacles familiar to us all. Lorraine López moves effortlessly between humor and heartache, opening us up to the possibility that what seems coincidental is truly magical."

—Blas Falconer, author of *The Perfect Hour*

"Enchanting."

—*Good Housekeeping*

"*The Gifted Gabaldón Sisters* is about secrets and lies, dramas and scandals, big losses and deep resentments—the very stuff that makes life worth living. It's been a long time since I've encountered such a rambunctious and motley bunch of characters. And in López's hands, through her finely calibrated prose, they lift off the page with dignity and soul, and she makes you root and ache for each of them until the very end."

—Alex Espinoza, author of *Still Water Saints*

"This lyrical story is cleverly told…López folds in rich Pueblo Indian and Mexican American traditions and creates a loving, flawed, and interesting family that will entrance readers."

—*Booklist*

"Delightful...A new favorite author has been found."
—ReaderViews.com

"Magical."
—*Vanderbilt Magazine*

"Charming."
—*Latina Magazine*

"A master short-story writer and novelist."
—*Defining Trends Magazine*

"*Unique*...rich and believable."
—Unadorned Book Reviews
(unadorned-book.blogspot.com)

The Realm of Hungry Spirits

Lorraine López

GRAND CENTRAL
PUBLISHING

NEW YORK   BOSTON

LARGE PRINT EDITION

This book is a work of fiction. Names, characters, places, and incidents are the product of the author's imagination or are used fictitiously. Any resemblance to actual events, locales, or persons, living or dead, is coincidental.

Copyright © 2011 by Lorraine M. López
All rights reserved. Except as permitted under the U.S. Copyright Act of 1976, no part of this publication may be reproduced, distributed, or transmitted in any form or by any means, or stored in a database or retrieval system, without the prior written permission of the publisher.

Grand Central Publishing
Hachette Book Group
237 Park Avenue
New York, NY 10017
www.HachetteBookGroup.com

Printed in the United States of America

First Edition: May 2011
10 9 8 7 6 5 4 3 2 1

Grand Central Publishing is a division of Hachette Book Group, Inc.
The Grand Central Publishing name and logo is a trademark of Hachette Book Group, Inc.

Library of Congress Cataloging-in-Publication Data
López, Lorraine
    The realm of hungry spirits / Lorraine López.—1st ed.
        p. cm.
    Summary: "Marina Lucero appreciates peace and order. Unfortunately the people around her do not."—Provided by publisher.
    ISBN 978-0-446-54963-9 (hc) / 978-1-4555-9894-6 (lp)
    1. Hispanic Americans—Fiction. I. Title.
    PS3612.O635R43 2011
    813'.6—dc22   2010022243

*For my sister Debra Ann López,
who—despite often disappointing
results—never fails to inspire me through
the example of her life to be a more loving,
generous, and forgiving woman, a woman
with abundant faith in others.*

The weak-minded choose to hate. . . . It's the least painful thing to do.
   —*Yiyun Li*

The Realm of Hungry Spirits

Chapter One

First thing this morning, the phone's screaming its head off, and I can't find the stupid thing anywhere, so I'm wandering around in my empire-waist, lime nightgown, still half in a dream, like some dazed Josephine, minus her Napoleon. Has my nephew Kiko fallen asleep with it on the couch again? I flip a small plaid blanket off his lumpish, snoring form. Nope, not there. Kiko wrenches the flannel throw over his shoulder and flops on his side, turning his immense back to me. At least he's cut out the snoring. But the kid suffers from this sleep apnea thing. He ceases breathing every so often, like just now, and it's spooky. What if he croaks, right here? On my sectional sofa? Then he sucks in a wet, rattling breath, and I'm relieved, but kind of let down, too, in a weird way. I mean, at twenty-three, Kiko's only ten years younger than me. He still has a ways to go. Does he plan to spend the next fifty or sixty years of his life sleeping on my couch?

I glance at my kid sister's ex-boyfriend Reggie, passed out on the nearby love seat. Maybe *he* left the phone in the kitchen, which would be convenient. I could stand a cup of coffee. As I'm gristing the beans for a stiff espresso, a-*ha!* I notice one of the blackened bananas in the bowl on top of the fridge is actually the receiver. Of course, by now it's stopped ringing: my goal all along. I have no more desire to find out who's pestering me this early than I'd want to coochy-coo the rooster next door—a onelegged veterano rescued from the cockfights—that started shrieking just before five, driving me to wad my pillow into my ears.

I'm up for good now, and kind of enjoying the warmth of the linoleum on my bare feet. Summer mornings, this little rental house in Sylmar almost feels like a living body, pulsing with mild heat, expanding and contracting with the sleepy breathing of its occupants. But by afternoon, forget it, it's hotter here than inside a casket hurtling deep into the caverns of hell. Luckily, my backyard abuts the Angeles National Forest and corners of it, shaded by citrus trees and deep in the shadows of the pine and fir trees covering the foothills, stay as dark and cool as it is inside a well.

I'm humming to myself, dribbling water onto the

potted cactus and aloe plants, wiping the ceramic Buddhas, and straightening a framed snapshot of Gandhi on the windowsill, when the phone starts in again. I clear my throat and snatch the receiver from the banana bowl. "What's up?"

"Marina? Marina, is that you?" a sort of familiar male voice says.

"Yeah, who's this?"

"It's Nestor, Nestor Pérez, Rudy's friend."

Ah, yes, Nestor, my ex-boyfriend's old buddy, a Cubano, some kind of Santeria priest, a babalawo, who moved to Florida a few years ago. But he must be seriously out of touch with the orishas if he thinks he can find Rudy at my house these days. "Rudy's not here. We broke up about five months ago, back in February." I spoon ground coffee into the filter and fill the chamber from the tap. "Are you in LA?"

"Nah, I'm in Miami, and I ain't looking for Rudy. I want to talk to you."

"Yeah?" I press the on button on the espresso machine and make my way back into the living room. The machine clamors like a diesel engine once it gets going, making it impossible to hear a thing in the kitchen. It's only slightly less deafening in the living room, too, though this hardly wakes Kiko and Reggie.

No question Nestor hears the thing. He starts

shouting into the phone, "I want to do you a limpieza, you know, clean the evil spirits out of tu casa!"

Now, I've heard about this kind of thing before, so I'm wondering if he's lost his mind. The ceremony involves some kind of domesticated animal sacrifice. I picture goat blood pooling on my linty green carpet. And don't limpiezas cost a fortune? Nestor used to brag about what he charges, and I remember thinking it'd be cheaper (and more worthwhile) to have the house painted professionally. "No thanks. Don't need one," I say. He must have fallen on real hard times, if he's telemarketing his buddies' ex-girlfriends.

"Nah, man, listen, *everybody* needs a limpieza, or the evil spirits just keep on accumulating and bringing all kinds of harm and shit."

I glance from Kiko, stop-and-start snoring on one couch, to Reggie, sprawled on the love seat with his thin, hairy legs dangling over the armrest like some lifeless insect's appendages. My nephew Kiko moved in when my older sister and her live-in boyfriend "tough-loved" him out of their house, and Reggie, his best friend, started staying over here after my youngest sister broke off their engagement, and he lost his job, car, apartment, the works. At the time, I was sorry for both of them, and feeling the sharp edge of breakup loneliness myself, I let them stay, thinking it would be at most a few days. But months have passed. And last week my neighbor Carlotta, who has run away from her bruto of a husband and three ignoramus teenage sons, moved into my guest room, after her baby—the thirteen-year-old—gave her a black eye.

"To be honest with you," I tell Nestor now, thinking evil spirits are *not* what I need cleared out of my house, "that kind of thing's not part of my culture, and no way do I have the money for it."

Carlotta's coppery curls emerge from the hall-way, followed by her girlish form, clad in a yellow nightie. She's lugging a basket of laundry, but she sees me on the phone and freezes, her hazel eyes wide and unblinking.

"Absolutely free. You understand?" Nestor says, sounding like one of those radio announcers offe-ring deep discounts on "pre-owned" vehicles. "I'm not going to charge you nothing."

I shake my head to clear my ears. Maybe I'm not hearing too well. "Let me get this straight—you want to do it for no money. I don't pay a penny."

"You got it."

"*Why?*" Knowing Nestor as I do, or any of Ru-dy's scheming friends for that matter, I have no doubt there's a catch of some kind.

"Es que, I had this dream about you, mujer, a nightmare with fiery lizards and poison toads. I can't tell it all. Me dió tanto susto that I woke up with two white hairs in my moustache. I could see, in this dream, that you're facing una tragedia, a terrible loss and a tremendous challenge, una lucha tan larga, that I says to myself, Nestor, you got to do something. I tossed the cowries, and you don't even want to *know* what I—"

"You can do a limpieza long distance from Miami?"

"Nah, man, I'll *fly* out there, and I ain't going to charge the airfare neither 'cause I'm heading out tomorrow for my cousin's wedding on Saturday, plan to spend a couple weeks in LA, so it's totally free."

"Who is it?" Carlotta whispers.

I cup the mouthpiece as Nestor explains all he plans to do in order to perform my limpieza, punctuating every sentence with "free of charge." "It's Nestor, Rudy's friend, the babalawo," I tell her. "He wants to do a limpieza here at the house."

Carlotta's face relaxes, but then she curls her upper lip. "*Ugh*—goat blood." She hefts the basket into the kitchen, where I keep the washer.

"Look, Nestor," I say when he finally pauses for breath. "I don't want a limpieza, not even a free one. I'm good the way things are." In truth,

I'm not too worried about evil-spirit buildup. At least these dark forces keep quiet. They don't break up with people on Valentine's Day or lose their jobs and come running to my house to stay for months. They never smell like foot funk or leave deep body impressions on my sectional cushions. I can't accuse them of smearing hair gel on my throw pillows. They have yet to use up all the hot water or borrow any of my major appliances, and they have not once disturbed my deep, delicious sleep. Even the wickedest of evil spirits would be a huge improvement over the neighbors' rooster.

Nestor assures me I will change my mind, and I tell him that I have to get ready for work.

"I thought you teachers were off in the summer."

"Ever hear of summer school?" I say, vaguely wondering how Nestor knows I'm a teacher now. He probably called Rudy earlier, made him the first offer of a free limpieza. To be polite, I cast about in my memory for Nestor's wife's name and reel up a possibility. "Hey, how's Dixie doing? And the kids?"

"You mean *Daisy*? Ah, you know women. They see someone has something, and they want it. She's bugging to get a job now, put the baby in preschool. She got all these gabacha ideas from her stupid friends."

"There are worse ideas to get," I say, thinking of my ex-boyfriend Rudy's former wife, Dolores, whose body was found right around Christmastime some years back, slumped on a bench in Echo Park, both arms so riddled with needle marks she looked like she had a flesh-eating disease. "Listen, I've got to go, or I'll be late."

"A'ight, that's cool. I'm going to give you my cell number, so call me when you change your mind. Just remember, this offer expires in a few days."

"I doubt I'll change my mind."

"Write it down anyway, okay? And I'm going to give you my website, too. You should check it out."

Amazed that Nestor has a website, I pretend to write everything down and finally hang up, replacing the phone, for once, in its cradle, which sits on a wooden bookcase near the love seat. The books are dust-furred, and the plum-colored love seat looks faded under a fine sifting of grit. Carlotta rattles the dishes piled in the sink, no doubt searching for a coffee cup to rinse out. Far be it from her to fill the basin with hot water, squirt in some dish soap, and actually wash a few plates. If Nestor could do a true limpieza in this house—one that involved pine-scented disinfectant, scouring powder, and furniture polish—

then, no problem, I'd certainly be down for that. I would even pay.

At Olive Branch Middle School, I teach English as a Second Language to eighth graders on an emergency teaching credential, which means I finished my bachelor of arts degree, but not the certification program yet. Since the district is so hard up for Chicana teachers, they went ahead and hired me anyway. Before last year, I worked in an insurance office, processing claims by day and taking courses at night to finish my degree. I was the bona fide vieja in all of my classes, the one-and-only over thirty. I'd hunch over my desk in the back, sweating pupusas, trying to write down everything the professor said, and pretending not to notice the cutting looks from stringy nineteen-year-old girls in low-rise skinny jeans and the snickering of bullet-headed punks with their 'chones hanging halfway out their pants. It was all worth it, more than worth it, not to face another day in my fluorescent tomb of a cubicle, not to deal with the liars, lunatics, hypochondriacs, and assorted nitwit opportunists who view a crumpled fender as a winning lottery ticket. People are not at their best, usually, just after car theft or collision. They can be pretty frazzled, irritated, shocked, or depressed. But more and more these days, they're gleeful, nearly smacking their lips with greed. And seeing this kind of thing daily creates a low-down and guilty feeling in a person, just by association.

At Olive Branch, these people, my students, *are* at their best, likely the best they'll ever be. They're fresh-faced, strong, healthy, hopeful, and eager— even the overweight and pimply kids have such promise. I want to take each one aside and say, *Stop a minute and enjoy this before it's too late. You will never feel so good in your lives. It is total bullshit about life experience and wisdom making up for what you will lose from here on out.* Of course, they'd never buy it. No one wants to believe that kind of thing. So I have to content myself with enjoying their great good fortune, however brief it is, in a secondhand way, while I'm at the middle school.

This summer, I'm teaching two reading classes— one beginning and the other advanced—on weekday mornings. For the beginners, I basically teach these fairy tales that are written in very simple English. For the advanced class, I picked out a book I thought would appeal to the students, a slender novel called *The Incredible Journey*. It has a picture of two dogs with a cat on the cover, and how could I resist? I figured, hey, kids like animals, especially dogs, so I ordered a set, not realizing how tough the thing would be. The vocabulary is what's *really* incredible about this book. I'm lunging for the dictionary at least half a dozen times with each chapter. Words like *sybaritic, somnolent,* and *hermetic* are all over the place. I guess *my* vocabulary's improving, and *that's* something, but in the meantime, I'm sweating all over again, just like in college, trying to rewrite the book, so I can crack the code for the middle schoolers and translate the words into plain English.

Today, after wrestling the high diction all morning and getting my butt whipped, I slink over to the office to pick up my mail and messages before heading home. I'm planning to cruise by Stop & Shop for a six-pack of beer. I'm craving some Kirin or Asahi, one of those clean, potent Japanese beers, with my nice solitary lunch of leftover grilled salmon out in the backyard. But there's a yellow slip in my cubby hole—until now I hadn't even noticed that I must have left my cell phone at home or else it's been swallowed up into the recesses of my trickster of a purse—a phone message from Leticia, my ex-boyfriend's daughter. *Come to the hospital right away*, someone, likely a student assistant, has scrawled in the message box. *Oh, shit*, I say, but silently because I'm in the office, and now that I'm a teacher, I have to cut back on the audible cursing while on school grounds. Wish I could moan it out loud though.

*   *   *

Just over six months ago, Letty and her husband, Miguel, had a baby boy, but he was born with a congenital disease, hypoparathyroidism, the doctors at Manzanita Vista Hospital said, after weeks of poking and prodding and testing. I know what this is now because I wrote the word down in a spiral-bound tablet I carry with me, so I could look it up on one of the school computers in the media center. But back then, when the baby was born, nobody knew a thing. We all thought he was fine. Rudy and I were together at the time, and I was even in the delivery room with Letty and Miguel when the baby popped out, though I hate the sight of blood and gore, slimy placentas and whatnot. It was a long, gross labor and delivery, but the baby seemed fine when he finally slithered out, a wet, rubbery thing with two lungs full of attitude. All of us sobbed. Even the midwife and nurse got a little damp eyed. Then I had to rush out and find Rudy, who was puffing Marlboros in the parking lot, to give him the good news. The baby looked to be in great shape: eight pounds, twenty-two inches long, red-faced, strong, and vocal. Rudy was especially proud because Letty and Miguel decided—after some heavy-duty campaigning on Rudy's part—to name their boy Rodolfo, after his abuelo.

But after six weeks, the little guy wasn't gaining much weight. It's shitty to say, but I secretly questioned Letty's decision to return to work, managing the food counter at Kmart, too soon and leaving him with Rosaura, Miguel's cranky old mother, without a second thought. *Failure to thrive*, the doctor said at the twelve-week visit. The bruja probably kept him locked in a closet all day, I thought, but I was also noticing his crooked crying, the left side of his lip dipping down, like it was being yanked by some unseen hook, and he cried *all* the time. Back and forth to the clinic and then to the hospital they went—usually hauling me along to talk to the doctors, translate the medical jargon into words they could understand. Again, I was sweating, papayas this time, and trying to copy everything down. *Cystic fibrosis*, they first said, then, after the salt test, no, not *cystic fibrosis*, but *hypocalcemia, diabetes mellitus, renal insufficiency, neurodegeneration*. In the media center, I looked each word up twice—Google and then Yahoo, though they led to the same websites. Despite this, I kept hoping to come up with different explanations or newer articles with groundbreaking discoveries. Nothing I found changed what I've known for weeks, which is what the doctors know and what Letty, Miguel, and even Rudy—wherever he is now—don't want to face at all.

At the hospital, I find Letty at the nurses' station, tapping her car keys on the counter. She keeps saying, "Can't you *do* something?" The nurses shuffle about uneasily, shifting file sleeves around and trading glances. It's impossible to find my bright and beautiful Letty, the eager-faced little girl I helped raise from the time she was nine years old, in this thin, tense young woman, tapping at the counter. With her unwashed hair and dark-ringed eyes, she looks more like an escapee from an institution for the criminally insane than the warm, funny girl I like to pretend is my own daughter. "He's all bloated," she says now to the nurses, her voice high and strained. "He can't even move his head. There's got to be something you can do to drain him out."

I call her name, and she rushes at me, nearly knocking me over.

Her thin arms encircle my rib cage, squeezing me so tightly it's hard to breathe. "He looks awful, Marina," she says in my ear, her breath hot and stale. "I can't stand to see him like this." Letty pulls away and searches my face, her fingers now digging painfully into my upper arms. "You *have* to help me!"

With these words, I remember the time I had to drive to the courthouse in San Fernando to pay Letty's bail after she was caught shoplifting a silk blouse from Neiman Marcus. She'd just turned seventeen and she was terrified her father would find out, so I was the one she called. "You *have* to help me!" I thought it was one of the worst things we'd ever face. Until now, I had no idea how easy it was to stroll into the courtroom, slap a serious look on my face, listen to the judge, and afterward, calmly write out a check. I actually *could* help my girl. But that was nothing compared to this.

"Okay, m'ija. It's okay. I'm here," I say, knowing full well there's little, if anything, I can do to help her now. "Let's go see the baby, all right?"

Before we leave the nurses' station, I give them a look, draw out my tablet, and say, "Please call the doctor." I'm gratified when the pudgy one at the desk lifts a receiver. I wish I'd known about the power of the writing pad when I had my miscarriages, that horrible time not two years ago.

Manzanita Vista Hospital is kind of a dump since the last earthquake. Overhead, you can see aluminum ducts, wires, and pink tufts of fiberglass insulation where the plaster has fallen out in chunks, but at least the children's wing is repaired and freshly painted with bright murals of circus scenes. Dancing elephants, balloon-bearing clowns, and flying trapeze artists scroll past as we make our way to little Rudy. The baby shares an aquamarine room with a six-year-old girl who has leukemia and a big family of mustachioed men and plump women who crowd around her bed, talking quietly whenever I come to visit. I imagine they are always there, eternally ringed around that bald kid, speaking in hushed tones like they're in church.

Poor baby Rudy has to take what he can get, visitorwise, as Letty continues to work, though she's cut back on her hours. Miguel has a full-time job laying and repairing pipe for the city, and he's doubled up on his Narcotics Anonymous meetings in his free time. And my ex—the *namesake*—forget about it. That useless fool can't be bothered with anything the slightest bit difficult or unpleasant. He hopped a plane to Santo Domingo as soon as we knew the baby's condition was serious. No one knows when or even *if* he'll be back.

"Buenos dias," I say to the quiet folks and the dying girl.

"Buenos," they murmur in unison without lifting their eyes to meet mine.

"Look at him." Letty points to the baby flat on his back in the hospital crib. "He can't even move."

Edema, I remember this from my previous notes, *fluid retention*. His stunted body looks inflated, like some grotesque balloon, the hospital band biting into his swollen wrist, but he's not crying. His face is calm, his puffy eyelids fluttering, as though he's lofting about in some gentle dream. "He looks peaceful." I touch his bunched and mottled fist, silky and warm as a puppy's belly.

"Don't say that." Letty wheels on me, her sour-smelling hair whipping her cheeks. "That's what they say at funerals."

The door swings open, and I'm impressed with the power of my writing tablet, but it's just Rudy, deeply tanned from the island, even wearing new sunglasses. I haven't seen him for months. My heart pitches against my ribs like some trapped, panicky bird. *Arrhythmia?* Immediately, I regret the loose blue blouse I threw on over black slacks that morning and bunching my long hair into a plastic clip. Rudy used to complain that baggy clothes made me look too skinny, and he liked me to wear my long hair down, so he could comb fingers through the soft brown tresses. But what does that matter now? I fold and then refold the extra crib blankets, not daring to look up.

"Where the hell have you been?" Letty asks him.

"How is he?" Rudy says. His husky, accented voice whooshes me back, over a decade ago, when he first told me, deep in the shaded dell of my backyard, that he couldn't stop thinking about me, and he asked me, real quietly, if he could kiss me. *Con permiso*, he'd said, and my eyes traveled to his lips, ripe as persimmons—full and sweet and sun-warmed. I lifted my face to his for a taste.

"Look, *look* at him," Letty says, now, hands on her hips. "What do you think?"

He stoops over the crib. "Hi, buddy," he says in that high, reedy voice people use when they have no idea how to talk to babies. "You get big and strong, so we can play some baseball, a'ight?"

Letty cuts me a look. "Like he ever played *anything* with me."

"Why don't you take a break, honey," I tell her. "Now that we're here, you can go downstairs, grab something to eat or freshen up, if you have to." The toilet in this room has been plugged for over a week, an OUT-OF-SERVICE sign hangs on the door-knob.

"I guess I could go to the bathroom. I've only had to pee for like three hours," she says, loudly, and the family nearby glances over. She glares back, grabs her back-pack—they don't carry purses anymore, these girls—and stalks out like an offended queen.

As soon as she's gone, I'm wishing I wasn't alone with Rudy. Rudy and the Quiet Family, that is. What can we say to each other? Sounds corny as something straight out of a telenovela, I know, but what is there *left* to say?

Rudy lifts his shades, clears his throat. "I hear you got a call from Nestor."

"Yeah, what about it?"

"He's offered to do a limpieza for you, and you said no."

I shrug. "What do I want with a limpieza?"

Rudy waves a hand over the crib. "Don't you think it would help?"

"Help what?"

"What is this, if not evil? How else can this happen to an innocent, little baby? The limpieza will expel the evil causing this harm."

I remember, again, why we broke up: Rudy is an idiot. "Are you out of your mind?" I ask rhetorically. "The baby has a congenital condition, meaning he was born with it. Will a limpieza in my house, of all places, reverse time, cram him back in the womb, so he can be reborn without this thing?"

"You know what, forget it," Rudy says. "You're so cold you won't do nothing to help no one. I should know by now." He pretends to shiver. "Fría, fría, tan fría."

"Have him do a limpieza here in the hospital or at your house, if you want it so bad. That's closer to the source," I say.

"He didn't offer us."

"Why not?"

He shakes his head. "Because we don't carry no weight."

"What do you mean?"

"Pues, I ain't even got my GED, but you, you're a teacher. You know children, what's best for them. A judge will listen to you, pay attention to what you say."

"*Judge?* What judge? What are you talking about?"

"The divorce, mensa. Nestor is divorcing Daisy. She's acting all gabacha now, wants a car, wants to work, everything. She don't care about him, so he's cutting her loose, but he wants to keep the kids."

Gooseflesh rises on my arms like I've experienced this precise moment before, but from another angle. The odious truth sinks in, what I have suspected in some dark corner of consciousness and must now embrace like a long-lost psychotic relative who's too eerily familiar to deny. I know exactly what I'm going to say and how Rudy will answer. "Let me guess, Nestor met someone else, and he's in love."

Rudy nods. "Real nice girl, just come from the island. *She* understands him."

His knowing frown, that phony sabiduría reminds me of Valentine's Day, when he told me in the waiting room of this very hospital, the first time we had to bring the baby in to stay, that it just wasn't that much fun to be with me anymore. I don't know how he thought it would be *fun* to have his gravely ill, newborn grandson admitted to the hospital. How on earth did he expect me to make this more amusing—crack some jokes, make funny faces, tickle his feet? Back then, though, it stung me, like I was caught *not* doing something I should be doing, like I'd just received some huge overdue bill, threatening legal action, in the mail.

When I got over being stunned, I flat-out didn't believe it. Even when he handed back the key to my house and asked me for his, I kept thinking, *This isn't real. No way.* I was sure he'd call in a few days or show up at my house after work with takeout from Wok This Way and a DVD, maybe even an armful of violets. We'd fought before, even returned house keys to one another, but he'd always come back. After Valentine's Day, though, weeks passed, then months. He never called, never turned up. Eventually I heard that he took off for the Dominican Republic, leaving me to comfort Letty and deal with the doctors, the pharmacies, the insurance, and such. The silence between us grew with each passing day, hardening into a thick, dull wall.

When I finally figured out he wasn't coming back, I determined to repair what I could on my side of the wall. I bought yoga DVDs, a.m. and p.m., and started performing the positions; I replaced the beer in my refrigerator with fresh vegetables, chicken, and fish; I shopped for books on spirituality, self-help guides for finding inner peace, and biographies of nonviolent leaders; and in this way, I encountered my spiritual guides: the Dalai Lama and Mahatma Gandhi. I'm not going to lie. This has been a solitary, mind-numbing struggle, but some days I really do feel closer to spirituality, and once in a while, it even seems like I will find the wisdom necessary for the serenity I'm after.

But not now, not while Rudy stands here telling me about Nestor's replacement for the willful Daisy, as if it's a retroactive cautionary tale, something *I* should have heeded.

"Do you even hear yourself when you talk?" I ask him in a low voice, so as not to disturb the Quiet Family. "You can't possibly believe half the stupid things you say. Tell Nestor, forget about it. I'm not talking to any judges, and I don't want a limpieza. Have you got that?"

"You know what?" Rudy tells me. "I'm leaving. It's no good being around you no more. You're so negative, Marina. All the sacrifices I make, and you won't do nothing for me or my kid, not even something as simple as letting Nestor do a sacred ritual that maybe could save this little baby's life. You just can't think about helping anyone but yourself, huh?"

I squint at him, thinking, boy, is he lucky there's

no avenging angel of irony hovering with a flaming sword, or surely he'd be split in two—*pffft*,
just like that. But then I waver, considering the spiritual plane and picturing the entrance to this, for
me, as a heavy door, padlocked shut. My deeply
devout mother who entered the convent, my de-
parted father with his Transcendental Meditation,
even Nestor, the babalawo, and countless others
must possess spiritual lives that grant them access
to spaces I am barred from. Like a tone-deaf liste-
ner at the symphony, I am cut off from the music,
utterly unable to apprehend things of the spirit.
Here, I picture vaporous twists seeping under that
door. Things must happen in realms I can't enter.
What if this thing could make a difference? How
would I even know?

And for sure Rudy reads the uncertainty in my
face because he seizes on it, saying, "At least you
got to think it over—for me, for him...even for
us." Rudy glances into the crib before shuffling toward the door and muttering "adios" to the assem-
bled members of the Quiet Family, who mumble
back like parishioners responding to a priest.

I push the plastic scoop visitor's chair up close
to the crib and lower one side, so I can put my arm
in and sort of hold the baby. I imagine him trying to nuzzle my arm, and I wish I could pick him
up. If not for the monitor wires and intravenous tu-

bing, I sure would. After all the stuff I've read on his condition, I can't believe how strong he is, how he fights for his scrap of this world, however bleak and tormenting his time in it has been. It's *his*, and he's not about to let it go, no way, not now.

Before Letty returns, one of the doctors finally appears. He's the young one, the borriqueño, tall and thin with a thick bush of black hair. He always seems nervous, like a great twitching rabbit in his white lab coat. "How are we doing?" he says.

"Well, he's bloated," I tell him, again stating the obvious.

"That's from the meds." He lifts the infant gown and puts his stethoscope to the baby's chest. Little Rudy flinches. The doctor then checks the monitors and makes notes on his writing pad, attached to a clipboard. "I can prescribe a mild diuretic."

I pull out my tablet, thinking maybe *I* should get a clipboard. "Where are we at?"

He shakes his head, meets my eyes for a split second before blinking several times in rapid succession. "It's a matter of days now."

I drop my gaze, hold my pen steady, but the blue, college-rule lines on the notepad wobble and blur. My face grows hot and salty. "But what do I tell *them*?"

"What we're dealing with here is an infant who has *multiple endocrinopathies* with *fatal neuro-*

degenerative disease." He scribbles all this on a prescription pad, rips off the sheet, and hands it over, so I don't have to copy everything down. "We're trying to make him comfortable. Palliative care—that's all we can do."

The door bursts open once more. This time, a noxious gust of cheap lilac scent ushers in Miguel's mother, la bruja herself, tottering on cracked patent leather heels and clutching this fake leopard-skin coat about her as though it's thirty below, instead of in the upper eighties and smoggier than the sulfuric pit of hell. Old Rosaura scans the room with an expression on her face that she'd wear if she accidentally stepped into an outhouse. Then she looks me up and down and pinches her nostrils together. "It smells like a skunk *died* in here!"

Chapter Two

Back home that afternoon, I snap open a beer in the backyard. Though overgrown with crab-grass, dandelions, and foxtails that reach to my knees, this is the only cool place on the property this time of day, so of course, I have to share it with los housemates: my nephew Kiko and my sister's ex-boyfriend Reggie, who have roused themselves for the purpose of smoking joints at the dinette table I use for picnics and barbacoa. At least they've left me my plastic-weave lounge chair under the mutant grapefruit tree, where I'm sprawled, staring at the bumpy globes that have fallen from its deformed branches and wondering what's made this tree so strange and sick.

Meanwhile, Kiko's finally unveiling an action plan for changing his life's direction after getting fired from his job as a janitor six months ago. "Yeah, I'm going to meet me some fine, rich babe, with tetas out to here, pop her the question. She'll be so happy, she'll be all, like"—here, he affects a syrupy falsetto—"'*Honey, what kind of car can I buy you?*' 'Cause chicks, man, they'll do like *anything* to get married, know what I mean?"

"Got that right," says Reggie, despite the fact that not too long ago my kid sister chipped his eyetooth trying to cram the engagement ring he gave her down his throat.

I put my beer can to my cheeks, my forehead, letting the condensation trickle down my face like icy tears. "Where's Carlotta?"

"I ain't seen her." Kiko drags on the joint noisily. He's a heavy kid with pebbly gray eyes imbedded in his pale slab of a face.

"I think she went back home again," Reggie tells me. "She borrowed some harina de maiz. Said to tell you she'd pay it back."

"Talk about sufridas, this is a textbook case." I gulp my Japanese beer. It isn't the first time Carlotta has snuck home to fix food for that houseful of ungrateful babosos. I can almost see her flipping corn tortillas on her comal and shooting furtive glances at the door. She'll scuttle back here before her husband and sohs get home, leaving behind a plate of steamy tortillas at the center of the table and a bubbling asopao on the stove. Maybe Kiko's plan is not so far off the mark if attractive and otherwise intelligent women like Carlotta can stomach twenty years of mistreatment and still scurry home on the sly to fix hot meals for their abusers.

"Eh, I think she took some paper towels too." Reggie relights the roach, sucks at it. "By the way," he whispers hoarsely, holding the smoke in his lungs, "we're almost out of toilet paper."

"You ever hear of a place called the *store*?" I say, picturing *my* paper towels tucked under the chins of those four wolfish louts next door, *my* masa in their bellies.

"I'm just saying—"

I vault from my chair, nearly spilling my beer. "I know what you're saying. You're saying, Marina, go get some toilet paper, since you're buying all the groceries all the time anyways. You two lazy parasites sleep almost all day long, sit on your asses the rest of the time, smoking mota and hatching stupid plans, and then when I get home from work, from seeing that poor baby in the hospital, you tell me we need *toilet* paper!"

"Jeez," Kiko says, gathering up his stash box, rolling papers, roach clip, and lighter. He's been around me long enough to know what's coming.

"Hey, hey, take it easy," Reggie tells me.

I turn to him. "What are *you* doing here anyway? Whoever heard of getting dumped by your girlfriend and then moving in with her *sister*?" Sure,

I felt sorry for him when he showed up at my door, all weepy when my sister kicked him to the curb. This wasn't long after Rudy and I split up, so looking at Reggie's mopey face was kind of like glancing in a mirror for me, but that feeling's wearing mighty thin these days.

"We better go," Kiko tells Reggie, whose red-rimmed eyes bug out with alarm.

"A'ight," he says and rises from the table with a shrug.

"We'll be back later, tía, when you're feeling better, okay?"

"Later, ese," Reggie says. "We'll even bring some toilet paper."

They head for the side gate, buzz-cut heads lowered like they're leaving a funeral. Kiko tosses a last look over his shoulder. "Hey, tía, can we borrow your car?"

Minutes later, my hands are still buzzing when I pick up the ringing phone, after I manage to locate it, this time on the edge of the bathtub. "Hello?"

"Hey, it's Nestor. Listen, I just got off the phone with Rudy. He says you're thinking it over, about the limpieza."

"Does he?" I lower the toilet lid to sit until my breathing slows down and the hot pounding in my temples subsides. The tub is sooty with filth, and some greenish fuzz sprouts from around the fixtures.

"Yeah, and like I said, I ain't going to charge you nothing."

I'm gazing now at the framed black-and-white photo of Gandhi mounted near the towel rack. I bought it at a yard sale to hang where I can see it every day—a reminder to be strong, to be peaceful. Wearing no more than a dhoti, old Gandhi stares back with such bony seriousness that it feels like he's taunting me, double-dog daring me to chill out. The quote below the picture reads: *You must be the change you wish to see in the world.* I close my eyes, breathe deeply. Maybe this thing of Nestor's, this limpieza, can work. Clearly, the world of science and medicine is out of options for little Rudy. What if the spiritual realm can offer him a chance? And if there is any chance of helping the baby, shouldn't I take it? How can it hurt? So I tell him, "You do what you have to do."

"Like I said, this is totally free, no charge to you. Rudy told you the situation, right? You'll just give a deposition in an office. Just say what's best for my girls is to live with their daddy, got it? My abogado has a whaddayacallit—a relationship with a law firm in Reseda, so you don't have to fly to Miami. You don't even have to appear in court nor see Daisy nor nothing like that. It's an I-scratch-your-back-you-scratch-mine kind of thing. Are we straight? So you know the deal?"

The last time I saw Daisy, she was packing boxes for their cross-country move, after Nestor figured out there's more opportunity for a Santeria priest in Miami than in Los Angeles. She had her little daughters helping her, wadding newspaper to jam into cups and glassware. She blew a strand of honey-colored hair from her face and grinned at me, looking like a young girl herself. Now Nestor wants me to help him do to her what Rudy did to Dolores years ago when he met me. "Believe me, I know the deal," I say, thinking, *This is how it can hurt.*

After work the next day, I head straight for the hospital, not even bothering to look for my missing cell phone or check for messages in my mailbox. After all that Asahi last night, my head throbs and my chest burns, like I just scarfed down a double helping of mole rico, though I haven't eaten a thing all day. Scorching gulps bubble up, searing my esophagus, but I keep plugging ahead, and soon I'm turning into the visitors' parking lot at the hospital.

This time, both Miguel and Letty huddle around the baby's crib with Miguel's mother and a cluster of people who look like they belong in a motorcycle gang. After a confused moment, I recognize these as the cristianos from Miguel's church—ex-junkies and former cons, who've given over their scarred, tattooed bodies and depleted souls to Jesus. Usually, Miguel's crew creeps me out, but today I look from one battered but serene face to the next and the next, and longing for their faith twists in my stomach. Eyes closed, they're bowing their heads as the pastor—wearing black leather, chains, and a red paisley do-rag over his skinhead—leads them in prayer. No one notices me but Miguel's mother, who puts a finger to her lips, unnecessarily, to silence me.

The prayer is about what you'd expect, with so many references to our transgressions and all of us being sinners that it seems like the guy holds everyone in the room personally responsible for the baby's condition. At long last, he wraps it up, with a string of loving references to Jesucristo, and they all hug Letty, who looks stiff enough to break. Then, the group trickles out, leaving Rosaura, Miguel, Letty, and me, standing before the baby's crib, as the Quiet Family beside us murmurs at the doomed girl.

Little Rudy is less swollen, but his skin has gone gray. When I stoop to kiss him, his cheek feels as clammy as potting putty. His eyelids jerk open, and he focuses on Letty, his eyes round with recognition. She leans in like she thinks he's going to speak to her. And his chapped lips part, but he emits a soft, soft sigh, like the whisper of a butterfly's wing, the breeze that ruffles the fluff on a dandelion's head. He blinks a few times, closes his eyes, and his entire body sinks into the crib. I hold my breath, watching, waiting for his chest to rise.

Late that afternoon, I give Letty the pill the doctor said would help her sleep and settle her in bed. Miguel, afraid to take as much as an aspirin these days, stretches out alongside her staring at music videos with the sound turned off, and I head for home. It's no good to cry on the freeway, so I clench my jaw and squeeze that steering wheel until my fingertips grow numb. If I let myself go, my sunglasses will fog up and I'll be driving blind. Naturally, Kiko and Reggie forgot the toilet tissue, so they took all the Kleenex out of my car to use in the bathroom. I have nothing to blot my face. As I pull up to my little house, I spot Rudy's truck parked right in my driveway. Now I've got to tell *him*. I'm tempted to keep on driving right past the house, maybe take one of those winding roads up into the Angeles National Forest and find a place where I can sit by myself and not hear anyone talking. But wait a minute, that's what my home is supposed to be, the place where I can be alone in silence, the sanctuary where I'm supposed to find the peace of mind that always eludes me, so I park the car alongside Rudy's, giving him plenty of space, and haul myself out.

Voices spill over the backyard fence. No doubt, Reggie and Kiko have bestirred themselves to smoke mota with Rudy out back, so I don't bother to go inside. Instead I slip through the side gate and up the stone path where I hear this weird squawking mixed in with the voices. Standing with Rudy beside my diseased grapefruit tree is Nestor. He's holding on to the one leg of my neighbor's rooster, the cockfight survivor. The upside-down bird is flapping its reddish wings, shrieking, and twisting to peck Nestor's hand. But Nestor beams at me like he's arrived for a party. He's spruced himself up since I saw him last, no doubt prompted by new love to do some overhauling. He's trimmer now, wearing a pastel-blue oxford shirt that's still creased from its fold like he just tore it out of the cellophane wrapper this morning, and he's got a fresh haircut—stylish spikes twisted into creosote peaks that crown the closely shorn sides. If he found white hairs in his thick moustache, he's surely plucked them out; it's as black and glossy as a sable brush. His hair gel glints, his sunglasses glitter, and the rosy tips of his ears practically twitch with eager pride. "Where do I set up?"

But it looks like he's already started setting up. He's removed my folding chair and cleared away some of the cankerous fruit to arrange about half a dozen apples, a red cloth, some big leaves, and a planting tray with blood-colored vines in it. Plus he's got some stones in this wooden bowl and a silvery dagger thing on my table. I don't yet trust myself to talk, so I glance over at Rudy, who sneaks me a shy smile and a begging look, the same face he pulled when he asked me to call the IRS last spring and explain to them why he hadn't paid taxes for four years straight.

The rooster stretches its neck and manages to pierce Nestor's hand with its beak. A blood bubble appears on his knuckle. "¡Cabrón!" Nestor shifts the bird to his other hand, and brings the torn flesh to his mouth. The rooster squawks, flapping crazily.

"Let it go," I say.

"Nah, man, you have any idea how hard it was to catch this thing?" Nestor asks me. "We need it for the limpieza."

I fold my arms over my breasts, shake my head. "I changed my mind."

"Aw, come on, querida," Rudy says, his voice all sticky and oozy. "This will give us a new chance, a clean start together. Don't you want that?"

I hesitate, recalling that first taste of his lips,

nectar-sweet, but sharp with salt—persimmons rinsed in the sea. "No," I finally say. "Not anymore."

The rooster rips off a scream that sounds almost human.

"Fool, let that thing go," I say. "That's my neighbors' rooster." I shoot a look at the blade on my table. "They're not going to be too cool if anything happens to it."

"Relax. I paid them fifty bucks for it." Nestor gives the bird a shake.

"Hey, don't you want the baby to get better?" Rudy asks.

"Rudy, the baby is not going to get better."

"Listen to you. You're so negative, mujer, always looking to the bad—"

"The baby's *dead*." I step close to Rudy and put my hands on his forearms. "Do you hear me? Little Rudy died this afternoon."

Rudy's face goes blank. He jerks away from me.

"Abikú," Nestor says, not missing a beat. "His spirit twin, Emere, has called him back. That's what I was afraid of. Now we need bitter broom and espanta muerto to help him to the other world."

I ignore him. "Rudy, you've got to go see Letty. She's sleeping now, but you should be there when she wakes up. She needs you."

"We'll finish here first." Nestor advances on me with the rooster. He's clutching the breast and wings, and he tries to rub the thing on my arms.

"Get that off me! You know what, Nestor? I don't believe you're a real babalawo. You're just some con artist. I looked on the Internet. A true babalawo doesn't go for crap like this, for using up one wife to change her for another."

"You better watch out," he says, holding the rooster over my face. "I can do limpiezas, and I can put the evil eye, lay a curse." He snaps his fingers. "Like this."

"Give me that." I snatch the bird away. It's a hot, quaking bundle, the heart tick-tocking in my palms like a wind-up clock. I dash to the fence, but not before it razors my thumb. "You stupid thing," I say, dumping it over the chain link.

"It's all your doing," Rudy tells me, shaking his head. "This is what you've done to me, to my family. You have such bad energy."

"You're going to regret this shit," Nestor says.

"Get off my property—both of you!" If I'm going to regret shit, I want to be sure it's purely regrettable, so I grab a few lumpy grapefruits from beneath the tree. These are hard with tumors but also squishy with rot—perfecto! I aim one right at Nestor and hit him square in the chest.

He buckles with the blow. "Hey, that hurt!" Nestor brushes off his new shirt. There's a dark stain where I imagine his heart would be.

Then I land another on Rudy's elbow.

"You know what? You're crazy," he tells me, rubbing his arm.

The third one strikes Nestor's hip. I gather more damaged fruit and throw it as hard as I can. "Get out of here or I'll kill you with these things!" Let them think I'm raving, if it scares them. Let them think I'm combustible with rage. It's not too far from the truth, though the truth is also that I am brimming like an overfull glass. As long as I can chuck the grapefruits, I won't spill a single teardrop. My cheeks flame and blood drums in my ears like a summons to war. "In the name of Obba," I shout, remembering this from my Internet search, "in the name of Santa Rita of Cascia and all wounded women and thrown-away wives, I demand you remove your stupid asses from my yard!"

At the mention of Obba, Nestor's face drains of color. He grabs Rudy's arm, whispers in his ear. They scurry around gathering up his junk while I chuck grapefruits at them as fast as I can scoop them out of the grass.

In my bedroom, I kick off my pumps, step out of my skirt, and unbutton my blouse. I slip on some gym shorts and a raggedy old T-shirt. I find my tablet and scribble out a list, bearing down so hard I nearly rip the paper. Then I make another and one last one before heading to the kitchen, where I fill a bucket with hot, soapy water. As the tap rushes, my throat thickens. In this sink, Letty and I gave little Rudy his first bath. After which, I'd swaddled him in a receiving blanket to suds his tight ringlets. But I shake myself hard—not now, not yet—and grab a mop from the pantry. "Kiko," I holler over the running water. When he doesn't reply, I stomp over to the couch, bearing the mop like a rifle. Unbelievably, after the racket in the backyard, he and Reggie are snoring away at four in the afternoon, making it sound like I keep a pig farm in my living room. I thunk the handle on his meaty shoulder a few times until he sits up, rubbing his eyes.

"What up, tía?"

"*You're* up, that's what up. You're up, and you're mopping the floors. Got it?"

Reggie emits a snort of laughter from the love seat.

"Glad you think that's funny." I head to the kitchen for my lists and stride over to the love seat. "'Cause you're going to have a hilarious time scrubbing out the toilet." Sometimes you have to write things down for people, spell it out for them to get the point, so I hand each of them a list.

I push open the door to the guest room. The bed is empty, neatly made. I yank the closet door wide, empty hangers rattling like bones. "Where's Carlotta?"

No one bothers to answer.

I set the third list on the dresser, weight it with a fat, unlit candle, for when she comes back. In the living room, I clap my hands, hollowing my palms for that explosive sound. "Now get up! Get to work, or get the hell out of this house."

Of course, they grumble, and Reggie mutters something about PMS, but they roll off my living-room furniture, and soon, sharp pine smells fill the house. I rumble the vacuum over the living-room carpet, dust the woodwork with an oiled rag, and lug the furniture cushions out front to air them in the sun. Rain streaks, grime, and smudges cloud the front windows, so I tiptoe across the wet kitchen floor to fill another bucket with steaming water and a cup of vinegar. As I swipe the glass with my sopping sponge, Reggie calls out, "Hey, Marina!"

"What?" I plunge the sponge deep in the hot, bitter water, soaking it through.

"Rudy called, I forgot to tell you. Said he was coming over, something about a limpieza. I didn't get the whole thing. You should probably call him back."

"Nah, I don't need to—I'm doing it myself." I say this loud and clear, then translate, "Lo hago yo misma," just so it will be clear.

Chapter Three

You wouldn't expect so many people to make it out on a Friday morning to attend a funeral for a six-month-old baby, but the chapel is so jam-packed with cristianos and the parking lot arrayed with so many motorcycles that it looks like a breakout session at Bike Week in Daytona. The place reeks of exhaust emissions, sweat, and stale cigarette smoke. I'm sure it means a lot to Miguel that his church group turns out big-time to support him on the horrible day when he and Letty will bury their son, but I can't help wondering where and if any of these people work. Who would hire them? Pew after pew is crammed with beefy bare-armed, tattoo-stained, and sun-leathered toughs and their big-haired mamas in skintight jeans and clingy low-cut tops. If not for my sisters and Carlotta in their black dresses, I would be ridiculously overdressed in my navy pencil skirt and ivory silk blouse.

I arrive a little late since I forced those two babosos to come with me. Both of them have known
Letty since she was a little girl. No question that
they should be here for her now. Getting Kiko and
Reggie up for the funeral was no easy trick, but the
godforsaken ties are what caused the greatest delay. I insisted they both wear ties that belonged to
my father, rest his soul, and not a one of us had any
idea how to knot the damn things. Finally, Carlotta stopped by for directions to the funeral. After
three sons, she knew the complicated loops and
twists, fixing them both up in no time. Now, Reggie and Kiko stumble into the chapel behind me,
surely flinging ocular daggers at my back as they
are the only two in ties. Even Miguel wears just a
navy hoodie and baggy jeans.

In the front pew, Letty sits upright, but she still
looks as breakable as a porcelain shepherdess. She
glances around, this way and that, her dark eyes
overlarge and her pale face taut with strain. When
she spots us, Letty signals me over to a spot between her and Rosaura, who is, as ever, garbed in
faux leopard. Letty points at Reggie and Kiko and
makes a downward waving motion, indicating that
they should sit elsewhere, preferably at some distance from us. When I wheel around to face them,
Kiko stops short and Reggie crashes into him. "Go
sit over in back," I whisper, "and act right, will

you?" They roll their eyes, but retreat obediently to the rear of the chapel. I'm hoping that Kiko will take a seat near his mother, my oldest sister Della, but she has her live-in boyfriend, Duffy, at her side, to monitor—as in prevent—any contact between her and her son.

I kiss Miguel's raspy, unshaven cheek and slip past him to embrace Letty. I wince at how sharp her bones feel in my arms. Her thin neck is so stiff with tension that a vertebra pops when I pull her tight. I don't see Rudy anywhere, but that's no surprise. Two years ago, he refused to attend the services for my father, claiming that funerals are not his "thing," as if they were some little hobby of mine he just didn't happen to share. His "thing" or not, he should be here for Letty, and if his so-called friend Nestor, the fake, is still around, he ought to be here, too. I hesitate before taking my seat, wondering if I should hug Rosaura or at least pat her arm, but face it—neither of us would enjoy that. So I smile instead and lower myself onto the hard bench. She frowns, fixes me with an accusing stare. I just shrug and face forward, averting my eyes from the tiny casket in front. The altar is unadorned, almost secular—wood and granite, no hint of a cross. Long windows on either side of it imbue the room with natural light, a pleasant airiness, despite the imposing altar. Letty reaches for my hand. Her fingers are chilly and moist.

At the icy shock of her touch, I can't look away anymore. The mahogany box up front is way too small. It looks stunted. How wrong it feels to sink something so undersized into the ground. Heat stings my eyes. I blink hard and weave my fingers, warm and dry, through Letty's. I steal a sideways glance to see how she's bearing up. She's tearless, though her jaw is clenched, the mandible pulsing. Beyond her, Miguel coughs and clears his throat, sounds echoing in the now-silent church. He lifts a green hymnal from the pew's pocket, rifles its pages, and drops it back in its holder, this noise amplified like a gunshot. The minister emerges from a side door in front and steps to the podium, his vestment rustling. Minus the do-rag, his bald head has a watery sheen in the sunlight streaming from the tall windows. His gaze sweeps through the chapel, as if he's taking measure of the lot of us. His scarred and solemn face transforms into a mask of wolfish satisfaction, and he begins afresh to harangue us for our trespasses.

At the grave site, which we actually had to use maps to find in this unbelievably labyrinthine cemetery, Rudy finally turns up, with Nestor, both of them puffy-faced and ashen, looking spectacularly hungover, despite their oversized sunglasses. Nestor, I notice, wears another factorycrisp oxford shirt, pale gray this time. They make a big deal of shunning me and my sisters when they step up to embrace Letty and shake hands with Miguel. Though it's already hotter than the devil's breath, these furnaceblast winds kick up. Dry, torrid Santa Anas whoosh in from the east, and I remember the KROQ deejay warning listeners to watch out for "Santa-animosity" during our drive out to the funeral. The Santa Anas are bad for gusting up trouble, even worse than the full moon here in the Valley. In the cemetery, torrid currents overturn floral displays, scattering petals and flinging grass clippings like confetti. Foot-high funnel clouds of debris whirl before headstones, lofting skirts of nearby mourners and whipping grit into our eyes. The minister's robes billow and snap.

Carlotta's copper curls unfurl, flipping this way and that, exposing her dark roots at the scalp. Letty's lank tresses wrap around her washed-out face, veiling and unveiling it again and again. I don't want to think about what my flyaway hair is doing, but when I try smoothing it down, it feels as limp and matted as the pelt of some diseased animal. Only the cristianos—the men, that is, with their shaved heads or convict buzz cuts—maintain hairstyle integrity in these conditions. Usually I don't take advantage of sick days, and today on account of the funeral, the school counselor is covering my classes, but once in a while when I know the Santa Anas are blowing in bad, I will call the substitute hotline and stay home, if I can. Here, I'm kind of grateful for the distraction of the wind. Rudy's deliberate snub and Rosaura's disgusted expression are hurled skyward, like kites that have snapped their lines, jerking surely toward oblivion. The minister's last hectoring words are distorted, likewise carried off with the gusts. Little Rudy, in the end, is eulogized by the fiercely hot and howling wind.

Saturday, a week later, my house is still freaky clean. Apart from when I moved in, I have never, ever seen it like this. The windows and mirrors are crystalline, the woodwork gives off a lemony-scented sheen, and the carpet and furniture don't seem half so beat down and discouraged as usual. Even my sad sack of a couch looks like it's changed its mind about committing suicide. Maybe this is the way to find spiritual balance and peace— through order and cleanliness. I plan to make Reggie and Kiko help me keep things clean. Weekdays, I can leave them lists of daily chores to complete before I get back from school. "If you aren't going *to work*," I've told them, meaning if you don't engage in gainful employment, "then you *are* going to *work*," referring, of course, to housework. I may have tapped into their hidden talents.

Over the past few days, Reggie has revealed a flair for handling the vacuum cleaner, maneuvering it to get at tough-to-reach corners and under furniture; while Kiko, after his abbreviated stint as a school janitor, is emerging as something of a bathroom sanitation expert. Today, I even rearranged things, or more truthfully, forced those two lazy pendejos to move the sofa and love seat and shift the bookcase to another wall. I know, I *know*. I should have consulted a book on feng shui, but even without this, the energy flows through the place a lot better now. We work until sunset, when it occurs to me that I've been too busy to think of Rudy more than two or three, maybe four times, tops.

But my thoughts circled back to the baby, little Rudy, over and over, as I dusted and swept and put things away. While sorting the clothes hamper's contents, I wondered what he would have been like, a tough little guy like that, if he'd grown up. I picture a boy with his baby face in the size-three cowboy pajamas that I bought when he was born, thinking he would grow into them and wear them when he stayed overnight at my house. We would have popped corn in the microwave and watched cartoons together. I already collected half a closet shelf of books I planned to read to him. He might have called me, "'buela," like Letty sometimes calls me "mamí," especially when she wants something from me. He would have been my grandson, my step-grandson, and likely the closest I am to come to having such a person in my life. Again and again, like the tongue seeks a tender spot—the gap where a tooth has been yanked—my thoughts return to him, and to Letty. She's gotten quiet lately. Determined not to let the silence between us grow, I've called her and called her. I gave up on the lost cell phone and bought a disposable so I can try to reach her from work. When he's home, Miguel tells me she doesn't feel like talking, and when he's not, she won't answer the phone. That scares me. Our school counselor, Pancha, who works with the children of refugees from Central and South America, says she can tell that trauma victims will recover when they finally start speaking about what's happened.

This evening, after we've put the cleaning stuff away, the house nearly sparkles, and I offer to treat Kiko and Reggie to dinner at El Torito, but they're limping about and grousing like a couple of viejos secos, claiming to be too tired. They ask me to bring them takeout instead. "The heck with that," I say. "You can fix yourselves some eggs, but god help you, if I find one dirty dish, one smudged fork when I get back."

In the cool, dark restaurant, sipping my second margarita and scooping up a last bite of chile relleno with a wedge of tortilla, I relent and summon the waiter to order them some enchiladas verdes to go. The drive home is eerily peaceful. There are few cars, even on San Fernando Road. I whiz past the ferretería, the peluquería, gas stations, pawn shops, la panadería where they make the best pan dulce and bolillos in the valley, video rental places, liquor store after liquor store after liquor store, and las otras tiendas, including my favorite landmarks: La Ilusion, a bridal boutique, which is right next door to Sueños Vaqueros, Cowboy Dreams, a western-wear place that specializes in pointy-toed boots. It seems fitting that these two are conjoined—married, if you will—side by side in the same strip mall. In a few minutes, I'm threading my compact car through the side streets and pulling into my drive, feeling calm, nearly peaceful, tired, but ready to forgive and love, just like Gandhi and the Dalai Lama, even the most aggressively stupid people. Times like these, I feel close to that next level, enlightenment, nirvana, or whatever it's called, the place where no petty bullshit can bug you. I know it's silly, but I picture myself perched on my toes, reaching up with one arm to this platform over my head, then hauling myself all the way up and strolling around to check things out.

Then I climb out of the car, and a la chingada, there they are: Carlotta's oafish husband, Efrem, and her thirteen-year-old, Bobby, swaggering out of their house like a pair of pimps. It strikes me that Carlotta's other two sons—los dos huevónes, as I think of them—haven't shown face in the past few days. Efrem, their worthless father, has on this dingy wifebeater, appropriately, which his enormous panza stretches in ways surely unintended by the manufacturer, and the kid is in standard cholowear—khakis, bandanna, and Pendleton shirt, despite the muggy heat. They're cackling like jackals until they hear me slam my car door shut. Both of them cut me sharp looks. Efrem points at me and draws his index finger across his throat. Clearly, I have no choice but to fling an arm up and pop them the finger. Without waiting for a reaction, I pivot, stride into my house, and shut the door behind me.

Naturally, I find Kiko and Reggie both crashed on their respective pieces of living-room furniture, this time with the TV blaring. Lumpen, snoring bodies don't exactly contribute to the serene and orderly effect I was going for, but I'm glad they're too tired to pester me for my car so they can go out. I flick off the television and tiptoe into the kitchen to stow the Styrofoam cartons in the fridge. The clean plates in the dish rack are undisturbed. Those two haven't even bothered to fix themselves bowls of cereal. Now *that* is some kind of lazy. You almost have to admire slothfulness of this ma-

52   Lorraine López

I poke my head in the guest bedroom—the bed still tightly made up, my list flat under the candle, the curtains fluttering softly with a breeze from the slightly opened window. Though Carlotta has not returned, neither Kiko nor Reggie has mustered the nerve to ask about staying in here and stretching out in a proper bed. Not a one of us has seen her since the funeral, but we all know she will be back.

As I brush my teeth, I gaze at Gandhi—his bristly moustache, those round glasses, that wedgelike putty nose, the pointy chin, and I'm goofily trying to transmit my thoughts to a photograph that's not even in color. It's like I want him to know I feel kind of bad about flipping off my friend's husband and son. Not incredibly mature behavior, I admit, in no way a gesture of tolerance or a move toward that inner peace I'm after. Even so, I search Gandhi for some flicker of understanding. But old Mahatma just continues looking stringy, maybe slightly forgiving, but more stern than that, as if to say, *I may let it go this time, Marina, but I've got my eye on you.*

My room is so immaculate that it's gratifying to go to bed. These days it's the most enjoyable thing I do. My burgundy-shaded lamp casts a rosy glow against the stucco walls, imbuing my now dust-free, secondhand (soon-to-be antique) bedroom set with an unaccustomed high gloss. On the chest of drawers, between framed photos of Letty, my earring tree sparkles in the lamplight, like it's strung with fairy lights, real pretty, right under my poster print of Frida Kahlo's *Self-Portrait with Monkey*. In bed, I sniff the fresh linen, still redolent of fabric softener with a touch of chlorine bleach, before opening my copy of *Awakening the Mind, Lightening the Heart*, by His Holiness the Dalai Lama. It's a book on how to develop compassion in daily life, but I'm so brutally tired, I really can't concentrate on what the Dalai Lama is trying to get across. I read the same passage four times— something about cherishing ill-natured beings, viewing those that betray us as spiritual guides, and acting by force of generosity. I like that last phrase, but I let the book thunk to the floor and snap off the lamp, sufficiently prepared to bear that ungrateful rooster I rescued no murderous wishes when he shrieks before dawn. "By force of generosity," I say the phrase aloud in the dark, imagining a gigantic fleshy fist opening itself gradually in supplication.

My father was into Transcendental Meditation in a big way in the last two decades of his life. He persuaded me to try it when I was a teenager, even went so far as to purchase a mantra for me from his teacher. *Shri Ram*. It was supposed to be specially chosen for me, but nonetheless a meaningless word. Practitioners of TM focus only on the sound of the mantra, not the meaning. But I couldn't avoid hearing the phrase, *Sure I am*, whenever I concentrated on my mantra, invariably thinking: *Sure, I am* not. That was truer to the way I felt about the whole meditation thing. I just couldn't concentrate on nothing. My mind insists on sniffing around like a hound for crumbs of meaning and scraps of significance, thoughts and more busy thoughts.

Years later, I researched the whole TM thing on the Internet at school, and I found out the so-called personally customized mantras were issued from a list determined by age and sex of the meditating person. In effect, my father paid his teacher seventy-five dollars to look up my mantra on some list. While my father never knew about the lists, this angered a lot of people who were into TM, and more were outraged when investigators discovered the words are derivations of Hindu gods' names, and not meaningless at all. TM was supposed to be this secular thing, drawing people from different faiths to the healthy practice of meditating. Of course, some felt betrayed, the way a Jew might feel learning that for years he had been chanting Jesus Christ's name to relax his mind.

After learning all that, I'm not big on mantras,

but I say the phrase again, "By force of generosity," liking the idea of it—something positive and beneficial as a force impelling people to act against personal interest, even against human nature, to help others. But my last sleepy thoughts wander toward plans to see Letty tomorrow, to take her something (*but what?*), and then I wonder where I can get a portrait of the Dalai Lama, something framed to hang in the bathroom alongside Gandhi...

What wakes me, though, isn't that strutting feather duster. Instead sirens pierce my dreams, the throbbing wail of squad cars and maybe a fire engine or an ambulance blaring right up to the house. I lunge out of bed and throw on my kimono, wondering what my nephew and that other dummy have done to bring the police down on us. I dash to the front room to peer out the window that faces the street. Kiko and Reggie are still snoring away. A squad car pulls into my driveway, its blue flashing light pulsing through the sheer curtains like a disco strobe. An ambulance shrieks to the curb in front of Carlotta's house.

The paramedics scramble out and the police emerge from the squad car, one of them shouting into a megaphone. Then everyone rushes about, and I can't see much from the window until two cops loom back into view, leading Carlotta's husband, Efrem, head lowered as he stumbles across his front lawn. Reggie jerks into a sitting position, and Kiko raises his head from the sectional cushion. "What up, tía?"

"I don't know," I say, though anyone can probably guess.

I fling open the front door and pick my way over the prickly crabgrass and cold cement in bare feet to the sidewalk to join the other rumpled and yawning neighbors gathered now in front of my house. "What's going on?" I ask Henry Fuentes, my across-the-street neighbor, a fifty-something bus driver with more kids and grandkids than I can estimate without a calculator, all of them living with him and his immense wife in their stucco two-storey. Privately, I call them the Vehicle Family. Every Fuentes over sixteen has a car. Henry, his wife, their sons, daughters, and many friends take up all the available curb space in a four-block radius. And their dusty front yard looks like a used Big Wheel, tricycle, and ten-speed bike dealership.

He juts a thumb at Efrem, who's being guided into the backseat of the police car in my driveway. "Didn't you hear all that racket?"

I shake my head and point at the six-foot cinderblock wall separating my house from Carlotta's. "Noise from their place doesn't climb that high."

"That pinché panzon beat up on Carlotta, so I called the cops."

"You motherfucker!" bellows Efrem. "I'll kill you, I swear. I'll kill you *first* when I get out."

Henry rolls his eyes, and the two cops trade amused looks before shoving Efrem in and clicking the door shut, which has the same effect as hitting mute on the remote control when an obnoxious commercial starts blaring. Efrem's face contorts with rage, mouthing all nature of curses—spittle flies and the glass clouds up from the heat of it—but we can't hear a peep. Now, I'm no lawyer, but anyone knows it's probably not the smartest thing in the world to threaten premeditated murder while being arrested for battery. I grin and flutter fingers at him—*Bye-bye, bad boy.* "Is Carlotta okay?" I ask Henry.

He shrugs. "Look. They're bringing her out now."

I head for the paramedics who are wheeling my neighbor toward the ambulance when some punk cop, a freckled redhead who looks younger than Kiko, says, "Ma'am, step back. Let the paramedics do their job."

"She's my friend. I just want to see if she needs anything."

"Step back, ma'am," he repeats, slipping into broken-record mode. It's no use arguing with these officious types who'd rather recite rules than go to the trouble of thinking for themselves. Instead I crane my neck to glance over his shoulder at Carlotta.

She sees me and calls, "Marina! Marina! I got to talk to Marina!"

"That's me," I shout, and a paramedic signals me over, so I slip past the junior cop and make my way to the ambulance, where they have loaded Carlotta into the back. The paramedics step aside. One guy jumps off and the other remains in back, adjusting this and securing that. I climb on board and try to stay out of his way.

I suck in a hard breath. Carlotta's lip is split like rotted fruit, blood bubbles in one nostril, and her left eye is puffed shut. There's something dripping into her arm from an upturned bottle on a stand near the stretcher. "Jesus, Carlotta." I stoop down to take her hand which is marble cold. "You want me to come with you to the hospital?"

She licks her upper lip, shivers, and says, "No, stay here. Take care of my boys for me. Someone needs to stay with Bobby tonight."

I nearly drop her hand, thinking, *no way*, but under these circumstances, I have no choice but to nod.

"You *will*?" Carlotta strobes my face with her undamaged eye. "You'll take care of him?"

I hesitate, thinking of Gandhi and getting to the next level, attaining peace and enlightenment, that business in the Dalai Lama's book about cherishing the ill-natured, that force of generosity. Maybe this is the way. I nod. "I'll make sure he's taken care of." And then again, maybe this isn't the way at all, and just another tormento. I don't want to flat-out lie here. Face it—I'll have the little jerk thrown into lock-up if he tries anything violent with me. And that would be one way to take care of him.

"And Efrem," she says. "Can you call his father? The number's on the fridge. He can put up his house to bond him out."

"Okay, Carlotta, now you're pushing it." I straighten up, ready to climb off the bus. They ought to get her to the hospital. She must be altered, delirious as hell. The paramedic, a tall black guy, gives me a look, as if to ask, *So are we done here?*

"Efrem's hurting, too, you know," Carlotta says.

"Good." I leap off the ambulance, landing harder than anyone should without shoes.

"You don't understand," she says, raising her voice. "I should never have left him, never have come to stay with you. It's my fault."

"*Your* fault?"

"Don't you see? I ruined his reputation. When I came running over to your house and talked all kinds of smack on him, you lost respect for Efrem."

"Honestly, Car, I never had one molecule, not one atom particle of respect for that bastard." And it's true. Before I ever met Carlotta, when they first moved into the rental next door, I overheard Efrem in the street, cursing out his sons as they hauled in bed frames and mattresses, and I formed an immediate and lasting impression: *total asshole*.

"That's my husband," she says. "He told me what you did. You disrespected him, and it's my fault." The engine churns to life with a roar.

"Carlotta," I tell her, shouting now to be heard, "you need to concentrate on getting well, in more ways than one."

The paramedic pulls the door shut. *Blam!*

I limp home thinking of that fairy tale I taught recently about the old woman and her pig. The one where the vieja has to have all these things happen—a cat has to bite a rat, the rat must gnaw a rope, the rope needs to whip the butcher, and so on, in order to get this stubborn pig into its sty that night. In this case, I flipped off Efrem, so he beat up Carlotta, and Henry called the police. I got the pig locked up all right, but if I look at it another way, and flash on the image of Carlotta's pulpy lip and swollen eye, I went about it all wrong and feel almost as low-down as if I'd slugged her myself. But that's if I buy into her version, which is really Efrem's spin on the story. Even in the fairy tale, it all begins with a stupid pig.

At my house, Kiko and Reggie crouch near the front window in their 'chones, watching the scene. I tell them what happened, and Reggie says to Kiko, "What'd I tell you, man. I *knew* that old guy Henry was a narc."

"A *narc*?" I say, purely mystified.

"Yeah, a fink," Reggie says. "He'll call the cops on anyone."

"Shut up," I tell him. "That's the only decent man around here for miles." And it's true. Henry Fuentes is as honest and true a man as you can find. He's been with his wife, Imelda, for nearly thirty years, through thick and thin, though mostly thick as Imelda is pura nalgona. "Henry Fuentes is the only one with the cojones to do the right thing, and you call him a *narc*? If he's a narc, then I say march all the stupid clowns off the planet and bring on the narcs." I picture a parade of grease-painted fools in fright wigs and baggy polka-dot suits goose-stepping off the edge of a cliff, and an army of stocky and purposeful Henry Fuenteses appearing over another ridge to replace them. I tap my forehead to clear out this nonsense and turn to Kiko. "Get your clothes on."

"How come?"

"'Cause you're going to babysit that cholo mocoso, that punk Bobby next door," I say, but I wonder just where the heck the kid is, where any of those boys are. Not a one of them showed face, neither during the fracas nor after the police and ambulance pulled away. "He might not even be there, and you can come back, if no one's home."

"I don't want to go over there," Kiko whines. "I want to stay here."

I look him up and down. He's even heavier, pastier, and dimmer looking than usual in boxers and a stained T-shirt. "That's too damn bad," I tell him. "Now put some pantalones on."

He sucks his teeth, but reaches for his Levi's. Reggie hoots with laugher, so I grab his khakis from the love seat and chuck them in his face. "You, too. Put your stupid clothes on. You're going with him. Think you're staying here? You're out of your mind." I head for my serene and exquisitely appointed bedroom, before closing the door on their useless grumbling.

Soon enough they slam out of the house, and for the second time, I snap off the light. Carlotta, I recall, has a sister named Consuelo, a big-mouth with a pumpkin face and long, straight, black hair. I met her at a party once, where she blabbed so much I got a stabbing headache just from being introduced to her. I figure tomorrow I can hunt Consuelo down and make her look after her nephews. Like Kiko, I really do not want to go over there. Not one bit.

In the morning, I don't even hear the damn rooster. That's how tired I am. Around ten, I wake to blinding sunshine, my temples hammering. I need caffeine, and fast. On my way to the kitchen, I see those two nitwits didn't bother to fold up their bedding. The front room already has that familiar ransacked look. I'll have to straighten it right after coffee and my *A.M. Yoga* exercises. Church bells from Our Lady of Whatchamacallit dong ten annoying times, and I peer' out the window at the Vehicle Family pouring out of their duplex into their various cars. Like me, Henry and Imelda must have gotten a late start. Idly, I try to tally the herd. *One, two, three, four, five—now is that a Fuentes or a Fuentes cousin?—six-seven-eight—*then a closely clustered bunch stampedes out, and I lose track. All of them scrubbed, combed, crisply dressed for Mass, and I have to admire the organization behind this, though I do not do church or practice any form of organized religion. Lately, though, in my search for inner peace through spirituality, I've considered becoming a Buddhist because I don't think you have to leave the house, much less pull on pantyhose, to do that.

By the time I slap on some sweats, unfurl my

mat, and fast-forward my yoga DVD past the cre-
dits, the coffee-machine diesel commences juddering into the station, obliterating all sound, so I
don't know how long the knocking's been going
on. I don't even hear it until the last gasps of steam.
Did those lunatics forget their keys again? I stride
to the front door and swing it wide.

It's Rudy, standing on the front step, smiling
in a nervous way. "Hey, Marina," he says, softly.
Without the shades, his brown eyes are wide and
moist, like those of some tender woodland creature
startled in its nest. He's wearing an overlarge soccer jersey and longish shorts that expose his thin
calves. "Mujer, can we talk?"

"You tell me." I clamp my jaw and fold my arms
over my chest, regretting with all my heart that I
have not shaved my legs since Friday.

But we don't talk. Not much. He gives me a
look, opens his arms for me, and I just kind of flow
into him like water, but thicker and sweeter, like
nectar or honey.

No way is Rudy what any seeing person would
call eye-candy. With his concave chest and knobby
spine, he's more a splinter than a hunk—a splinter
with a potbelly. Add this to his sallow complexion,
that crooked honker, the frizzy hair, and about all
Rudy has going for him are those eyes. And pheromones, which he seems to have in spades. Plus,

after nearly ten years, he's finally figured out what I like: the long, stinging kisses; his hands sure and strong gathering my breasts, guiding both nipples to his lips; the always unexpected but inevitable shock of his thrust. And sometimes, he knows exactly what to say, like this very morning in my still-unmade bed, when he turns to me after we've made love and he strokes my cheek. "You are so beautiful, Marina. I swear it hurts me to look at you."

Times like this I can almost forget Rudy's absence from my father's funeral, his obvious relief after both of my ectopic pregnancies, the Valentine's Day breakup, even his stunt to enlist me in Nestor's attempt to win custody of his two girls. Instead, with the moist warmth of his breath on my neck and our bare bodies curled together, I remember how, after a shower, he would push his wet bangs over his forehead and wind the towel about his body, toga-style, and do jumping jacks, claiming to be "Julius Scissor." I recall the sharply spiced albondigas soup he made for me when I had pneumonia last winter and that he would pack the wheelchair in his truck and take my ailing father to the racetrack on Saturdays when the weather was fine. And in this moment, I actually stop worrying that this, *this* will have been our last time. I pull him close for an embrace, thinking maybe we do still have a chance. I kiss his eyes shut.

Usually, though, he has no clue and therefore blurts out the stupidest things, like right now, when he says, "I wish I could take a picture of you like this."

I jackknife upright. "Hell, *no!*" Does he not remember the fit I threw when I discovered those Polaroid snapshots in his closet? Boob-baring, bum-flaunting, snatch-flashing chick after lewdly grinning chick—a regular rogues' gallery of naked ex-girlfriends preserved for posterity in a Nike shoebox. (The only one not smiling in her photos was his ex-wife; hers looked like naked mug shots.) Finding these, I was so enraged I nearly spoke in tongues. Has Rudy forgotten this? How could being struck repeatedly with a plastic hanger not have made a lasting impression on him? "You are *not* taking my goddamn picture." I strip off the top sheet and wind it around me as close to burqa-style as I can manage. "What are you even doing here?" I'm out of bed by now, ready to brush him off my mattress like grit.

"Hey, relax," he says. "I was just kidding. You get so worked up."

"Get out," I tell him, remembering now that I've got to find that sister of Carlotta's, that Consuelo. I should also go by the hospital and check up on my neighbor, and I promised myself to see Letty, take her something. Plus, I need to swing by the supermarket to pick up supplies for the culminating project in my beginning class. "I've got a ton of stuff to do, and *you* are just in my way."

"It's always about you, isn't it?" he says, not budging from my bed. "You got things to do, you this and you that. You, you, *you*. You don't care nothing about me, my family, or my friends. You could really help Nestor out, you know."

"*Nestor?*"

"There's still time. The deposition's at four in Reseda, at that law firm next to the travel agency— Berger, Rivera, and something or other, just across the boulevard from the college. You could make a big difference, Marina. Help those girls of his have a decent life with their father."

"You're tripping," I tell him, shaking my head.

Rudy narrows those woodland-creature eyes at me. "You don't know what it's like to be raised without a father. You have no idea. They could turn out all selfish and demanding, all agringada like their mother."

I wonder if in Buddhism or Hinduism there is some jolly deity with a club who settles scores. I know there's karma, but honestly, that's just not quick and dirty enough. "Look, do me a favor here and get out of my house," I tell him, struggling to stay calm, though I am about to lose my cool in a very un-Buddhist way, possibly involving another handy hanger.

He rolls out of bed, steps into his boxers, muttering, "I don't even know why I came here."

"I do—same reason I let you in and we wound
up here. Sometimes, Rudy, I miss you so much it
hurts like my arm has been cut off, even though
I know that arm was bad, rotted with gangrene or
cancer. It would kill me to keep it," I tell him, for-
cing myself to use a quiet, controlled voice. "Still
it hurts so much that—" I turn away from him, my
eyes burning. "Please just lock the door on your
way out."

Clutching the sheet tightly around me, I stumble
for the bathroom. The rusted tap shrieks when I
turn the faucet handle to full pressure, and hot
water splashing from the showerhead deafens me.
Billowing steam fills my bathroom like a crowd of
plump and bumbling ghosts. These grow so full, so
dense that before long I can't make out the Mahatma's face at all.

Chapter Four

When Rudy is really and truly gone, the smell of him lingers, as unshakable as a bad feeling, like guilt or grief, but with an undeserved aspect to it, like a hangover the morning after drinking no more than two beers. It's a salty, dusty odor that's part sweat, part cigarette smoke, and part sports equipment. Though he doesn't play on a regular basis, he somehow smells like a soccer ball pressed up close to the nose. Maybe it's the cologne he uses—*eau de fútbol*—or some such thing. Whatever it is, it hangs heavily, clinging to the linen, even my drapes, indelible for hours. I light half a dozen joss sticks—*Sandalwood Serenity*—and place these strategically around my bedroom. I also pull the window wide open.

Of course, *A.M. Yoga* is out of the question now, after my shower and with the temperature already galloping toward the nineties, unless I want to

shower all over again. "Mensa," I say aloud, promising myself to perform the positions before bed
somehow, even, if I must, with my living-room
dwellers, Reggie and Kiko, in audience. "Pura
mensa," I say again, thinking of Rudy, my little
transgression. Hey, I'm no nun. The time seemed
right, with those two babosos out of the house for
once. But didn't Gandhi go years without gratifying the flesh? I ought to check out the video again,
see how he managed that.

But who am I kidding? It isn't just the sex. It's
the fact of me, Marina, alone, day after day after
day. I feel it like hollowness, a cavity that aches,
even living with those two goofs or, I should say,
especially living with those two goofs. Unlike
grief or physical pain, my aloneness grows sharper
instead of duller with time. When I was a little
kid and wanted attention, I would grumble that nobody loved me, and my mother would scoop me
in her thin arms and lift me to see the big crucifix hanging over our living-room couch. She'd
tell me that she loved me, but that was nothing
compared to how He loved me. He loved me so
much He gave His life for me. Staring at the red
paint streaming from the crown of thorns onto those anguished plaster cheekbones always creeped
me out, but I guess on some level it was reassuring.
Nowadays, if I complain that nobody loves me,

who's around to dispute it convincingly?

As I eject my yoga DVD, the front door flies open and Kiko crashes in. "Hey, tía," he says. "What up?"

"Nothing," I tell him, wondering again how it is that loneliness cuts more deeply when other people are around. "How's Bobby?"

"Aw, he's okay. They don't got no Raisin Flakes over there," Kiko says on his way to the kitchen. "I got to have my Raisin Flakes." It's true. My nephew only eats one thing for breakfast—generic raisin bran. I buy it in the economy size. He reappears in the living room with the large purple-and-white box tucked under one arm. "You should see. They got tons of cool stuff over there, tía. They got Xbox 360, and all kinds of great games. We been playing Grand Theft Auto, and I got to get back for my turn."

"Did those other boys show up?"

"Huh?" He stops in his tracks, brow furrowed.

"Bobby's brothers?"

"Nah, I ain't seen them." Kiko heads for the front door, pulls it open, and turns to me. "We should get an Xbox, tía."

Apart from gleaning some connection to video games, I am not really sure what an Xbox is. "No," I tell him, "no Xboxes. They damage the mind."

"Shoot." Kiko's pudding face wobbles, but only

briefly. "Okay, well, later, tía." He gives a friendly wave and lumbers out the front door.

I'm about ready to fold up the tumble of bedding left in Reggie and Kiko's wake when the phone rings—all nice and charged these days in its cradle on the bookcase. I lift it briskly. "Hello?"

"Hey, Marina," my oldest sister says. "It's me, Della," she says as if I wouldn't recognize the distinctive donkey voice of the person I have known longest in my life, apart from my mother. Since my mother joined the Carmelite cloister, taking the vow of silence nearly two decades ago, I no longer hear *her* voice at all. In fact, unlike my sister's raucous but familiar braying, I don't know if I would even recognize my mother's voice after all this time.

"What's up?" I ask, immediately regretting how brusque this sounds.

"Nothing, really," she says. "I just…well…Is Kiko around?"

"No, he's next door babysitting my neighbor's kid."

"He has a *job*?" Her voice rises with such enthusiasm that I feel a twinge of regret having to let her down.

"No, not really. There was an emergency last night, so I asked him to go over to Carlotta's and stay with Bobby. No one's paying him or anything."

"Oh," she says, dully.

I explain the situation, not going into the details too much, so as not to worry her.

"Is he okay? Kiko, I mean?"

"He's fine," I tell her. "Why don't you come over and see for yourself?"

"Maybe I will," she says, both of us knowing she won't. Her boyfriend, Duffy, insists they use the "tough love" approach with my poor nephew since Kiko lost his job cleaning classrooms in January. As Duffy interprets this method, they will have nothing to do with the kid until he's employed and self-sufficient, though why this short, balding güero, who is neither father nor friend to my nephew, has taken charge of how to handle Kiko is beyond me. I stare out the living-room window, willing Kiko to loom back into sight, so I can hand the phone over and *make* Della talk to him. But only Vehicle Family cars glide into their parking spaces, disgorging Henry, Imelda, their many children and grandchildren. Apparently, they've stopped for pan dulce after church. Imelda and a few of the older girls bear pink bakery boxes into the family's duplex.

"Did he get that stuff I sent?" my sister asks.

My stomach gurgles, my mouth all juicy at the thought of those yeasty sweet rolls, fragrant and moist under their sugar-crust shells. I mix this up with what Della's saying and wonder when she ever had anything tasty delivered here. "What stuff?"

"Those articles I clipped. I mailed them last week, and I sent him a package on Thursday."

"Yeah, he got the articles, but no package," I say. My sister keeps mailing magazine and newspaper clippings to Kiko, never mind that he's so dyslexic that he has trouble making out street signs. "Whether he's read them or not," I tell her, "I can't say." *I've* read the things, though, and the advice is so obvious—*dress tastefully, arrive on time, show an interest in your potential employer*, and so on—that I wonder why anyone bothers to print them.

"And you get the Sunday *LA Times*, right?"

"Yep." In fact, it's likely still sitting in my driveway, baking in the late morning sunshine.

"There are tons of classifieds this week," Della says. "All kinds of ads for dispatchers, marketing reps, retail sales, data entry—I mean, he could take his pick." Her voice is breathless, the pitch rising again.

I want to say, *Yeah, if only the kid could read*, but there's no point in broaching reality with my sister. Instead, I tell her I'll be sure he sees the paper.

"You know, Marina," Della starts in, "Duffy says you're really not helping Kiko by letting him stay with you like that. He says you're just enabling him, making it easy for him not to take responsibility and find work."

"Oh, really," I say, keeping my tone cool. Where was she that rainy night in early February, following the birthday dinner I had here for our youngest sister, Xochi? And what would she have done in my place? A few hours after everyone had left, thunder cracked and thick, heavy raindrops thumped on the roof. I rushed out to check whether the car windows were rolled up. Who do I find parked in my driveway behind me, sound asleep and fogging up the windshield so much that at first I thought he had a girl in there with him? Kiko, that's who. This was back when his car, now deceased, was still running. I rapped on the driver's side window until he woke up. "Aren't you okay to drive?" I'd asked him. He'd had maybe a beer or two with dinner, not enough for a big guy like him to be impaired. And that's when he explained he'd been "tough-loved" into sleeping in his car after he lost his job a few weeks earlier.

I couldn't believe my ears. Mi sobrino único, who was born when I was just ten and who is like a cross between a son and an only brother to me, thrown out of his mother's house and forced to sleep in his car! I ordered him inside, marched straight to the linen closet, pulled out a stack of blankets and a set of sheets. I tossed these on the couch—even then, the guest bedroom was reserved as Carlotta's refuge. "You're staying here," I'd told him. "You stay with me, hijo, however long it takes you to find work and get a place of your own." It had been the only thing to say at the time, though obviously I've had reason to reconsider the terms of my offer since then.

"Yeah," Della says now. "Duffy says you aren't doing him or us any favors."

"Is that right?" I say, convinced that I'd acted correctly and compassionately in taking Kiko in. The Dalai Lama himself points out that Buddhahood is attained only "by the force of generosity and other virtues." He would definitely have approved of this. "Is that what Duffy thinks? But what about you, Della, what do you think about your boy, your only child staying in my house instead of sleeping in his car or on the street? What's *your* opinion on that?"

She goes quiet a superlong time, and then she says, "Just make sure he sees the want ads, Marina. There are so many opportunities, if only he'd open his eyes and look."

I tell her I have to go.

"Marina, one thing."

"What?"

"Take care of him." Della's voice is low and muffled now. I picture her cupping the phone, Duffy puttering around nearby, pretending he's not really listening in. "And tell him I called, will you?" my sister whispers before hanging up.

First stop: the hospital. Otra vez. Though I toyed with the idea of swinging by Letty's apartment first and asking her to come with me to see Carlotta, I threw that plan out when I realized Letty might not be too eager to return to the same hospital where little Rudy died, at least not right off the bat. Besides, I still haven't come up with what I should bring the girl—nothing as insensitively cheerful as balloons or as morbidly redundant as flowers. What, though? Maybe better ideas will come to me after visiting Carlotta.

It feels like old times, but not in a good way, as I pull into the visitors' parking lot for Manzanita Vista. My little car practically knows the way on its own. I even find my usual spot, a narrow space near two pillars, open and waiting for me. The familiar hum of the automatic door, the whoosh of air-conditioning, and the snowy-haired volunteer at the information desk all greet me. "There you are," she says with a smile. "I haven't seen you around in a while."

I don't want to tell this mild, grandmotherly type that, well, the baby died and now I'm here to visit my neighbor who's been beaten by her lousy husband, so instead I say, "It *has* been a while," hoping she'll think I'm a social worker or some such person whose job it is to visit random hospital patients now and again. "This time I'm here to see Carlotta Valenzuela. She was admitted around two or three this morning."

The kindly receptionist lifts the receiver of her desk phone, punches in a few buttons, and locates Carlotta's room number for me. I thank her, jokingly warn her not to work too hard, and pace the familiar path to the elevator. I admire the fit of my cotton sun dress, how it molds to what curves I do have and how the humidity has given my hair some bounce in the reflecting aluminum doors, before these slide apart, splitting my image vertically, and I have no choice but to step on board with an ancient nun. She grins at me, and I nod without returning the smile. Last thing I need to do is get stuck in a conversation with some sister. Since my mother abruptly entered the cloister, I'm not all that wild about nuns.

To be honest, they've always spooked me some. But they see my olive skin and dark hair and right away assume that if not Roman Catholic, I'm some kind of Christian, like most Latinas. Though nothing could be further from the truth, these nuns often approach me, their plain yogurt-colored faces wreathed in smiles as they embark on all nature of pleasantries, one-Christian-to-another exchanges designed to uncover my specific church affiliation. Straight away, I want to tell them, *No offense, but just keep your distance there. You people freak me out, and though it's none of your business, I'll be converting to Buddhism soon.* To avoid talking to this one, I face the elevator's control panel, pretending to be mesmerized by its illuminated buttons.

Of course, since Carlotta is not a child, her room is in a different wing from where little Rudy had been. She's up a few floors, but I'm tempted to hop off at the pediatric level, just to get shut of the nun and to check in on the Quiet Family, see if they're still surrounding the bald girl. But it would be too heartbreaking if that kid's bed is empty and no one is there. I can't risk this, so I endure two more floors with the nun, her musty nunnish odor permeating my pores, sickening me slightly, the way church incense does. By the time we reach Carlotta's floor, though, I begin to feel pretty lousy about my prejudice against women of the cloth. It's not her fault my mother skipped out on me to take the veil. The Dalai Lama tries to love everybody, especially spiritual people. I bet Gandhi was kind to nuns, too. And wasn't Mother Teresa, whom I also admire, an actual nun herself?

When the elevator finally dings at Carlotta's floor, I figure it's safe to tell the old sister to have a nice day. But does she wish me one back or even thank me? No, she does not. She just continues standing in the elevator, grinning at me, in silence. I step out, feeling foolish, until I turn my attention to finding Carlotta's room, which is just past the nurses' station. Turns out, she shares a darkened double room with someone behind a beige curtain just past her bed. Carlotta, head lolling to one side and eyes shut, appears to be napping. Her face now has eggplant-colored blotches on the chin and cheekbone. One eye is covered with a perforated metal cup that looks like half of a tea strainer. Her lower lip protrudes with swelling, and bristly black sutures trace the gash in it. Idly, I lift her chart. I've somewhat gotten the hang of reading these, so I scan the BP (very low) and pulse (also low) before getting to the nitty-gritty: fractured ulna, fractured rib, detached retina—*Jesus!*—and the meds. I'm reading away, ready to take notes, when a white-coated figure in aqua scrubs scampers past. It's the borriqueño bunny again. I thought he was in pediatrics.

He catches sight of me and looks as startled as I am, but recovers enough to backpedal, step into Carlotta's room, and reach for the chart, which I hand over. He's still twitchy, blinking like crazy and running his hand through his bushy black hair. "Marina?" he says. "What are you doing here?"

"I'm here to see my friend." I point to Carlotta. The guy probably thinks I'm some kind of hospital groupie, a Munchausen's type, seeking attention and sympathy just for *knowing* sick people. To distract him from this impression, I say, "What about you? I thought you were a children's doctor."

He blushes violently. Even the tips of his ears go scarlet. "I'm a resident, in general medicine," he explains, as if this would make any sense to me. "I have round rotations. I completed my assignment in pediatrics and now I'm here."

"Oh."

"I'm sorry about the baby. There was nothing that could be done."

"I know."

"Your step-daughter?" he asks. "How is she doing?"

"Letty is my *ex*-boyfriend's daughter." I don't know why I feel the need to clarify this, but I do. "And she's not doing all that well."

He glances at the chart and gestures at Carlotta. "She's listed you as an emergency contact."

"That's right."

"Well, I'm glad you're here. I wanted to give

you some referrals for Letty," he says. "There are support groups and grief counselors. They can really help. Are you going to be here a while? My shift ends in half an hour. I can bring you the information."

I shrug. "I suppose I'll stay to see if Carlotta wakes up. I need to talk to her."

He flashes this toothy smile, but catches himself, no doubt remembering the circumstances, and makes his face serious again. He lilts his chin toward Carlotta. "You seem to know a lot of people," he says, "people who have problems."

"That is true."

A long, twitch-filled silence ensues before he clears his throat to say, "Okay, well, then, I'll be back in a bit." And he scurries off, his white coat bobbing behind him.

I lower myself into a plastic chair at the foot of the bed, wondering who the heck's on the other side of the curtain dividing the room. Slow, regular breathing emanates from behind it. It's not quite snoring, but obviously that other person is also sleeping. It must be a woman. No way can these rooms be coed.

I flip open my Dalai Lama, straining to figure out why I should be grateful to those who turn on me and how on earth they can possibly be my spiritual guides. I think of Rudy dumping me all those months ago, then returning today for a booty call. He's no more capable of providing spiritual direction than he is ready to perform neurosurgery. In both cases, the results of his efforts would be disastrous.

Maybe sensing my presence, Carlotta finally stirs. "Marina?" She turns to regard me with her uncovered eye. "Is that you?"

I put a marker in my book and stand beside her.

"How long have I been asleep?"

"I have no idea. I just got here about fifteen minutes ago."

She glances toward the door, smoothes down her hair. "Did you bring Bobby? The boys?"

"No, I..." I don't want to admit that Bobby's blithely playing Grand Theft Auto with Kiko and Reggie. Who knows where the other two punks are? "I left Bobby with my nephew. Kiko's looking after him."

"Where are my other sons?"

I shrug and say, "Well, you know boys," as if they were off on some Hardy Boys adventure instead of engaging in antisocial behavior likely to get them arrested, just like their father. "They'll probably come around later."

Carlotta's face droops, her lip quirks, but then she whispers, "I hate him." She cups her mouth quickly, her good eye wide and alarmed, as though

Efrem might pop out of the closet with fists raised and snarling upon overhearing this. When no such thing happens, she says it again. "I really, *really* hate him."

In all the years I have lived next door to her, I have observed that there are at least three distinct manifestations of Carlotta: (1) La Sufrida, who laps up whatever brutality Efrem and those other devils dish out and always, *always* returns for more; (2) La Llorona, who feels sorry for herself and spends so much time griping and complaining that even the most sincere potential Buddhist longs to smack her upside the head just to make her stop; and (3) La Chingada, the total bitch who hates everything and everyone, especially Efrem, with a thrilling vengeance.

"The fucking bastard," she says now, up-shifting full throttle into La Chingada mode. "I despise that son of a bitch. Thinks he knows everything, thinks he rules me. His chorizo is the size of a pimple. Half the time, he is too damn drunk to—"

"Easy, Carlotta," I tell her. La Chingada tends to grow shriller and coarser, her harpy's voice ratcheting up with each syllable. The smooth, sleepy breathing from beyond the curtain cuts off with a gasp. "Take it easy. It's not that good to vent." I read this somewhere, and if my experience with my neighbor is any indicator, it must be true. Cursing Efrem just makes Carlotta even more pissed off, more vehement. It's like picking at a scab when the wound isn't anywhere near healed. Some people could seriously stand to chill, to detach and view things objectively. Besides, her ranting sounds as disturbingly passionate as her insistence that she loves the brute when she's in La Sufrida mode.

It's no use trying to reason with my neighbor in any of her settings. I just have to wait until she gets tired and winds down with a final "motherfucking-piece-of-shit-joker-pinché-puto-cabrón-hope-he-rots-in-fucking-jail-never-want-to-see-his-fat-ass-again-and-I-mean-it."

"Okay," I say, "okay, I get it. Relax, Car. I just came to see how you're doing, not to get you all riled up."

"You better not have phoned his psycho father to bail him out."

"Trust me, I would never do that," I assure her. "Carlotta, have you called your family yet? I mean—do they know what happened?"

She sinks back into her pillow, looking small and spent, her expression reminds me of the little bald girl a few floors down. "No, I...I couldn't..."

"Listen, why don't I call them for you? I should at least call Consuelo. She can help take care of the boys, like when I have to work."

"No, don't tell Consuelo. Please. She hates Efrem. My whole family does. They never even gave him half a chance," Carlotta says, schizophrenically teetering now toward Sufrida.

"Look, Carlotta, I have to call Consuelo or somebody to help with the boys. Tomorrow's Monday. I need to go back to work. Who's going to watch Bobby, see that he stays out of trouble then, huh?" It doesn't suit my cause to mention that Kiko has enough time on his hands to look after Bobby, at least until the kid's old enough to vote.

"I don't even know where Consuelo is these days," Carlotta says. "I haven't seen her in like a year. Efrem can't stand her. I'm not supposed to see her or call her since the time she told him to go fuck himself at our Fourth of July barbecue. I don't even know where she's staying these days."

"I should call your dad then."

Carlotta grumbles, but eventually she gives me his number. "Ask him where to find Consuelo so she can take care of Bobby, but don't tell my dad nothing, okay? *I'll* call him. I'll tell him," she says. "He's going to be really pissed."

"Good, that's exactly what Efrem deserves."

"Not at Efrem." She shakes her head, wincing. "At me."

I'm hoping something in the Vallarta Market will inspire me with regard to Letty. After spending all that time with Carlotta and then waiting forever for that doctor-in-training to bring the grief information, which he never does, I don't get away from the hospital until early afternoon. I still hope to make it over to Letty's well before dinnertime, when Rosaura will likely turn up, bearing one of her foul-smelling asopaos along with her equally noxious attitude. As I trundle the shopping cart through the aisles, I remember Letty's favorite foods.

She was just nine when I started seeing Rudy, and boy, did she ever hate my guts when she first met me. Though her mother was a full-blown addict by then, Letty blamed me for the breakup of her parents' marriage. The first few months I was seeing Rudy, she refused to speak to me, would walk right out of any room I entered. Fierce, little bug-eyed thing with braids and crooked teeth, she used to freak me out. And then one day, Rudy's truck broke down when he was working in Downey, and he called me to pick Letty up from her mother's house. Letty would visit Dolores every other weekend, returning on Sunday afternoons for school on Monday. I drove out to Compton that particular afternoon to get Letty, and first thing, I can't find the damn building where Dolores had her apartment. It was somewhere in the projects. I didn't understand how the setup worked, but odd and even numbered apartments were, for some reason, located in separate buildings. Loads of people milled around, smoking, listening to headphones, though no one I asked was willing to help me out. Finally, near tears, I just stood in the parking lot, and cried, "Letty, Letty! Where are you?" And this little pigtailed head appeared in a window on an upper level of one of the brick buildings. Letty rapped on the glass and waved me up.

I tore up the stairs two at a time, so as not to lose her in the maze, but she pulled open the door before I even knocked. "My mama's sick," she told me. She led me into the kitchenette of the filthiest apartment I ever hope to set foot in, and there, heaped on the linoleum like a pile of soiled laundry was Dolores, unconscious—yellow tubing still constricting her upper arm, the melting spoon and needle on the gritty floor beside her. I knelt to put my finger on her cool throat, to find just a whisper of a pulse. I called 9-1-1. It took the paramedics forever to arrive, and while we waited, I put a grungy pillow under Dolores's head and covered her with a beach towel. Then I unloaded dirty dishes from the sink to wash them, all the while talking to Letty, telling her how things would be okay, how sometimes people can't help what they do and on and on.

Letty didn't say a word or even cry until after the paramedics hefted her mother onto a stretcher. The whole ride to the hospital—I took her in my car— I kept talking and talking, asking her about school, her friends, her favorite colors and foods, and not minding at all that she didn't answer or even look in my direction. The passenger-side window fogged with her hot, ragged breath, and she drew a face in that with her finger: two dots for eyes and the mouth an astonished *O*.

After that day, and over the next few weeks, I discovered Letty liked social studies and language arts, but not earth science, which was taught at her school by mean old Mrs. Sheriff, who had mocked Letty the previous week for not understanding the homework assignment. (Letty pinched her nostrils together to mimic the woman's stuffy-sounding speech: "If you had *read* the directions, young lady, it should have been *crystal* clear.") I found out Letty's friends were Diane and Diana, two separate people, but both with the same last name: Garcia. She used to be friends with Juanita until Juanita told Gustavo that Letty wanted to go out with him because Juanita used to go out with him and actually still wanted to, but it was complicated, and now Letty wasn't speaking to Juanita or Gustavo anymore. And I learned that Letty's "most favorite color ever, ever" was pink—not the yucky pink of bottled antacid, but shiny pale pink, the color that you see inside conch shells, and did I really believe you can hear the ocean inside of a conch shell? Is that *really* the ocean? And frequently she named her favorite foods.

She listed these, using her stubby fingers to count off Necco wafers, SweetTarts, Snickers bars, cold milk with Hershey's syrup poured into it, crustless tuna sandwiches made with sweet pickle relish and mayo, hot dogs, those manatee-sized dill pickles that come individually wrapped in plastic. Like most kids, she craved sweets, but she also loved anything bitter, anything steeped in brine. She even went through a phase where she peeled and devoured lemons and limes, the way most people eat oranges or tangerines, until I told her this could damage the enamel on her teeth.

Now in the Vallarta Market, I consider buying one of those mesh sacks of Key limes and baking a pie for her, but since the baby first got sick, she's complained that everything tastes "exactly like nothing" to her. I steer the cart away from the produce section, the dairy case, and the canned goods, heading for the laundry detergent aisle. I have to buy starch for piñatas: the culminating project for the beginning class. All along, we've been incorporating art into the class any chance we get, composing storyboards, making collages, and designing sets to act out scenes from the fairy tales. The fact is, I love to draw, paint, and sculpt, and I'm not half bad at this stuff. Also, it plain pisses me off that the district budgeted out the art program at our school, so I try to compensate, especially in the beginning classes, where I can get away with such things. Tomorrow, we start piñatas in the forms of favorite fairy-tale characters. Of course, this will be in connection with a story report of sorts, so there's a pedagogical connection, or at least so it says in my lesson plan book.

Stupidly, I left the instructions for making piñatas on my desk at school, so I'm not sure exactly how many bottles of starch I need, though I do recall it had been a round number, a single digit. I also remember that I didn't buy enough the last time my class undertook this project, and I had to make a return trip to the store during my lunch break. I settle eight plastic jugs of milky blue starch in my cart, lining them against one another so they don't topple over.

Across the aisle are the pet products. I often find myself lingering before the displayed treats and toys, imagining what I would buy if I had a little dog. I catch sight of an aerosol can of something called "Doggy-No!" Apparently, it keeps pets from fouling certain parts of the house and yard, and my mind wanders to Nestor. Finally, an idea occurs, something that might make Letty feel a little better—a limpieza. Of course, I'm thinking of the sensible version of this, involving cleaning supplies, scouring powder, and pine-scented disinfectant. I push the cart a few feet this way and that in the very same aisle. I throw in a pair of rubber gloves, some sponges, a bucket, and this innovative mop that is supposed to practically wring itself out. I don't kid myself that this is the answer to everything, but remembering what a difference a clean house made for me when I felt lower than a pigeon dropping, I'm kind of relieved to have come up with the idea.

As usual, when I'm ready to check out, everyone in the store gets exactly the same idea. Customers swarm the registers, and the lines wind back into the aisles. I consider all the bottles of starch to be one purchase, so I slip into the ten-items-or-less, cash-only line. More people queue up after me, and I glance at the faces of those standing behind. They're washed out in the fluorescent lighting, drained of color, but definitely hostile looking, as if daring the people in front to have the nerve to demand a price check or take the time to write out a check. When it's finally my turn to pony up, I arrange the bottles of starch carefully on the rotating rubber mat and hand the mop over because it's too long to fit. The cashier, whose nametag reads "Pinkee," looks like she could be from India or Pakistan. She scans each bottle of starch for emphasis, instead of entering just one code and punching in the quantity.

When she finishes, Pinkee grins at me, her nose ring glinting. "You certainly have got a lot of starch, haven't you?" she says in a choppy, British-sounding way.

"Yeah, well," I say as the upright bottles jerk along on the conveyor belt, like bowling pins so impatient for a ball to thunder down the alley that they lurch forward dutifully to topple themselves on the counter rail, "for the kind of thing I'm doing, I only hope it turns out to be enough."

Chapter Five

I knock and knock. No one answers the door at Letty and Miguel's. After lugging the cleansers, bucket, and mop all the way up three flights of stairs and dodging the rusty water trickling from air-conditioning units and slicking the walkway, I'm tempted to leave everything I bought outside the door for them. But they might take it the wrong way. It might come across as an insult to their housekeeping practices, like when someone prints "Wash me!" in the film on a car's windshield. I remember how 'Buela Lupita, my father's mother, would scrawl "cochina" in the dust on our windowsills when she visited. My mother, already tripping on Jesus in those days, never seemed to notice or care that my grandma was basically calling her a filthy pig, even when I pointed this out to her, but it sure made me hot—definitely *not* the effect I'm going for with poor Letty and Miguel.

Banging the mop handle on banister slats, the bucket bumping against my thigh as I make my way downstairs to the parking lot, I'm reminded of the time right after Valentine's Day, when Rudy dumped me for not providing more laughs. Before this, I'd bought him this fancy bedding—comforter, sheets, pillows, pillowcases, shams, skirt, the works—for his birthday on the nineteenth of February. I was tired of sharing the mildewy camouflage sleeping bag he used as both bedspread and blanket when I slept over at his place. No way would I settle for the handy bed-in-a-bag you can get at the discount department stores. Instead I went all out, calidad all the way. Of course, after our breakup, I had to return every individually wrapped item to Macy's in the Galleria. Problem was that it was some stupid President's Day sale and the parking lot was completely filled near the store. I had to leave my car clear on the other side of the mall, near some sporting goods megastore.

I wound up trudging like a pack animal—some stupid burra!—with all these slippery bundles, bulky bales of Egyptian cotton with absurdly high thread count that kept sliding around and tumbling down, through acres of gym shoes, elliptical equipment, tennis rackets, golf clubs, and balls, balls, balls of every shape, size, and texture. I even plodded past a fake rock-climbing wall that seemed to extend toward infinity before I made it to the mall's entrance. Shoppers stopped to gawk, little kids pointed, and some guy, all decked out like Abraham Lincoln and walking on stilts, practically laughed his craggy face off when he saw me bearing my load up the escalator. A grown man, wearing a stovepipe hat, tail coat, and fake whiskers, lurching around the shopping mall on wooden posts, and he found *me* a hoot?

Of course, no one bothered to lend a hand, not even when I blindly smacked into a pillar and everything tumbled to the floor. When I wasn't cursing Rudy, his worthless ancestors, and the entire Dominican Republic for having spawned such a particularly persistent strain of pendejo, I flashed on the Stations of the Cross, Jesus bracing the cross on his back, stumbling under its weight on the way to Calvary. There's no comparison, of course, given the outcome—if you believe that. But this popped into my head to remind me, I suppose, that my pilgrimage was at least a thousand times more inane and way, way more humiliating than that.

Again I'm burdened with un-given gifts, though these are more manageable despite the mop that nearly takes out an overhead light fixture at one point. Thinking of that phony babalawo Nestor, I shoot swift thanks to the orishas for Plexiglas. I manage to get down the slippery stairs, stow everything but the mop in my trunk, and head home wondering where Letty and Miguel could be. It's not like she's gone back to work. According to Miguel, she's pretty much stopped showering or even changing out of the cornflower blue night-gown I gave her last Christmas, so there's no way to imagine that she has places to go and people to see. Though there's probably some totally or-dinary explanation, I'm a little worried. Maybe Miguel has managed to drag her to Rosaura's for Sunday supper or to some church function. I pic-ture Letty, her hair shampooed and shiny, wearing that bronze lipstick she favors, as she sits at a ta-ble sharing a meal with others. This could be a good sign, I tell myself. With all my heart, I hope it is as I angle the mop handle behind the driver's seat, so the head is propped over the passenger's side headrest, leaning forward like a shaggy but eager passenger.

At my house, naturally, no one's bothered to put up the pillows, throws, and assorted blankets dra-ping the love seat and couch, and the front door gapes wide open. "Kiko!" I yell. "Reggie?" The bathroom door is shut. A seam of light glows under it. "Who's here?"

Snuffling sounds emanate. Then Reggie's muffled voice: "It's me." The toilet-paper roller rattles and nose-honking resonates from within. "I'll be right out."

Citric sweetness—a saccharine, but fittingly tart fragrance—stings my nostrils. "Did Xochi stop by?" I ask Reggie when he emerges, eyes red rimmed and swollen. His lower lip quirks and he gives a terse nod.

"Are you okay?"

"Yeah," he says, but he shakes his head. Then he releases these low *whoo*-ing puffs of sound, like this: *ahwhoo, whoo, whoo, whoo, ah-whoo, whoo, whoo, whoo*.

Guys—no matter how they try—just can't get the crying thing right. Most women have crafted crying so it is nearly at the level of artistic expression. Though not a vain person, I myself have spent some mirror-time practicing my weeping—from the mute tear welling and the judicious solitary trickle to the full-throated, madwoman's squall. After working to develop my art, I struggle not to laugh at these amateurish efforts. But do I even let myself smile? I do not. Instead, I fold bony old Reggie in my arms and say, "M'ijo, m'ijo, what happened?"

He's hot to the touch, reeks like a pot of chicken-noodle soup that's been simmering on the stove for hours. Reggie weeps until he hiccups, and when this trails off, he finally says, "She-she-

she...doesn't love me anymore."

And *this* is news? Nevertheless, I pat his shoulder as if burping a newborn. "How about a glass of water? Okay? Sit down, m'ijo, and I'll get you some water."

He collapses on the love seat, buries his head in his stringy arms, surrendering himself to the ridiculous *whoo*-ing noises. While I fill a glass from the tap, I bite my lower lip to keep from mocking his strange cries that take on distinctly avian—whooping crane, maybe hoot owl—traits. At the same time, I feel awful for the poor inocente. He's right and he's wrong about Xochi. Of course she doesn't love him, but as for the "anymore," well, she never really did. Love is an impossibly tough gig for budding young narcissists like my kid sister. I hand Reggie the glass of water, raking my memory for something the Dalai Lama might say at a time like this, something to expand the mind and deepen the meaning of the moment. I remember that bit about cherishing illnatured beings and regarding those who hurt you badly for no reason as splendid spiritual guides, but that still doesn't make too much sense, so I doubt I can explain it.

Reggie gulps the water, sounding like a gerbil lapping feverishly at its dispensing bottle, and he sets the empty glass on the bookcase. His ferrety face is a mask of anguish: his nose is puffy, purplish, and shiny, and his brown eyes watery and bloodshot, threatening to fill with fresh tears. What exactly *does* the Dalai have to say about disappointment in love? The refrigerator hums. Outside, somewhere, a dog barks—*woof, a-woof-woof*—and a car with a bad muffler rumbles past. Another follows, mariachi music blasting from its open windows. "She's too old for you," I finally tell him. "And crying like that just makes your forehead ache."

"She's *not* too old," he says, his voice cracking. "Just two years. In Japan, you're supposed to marry a woman who's a little older than you. That's considered, like, a perfect match. I always loved her. I can't love anybody else."

The weird thing is, he *has* always been nuts about my kid sister. His mom—a teen pregnancy statistic, just like my sister Della—lived with her parents next door to us practically from the beginning of time, and Reggie and Kiko have been best friends since they were in diapers. He fell for old Xochi the first time he laid his beady eyes on her. As soon as Reggie could wobble around on two feet, he trailed after her like a stink. When he was a toddler, he would flirt with her by not allowing anyone but her to push his stroller when we all tramped to the park on summer evenings when our apartment steamed up like a sauna. His mother told us that Xochi, or "So-she," as he pronounced her name, was all he could talk about. "What So-she doing?" he would ask over and over. And when we were all together for, say, a picnic or birthday party, he'd insist on sitting beside her and asking her himself, again and again: "What you doing, So-she? What you doing now?" And my sister, who was a lot kinder in those days, would at least answer him, saying stuff like, "Um, chewing" or "Just breathing."

When they got older, she must have told him to knock it off because Reggie went through a phase where he left her pretty much alone. He would watch her from a distance instead, a moony look on his face. After high school, he got a job with a cable company, setting up service and repairing connections for about six years before he earned enough to buy her the enormous rock he found. Though I don't know much about jewels, I'm pretty sure it had to be cubic zirconium. It was as huge as a fake Hope Diamond—crass as can be and chock-full of doom. I guess they were kind of dating before that time, which is to say Xochi would once in a while go with him to a concert or a movie if she had absolutely nothing better to do. And if I know my sister, I have no doubt she slept with him at least once, out of curiosity.

For reasons that baffled my older sister Della

and me at the time but soon revealed themselves in kind of an expected yet appalling way, old Xochi accepted Reggie's ring. And then, he scored Xochi, a part-time perfume spritzer at the mall, a job with the cable company, a good one that came with its own desk, personal computer, and somewhat spacious cubicle. It was also a job that suited her natural affinity for kicking people to the curb. She's the bitchy voice that tells people they haven't paid their cable bill, so too bad, the service is being discontinued. Since Xochi was keeping his ring (though not often wearing it), working at the same company with him, and dating him when she couldn't possibly avoid it, Reggie bubbled with joy—for almost two weeks. Until my kid sis started lunching with the division manager, that is.

Still, Reggie hoped to marry Xochi, so he continued plying her with phone calls, text messages, sappy greeting cards, stuffed animals, CDs, bottles of perfume, chocolates, roses—the works. He even turned over the keys to his Toyota Corolla to her. That's when Xochi started seeing the boss after work and on weekends, canceling dates with Reggie right and left. When he complained about this turn of events, she promptly filed a sexual harassment complaint, and the unfortunate nitwit lost his job.

Of course, after being fired, his resources ran out about the time Xochi's patience with him expired. He was evicted from his apartment the same week that she officially terminated their engagement, with extreme prejudice, as they say—hence, the chipped eyetooth, the weeping on my doorstep, and the initiation of his tenancy on my love seat. Now, Xochi, like Della, is pissed off at me for opening my home to a sad case. "It's so inconvenient," she says these days about the trouble of having to see Reggie when she wants to come by and borrow my stuff. "You should kick his stupid ass out," she tells me again and again. This phrase is the mantra she lives by, the words that really should be etched on her gravestone.

Now, Reggie sighs long and hard and says, "She borrowed your black dress, the one without sleeves, and some earrings."

Disgusted, I suck my teeth.

"And shoes," he says before giving himself over to a fresh wave of *whoo-awhoo-whooing* and a new crop of tears.

After I finally settle the kid down, nesting him in a tumble of throws on the love seat, I snap on the television to some reality-show competition for models that seems to capture his attention. Then I retreat to my room with the telephone. The unmade bed, with its tangle of unwashed linen, confronts me like an accusation. I trade my heels for flip-flops and dial the number Carlotta gave me. To muffle the chattering television, I swing the door partly shut and tuck the receiver between my chin and collarbone, so I can peel off the sheets as the phone rings at her father's house.

"Who is it?" An old man's voice rasps over the line.

"This is Marina, Carlotta's neighbor."

"Carlotta?"

"Carlotta's *neighbor*," I say. "I live near her, and actually I want to get in touch with Consuelo."

"What's the difference? Las dos locas. They're both crazy as fleas and stupider than pinworms. The older one married to that comemierda, and the younger one, largo de cabello, corto de seso," the old man says, pretty aptly summing up my expe-rience of these sisters, especially Consuelo, being long on hair but short on smarts.

"Okay, well," I say. "I need to speak to Consue-lo, if you can—"

"She's right here, talking all the damn air out of the room. Ven aca, muchacha," he shouts, and I picture a wizened, vein-corded arm thrusting the receiver away in relief. "It's for you, mensa."

A low voice purrs seductively. "Raúl?"

"No, this is Marina. I live next door to Carlotta."

"Do I *know* you?"

"We met a couple years ago, at that party Carlotta had on the Fourth of July for Efrem."

"That fat fuck. You his friend?"

"No way. I live next door to them," I say, offering this as evidence that I could not possibly have friendly feelings toward Efrem.

"I don't remember you." The voice rises, accusingly.

"Anyway," I say, thinking, *that's because I didn't annoy the shit out of you, which is the only reason I remember you*, "I'm a friend of your sister's, and she's had some trouble. She really needs your help."

"What happened?"

"Efrem got violent with her last night, and she's in the hospital. She's going to be okay," I say quickly. "But Efrem was locked up and now Bobby—"

"You got a car?" Consuelo blurts.

"Yeah, but—"

"I'm coming right over," she says. The receiver clicks and the dial tone hums in my ear.

I bunch up the linen to haul it to the washing machine in the kitchen, curious about Consuelo's uncharacteristic conciseness in our conversation. There's no doubt in my mind, it was her voice I heard. It just didn't go on and on. Maybe she's not a phone person, or maybe she was zooming on speed at the barbecue and that's why she chattered at me like a chimp. I nudge my bedroom door open with a foot and glance at Frida Kahlo and her monkey. Both of them wear quizzical expressions as if they, too, are puzzled by the transformation in Carlotta's oncetalkative sister. Then I catch sight of my earring tree atop my chest of drawers. It no longer dazzles. Every limb, every branch is denuded. My tri-amber danglers, my Virgins of Guadalupe, my imitation corals, my turquoise and silvers, my jet bead studs, and my hoops—all of my hoops!—vanished so abruptly that I can still make out their glimmering afterimage. "Goddamn you, Xochi, selfish bitch," I say under my breath. All of my earrings gone, the thing looks barren and tragic, an arthritic crone holding out her many withered arms, reaching and reaching, for nothing.

While the linen spins before the rinse cycle, I consider tidying the front room, but my stomach grumbles, reminding me I haven't eaten lunch. In the kitchen, I slather two whole-wheat tortillas with reduced-fat chunky peanut butter for Reggie and me and try not to be too irritated at my kid sister. The Dalai Lama, who stresses that Buddha-hood is achieved by force of generosity, would probably give his sweetest, most radiant smile, his glasses glinting brightly, if his sister "borrowed" every earring he owned. He'd no doubt say something like, "Take, *take!* Everything I own belongs to the world!" And Gandhi, too, would likely hand over the matching necklaces and bracelets in a flash, if he discovered his hermanita had pillaged his earring tree. But come to think of it, those guys aren't really known for having great earrings. Or sisters. In fact, I'll bet a huge part of the Dalai's ecstatic serenity is due to the fact that he's not related to Xochi, or Della, for that matter.

I wrap Reggie's tortilla in a paper towel and take it to him in the living room.

"Look," he says. "They're about to kick the fake blonde out. She's kind of a bitch, calls herself 'Her Highness,' but I kind of like her." He grins, glances at the tortilla and at me. His eyes go shiny again. "You're too nice to me."

"Eat," I tell him. *"Eat."* Apparently, everything I own belongs to the world.

"Thanks, Marina."

"De nada," I say and bring my tortilla in to join him. "Hey, what's the story with Kiko and Bobby? Are they doing okay over there or what?"

"Yeah, I was going to say, one of us better go in after him, bring him out," Reggie tells me, as if Kiko's some comrade who's fallen behind enemy lines. "They're still playing that Grand Theft thing. We played all night and most of today. After a while, I just got sick of it." He shakes his head. "But they're still at it."

"Dang."

"Yeah, there's like nothing to eat over there, but that don't matter. They barely stop to piss. Kiko's eyes are all weirded out, too, with these dark circles and shit."

I picture my nephew hunched over the controls, a somehow more glazed and vacant look on his big pale face. As I'm chewing my tortilla de peanut butter, I think of ways to break this spell, even imagining myself cutting the main electrical line with pruning shears and wondering where I would even find such things. Then we both jump at the clatter of hooves on the pavement out front. It sounds like a herd of deer is about to trample down the front door. I leap up and pull it wide to admit Consuelo, staggering on lamé stilettos, her plump face slick with sweat. "You Marina?" she says.

I whiff the rush of hot air that's blasted in with her—*Boone's Farm? Thunderbird? Night Train?* "You're drunk."

"Not that much. Hey, you better be Marina. I already been to two wrong houses." Eyes bulging, she gags, cups a hand over her mouth, and mumbles, "Where's the toilet?"

I point the way, and she lunges for it.

"Wow," Reggie says. "Who's that weird chick?"

"Consuelo," I tell him, lowering my voice to encourage him to do likewise, though I doubt Consuelo can hear us over her retching.

"Like consolation? Isn't that what consuelo means? 'Cause if that's consolation…"

"I know," I tell him. "I *know*."

Consuelo yanks the door wide after puking and starts yakking at us while running the tap full blast. I can't hear her too well over that and the model show on television. So I step into the hallway. Reggie—more interested in the models, especially the pseudo-blonde who is pitching some kind of fit—doesn't budge from his nest.

"What's that, Consuelo?" I say, averting my nostrils.

"Connie," she says. "Call me Connie. I hate that Consuelo crap. It doesn't go with me, you know."

I nod.

"I'm just asking if you got any coffee."

"Instant." Despite the Dalai's emphasis on acting by force of generosity, I'm not about to all-aboard the Coffeeville Express at this time of day.

"Yeah, I need some." She examines her calabasa face in my mirror, dabs under her skunk eyes, smudging my cream-colored hand towel.

I slip away to fix her a cup, wondering whatever happened to words like *please* and *thank you*. Are they totally old school these days? Will they become extinct altogether or just fade into quaint anachronisms like *thee* and *thou*?

"Hey," Connie yells after me. "Who's the skinny old guy in this picture?"

I ignore this, busy myself filling the kettle, and then measure out a spoonful of Bustelo crystals into a chipped, pink cup that I never use because, well, it's chipped and tends to snag the lip. The sinking sun blazes through the kitchen windows, imbuing the room with that gauzy tangerine glow that always signals a Southern California setting in movies and television programs. Though fiery, it's a warm light that makes my window-ledge display of potted cacti and aloe plants look fuzzy, even cuddly, and in the framed photo between these, Gandhi's expression grows soft and pliant, somewhat wistful, rather than prickly and fierce.

When Connie finds me in the kitchen, she asks, "So what's up with Carlotta?"

Again, I explain the situation, filling in more details as we wait for the water to boil.

"Shit," she says, a pensive look on her face. "I got to go get my stuff if I'm going to have to stay here with Bobby."

"I can lend you a nightgown. We can pick up a toothbrush and whatever else you need at Save-More down the street," I tell her.

She stares at me, unblinking. "Yeah, but I got my prescriptions, my contact solution, and all that. I really got to have my things."

"That's fine," I tell her over the shrieking kettle. "Kiko can hang with him a little longer, at least until you get back."

"Until *we* get back," she says.

I fill the chipped cup, stir in the coffee crystals. "We?"

"Yeah, I ain't got no wheels, and I got to haul clear to Montebello for my junk."

"How'd you get here?"

She sips her coffee and winces. "The viejo brung me, and let me tell you, he wasn't too happy about it. Old bastard has nothing better to do, but he can't be bothered—"

"Have you even been next door?" I ask her. "Have you even stopped in to see how Bobby's doing?"

"Nah," she says, shifting her gaze to the kitchen clock. "I just got here. Quick as I could."

"Maybe you should go over there. Maybe you should check up on your nephew, see how he's doing."

She gulps down the coffee and thrusts her chin at my back door. "Can I go next door through there?"

"If you want to climb a six-foot cinder-block

wall, sure," I tell her, thinking of the padlock stupid Efrem clamped on the gate to keep Carlotta from slipping out back.

Connie shoots me an exasperated look and clip-clops out of the kitchen. I resist the urge to flip her off. I'm the one who deserves to throw the stink eye. I'm about as eager to drive her clear to Montebello as I am to rewind and replay this whole pointless day all over again, minute by minute, feeling even way more exhausted and discouraged this time through. But no way will I hand the keys over to Reggie, who invariably returns my car with the gas tank empty and the engine light flashing, or to Kiko, whose dyslexia will not have been improved by playing video games for the past twenty hours. I did promise Carlotta to look after Bobby, but I have zero desire to traipse next door and supervise the little jerk myself.

After Connie bangs out the front door, Reggie appears at my side to toss his napkin in the garbage can under the sink. "What's her trip?"

I shrug.

"Is she coming back?"

"I'm afraid so," I say, before rinsing out her cup and sponging away the sepia ring it left on my countertop.

Chapter Six

Montebello, from the Valley, is by no means an easy jaunt. The only lucky thing is that it's Sunday, so I don't have to deal with too much serious traffic. There's traffic, then there's *traffic*. What we have here is the bumper-to-bumper-but-flowing version of too many cars on the freeways. Connie intermittently gives directions while narrating the inconsequential details of her life. She turns out to be a true naviga*trix* with an emphasis on the "tricks," getting us lost several times as soon as we turn off the exit ramp, thereby stretching a forty-minute trip into well over an hour. She runs her mouth the whole way, which is part of the problem. She doesn't pay attention to much beyond narrating her life story.

"And so I took Raúl to meet my nina, Celsa, at Yvette's quinceañera," she says now as we likely pass a critical street where we ought to have turned.

Connie's the type of person who expects everyone to keep up with details of her life in the way fans track what's happening with movie stars. When I ask who Raúl is, she gets huffy with me.

"Raúl," she says. "Raúl *Rios*," as if giving his last name ought to crystallize his identity for me, like when someone says, "Oh, come on! Everyone knows Javier—Javier *Bardem*."

"Some friend?" I hazard a couple guesses. "A *relative*?"

She emits an annoyed puff of breath. "If you're a teacher, like you say, then you must have gone to college, and you don't *know* Raúl Rios? He writes that column for the *Daily News*. Don't tell me you've never read 'Ask a Cholo'? It's like 'Dear Abby,' but only comes out once a week, on Tuesdays."

I don't explain that I haven't seen the column because I read the *LA Times*. Instead, I bite my lower lip to simulate a thoughtful look, hoping to smooth over this hiccup in the conversation, so she can refocus on giving directions.

"It's the best thing in the damn paper. People all over the world write to Raúl. They want to know how come cholos like khakis so much, what's with the long-sleeve flannel shirts in summer, and what are those pocket chains for. But also they want to know deep shit, like where does the word *cholo* come from and what's a good first tattoo for a young cholo. Raúl knows all that stuff. He knows everything, and *everyone*," she tells me, "knows Raúl. He's even an adjunct professor at East LA College. He teaches introductory composition and basic cultural studies."

I lift an eyebrow.

"We've been going together for like two years now," she says, and I realize in a flash that if this fool is dating Connie, he's in no way possessed of the judgment necessary to advance beyond adjunct in this lifetime.

"Anyways," Connie says, "that's where we're going, to our apartment to get my stuff. We're engaged, me and Raúl."

"Congratulations."

She bares her gapped teeth in a grin. "Yeah, as soon as he divorces that ugly ho he married—right after the kid is born—we're going to elope to Las Vegas."

"Nice," I say.

"Honeymoon in Cabo." She sighs. "The Mexican Riviera."

"Sounds good."

"What's your story?" she asks, giving me an abrupt look. "You married?"

"I'm not married," I tell her.

"Boyfriend?"

I shake my head.

"A dyke," she says, slapping her thigh. "I *knew* it. I'm always winding up with the dykes."

"Look," I tell her. "It's none of your business, but I'm not gay. I had a boyfriend for a long time and we broke up." I have no idea why I bother to clarify my sexual preference and romantic status for her. The words just release themselves reflexively.

Connie squints at me as I drive. "He dumped you, right?"

"Not your business."

"A-ha," she says, waggling an index finger at me. "*He* dumped you. I can tell. The no makeup look, the draggy way you walk, the constant suspiros—"

"What?"

She inhales deeply and releases her breath noisily, a melodramatic sigh. "Like that," Connie says. "You've only done it like a million times since I first got to your place."

I swallow back a great gulp of air. "You're crazy."

"I knew it. Those pictures of that viejo all over your place," Connie says. "He's that old guy, isn't he? You got a thing for the senior citizen type."

I shake my head.

"Hey, I'm not judging. To each his own, right? I

go for brainy guys myself."

We likely sail past yet another crucial street and we will no doubt have to backtrack after half an hour to refind the damn thing. "Are we almost there?"

"Yeah, sure," Connie says, but she's been saying this for the past half hour or so. "It won't be long now," she tells me, but maybe this is in reference to her hopes related to her forthcoming nuptials. She yawns, goes silent. I steal a sideways glance. Her eyelids flutter shut.

"Don't we have to turn somewhere or do something?" I say, beseeching Buddha and the orishas not to let this nutty borracha pass out on me. "Connie! Connie! Come on. I can't drive around like this forever. Do you need to use my cell phone? Call for directions?"

"What? No, we're almost there, I swear." She pushes away my phone. "It's better not to call ahead." She sits upright, leans toward the windshield. "Look, *look*, there it is. The apartment complex is on that street. Turn right here."

"Turn *right* here?" I ask as I'm in the left lane. "Or right *here*?"

"Right, *right*," she says, pointing at last. "You have to make a right turn. The apartment complex is just up that street."

By this time, it's too late to turn, so I plow past

the street and make the first illegal U-turn I can manage to get us back to the shady little corner with no street sign that she claims to recognize. "This better be it," I say through gritted teeth.

She gives me an offended look. "You think I don't know my own place?"

"You didn't exactly get us here by the most direct route."

"Huh?" she says, now digging through the oversized and battered mailbag of a purse on her lap.

"Never mind." I brake to a crawl, scanning both sides of the street for an apartment complex before spotting a great beige stucco hive with barred windows at the end of the block.

"That's the place," Connie says. She twists the rearview mirror to see herself before outlining her lips with a chocolate-brown pencil.

I inch the car into a tight space near the complex. Over the entryway, rusted metal lettering spells out Polynesian Heights, and two unlit tiki-style torches stand sentry below that. A sign jabbed into the patchy lawn offers one month's rent free, and a wilted yellow balloon dangles from that, flapping listlessly in the breeze.

Connie's darkly lined lips make her look like a refugee from a superhero comic book, the bad guy's trampish girlfriend. She tosses the lip liner into her bag and snaps it shut.

"Aren't you going to finish?" I ask, gesturing at her mouth.

"Huh?" She clicks open the car door.

"The lipstick. Don't you want to fill it in? You've just got the outline."

She narrows her eyes at me. "That's the *style*," she says. "That's the way it's supposed to be."

I reach for my bag and unlatch my door.

"Um, Maria," she says.

"Marina," I tell her. "It's Marina, not Maria."

She gives a little shrug. "Listen, you better wait here until I check things out. You're cool with that, right?" Her inky pupils dart back and forth like there's some miniature Ping-Pong match being played on my face.

"You don't need me to help get your stuff?"

"Maybe," she says. "Let me see what's what first, okay? I got to make sure things are cool."

"Just hurry up, will you?" I slam the door shut, wishing I'd brought the Dalai Lama to read while I lop off another whopping segment of my mortal coil waiting for some fool. By force of generosity, I tell myself as I watch Connie teetering up the walk on those glittery heels. She picks her way past the torches, her blouse all rucked up and wrinkled in the back, and I wonder just how much time I have given over to waiting for idiots like this in my life.

I would have to begin by including the nights I struggled to stay up until my father returned home from work back when he was still living with us, and then again, after the divorce, when my mother split to join the nuns, and I moved in with him and his new wife, Xochi's mother. Once in a while I would get lucky back in those days, and he would stumble in around two or three in the morning, after which I would snatch a few hours of sleep before waking raw-eyed and dazed for school in the morning. But sometimes, he would not return at all, not for days. It was only after the cancer, when he got involved with Transcendental Meditation, that he got all spiritual and more considerate of others, that a person could depend on him to be home nights. Although when he was meditating and all fugued out, it still felt like he wasn't around.

On top of that wasted time, I'd have to count the incidents when I've been stood up by dates—there were not many, but they still sting. And then I'd throw in all the times I waited for Rudy to call or come over when he said he would but never actually showed up, and I add to that all the time I spent standing in lines or sitting in waiting rooms, just in a holding pattern, suspended like some useless scorpion in resin. If I tallied all the minutes and hours, I know it would come out to be something shocking, like the amount of salt a person consumes in a lifetime. I once watched a health program on television about this, and I was stunned by a tabletop loaded with sacks of the stuff. It put me off potato chips for the longest time. I'll bet the amount of time I've wasted waiting would turn out to be equally astonishing, like several months or even years.

An orange tabby cat with a loosely swinging gut strolls near the car, tossing me a disdainful look, and a turquoise Ford truck chugs past. Shadows lengthen, pooling on the sidewalk, welling like oil spills on the stubbly, faded grass. I wish I could meditate like my father used to do, empty my mind and refresh my spirit during all this lost time, but one thought jumps to another and another, like yappy circus dogs chasing after each other through flaming hula hoops. Before long, I have my replacement cell phone in hand and I'm dialing Letty's number. Miguel answers.

"It's me," I tell him. "How's Letty? I went by your place, but no one was there."

"Marina!" His voice is breathless, urgent. "Where've you *been*? Why didn't you come when my mom called?"

Rosaura call me? I can't even picture this. "No one's called, but I lost my cell phone, had to get another—"

"Letty's in the hospital," he says.

"In the hospital? *Why?* What happened?"

"She took her pills."

"What?"

"All of them," he says. "Those sleeping pills they gave her, she swallowed the whole bottle of them."

My heart lurches. A gasp, a true suspiro escapes me. My fingertips tingle, icy pinpricks of dread spreading into my palms and crawling up my arms. My tongue grows thick, clumsy. "Is she okay?"

"They pumped out her stomach. She's going to be okay. A'ight, don't worry. She's going to be fine. She's resting," Miguel says. "They'll keep her overnight, and then they want to put her somewhere—I don't know—some facility or something. You should have been there to talk to the doctors. I can't figure out half of what they say. Where *were* you? Why didn't you come?"

"I had no idea."

"My mom's right here. She says she did call you."

"I lost my cell phone," I say, thinking now about Rudy—poor Rudy!—and wondering how he's doing with this.

Bam! A slamming sound jolts me and I nearly drop the phone, my heart juddering against my rib cage. It's Connie banging on the passenger side window. I press the automatic door lock and put a hand up to signal her to stop, but she doesn't notice or else she doesn't care. Uselessly, she tries the locked door and then keeps pounding away. *Bam-bam-bam.*

"When can you go to the hospital?" Miguel asks. "She's been asking for you."

"Right now, I can be there in an hour or so." I gesture broadly at Connie, transmitting the universally recognized semaphore code for get away from me *now*.

Rosaura's voice buzzes in the background, and Miguel says, "You can't visit now. They just kicked us out. She's testing. Go in the morning, a'ight?"

"Okay," I say, waving off Connie, who's still pounding the window.

"It's the same place," he says, "where the baby—"

"I'll go first thing." I reach over to smack the passenger window myself and flash my hand, again palm up to get Connie to cease and desist.

"We didn't know—" he says again, his voice dissolving into static.

"I'll be there. I'll be there tomorrow. I better go. I'm losing you." The phone goes silent.

I press the release, snapping the locks open. Connie yanks her door wide and sticks her big head in to say, "What the fuck is wrong with you?"

"Damn it, I was on the phone," I tell her. "Couldn't you see? I just got some really bad news."

"Oh," she says, looking thoughtful, even serious for about a half second, but she isn't interested enough to ask about this. "Listen, I'm going to need your help now with my shit. It's more than I thought, and this is like the perfect time."

I heave myself out of the car to stand on buzzing legs that feel like they belong to someone else. That unrealness that overtakes me when I'm feverish descends on me now like a fog. *Letty tried to die.* I can't take it in, but deep in this gauzy cloud of otherness I can put one numb foot in front of the other and trudge robotically after Connie. In a way, I'm even grateful for this ridiculous errand, the petty distraction of it, but I tell her, "Let's make this fast, okay?"

She leads the way back into the complex, chattering the whole time about how lucky this is that Raúl's not home because he would really take it hard if he knew she was leaving, even for a few days, so with him out of the apartment, she can quietly just collect her stuff and she's even found these crates, so that's convenient, too, and on and on, until her flat, relentless voice jackhammers in my skull and I imagine tackling her to the ground, jamming a fistful of that straw-colored grass into her weirdly outlined mouth. But at least her non-stop babble crowds out worry about Letty. My dread shrinks to a dull, shadowy thing like an apricot pit lodged at the back of my throat, as we step through the courtyard. Finally, we approach a ground floor apartment near the rear of the complex. The front door stands ajar, and a window beside it is also flung open, its screen popped out and leaning against the outer wall. Connie strides right in. "Want a beer?" she asks.

"Are you insane? Let's just get your stuff and go. Come on, Connie. I haven't got all night."

"Yeah, okay," she says. Nevertheless, she heads for the kitchenette, swings the refrigerator door wide, and pops open a can of Budweiser. "We better make this quick. Who knows? They could be here any minute."

"*They*?" My eyes adjust to the shadowy apartment, and I make out a playpen at the heart of the green wall-to-wall shag carpet, a baby swing near the couch, a laundry basket filled with folded sleepers and receiving blankets on the coffee table, assorted infant toys strewn about here and there. "Hey, wait a minute. Who really lives here?"

"Raúl and that bitch wife of his *stay* here. For now. I'm moving all the way in after the divorce." She slugs back the beer.

"They had the baby?" I ask, pointing at the playpen.

"I guess so."

"You *guess*."

Connie shrugs.

"What's going on? Do you really have stuff here?"

Her lower lip pooches out. "Yeah, of course I do. What do you think? All my stuff is here." She bangs the can down on the kitchen counter and stomps over to a CD rack near the stereo. "My music," she says, randomly thrusting CDs into her capacious purse. "My pictures." She reaches for framed photos on the wall. The first one she removes is a wedding portrait in which she is definitely *not* the smiling, dimple-cheeked, clean, sane- and sober-looking bride. "That television belongs to me," she says over her shoulder. "Just unplug it and disconnect those wires in back. It's not that heavy. We can put it in your trunk. The stereo, too, that's mine. Come on. I thought you were in some big goddamn hurry."

This is where I fold my arms over my chest and plant my flip-flops in that avocado-colored shag. "Unh-uh," I tell her. "No way."

Footsteps scrape on the walk outside, followed by voices: a man and a woman chatting over the cranky sounds of a baby fussing.

"*Shit*," Connie says, freezing in mid-reach for

another framed portrait of the wedding couple. "Oh, shit."

A bolt of adrenaline strikes and I freeze, just as I do in nightmares where I know I've got to (a) scream, (b) run, or (c) be slain. My mouth feels cotton wadded, my numb legs turn to cement, and my heart knocks against my throat with such force that my hands and feet throb.

"Honey, you didn't leave the door open, did you?" the woman's voice asks. "Oh my god, *look*—the window!"

"Stay back with Yanira," the man says in a low voice.

Almost immediately, this hulking bullet-shaped form in khakis and a red polo shirt appears in the threshold, and Connie, face blanched but smiling sweetly, says, "Hey, Raúl! There you are. I was just talking about you." Still holding the portrait, she steps to the doorway and tilts her face toward Raúl as if offering her cheek for a kiss.

"*Connie?*" He flips on a light switch. "What are you doing here? And who are you?" He points an accusing finger at me, still standing statue-stiff, with my arms crossed. My jaw unhinges and my lips part, but I can only manage a shrug.

"*What* are you doing here?" Raúl's voice booms when he raises it, true basso profundo that reverberates against the walls, and he's puffing out his chest, ready to advance on us now that he's figured out we are beyond doubt stupid and crazy, but probably neither armed nor dangerous. He snatches the portrait from Connie. "You can't just break in here and mess with my stuff."

Connie forces a laugh. "Don't be silly, Raúl. No one broke in. I just came by for my things. I'm going away for a little while." She turns to me and winks. "I told you he can't stand it when I have to leave."

"These aren't your things," Raúl says, shaking the framed picture. "What do you have there?" He grabs her overstuffed purse, spills out the CDs on the floor, along with a jumble of grubby makeup, brushes, and balled up tissues. "This is *my* stuff. You're stealing my stuff, you stupid bitch. What else have you taken from here? Huh?"

Connie spreads those comic-book lips in another gaptoothed grin, looking like a beatifically insane person.

"Nothing," I say. "She drank part of that beer, grabbed the CDs, and took down a few pictures. That's all, I swear." My voice sounds distant, strange to me. The sense of unreality that filled me when I stepped out of the car seems to swell, inflating to encompass this small apartment and the people in it, and a strange calmness accompanies the feeling that this is not real—none of it, not Letty's suicide attempt, not this perceived burglary, not the large seething man standing between me and the door. It's not real, I tell myself, letting tranquility overtake me. An illusion, the Dalai Lama would say. Everything is an illusion, a dream. If I wanted, I could leave at any time, substitute this illusion for another.

"Who the hell are you?" he asks, squinting at me while still blocking the doorway.

"Um, look," I say and pull open my purse. "I can write you a check for any damage to the window and for the beer." But, shoot, where is my checkbook? I swear I possess the world's only Bermuda Triangle purse; I put things in, and they disappear for days, weeks, months even, before reappearing—without explanation—within its shadowy recesses. "I'll just write you a check," I say again, stalling for time while I rifle through the assorted pens, date book, compact mirror, brush, tampons, linty breath mints, tissues, glasses case, and *hello*, here's my long-lost gift card for Borders, a birthday present from Della, must still have at least twenty dollars on that—

"You think I'm stupid enough to take a check from some burglar?" he says, widening his eyes in disbelief. Now that he mentions it, with those smallish eyes agog and that beefy face that barely tapers into his thick neck, he *does* look kind of stupid. In fact, at the moment, I have trouble believing he really is qualified to be an adjunct.

Of course, I can't say this, so I tell him, "I'm not a burglar. I'm an educator, like you." I pull out the Borders card before it vanishes again and hand it to Raúl. "If you don't want my check, you can get about twenty bucks' worth of books with this, okay?"

The woman appears in the doorway behind him, holding a baby in her arms. "Raúl, what is going on?" She's the sane-looking bride in the portrait, now wearing an orange shift and sandals.

Raúl turns to her, shakes his head, and shrugs. "These, these people just broke in, started taking stuff."

"I've called 9-1-1," she says, narrowing her eyes at Connie and then at me. "The police are on their way."

"Raúl, honey," Connie says, "aren't you going to introduce us?"

Raúl's wife flashes him a hot look. "You *know* her?"

Suddenly, Raúl doesn't look all that fierce anymore. Instead, he's transfixed by the gift card in his meaty fist.

"So," I say, "I've really got to go now. Please use the gift card. There's no expiration, but you'd be surprised how easy it is to lose those things."

I wedge between the now-distracted Raúl and the door frame, slip past his wife, saying, "Nice baby."

"Just how do you know her?" she asks Raúl as I whoosh through the courtyard. My flip-flops smacking against my bare soles make the gladdest racket imaginable.

My trusty little car's engine churns at the flick of my key, and I steer through the darkening side streets for the main boulevard, listening for sirens. I nearly make it to the highway before the Dalai Lama's words funnel into my thoughts, penetrating my giddy relief at having gotten away. That one phrase—*force of generosity*—just won't leave me alone. And then the whole verse announces itself: *By force of generosity and other virtues, may I achieve Buddhahood to benefit all sentient beings.* Oh no, I tell myself, no way, but my pesky conscience nudges, nips, and nags, pushing me to consider karmic forces, kind acts to generate goodwill for those I love. *Letty!*

I yank a hard right to pull into a defunct gas station, mowing down the tall weeds that have pierced through the asphalt as I circle around to retrace my route. And there she is, the sentient being herself, tripping along the side street in those gilded stilettos, her empty purse swaying like a saddlebag at her side. I glide to the curb beside her and reach over to click the passenger door open. "Hey, Connie," I call, and she faces me, startled. One eye is puffed half-shut, promising to bloom into a royal shiner. Her resemblance to Carlotta comes across now in a kind of heartbreaking way. "Get in, okay? I'll take you home."

She trots to the car and scoots into the passenger seat. "She hit me," she says. "Didn't I tell you what a—"

"Shut up, Connie," I tell her, making my voice as sharp as it will go. "I'm taking you home on one condition: no talking. Not one word or I swear I will kick you out of this car." But I am curious, though, wondering how the woman smacked Connie with that baby in her arms. Or did she first hand the kid off to Raúl? And then I hear it: a pulse of sound at first, faint as a mosquito's whine that swiftly ratchets up the decibels, building to a mindscraping crescendo when the squad car rushes by, flashing its blue lights. Connie, predictably an expert in the lachrymal arts, releases a shuddery sob that is pretty close to elegant in its precision of pitch, and I pluck a small bouquet of tissues from the newly replaced box atop the console, thrust it in her direction. "Hey, hey, cut that out, will you? Seriously, I've had just about enough for one day."

Chapter Seven

I deposit Connie at her father's house, figuring she'll make a lousy babysitter. Even a cholo mocoso like Bobby deserves better than that. When I finally, *finally* pull into my driveway, I'm thinking, heck with it, I'll get the kid to come over to my house; he can stay in the guest room, his mother's old digs. If I bring Bobby home with me, I'll have a better chance of breaking Kiko out of his video game trance. One thing is sure: It promises to be a pain-in-the-nalgas night. Plus, I'll have to call in a substitute for tomorrow in order to see Letty first thing, which also means writing lesson plans and instructions so I can take these over to school before the first bell. "Como fregón," I mutter as I trudge up the walk, my flip-flops scuffling along, as if too worn out, too halfhearted even to slap at my heels.

But when I open the front door, unlocked as ever, a warm funky wave—the effluvia of unwashed male bodies combined with powerful foot odor—engulfs me, and I find Reggie *and* Kiko both camped out on the livingroom furniture, amid the bedding that no one has gotten around to stowing. And no one's bothered to flick on the lights. I stumble over a pair of gym shoes in the center of the carpet. The model competition is still blaring from the set, likely some marathon broadcast. "How come you're here?" I ask Kiko. "Where's Bobby?"

Bathed in bluish light emanating from the television screen, Kiko's face looks as broad and bland as the surface of the moon. He doesn't even bother to look up. "His old man came by."

"*What?*" I step in front of his face, blocking his view of the set.

Kiko cranes his neck to see the show, but a commercial pops on, a hectoring advertisement for miracle glue. He mutters something unintelligible, and I snatch the remote, mute the sound. "What old man?" I say. "His *grandfather*?" Maybe Efrem's parents are actually stepping up to take responsibility for their own family here.

"Nah, his dad. That ugly dude, that Efrem guy. He got in about six and kicked my ass out," Kiko tells me. "And, tía, he wasn't even nice about it, didn't even thank me nor nothing for staying with Bobby."

I shake my head, eyes wide. "Are you kidding me?"

"They must've bonded him out," Reggie pipes from the love seat. "Can you turn the sound up, Marina? The show's about to come back on. You won't believe it, man, but that bitchy blonde— that Her Highness chick—she's still in the game. I think she could even win."

"But it's Sunday. How can they bond anyone out on a Sunday?"

Kiko shrugs, and Reggie, with more truth than he realizes, says, "I got no clue."

"And, tía," Kiko says. "I wouldn't go over there or even call if I was you."

"Believe me, I'm not planning on it."

"He's pretty pissed off, that Efrem. Dude was talking all kinds of smack on you, tía. You don't even want to know."

"C'mon, Marina, put the volume on, *please*," Reggie says, his voice rising with eagerness. "They're about to do the catwalk."

I unmute the set and grab the phone to dial the substitute hotline, wondering how in the world Efrem managed to get a judge to set bail on a Sunday. Again, I'm no lawyer, but doesn't there need to be some kind of hearing for that?

"Tía," Kiko says, glancing at me with the phone. "Rudy called like around ten thousand times, sounded all upset, and that vieja kept calling, too. That Sour Rosa or whatever her name is, that mother of Miguel." He hauls himself upright on the couch and reaches to peel off his grime-stiffened socks with a groan. The kid's eyes have that hollowed, dull look that signals deep exhaustion. Even his plumpish cheeks seem drawn, paler than usual.

But I can't help myself and blurt out, "Kiko, wash your damn feet. Seriously, they stink like dog shit."

He winces, shoots me a big-eyed, startled look, like I just sucker-punched him in the gut. In the silence that follows this, Reggie glances at Kiko, then at me. "That's kind of cold, Marina," he says. "Kiko can't help his feet, you know. Heck, I bet he can't even smell them." He turns to Kiko. "Though, dude, she's right. They are pretty rank."

"Kiko, I…"

He tries a smile. "It's okay, tía, really. I'm going to shower in a minute."

"There's stuff going on with Letty, and I'm all— I don't even know—confused, pissed off, and shocked, really, that they let Efrem out. I mean, like, why is there no peace for me? *Ever?* Still, you got to know, m'ijo, that you were really great to watch Bobby. I didn't mean it to come out like that." Seriously feeble, I'll admit, but something of an apology nonetheless.

Kiko, still staring at the TV screen, says, "That's a'ight, tía. We cool."

And I retreat into my bedroom as the blond model, her hair snake-coiled atop her head and wearing a mini-dress that looks like it's made of cellophane, prances like some high-strung pony across the television screen.

Before I dial the substitute line, I plan to punch in Rudy's number. How terrible he must feel. Face it—I still care about the guy, even if he is a dick. After almost ten years, how can I not? And what's worse than to have your kid attempt suicide? In truth, Letty is like *our* kid. We were usually just the three of us at the dinner table, at the movies and amusement parks, on vacations. Not too long ago, at the Cineplex, I stepped to the window and ordered three tickets out of habit, though I was the only one there to see the film.

I remember Letty's mother, her body discovered in Echo Park by joggers. Wasn't that suicide, too? What an example for Letty, who was just a kid at the time. Still, some part of me just can't put this together—Letty and suicide. I rummage in my memory for hints or warning signs that should have alerted me to this. But instead a rush of images flash before me: Letty circling the block on the bicycle I gave her when she turned ten, tooting the horn on the handle and waving at me each time she passed; Letty after I took her to have purple streaks put in her hair for her first middle-school dance; Letty with her face buried in the hollow under my collarbone, weeping hot, snotty tears because a boy she liked said "Do I even know you?" when she finally mustered the courage to phone him; Letty, as a teenager, introducing me to Miguel, whom I did not like at first because he was older, an ex-junkie with tattooed arms; Letty on her wedding day, when Rudy gave her away, and I stood witness as her maid of honor. None of these memories jibe with the idea of Letty emptying that vial of pills into her hand and swallowing the lot of them. Where is she now, I wonder, that Letty I knew? And is there any way for me to bring her back?

I press in the familiar number, and Rudy picks up before the second ring. "Marina," he says, breathlessly, like he's just been staring at the caller ID, waiting for my name to flash. "Did you hear about Letty?"

"Yeah, I already talked to Miguel."

"My bebita," he says, his voice breaking. "Mi her-mosita, my sweet little girl. *How? How* can this happen?" His tone sharpens with accusation.

"She's having a hard, hard time," I say. "Neither of us can even imagine—"

"It's evil, mujer, just like Nestor predicted. A curse! He put the Evil Eye because of you!"

"Come on, Rudy. That's stupid," I tell him, gazing now at the stripped mattress and naked pillows on my bed. The blasted linen! I forgot to put it in the dryer, and stupidly, still in housecleaning mode, I threw the extra set in the washer, too, since the linen closet had a musty smell. "You can't possibly believe—"

"You're so stubborn, Marina. That's what's wrong with you. You don't care who you hurt, just so you can be the one who's right."

"Think about it, Rudy. Nestor's supposedly your friend. Why would he harm Letty like this?"

"He just throws curses," Rudy explains. "He can't know how far they'll fly nor where they're going to land. He told me himself, and that's why I called you. You got to change your mind, Marina. Come down to that law office tomorrow. You got to, so he can do the limpieza before worse shit happens."

"Be real, will you?" I tell him. "My going or not going to that law office isn't going to change a damn thing. If I thought it would make a difference, I—"

"Ah, forget it," he says. "You don't care. I should know by now. When the baby was born, you could have taken time off from work to help

Letty."

"What?"

"Don't 'what' me. You know I asked you, I begged you, and you refused."

A dim recollection of Rudy contemplating hiring a nurse to help Letty when the baby was born emerges for me. We were drinking coffee before work and Rudy was, as usual, coming up with reasons not to spend money on anyone other than himself. He *did* throw out the idea of me taking off time to be with Letty and the baby, but I assumed he was just thinking out loud, listing possibilities. I dismissed that one pretty quickly. At the time, I had no way of knowing the baby would be ill, that he would die, and Letty would try to take her life. I was just finishing my first semester at Olive Branch Middle School, building relationships with students and colleagues, looking forward to advising the literary magazine in the spring. I think I said something like, "Are you kidding? There's no way I can take a leave when I haven't even been teaching a year." Rudy dropped it, and eventually Miguel enlisted his mother to help out with child care.

Now, I say, "Oh, come on, Rudy. That's not fair."

"No, it's not fair, and it's not right. The world is off-balance when women put themselves first—

their precious careers ahead of human beings, human life." His voice takes on a nasty edge. "You know what, Marina? It's a lucky thing you can't have kids. You'd make a real shitty mother." And he hangs up.

I drop the phone, recoiling from it like it's a rattlesnake or a tarantula. With one deft kick, I send it skittering under my bed. Then I breathe deeply, close my eyes, think of the Dalai Lama, those perplexing words about cherishing those who treat us badly. I still don't get how this is supposed to work, but after a few moments, I'm at least calm enough to make the bed.

I plan to sleep on top of the comforter and cover the pillows with soft towels since there's no time to dry the sheets. I snap the down-filled quilt, unfurling it over my bare mattress, thinking Rudy's wrong, way wrong. The trouble is that I care too much. "About everything," I murmur. I round the corner of the bed to smooth out a little hillock, gasping when I catch sight of a face in my darkened bedroom window—a blurry, tortured-looking mask of fury. I back away, thinking, *Efrem!* But the face retreats, too, and I recognize my own stupid self, my reflection distorted in the shadowy glass. With shaking fingers, I twist the latch, locking the window, and yank the curtains shut.

After the bed is made, I crawl underneath to

retrieve the phone so I can call the substitute hotline and, unbelievably, I get the automatic this-
number-is-no-longer-inservice message. Thinking
I misdialed, I try again, but the same recording
drones in my ear. Don't they have subs during
summer sessions? Did they change the number without telling me? That would be typical of my
school, where vital information, especially for teachers, is generally not divulged. Summer school
sessions are only half-day, so maybe I should just
teach my damn classes and visit Letty afterward,
around one.

Then I remember someone Rudy and I met at a
party for his cousin, Mateo. This guy said he was
a graphic artist who worked as a substitute teacher
to "feed his habit," meaning printmaking. He gave me his card, which I, of course, tossed into the
Black Hole, also known as my purse. I snatch my
bag from the dresser and dump its contents out on
my bed, knowing my chances of finding the thing
are pretty poor. Even so, in my wallet and oddly
stuck to the back of my health insurance card, I
discover an embossed gray rectangle of cardstock,
a tasteful thing with handsome black lettering that
reads: Carlos Lozano, Graphic Designer/Substitu-
te Teacher, and below that, blessedly, is his phone
number.

I sit on top of my bed, phone in hand, and then

I press in the unfamiliar number with care. After a few rings, a sleepy voice answers. "'Lo?"

"Hi, is this Carlos? Carlos Lozano?"

"Yeah, who's this?" After so many months without waking up next to Rudy, I'd forgotten how sexy some men sound when their sleep is disturbed, that husky rumble of their deep voices.

All at once, I'm tongue-tied. I hadn't planned out this part of the conversation. There's way too much to explain and really not a lot to say. "I, uh, I don't know if you remember me. I met you at Mateo's party last fall. I teach over at Olive Branch Middle—"

"Marina, right?" His voice sounds much less sleepy.

"Yeah," I say, impressed. "Say, you've got a pretty good memory."

"You still with that Reuben?"

"You mean Rudy," I say, "and no, that's over. We broke up months ago."

"O-*kay*, then."

"Listen, I remembered you sub sometimes, and I need someone to cover for me tomorrow."

"Oh," he says, a little flatly.

"It's just half-day because it's summer session, so it's probably less money."

"It is less," he tells me.

"Can you do it, though? Will you cover my classes for tomorrow? Something important came up for me, and I just can't put it off."

"I guess," he says with a yawn.

"Great! I'll make up the lesson plans and copy the roll sheets."

"Wait a minute," he says. "I just remembered I got to take my moms to the dentist in the morning. I don't think I can actually be there before ten."

Two hours of substitution is hardly worth it to either of us. "Maybe another time," I say.

"Listen, Marina, I want to do it. I need the hours, especially over the summer," he tells me. "Plus, I might get a long-term gig at your school. You know Alva Reyes? Teaches math?"

I picture the chirpy, apple-cheeked, and pregnant pre-Algebra teacher who was hired a year before me. "Yeah."

He tells me she's been talking to him about covering her classes while she's on maternity leave, explaining that he'd been planning to meet with her anyway this week. Since the district pays, it doesn't cost me a dime to call in a sub, even if it's just for a couple of hours, so I go ahead and give him directions to my classroom, thank him for doing this, and we hang up. Then before I stuff everything back in my purse, I pull my phone book from the pile. I have one more call to make before crawling into the makeshift bedding. The line rings and rings as I scan my closet trying to assess exactly which shoes and what else my thieving sister took from me and hoping whichever pair she chose, those shoes are pinching her toes mercilessly right now since her feet are at least a half-size larger than mine. Whatever Xochi took, she sure left a sloppy mess in her wake. Dresses puddle the closet floor, skirts hang askew, silk blouses and scarves are tangled in my high heels, misshapen sweaters dangle halfway off their hangers—I can hardly bear to look.

Finally, another sleepy voice, this one is higher pitched, sounding more scared than in any way sexy: "Hello?"

"Daisy? Hi, it's Marina. Remember me? I was going with Rudy, Nestor's friend, when you guys lived here in LA."

It takes her a few seconds, but she says she knows who I am and asks what's up.

"Not that much, really," I tell her. "I just wondered...well, can we talk?" While she considers this, I tuck the phone between my chin and collarbone and pull both closet doors wide open. While we talk, I can sort through the jumble of shoes and clothing. This would be a good time to put things back where they belong.

Chapter Eight

The next morning, after I pull into the teacher's parking lot behind Olive Branch Middle School, I pop the trunk to unload the piñata supplies into the handy collapsible rolling cart I bought at some discount office supply store. Really, it's one of my proudest possessions, and I wish I'd had it with me when bringing cleaning supplies to Letty; though—come to think of it—it wouldn't have helped with the mop or done much good on the stairs. Here I just unfold the sides, snap down the bottom flaps, extend the handle, and voilà! I can haul just about anything that fits in a crate anywhere with ease, if I ignore the mind-crunching rumble of hard plastic wheels over concrete. Soon I'm rolling toward my bungalow classroom, happily deaf to the roar from the nearby freeway. In the distance, I spy three compact figures standing before the door to my classroom: a man with two familiarly similar boys, and I'm thinking, *No way!* But yes, as I draw nearer I make out the Ahuaul twins, and most likely an older brother or their father.

Weeks ago, I'd given both brothers after-school detention, which—for me—means about ten minutes of extemporaneous lecture about the consequences if they continue to act like fools in my classes. Armando and Felipe are identical twins, but Armando, more skilled at language acquisition than his brother, is engaged in la lucha with *The Incredible Journey* in the advanced course, while Felipe will soon be making fairy-tale piñatas in beginning reading. Despite the difference in English language proficiency, each brother seems to think he is Cantínflas himself, reincarnated. Puros payasos, those two, and about a dozen days ago, I got fed up with their clownish antics—clapping chalky erasers on other students, snaking their legs out into the aisles to trip kids, making spitballs and farting noises, all of it—I'd just had it, so I made them stay after and harangued them in Spanish about straightening out. The whole time they grinned at me in a mocking way, irritating me to the point that I blurted out that if they couldn't behave themselves in school, they'd better prepare themselves for future employment collecting garbage, or cleaning toilets, or, or, or ... selling paletas.

With that word, the mocking grins vanished. The boys lowered their eyes to their desktops, their identical Dutchcut black bangs curtaining their expressions. Encouraged by this reaction, I continued outlining the limitations they'd face due to lack of education, elaborating on how stultifying it would be to sell fruit popsicles from a freezer cart day after day. "You will have next to nothing apart from frostbitten fingers," I told them. "Is that what you want? Is it? Do you want to wind up like the paleta man?" I asked, specifically referencing the wiry white-haired baboso, clearly not quite right in the head, who parks his cart just outside school grounds, selling not only crushed fruit-sicles, but wedges of pineapple, watermelon, and corn on the cob—butter slathered, sprinkled with powdered chili, and jammed on a sharp stick. I then told the boys I wanted a meeting with their padres as soon as possible and kicked their butts out of the classroom, so I could pack up and go home.

Afterward, they both behaved like model students, even completing homework assignments— a first for both boys. And if I caught one or the other about to transgress, I simply swooped to his side and whispered "Paletas." It worked like magic every time. I forgot about the parent conference thing altogether, and now here they are, los gemelos idénticos, and from the look of it, their father—who resembles the boys so closely he could pass for a third brother, a slightly oversized and oddly superannuated triplet—on this, the worst possible morning for me to meet with them. Nevertheless I greet the brothers and shake hands with the man, who introduces himself in Spanish as Gaspar Ahuaul, the father of Armando and Felipe. He has come, he says, for the meeting I requested. I unlock the door, roll in the cart, flip on the lights, and invite the Ahuauls to take a seat in my dusty classroom.

Before I even reach my chair, Señor Ahuaul releases a torrent of words, most of them in praise of his parenting style and his firm stand against drugs. Apparently, he allows no drugs in his house, will not tolerate them under any circumstances. He says this over and over and then he goes on to tell me the boys' mother is a drug addict. Basura, he calls her, right in front of the boys, who flinch upon hearing their mother called trash. There are no women in his house, the twins' father says, in the same tone he used to denounce drugs. Señor Ahuaul and his father do fine on their own—cooking and cleaning and looking after the boys. He takes good care of his sons, he tells me, but if they ever bring drogas into his house, and here he shakes his head and brushes his palms together as if to remove dirt, that's it. He will have nothing more to do with them. That they should go straight to el carajo con su madre sucia.

I'm barely able to interject the occasional "claro" and "de veras" when he takes a breath.

He adds that he works very hard and again shows his smallish coppery hands for emphasis. Señor Ahuaul assures me that he provides everything the boys need.

When he finally pauses, possibly for praise, I ask what he does for a living.

He straightens up in his seat, throws back his thin shoulders, thrusts out his chest, looking me right in the eye. Why, he sells paletas, of course. He owns a freezer stand on wheels that he takes to the elementary school a few blocks away every weekday before and after school. It's a family business, he says with pride. His father mans the paleta troca that operates near this campus. Perhaps I have seen the grandfather of Felipe and Armando, he says, selling paletas out there en la yarda.

I nod, my cheeks suffusing with heat. The Dalai Lama's gentle face appears in my mind's eye, his expression sharpening into disapproval, even disgust. Compassion, he writes, is built upon connections forged through recognizing similarities, not by fixating on differences and holding in contempt those who are different, as if they are lower than the self. I have to marvel at my own blindness. Of course, Señor Ahuaul sells paletas. But if he had driven a garbage truck or scrubbed out the school's bathrooms, as the venerable Mr. Gustafson does here at Olive Branch, I would be in the same shameful place. I have no business suggesting school as an antidote to lives that many live with fullness and dignity. I deserve the full force of the Dalai's scorn. That he himself would be too compassionate to mete this out is no comfort here.

The paletas, the boys' father tells me, are made with fresh ingredients, all natural, no productos aditivos ni químicos. From there, he re-emphasizes his abhorrence of drugs and drug addicts, and his two sons stare downward as if again mesmerized by their desktops. Finally, Señor Ahuaul rises, asking me to let him know if the boys behave badly or if I suspect they are involved with drugs of any kind. We shake hands once more, trade muchos gustos, say adios, and he strides out of the bungalow, the silent twins shuffling in his wake.

After they leave, I barely have time to unload my supplies before students begin trickling in. Only then do I realize that Señor Ahuaul never once asked why I called the parent conference. Come to think of it, he didn't ask me anything at all about the boys or their progress in my classes, but I don't have time to dwell on this. There's not even half a minute to dash to the office to duplicate my roll sheet for the substitute. I'll have to find the time to copy all the students' names by hand, so Carlos can take roll in the second class. There's no way I will leave my roll book—listing grades and student contact information—with a sub, no matter how nice he sounds on the telephone.

A recording of the Pledge of Allegiance sputters and croaks from the staticky PA system, and following that, a series of useless and mostly unintelligible announcements, and then I take roll. The first day of piñata-making is usually a big hit, so I'm not surprised that nearly every kid is present and on time—all except for one: Felipe Ahuaul. And though I take my time handing out the jumbo-sized balloons, distributing stacks of old newspapers, and measuring out the starch into empty margarine tubs that I collect for this purpose, Felipe still doesn't show up. He must have cut out as soon as his father left the school grounds. At fifteen minutes after the hour, I give up waiting and tell his partners, Elias and Maritza, they will have to work without him.

The next ninety minutes I spend dashing from group to group, making sure no one is taking shortcuts. It's probably not surprising how many kids, especially boys, think they can get away with drenching a full sheet of newsprint in the thick blue starch and swathing their balloons with that, even though I warn them repeatedly that their piñatas will turn out looking like boulders, instead of pear or apple shapes that can be made into animal bodies or heads. I remind them that we haven't read any fairy tales featuring boulders. Corten el papel in narrow strips, douse each individually in the starch, and dios mio, practice speaking English. There are only fifteen kids in the class, fourteen with Felipe missing, but they can sure raise a solid wall of sound, gabbing to one another and laughing. Only a few, the diligent ones, abide by our rule to speak in English, but the Spanish flows so sweetly and eagerly that I don't really enforce this.

When the piñatas are covered with several layers of starch-soaked newspaper strips, we hang them on a clothesline I've strung at the back of the classroom, where they can slowly drip excess starch onto the tarp spread below as they dry. Suspended in air and oozing bluish gunk, these nascent piñatas look like pods from a low-budget science fiction flick, dark gray shells that will ultimately hatch gooey aliens. At least that's what Elias Delatorre tells me before complaining about bluish splotches on his new guayabera. I tell him it's just starch, a laundry product, and I swear it will wash right out. The other baker's dozen of kids are lining up to wash their hands in the sinks along the side wall, and still thinking about Elias's aliens, I suck in a sharp breath at the sight of a black leather-clad form wearing a shiny silver helmet and standing in the doorway. He removes the helmet, revealing a vaguely recognizable head of thick black hair tapering to a widow's peak above a flatnosed, grinning face. "Remember me?" he says, advancing with a gloved hand extended.

"Carlos," I say. "Let me wash my hands. You don't want starch on your gloves."

At my elbow, Elias says, "Why not? It washes out, qué no?"

I ignore this, cut in line to rinse my hands in the chilly water and blot them with the cheap brownish paper towels the school provides before returning to Carlos, who is examining the dripping pods. "Ah, piñatas," he says, no longer offering me his hand.

"Yep, you can't tell it now, but that's Jack the Giant Killer, next to Jack is one of the three little pigs—"

"No, no, maestra," Cecilia Valdez says. "Es el lobo."

"Okay, the wolf, then. That's Goldilocks, there's Rapunzel and Rumpelstiltskin, and some other characters I can't remember. I should have had them label the things," I say. "It's a beginning reading class, and this is the culminating project."

The bell rings, and the students grab their backpacks and trample out, a few of them shaking their wet hands dry.

"Nice," says Carlos, holding his helmet under one arm and standing awkwardly at the rear of the classroom. "I always like to see teachers sneaking in a little art."

"That's right, you're an artist." I smile at him, and then say, "Oh, no! The roll. I forgot to copy it for the next period."

"That's okay," he says. "I can have them use a sign-in sheet."

"Not such a good idea," I tell him. Last semester, I tried the sign-in roll sheet, the substitute passed it around, instructing everyone to sign their "John Hancock." I returned the next day to find a binder sheet with "John Hand Cock" scrawled twenty-three times. Another time, some joker thought it would be fun to put down a fake name. After that class, the substitute's notes reported that Pedro Infante had really acted up and been assigned detention, and Maria Felix had to leave early for a dentist appointment.

"Just leave me your roll book, then," he says.

"I don't know," I say, though apart from the motorcycle gear, he looks pretty trustworthy.

His wide face has an open expression, the dark almond-shaped eyes gaze directly into mine.

"Look, just tell me where you live, and I'll bring it by tonight."

"You'd do that?" I hesitate, considering the repercussions if I should lose the roll book; a *legal* document, I was told when first hired. "You have some place to secure it on your—" I point to his helmet—"motorcycle?"

"Sure, I have a storage compartment on the bike. I'd be glad to bring it to you, along with my notes."

During all this time we spend yakking about the thing, I could have hiked all the way to the office and back to copy the roll sheet, but I kind of like the idea of this guy coming by my place to bring the thing to me, and I really ought to get going to see Letty, so I say, "I guess that would be okay," and I scribble my address on a Post-it note for him. "I'm just curious," I say, flashing on an image of some vieja around Rosaura's age hunched on the back of a motorcycle, clutching onto a fake leopard-skin coat to keep it from whipping in the wind. "Did you take your mother to the dentist on your bike?"

He laughs. "No, we used her car. She has cataracts, can't drive anymore, so I ride over there, and we take her car when she needs to go out."

I tear off the Post-it, and on an impulse, I stick it to his jacket sleeve, but it flutters off the smooth worn leather. Carlos deftly snatches it in midair, tucks it into his helmet, and gives me a wink.

Back at the hospital, I wonder how people can stand to work here without becoming discouraged, even deeply depressed. The sprawling granite complex barely stands out in contrast on this muggy, smoggy day. Dull gray against duller gray, it looks like something designed more for prisoners than patients, except that the glass doors whoosh open freely when I step on the long rubber mat. This time, my old friend the receptionist asks me if I'm a social worker before picking up the phone to find out Letty's room number. "Something like that," I tell her.

"I thought so," she says and then dials the information operator. But after giving Letty's name, she listens briefly, frowns, and covers the receiver with one hand. "That patient was checked out this morning for transfer to another facility."

"Where? What facility?"

She asks the operator and cups the phone again to tell me, "They only give that information to family members. I'm sorry."

After purporting to be a social worker, I can't very well tell her I'm family, which technically I am not. I thank her and step into the lobby to call Miguel on my cell phone. The hospital is bad for reception, though I've discovered the best place to make a call is a spot between the fake potted plants, plastic palm things on either side of the coffee table surrounded by foam-filled plastic lounge chairs. I have to crouch way down, squatting so I'm nearly eye level with the coffee table to get a signal. This is not easy in a tight skirt, but fortunately, in the waiting area, only one oldster, with plastic tubes snaking from an oxygen tank into his nostrils, sits gaping at me in leapfrog position as I make the call. Miguel's home and cell phone ring and ring—no answer, so I leave two messages. No way will I call Rudy after last night.

After I rise to smooth my skirt, the elderly man with oxygen tubing flutters his fingers, beckoning me to approach him. I glance about in case he's summoning someone else, but he points at me, urging me to come closer. Poor viejo, abandoned in the lobby for who knows how long. Lucky for him I turned up. I imagine myself wheeling him to the front desk for help or even up to his room.

I step to his wheelchair and stoop to hear his wheezy words. "I seen that pussy," he says, his filmy eyes filling with tears of mirth. He points a knobby finger at my crotch.

"You did *not*." My palm tingles, so strong is the impulse to slap the lewd grin from his ancient face, but striking an old man is surely no way to attain Buddhahood. I picture the Dalai Lama shaking his head, frowning at me. "For your information," I tell the codger in a calm voice, "I am wearing underwear." I scan my short-term memory for an image of the exact pair I pulled on that morning: navy cotton bikini briefs. "My panties are dark blue, so your mistake is understandable."

"I seen it. I sure did."

I turn away from his rasping laughter, take brisk steps toward the elevators. Since I'm here, I figure I should drop in on Carlotta. I'd kind of planned on doing this after seeing Letty. I should find out if she knows about Efrem getting out of jail. In Carlotta's room, I find her standing beside her bed, shedding the hospital-issue gown, her clothes— the blood-spattered nightgown and robe she was wearing when Efrem attacked her—arrayed on the bed, and a wheelchair parked alongside the swing-arm bed tray which now holds a vase full of pink carnations.

"Marina," she says, the metal cup over her eye tipped slightly askew. "How come you never answer your cell?"

"I lost that phone."

"Well," she says, clearly not listening, "at least you got my message. I was afraid I'd have to call a cab."

"What message?"

"The message telling you they're releasing me. I

need a ride home."

"*Home*?" I say, thinking of Efrem, likely still en-raged—even vengeful—already installed in their small house next to mine. "But that's impossible," I tell her. "You can't go home."

"They're releasing me. I can't stay here. I have to go home. I miss the boys and I got like a million things to do." She pulls the stained nightgown over her head.

"You can't wear that, Carlotta. It's got blood all over it. Let me bring you something else to wear. I'm sure you can stay a little longer while I pick up some clothes for you."

"I can't. There's no time." Gingerly, she threads her arms through the sleeves. She stands to smooth it out and reaches for the robe. "I got way too much to do. There's the boys and then I got to help Efrem—"

"What the hell are you talking about? I thought you hated Efrem. Yesterday you wanted him to rot in jail. Can't you see what he's done to you?" Too bad there's no mirror in this room. I'd like to push her in front of it, force her to see the amber-edged purpling around her eye, that crazy metallic cup, and the cross-hatched stitches like miniature bar-bed wire imbedded in her lower lip.

She points to the flowers on the swing-arm stand, plucks out the small card affixed to a plastic fork in the bouquet. "He loves me," she says with a smile that makes her wince. "Listen to this: *Carlotta, you know you are the only one for me. I love you so much it hurts. Tu amor por vida, Efrem.*"

I nearly shudder with that *tu amor por vida* business, which sounds to me like a life sentence with no hope of parole. "He always says things like that after he hurts you, Car. You know this better than I do. Don't tell me some cheap flowers and a florist's card are all it takes. You're worth way more than that."

"He's the love of my life," she says, leveling her good eye at me. "That's something I don't expect *you* to ever understand. Now help me gather up my stuff so I can go home and change. I got to see the boys and—"

"Efrem's out," I tell her. "Don't ask me how, but they let him out last night. He's home with Bobby. I have no idea where the other two boys are. I haven't seen them in days."

She sits on the bed, her face pale. "Then it's true."

"What's true?" I ask, purely puzzled.

"They must have really enlisted," she says quietly, more to herself than to me. "Efrem said they'd signed up, that they were going away for basic training. They haven't shown up since I went home from your place. But I didn't believe him because they sometimes stay with their girlfriends. Efrem was always threatening to send them to military school, always egging them on to 'man-up' and go into the service like he did."

"But they're not old enough. They're just kids."

"They *were* kids, Marina, when we first moved in. Think about it. That was like six years ago. Junior is twenty, and Ramón turns nineteen in July. That's what we fought about that night—the boys. He was on and on about them going into the army and all that shit, lying to me, I thought, and so I told him to shut his fucking fat—"

"*That's* what you fought about," I say with a whoosh of relief. "I thought it was me. I thought you said it was because I flipped him off that afternoon."

"Oh, it was you, too," she says quickly. "He started tripping on how disrespectful I am to him, una desgracia, just like you."

Though we go back and forth like this for some time and she's stunned about her sons signing up, there's no way I can convince Carlotta not to return home. I do, however, persuade her to wait until I pick up something other than that bloodsplotched nightgown and robe to wear out of the hospital. There's a Kmart not too far from here, where I can at least buy a T-shirt and sweatpants for her to wear.

On my way to the elevator, I catch sight of the tall, jumpy Puerto Rican doctor or resident or whatever he is at the nurses' station. I avert my eyes, quicken my pace, pretending not to have seen him. But he steps into my path, saying, "Marina, wait."

Again, I'm surprised he remembers my name, when I haven't even thought to ask what his is. I tell him, "I really don't have a lot of time right now."

"Listen," he says, "I'm sorry I couldn't get back with that information yesterday. There was an emergency. A patient coded."

Unsure exactly what that means, I glance at his name tag. "It's no problem, Dr. Ortiz. You're a doctor—or going to be—so, of course, you're busy. Other people, non-doctors, are also sometimes busy. Like right now, I really do have to go," I say, wondering if there could possibly be a more awkward or unintentionally hostile way of putting this and wishing I could reverse time and suck my rude-sounding words back into my mouth. By force of generosity, I should have just smiled beatifically and thanked him for all his hard work to bring relief to those who are ill.

"Well, then," he says, blinking fiercely and turning a rich radish color, "can I call you?"

Here, I back up and look up at his longish, twitching face in astonishment. The nurses at the station freeze, suspended in their motions—one with a pen in midair; another half-bent for a file; and the third just sitting stock still, her mouth wide open—all of them listening so hard I can almost feel the suction from their ears.

"I mean, with the information I promised."

"It's kind of late for that," I tell him. "Letty's being admitted somewhere. You see, she…" My eyes burn, my throat thickens, and I can't say it. I couldn't tell Kiko and Reggie last night, didn't call my sisters to tell them, couldn't bring myself to tell Daisy even though we talked for almost an hour, and I certainly can't tell this white-coated resident I barely know. As long as I don't say it, as long as I stay busy, rushing here and there, I can keep everything inside. Once I let a word out, all of it threatens to spill. I fan my face with a free hand. "It's just too late, okay?"

"I see," he says and steps aside so I can pass.

I hurry by, my head lowered, so my hair drapes my face.

"Can I phone you anyway?" he calls after me.

I stop in my tracks, half turn to see if he's kidding, but he seems to be serious, if nervous, standing there clutching at his own hands, wringing them even. I give a jerky shrug—more yes than no—before striding off without looking back. I wonder what it is about suffering and stress that's somehow attractive to men. When everything's cool, no one gives me a second look, but now, during what's turning out to be the most tormenting week of my entire life, I'm suddenly Señorita Popular, first with that Carlos and now with this resident.

I punch the elevator button, thinking how embarrassing that I will have to return here and likely re-encounter the guy in around fifteen minutes with clothes for Carlotta. It reminds me of that time I exploded at Rudy after finding those nasty Polaroids of his ex-girlfriends. I stormed out of his place, slamming the door hard enough to shake the walls. I was so furious I didn't realize I'd left behind my purse and car keys until I was outside, staring at my locked compact car neatly parked on the street.

When I return with clothes for her, I persuade Carlotta to let me buy her lunch at a place called Jigglers, a chain restaurant that's famous for big-breasted waitresses, the kind of place I would ordinarily never step foot in, but it's conveniently located between the hospital and the freeway. Maybe if we stop there for a while I will be able to dissuade her from going home. But no such luck—she eats her chicken Caesar salad in silence while I go on and on about how bad it will be for her to get back together with Efrem. These people only get worse, I tell her. And I stress what a terrible example he is setting for Bobby. I even bring up Oprah Winfrey, whom Carlotta idolizes, and remind her of what her heroine has to say about abusive partners: *If he does it once, he'll do it again.* "How will you ever be able to face Oprah?" I ask her. Carlotta's dream is to get tickets to the Oprah Winfrey show, fly to Chicago, and sit in the audience, preferably on a day when Oprah is giving away cars or laptop computers. But now Carlotta's barely listening. She just chews and swallows, inserting forkfuls of lettuce and meat sideways, so as not to re-injure her damaged lip. Finally, she finishes, blots her mouth with the napkin, and says, "You don't understand, Marina. It's going to be different this time."

"Why on earth do you think it's going to be any different than it's always been?"

"Because now I have a TRO," she says, her eyes dancing with delight.

"A TRO?"

"It's a temporary restraining order, a condition of release. He's not supposed to be within a hundred yards of me, or they'll slam his ass back in jail, even send him to prison this time."

"Wait a minute. I don't get it. You mean *you* had Efrem released?"

"Nah, the jail was overcrowded. A sheriff's deputy called me at the hospital to tell me. He said Efrem's not supposed to be anywhere near me. So don't you see? I can make all the rules." She gives a tight, demented smile, reminding me very much of her sister, Connie. "If I don't like what he says or does or even the way he looks at me, I can just pick up the phone." Here, she pantomimes lifting a receiver.

What happens, I wonder, when he rips that phone out of her hands and bashes her skull in with it? How will she call with his thick, hairy fingers wrapped around her throat, crushing her larynx? And good luck dialing from a shallow grave.

The buxom waitress—clad in a tight low-cut T-shirt and short-shorts that reveal a good bit of nalga—hesitates at our table. She's no doubt spooked by Carlotta's banged-up face. "Is everything okay here?"

No, I want to say, not at all. Nothing is okay.

But Carlotta nods, and I ask la tetona to please bring me a box for my untouched salad along with the check. While we wait, Carlotta elaborates on How Things Will Be Now That She Is In Charge, and I stare at my full water glass, beads of condensation trickling, one then another and another, to puddle the laminated tabletop.

After dropping Carlotta off, I yank my mail out of

the box—bills and a package for Kiko, something from Calvary Crosses, Incorporated, no doubt some work-at-home kit, the package Della mentioned sending. I only have time to chuck the stuff on the dining table, stow my salad in the fridge; and then, I jump back in my little car and peel off for the freeway. At ten to three, after having no luck finding a place to park near the law office, I swoop into an adjacent lot designated for a travel agency, figuring if I slip in to inquire about a flight, they will at least think twice about towing my car, despite the many posted warnings promising this.

It's around five hundred bucks to fly round-trip to Mexico City. I bet I can do a damn sight better on the Internet, but I thank the helpful guapo— with honey-colored eyes and thick black lashes— at the desk, tell him I will think about this and return shortly with my decision. And then I slip over to the law office next door, wondering why the heck I asked about Mexico City. Who do I even know there? Except for my mother in that cloister just outside of the capital, and what's the point of visiting someone sworn to silence in a Carmelite cloister? I picture a shadowy, shrouded figure through a mesh screen, though why I imagine visiting her in a confessional box, I can't say. I quickly push this out of my head as I step into the cool mauve-and-pink reception area to the law offices.

"Hi," I say to the receptionist, a pretty girl with long, dark hair who reminds me so much of Letty, or rather of what Letty looked like before all this, that I have to swallow hard and clear my throat before I can speak. "I'm here for the Nestor Perez deposition."

The girl asks me to have a seat, says she will be right back. Soundlessly, she glides into an inner office. I sink into the leather sofa and settle my purse in my lap. I stroke the broad, buttery-smooth armrest, admiring the abstract paintings on the walls: fields of confetti colors that seem to undulate as the hue deepens and fades. These are not reproductions or prints; they are signed originals, textured oil paintings behind glass and handsomely framed in pewter. Calidad, I nearly say the word out loud. The sparkling candy dish on the coffee table catches my eye, the crystal prisms refracting rainbow lights on the polished wood. I select a wrapped candy, peel away the shiny pink-and-silver paper, and pop it into my mouth: English toffee with roasted almond slivers coated with smoky, rich dark chocolate. Calidad—you can taste it, touch it, even smell it, and it is unmistakable, as undeniable as truth. Why would anyone settle for anything less?

Chapter Nine

After a few minutes, the receptionist leads me into a conference room where the others are already seated. A broad smile blooms on Rudy's freshly shaven face, and those woodland-creature eyes twinkle tenderly when he sees me. No matter that last night he said about the cruelest thing he could to me and no matter that his daughter has nearly taken her life and he should be at her side right now, Rudy, instead, is actually beaming at me, seated right beside his buddy. Nestor's now wearing a pink oxford shirt with factory creases, just like the blue one he wore to perform the limpieza at my house and the other, the gray, he donned for little Rudy's funeral. These, I'm thinking, must come three to a package. On the other side of Nestor sits the pretty young thing that I take to be his island honey, Daisy's replacement.

She's all golden-tanned with a glossy mass of

hair so black it casts a bluish hue, and she has the wide, imperturbable espresso-brown eyes of a true inocente. She's wearing a sleeveless magenta blouse, comprised of all these triangular swaths of silky fabric that remind me of bougainvillea petals. A small crucifix dangles from a slender gold chain around her neck, and I marvel anew at the way Christians blithely display artifacts commemorating the sadistic torture and murder of their founding leader. I mean, I know Christ is supposed to have died for their sins and all that, but still, adorning oneself with his crucified body, doesn't that strike anyone but me as weird? The tawny skin at the girl's throat is irritated, streaked with reddish claw marks. After nodding at me, she rakes her stubby fingernails over and over the front of her neck. I think of the twitchy resident at the hospital, wondering if this is homesickness, if he, too, is ill at ease with place. Maybe like this girl, he misses his island.

I slip into a plushly upholstered throne across from the three of them. A bald-headed guy with red-rimmed, streaming eyes hurries into the room, slaps down a pad of paper, and introduces himself as Joel Rivera. He explains that he's acting as proxy for Nestor's lawyer in Miami. Then he apologizes for his allergies, before sliding into another monolithic chair at one end of the long table. The transcriber, an olive-skinned woman with a helmet of auburn hair, hunches before something that looks like a fancy adding machine opposite the attorney, across the vast sea of high-sheen mahogany. Though names are exchanged all around and she pecks swiftly at the small keyboard the whole while, no one bothers to introduce her.

Rivera begins the deposition by questioning Nestor's island honey in his slow and choppy Spanish, lobbing softballs about her full name (Loída Esmeralda Reyes de Toro), where she was born—I notice he doesn't ask *when*—and what she does for a living. Even these simple questions fluster the kid, especially the last one, and I'm stunned to learn she is from Santo Domingo, not Cuba. No doubt Nestor met her through Rudy on one of their jaunts to visit Rudy's family. Rudy's only taken me once, but Nestor has gone with him at least half a dozen times. Finally, Rivera asks about her relationship to Nestor, and she smiles shyly for the first time. They are novios, Loída says. They will soon be married, and she scratches at her raw-looking neck with vigor until Nestor guides her hand away, cups it in his atop the table.

When Rivera asks how they met, she tells this convoluted story about her parish priest who introduced them, encouraging her to make more of her life than the island could offer. Here, Nestor clears his throat, and Loída glances at him before switching tracks to talk about love at first sight and writing a letter to Nestor when he returned to the States after that visit so he would not forget her and not forget the love that they shared with the blessing of Jesus Christ and that wise Cupid of a parish priest, whom I am beginning to suspect is Loída's biological father from a few slips of her tongue, wherein she refers to him as "ápa," instead of "padre." Rivera, no doubt aiming for some touching recollection, asks what she wrote in her letter.

With a fetching smile, Loída says that she asked Nestor to send her a pair of jeans, size six, in the color of brown.

The transcriber emits a snort of laughter that she quickly masks with a cough.

Nobody on the island, Loída tells us, has jeans like these, with burnished copper studs and diamond shapes embroidered on the back pockets. She had seen a pair in a magazine and knew at once that only someone as powerful, manly, and intelligent as Nestor could obtain such jeans for her. She stands to show us that she's wearing them now. "Siempre me los uso," she says, proud of herself for always wearing them.

Nestor turns plum-colored, and Rudy's mouth hangs open, amazement and alarm on his face.

Swiftly, Rivera turns his questions to the matter at hand: child custody. He asks Loída how she feels about Nestor's girls.

At this her face lengthens with seriousness and Loída says that she is not a jealous woman. She does not mind the girls that Nestor has had or even if he has more girls in the future. "No me las importa," she says. Unlike the much-coveted brown jeans, Nestor's philandering is of no significance to her.

Rivera mops his teary eyes with a handkerchief and clarifies, telling her he means "las hijas de Nestor," his daughters.

"Oh," Loída exclaims, "las chicas." She goes on to say that she loves children, all children, no matter what children or whose children. Children are wonderful and beautiful. Jesus loves every child, and she does, too. And why not?

Rivera wants to know if she has met Nestor's children, and Loída again glances up at Nestor, who nods.

"Si," she says before elaborating on how marvelous Nestor's daughters are, sweet as little sugar cookies that she would like to—

Rivera cuts her off, and turns to question Rudy, whom Nestor apparently has asked to be a character reference, despite the fact that he never earned his GED. With obvious relief, the lawyer drops his labored Spanish, switching to English for this part of the deposition. After gathering the basic information, he asks Rudy a few questions about Nestor, and Rudy provides all the right answers to present his friend as a stand-up guy: a dependable provider, a caring father, a spiritual leader, even. Then, Rivera asks about Daisy, what kind of mother she is.

Rudy furrows his sallow forehead and knits his wellshaped eyebrows, wearing the expression he adopts when he wants to look smarter than he actually is, and he deepens his voice to sound like some kind of authority. "Daisy has some issues, and she's, well, maybe not ready to be a real good mother. She's immature. Nestor says she wants to go out all the time. He says—"

I have to give the weepy-eyed Rivera props here for interrupting to remind Rudy to confine his remarks to what he has seen firsthand and not to discuss what Nestor has told him. "Have you seen Mrs. Perez, say, going out and leaving the children unattended or neglecting them in other ways?"

"No, but Nestor says—"

"Have *you* seen this?"

"No, but I ain't seen Daisy nor the kids in a few years, since they moved to Miami."

"What was your impression of Mrs. Perez before the family relocated?" asks Rivera. "What kind of mother was she to the children?"

"She was..." Rudy's jaw twists this way and that, the phony sabiduría wiped clean off his face. Inwardly, I wince as he fidgets in his seat, rubs at his nose, and chews his lower lip. There's bros over hos, and then there's the truth, the real ass-kicker. "She was fine, I guess," he finally says. "I didn't like the way she cooked. The rice she fixed was all watery with hard bits in it, but she was nice with the girls."

Rivera lets Rudy reel off a longish monologue in praise of Nestor before finally turning to me. Discreetly, I tug on a pinching bra strap and straighten the shoulder seams of my blouse. I sit back in the chair, making my spine as straight as it will go. He has me give my full name and occupation, and he asks how I know Nestor and Daisy, which I answer by saying I met them through Rudy, before they moved to Florida.

"As a teacher, Ms. Lucero," Rivera says to me, blotting his eyes once more, "you were required to take courses in child psychology and child development as part of your training. Is that true?"

"Yes," I say, inclining toward the transcriber and raising my voice.

"And you work with children on a daily basis?"

"I do."

"What is your opinion in this matter?"

I glance from Nestor's smug face to Rudy's eager look, and I clear my throat to speak clearly, so every word will be recorded. I recite what I practiced in the car, a three-point list: "As an educator, as someone trained in child development, I have the opinion that the children will be better off with Daisy than with someone as manipulative, opportunistic, and mean-spirited as Nestor."

Rudy says, "Marina, what are you saying?"

"You stupid bitch, do you even know what you're doing?" Nestor's eyes flatten, while Loída's are vacant with incomprehension.

"You cannot speak," Rivera warns Nestor and Rudy, "during this witness's deposition."

I go on to tell that bald abogado about Nestor's offer of a limpieza, my refusal, and the Evil-Eye business, the so-called curse. I spell out the whole story from Nestor's first phone call to my late-night conversation with Daisy.

The silent transcriber pecks at the keyboard with jaunty vigor, and Rivera looks disgusted enough to resign from the practice of law. "It's unusable," he says, stroking his bald head repeatedly. "All of this will do more harm than good."

"Can I get a copy?" I ask.

Rivera shoots me a flabbergasted look before sneezing three times in rapid succession.

I point at the woman relentlessly typing away,

idly wondering if she is required to record the sneezes. "Can I get a copy of that thing, the transcription?"

"No!" says Nestor. "No fucking way."

"It's his deposition," the lawyer tells me. "Even if his lawyers can't use it, he's paying for it, so he owns the thing."

"You're tripping," says Nestor. "I ain't paying one penny for this."

Rivera just gives him a look, and in this moment, we all know Nestor will pay and pay, if he hasn't already, by shelling out big bucks to his attorney in Miami for the retainer. *That* is a foregone conclusion.

"Are we done then?" I ask, looking straight at Rudy. He turns away, and Rivera says that I'm free to go. I thank him, shoot a "mucho gusto" at Loída, who, in turn, says, "Me encanto," though I am sure neither of us can imagine how meeting me was in any way enchanting to her. I gather up the Black Hole, heave the mammoth chair away from the table, and hurry out. No way do I want to get stuck in the elevator with that little party, but in the reception area, I pause to scoop up a handful of that sublime English toffee, thinking Kiko and Reggie should get to taste some of this.

Back home, a sharp, astringent odor, something like fruity nail-polish remover, stings my nostrils as soon as I walk through the front door. The television flashes some step-by-step infomercial thing, and the living-room carpet is littered with longish carpenter nails and wires, plastic coated in a variety of colors. Kiko, Reggie, and that cholo mocoso, Bobby from next door, are sitting cross-legged on the floor, winding colored wire around the nails crisscrossed in the shape of the letter "X."

"What the...," I say, and they look up at me: three sets of bashful and beseeching eyes. "What is that smell and why are you making those exes?" I ask.

"They're not exes," Kiko tells me. "They're Calvary crosses. My moms sent me the kit. You can make like thousands of dollars putting these together. Look, the DVD shows how."

On television, a stringy-looking gringo with an oversized Adam's apple narrates directions for assembling the things in the slow and patient tone one would use for telling preschoolers to wash their hands after using the toilet, but somehow the sample he's working on has sharp right angles and actually looks like a cross, not an *X*. "What's that smell, though?" I ask. "It's giving me a headache." The sharp chemical stench travels up my nasal passages into my skull in a painful way.

"It's clear-coat acrylic," Reggie says. "The finishing touch." He points to a couple of opened cans next to a few uneven exes that are completely wire-wrapped and glistening atop my cutting board.

"In the *house*?" I stare at all three of them in disbelief, my face hot and my toes throbbing. *Compassion*, I remind myself, *by force of generosity*. Despite the odor, I take a deep breath and make my voice steady and low. "Listen to me, will you? Take that stuff outdoors. This is a home, not an auto-body shop. Are you trying to give us all brain damage?"

Bobby's eyes widen, and Kiko sighs, begins gathering the nails and wires, but Reggie says, "We can't see the DVD out there, Marina. We got to see how to make these things."

"That DVD isn't helping much," I say, pointing at the cutting board. "Those look like sloppy exes." Here I think fleetingly of Rudy, flash on the last time I let him into this house wearing those long shorts and a soccer jersey, and sporting a five-o'clock shadow before it was even noon. Talk about a sloppy ex.

"Nah," Kiko tells me, "they're fine. That guy on the DVD, that pastor, he buys them back at five dollars a pop. Or we can sell them ourselves for more money to church supply places and gift shops. The three of us can make some serious—"

"Fine, but get this junk out of my living room," I tell them, my voice rising in spite of myself. The odor's making me dizzy, causing my stomach's contents to roil. "Get it out *now*, and put up the blankets. I can't believe you still haven't done that." I glance at Bobby. "And what's your story? Why are you here?"

He lifts his bony shoulders, looking all timid and mousy in his oversized tank top—no vestige of the swaggering pimp in his big-eyed face. His lips curl in a shy smile and for the first time, I feel a pang for the kid.

"His folks are all lovey-dovey," Kiko tells me, still collecting the craft supplies.

"The big reunion, you know, the honeymoon scene," Reggie says. "It's embarrassing, so the kid came over here."

Kiko loads junk into the packing box. "He can stay, right?"

I sigh. "Just clean this mess up. Go outside with all that, and don't *ever* use that toxic-smelling stuff indoors, you hear me?"

I fling open the front door, lift the windows, and set up the rotating fan while they haul the tools, materials, and acrylic outdoors. Then I head to my room for breathable air, taking the phone to call Miguel, who surprisingly answers this time. "How's Letty?" I ask. "*Where* is she?"

"She's okay, just real sad, you know. She's at this residential place in La Crescenta. They've got her taking antidepressants and talking to a counselor. She'll be there, I guess, until the insurance runs out."

"Can I see her?"

"Nah," he says. "They got all these rules and visiting schedules, plus some kind of problem with another facility they manage, so there's no visiting hours for a few days. I think Wednesday afternoon is the next time we can see her. I can pick you up at two, if you want to go over there with me."

"That'd be good," I tell him. "Hey, Miguel, listen. You might hear some bad chisme about me, especially from Rudy, but I swear it's not true."

"Este idiota. Man, no one pays attention to that guy. He's a joke. He already called to tell me some shit about a curse that you supposedly caused, like I need to hear that kind of thing right now. In my church we don't believe any of that superstitious crap. Letty and me, we mainly just humor the dude."

I feel a twinge, a residual tug of feeling for Rudy, whose own daughter doesn't take him seriously. "I just want you to know I would never, *ever* do anything to hurt Letty or you."

"We know that, Marina. Believe me, we do."

I grip the receiver a little tighter. "How are *you*

doing, Miguel? How are you coping with all this?"

"Well, it's not easy, you know. But I'm talking to my sponsor sometimes two or three times a day. He's been great. And I'm going to meetings every day. In fact, I got a meeting in about fifteen, so I got to book," he says. "I'll see you on Wednesday, okay? Pick you up at your house around two, a'ight?"

"Okay, Miguel," I say. "I'll see you then."

"Oh, and Marina, about Rudy, he's not like evil or anything. He's just kind of limited, a little blind. Everyone's got problems, you know, and that's his. Don't hate the dude, is what I'm saying."

"But I don't hate—"

"I mean, it's more than that. You got to forgive, you got to let go of what you can't change. Let go of the anger. I know you must be pissed off, the things he's saying about you. Those bad feelings, *oigame*, they're like corrosion. That shit will eat you from the inside out," Miguel, pipelayer for the city and ex–heroin addict, tells me. "Okay, got to book. Later, ese."

After we hang up, I sit on my bed in silence, considering what Miguel has said. He's right. I think of Nelson Mandela's words when asked by an interviewer if he hated those who imprisoned him for over twenty years. I remember his words because I wrote them down when I heard them, and then I learned them. He said, "Harboring bitterness and hatred toward others imprisons a person far more than the four walls of my prison cell have imprisoned me." Then he goes on to describe the lightness and freedom experienced when forgiving those who commit wrongs. Of course, I can't compare Rudy's behavior to the atrocities and deprivation Mandela endured, but if I ever want to be free of him, I have to let go of my anger, the shameful desire for revenge, which was—I have to face it—partly why I drove out to that lawyer's office this afternoon.

Noises from the kitchen interrupt this reverie. Reggie and Kiko keep slamming through the screen door from the backyard to check out the DVD at various intervals, while Bobby remains outside putting together the Calvary crosses with their instructions. I call out to whoever has just banged in the back door. "Don't you dare smoke mota out there in front of that kid, and I bet that acrylic is flammable, so don't even think about lighting any matches unless you want to blow us all to kingdom come."

After a moment, Kiko pushes open my bedroom door, his face a study in fake innocence. "Jeez, tía, we're busy working out there. No one's smoking anything, I swear."

"Good," I say, and then it hits me that I haven't

heard that damn cock shrieking the last few mornings. "Kiko, whatever happened to that old rooster next door?"

"Caldo," says Kiko, who keeps up with goings-on in the barrio. "The old lady wrung his neck and they scalded him on Friday night. I helped pluck the feathers, and they made this big old soup with corn and rice. They gave me a bowl. The meat was all stringy and tough, but the juice wasn't too bad. In fact, tía, I wish I had some more of that right now."

"There's a giant salad in the fridge," I tell him. "Go ahead and have it, if you're hungry, and I've got some really great candy in my purse." If Miguel, who's never even read the Dalai Lama's books or studied Nelson Mandela's words, can forgive and let go of disappointment with others, I suppose I can, too. Why not? I am determined to be tolerant, compassionate, and generous. That sweet solvent smell gradually dissipates and with it my headache diminishes, and the queasiness in my stomach subsides. Instead, a wave of weariness overtakes me. After Kiko steps away, I replace the sheets and make up the bed, planning to curl up with the Dalai, anticipating the comfort of a nap.

There are those, like Kiko and Reggie, who smoke mota to relax, which I cannot do, owing to the paranoia it creates in me, the certainty that I will be arrested for it and lose my job at Olive Branch. There are others, like Rudy, who drink, and yes, I would drink with him, but rarely ever to excess and not much at all now that we're not together. And there are even people like Miguel, who would shoot up smack and now substitute this with NA meetings, sometimes two a day, to find some equilibrium, some temporary peace of mind. For me, nothing beats a nap. When everything seems like too much and I don't know where to start when it comes to making things right, the best I can do is crawl into bed in the middle of the day and sleep. This nicely cuts the day in half, giving me two opportunities to confront challenges when rested and refreshed.

So I snuggle under the comforter, imagining the Dalai's deep voice in my ears as I read until the sentences no longer make sense. My eyelids flutter. I set the book down and turn on my side. In the kitchen, the refrigerator door sucks open, plates clatter, and then a drawer rattles as it slides out. The abrupt and arrhythmic music of utensils chiming against one another is the last thing I hear before fading into the blankness of sleep.

In this twilight stage, this half-dream where I'm sure I must be awake, but every move I make is syrupy slow, my arms and legs leaden, buzzing with numbness, a miniature-sized Rudy, no bigger than a fruit bat, flits about the room, flying somehow just below the ceiling before perching at the foot of my bed. He's wearing a beaked, red mask, but I recognize the long shorts, the knobby knees. Without speaking, he urges me to cough. I can't though; my throat is too dry. A heavy hand inches to my mouth, and gradually I remove a feather from between my lips, then another. I reach in farther, gagging as my fingers push past the uvula to dislodge a small, slippery lump, and I extract a dead chick from my throat. Rudy nods, saying, "See, I brought your earrings back."

My eyes snap open. Xochi sits on my bed, dangling a velvety black pouch in front of my face. My smooth-faced sister looks pale, even a little haggard. Her green eyes are underscored with faint shadows, but her skin is as firm and poreless as a child's. *Orchidaceous*—a word I encountered in my horticulture class—is what comes to mind when I look at Xochi's cheeks, which are as translucent and dewy as the milky blooms we tended in the university's dank greenhouse. "Why are you waking me up?" I pull the comforter over one shoulder, wrenching away from my pretty but tired-looking sister.

"I'm returning your earrings," she says. "I thought you should know."

"What about the dress?" I murmur. "The shoes?"

"In your closet, Ms. Suspicious."

"Thrown in a heap or put away neatly like you found them?"

"Don't you even want to know why I borrowed your stuff?" she asks, and for sure I will find a wrinkled bundle—shoes swaddled in the unlaundered dress—on the floor of my closet.

"You always borrow my stuff. Why should I ask this time?" I squeeze my eyes shut, hoping that when I open them again—*poof*—she will be gone.

"Listen." She shakes my shoulder. "Listen, will you? I joined a club."

I groan, roll onto my back and prop up my head on the pillow to see her better. "You joined a club." The only way to get rid of people like my self-centered sister is to pretend to pay attention. "Yay, a club," I say, flatly.

"It's not just any club, Ms. Total-Lack-of-Enthusiasm. It's an activities club for single professionals." Her eyes twinkle and she grins. Catching sight of her reflection in the dresser mirror, she lifts a hank of golden hair, twists it into a knot, and turns her face this way and that.

"Single professional whats?" I rotate my wrist, indicating more information is needed.

"Professional professionals," she says. "Doctors, lawyers, architects, college professors, there's even a priest."

"A priest in a *singles* club?"

"Well, maybe he's not exactly a priest, but a clergyman of some kind, probably not Catholic." She narrows her eyes and twists her mouth, puzzling this out. "He does wear a collar, though, and he is *smoking* hot." Xochi licks her gloss-coated lips.

"And you?"

"What about me?"

"What kind of professional are you supposed to be? Doctor? Lawyer? Or are you supposed to be in the clergy, too?" I ask as if questioning a child about an ambiguous Halloween costume ("So, dearie, are you an angel or a fairy?").

"That's cold, Marina," she says in a hurt tone, slyly checking out her wounded expression in my mirror. "You know I do accounts for a major communications company."

Maybe if she hadn't interrupted my nap, I would have more patience for this silliness or even some sympathy for the diminished sense of self that drives her to misrepresent herself to others, but at the moment, I can't help myself and let out a snort. "You are *not* going around telling people you're an accountant. You may not realize it, but that is something totally different from what you do. People have to go to college and get certified for that.

They know what amortization, options, and dividends are. Do you even know what those words mean? Accountants have to be able to count without using fingers, to add and sub—"

"I thought you would be happy for me. You're always telling me to go out and meet more interesting people." Xochi glances down at her manicured hands; the press-on ruby nails overlong and talon curved so as to make any kind of manual task a challenge.

"That's not what I tell you." I push off the comforter, trying not to be irritated at having my sleep interrupted for this nonsense, and swing my legs over the side of the bed. If she's not going to leave me alone, I may as well get out of bed and pick my dress up off the closet floor. "What I tell you is to *act* like you're interested in people."

"I am acting interested," she insists. "And I've made a bunch of dates. That's why I needed the earrings and another outfit, but that dress was way too big for me." She pats her flat stomach and crosses her slender legs. "You really should work out."

When I shake out the dress, my black leather pumps roll out. I catch a salty whiff of the fabric, toss the thing into the clothes hamper, and kick my shoes into the closet. "You know I don't like you borrowing my things when I'm not home, but what I really dislike most is how you treat Reggie. He was pretty upset after seeing you yesterday." Since I'm up and near the closet, I reach for a pair of Levi's and an embroidered peasant blouse.

Xochi clicks her tongue. "That wuss, that stupid, crybaby huevón. Seriously, it's so inconvenient. You should kick—"

"Shush! He might hear you." I step into the jeans, pull them up, and zip.

"No, he won't. He's outside with Kiko and some kid, in the backyard."

"Still working on the crosses?" I say before pulling the blouse over my head. If so, I'm amazed the project has kept their interest this long. Maybe they will get the knack of constructing these and gain some confidence from this. Who knows? They might even sell a few and make a little spending money.

"I have no fucking idea what they're doing," Xochi tells me. "Go look if it's that important to you. Yeah, why not? Just go ahead and walk away when I'm trying to talk to you about something important. Go check on those idiots, Ms. Doesn't-Give-a-Damn-about-Her-Own-Sister. It's no secret you love Kiko more than me."

No way to deny or disprove this, so I stand at the middle of the room, my hands on my hips, facing my kid sister. "Talk then. Let's have it."

"It's that I'm not young anymore," she says.

"You're just twenty-five."

"Yeah, I know, I know. And I still look great, better than ever, in fact." Xochi rises from the bed and steps before the mirror, pivoting one way and then another before doing an about-face and craning her neck to check out her butt in a Spandex miniskirt. "But time is running out. My clock is ticking."

"What clock?" I ask, straining to imagine this *egoista* with some poor helpless infant to neglect. "Good god, you're not thinking of having a baby."

"Oh, *hell* no! Are you insane?" A look of horror disrupts the lovely symmetry of my sister's face. "I'm thinking about marriage. It's time for me to start getting married, even my mom says so."

"What do you mean '*start* getting married,'" I ask, though knowing my much-married and acquisitive stepmother I have a pretty good idea.

"I can't work at that fucking cable company forever. It's boring to have to get up and be somewhere at nine every Monday through Friday, and I'm tired of paying for groceries and stuff with my own money."

"Xochi," I start, "people have to work—"

"Have you seen my stupid apartment? It's a goddamn mess, a fire hazard, even, there's so much clutter and junk. It's worse than this pigsty. I can't do everything. Not everyone gets to go to school, you know, to become a teacher with all the vacations and stuff." Here, my sister's wide eyes fill with true tears of self-pity, which she wisely allows to well, but not trickle, on account of the eyeliner and mascara she's wearing. "I don't want a baby. I want a maid," she says. "So, it's high time I started getting married and divorced and remarried a few times to build a little capital." From anyone else, this would be laughable, but Xochi is being completely sincere, and she's quoting, too. This is the gospel according to my stepmother, the ideas behind them drummed into my sister since she was old enough to understand language.

While I'd like to point out that anyone with an ounce of brains and willing to work at it *can*, in fact, go to school and become a bona fide professional, a warm rush of tenderness overtakes me. I remember Xochi as a toddler, dressed in scratchy flounced dresses and stiff patent-leather shoes on Saturday mornings at dawn. My stepmother would ferry her all over Southern California for Little Miss pageants. I can still see my kid sister's waxy pink lips stretching to yawn, her emerald eyes staring off into the middle distance, as if she were in a hypnotic trance, while my stepmother hissed a noxious cloud of hairspray over her amber curls for the finishing touch. Xochi never won a single competition, never even placed as a runner-up, but at

least three years passed before my stepmother gave up in disgust. So instead of criticizing her lack
of initiative to educate herself, I step to my sister's side, drape an arm over her shoulders and say,
"Xochi, querida, you don't have to—"

My bedroom door bangs open and Kiko's large
head looms in. "Hey, Xochi," he says with a nod
at my kid sister before turning to me. "Tía, you got
somebody here to see you, some biker dude at the
door."

The roll book! How long had I been asleep? In
no way did I expect it to be returned this early.
"That's Carlos. Let him in and have him sit down
in the living room. Oh, damn, the living room! Did
you guys ever pick up those blankets and straighten out that mess in there?"

Kiko reddens, stares at the floor.

I release a sigh. "Let him in anyway. Offer him
some bottled water or a beer or something." I tuck
in my blouse and wedge between Xochi and the
mirror.

Kiko pulls the door shut, and Xochi says, "Don't
tell me *you* have a date."

"He's just the substitute who covered a class for
me today. He's bringing the roll book." My face
is sleep swollen, one cheek waffled from the che-
nille bedspread, and my eye makeup smudged. No
time to wash up. Besides. the way this house is set

up, how can I possibly slip from my bedroom to the bathroom without being noticed from the living room? And once he's seen me to say hello, seen me looking like warmed-over doo-doo, what's the point of cleaning up?

Xochi regards me now swiftly brushing my hair. "Oh, really? Just a substitute?" And she opens a dresser drawer to pull out a lipstick called Hawaiian Dusk that I bought on an impulse but never use because it is too aggressively orange and red, more suggestive of flames raging through a muumuu factory than a sultry sunset. Xochi applies a few deft strokes, though, and on her, it's still tropically combustible, but in a daring, even sexy, way. She puckers up, blows a kiss at her image in the mirror, and hips swaying, she saunters out of my bedroom. I shut the drawer and glance up at my own washed-out, puffy, and ruefullooking face.

Chapter Ten

I pause at the threshold, half-hidden in the hall. In the squalid mess that passes for my living room, Carlos sits on the couch, nursing a bottle of Alpine Spring. In profile, he looks expectant and maybe a bit anxious, but wholesomely sober. I think of the time after a party—Mateo's, in fact, to which Rudy and I arrived in separate vehicles because we were coming from different parts of the city—when we stood near our respective cars, bickering. Rudy, as is his custom, drank too much and wouldn't listen to me when I offered to drive him home. With drunken conviction, he insisted he could drive, and the argument got ugly. I could see it devolving—if we stayed together—into one of those I'm-less-senile-than-you-are disputes, when we'd get to the golden years. Of course, my suggestion offended his manhood. Cursing me, he slammed into his truck and tore off before I even unlocked my driver's side door. Just before I reached the freeway entrance, I noticed pulsing blue lights. The cops had pulled over a truck very much like Rudy's. I eased off the gas for a better look.

Sure enough, it was Rudy's truck with Rudy standing beside it, his arms up and fingers laced behind his neck, while one cop shone a flashlight in his squinting face and the other sat in the squad car talking into a mouthpiece. Thinking I should stop and offer to drive him home, I nevertheless sped up the on-ramp and drove home without a backward glance. I was still angry at him, true, but moreover, I had been drinking, too, as was *my* habit when I went out with Rudy, though I never drank as much as he did. The shameful truth: I didn't want to tangle with the police, tipsy as I was. Another shameful truth: This was not the first time Rudy was stopped for driving under the influence.

Not that it matters, but seeing Carlos with the bottled water buoys my spirit in a small way, though Kiko, ever forgetful, may not have offered him a beer. "Hi, Carlos," I say, pointing at the Alpine Spring. "Did you want a beer?"

"Nah," he tells me. "I'm good."

I imagine seeing this place the way he would, and no way around it, the front room looks like an indoor tent city with blankets humped here and there and clothing strewn about. An empty, milk-coated cereal bowl sits atop the television set. Grateful that someone has at least clicked the TV off, I lower myself onto the couch across from him, and Xochi sashays in from the kitchen, bearing a long-necked Dos Equis.

"Have you met my sister Xochi?"

"Yeah," Carlos says. "We've introduced oursel-ves."

"So what's your story?" Xochi asks. "You don't drink?" She plops onto the love seat—Reg-gie's bed—beside Carlos, crosses her legs, and gives him a toothy smile. I'm hoping with all my heart that Reggie doesn't wander in, provoking her to amp up the flirtation for the twofer bonus of tormenting us both.

"I'm on my bike," he says. "I don't drink when I ride." He lifts my roll book out of a battered accordion file at his feet. "Here's your attendance. Only one absence."

"Armando Ahuaul," I say.

"Yeah, how'd you know?"

"Long story," I tell him.

"Well, I got time." He looks across the room at me. "In fact, I was wondering if you might be free to have dinner with me tonight."

"Tonight?"

"Short notice, I know," he says. "But I just

thought, I mean, if you haven't eaten yet." He gazes down at his hands, so I regard him freely. He's nailed the middle part of tall, dark, and handsome. He's short and thick-bodied, his eyebrows a bit too bristly and his nose too wide and pushed in, but he's not exactly *bad* looking.

"No," Xochi says, "none of us have." She sips her beer and smiles at him again.

Carlos looks startled. "Um, I just have my motorcycle, and it seats only one passenger..."

"Right, I know that," Xochi tells him. "Of course, I'm just saying that my sister hasn't eaten. None of us have, so she should go and eat with you because it's not like anyone else will ask her." She recrosses her legs, examines her fingernails. "I have a date, so I can't hang around here forever, Marina. Seriously, I have to go." She makes no move, and I'm thinking that if it weren't for Della, who's handed over her free will to someone as lame and stupid as Duffy, Xochi would definitely be my least favorite sister. At the moment, I have to struggle to recall the compassion for her that stirred in me earlier.

"Well," Carlos turns to me with a smile. "Now that we have that squared away, would you like to have dinner with me? I know a place not too far from here that's pretty good."

"Okay, but can we take my car? I've actually never been on a motorcycle…"

"It's really safe," he tells me. "I even have a spare helmet."

"Don't be such a sissy," Xochi says. "It's nothing to ride on a motorcycle. It's exciting—the wind in your face, the roar of the engine between—"

"So if it's all the same to you," I tell Carlos, "let's take my car, okay?"

"Sure," Carlos says. "That's fine, too."

The back door slams open, and Kiko soon appears from the kitchen, trailed by Bobby, whose cheeks are flushed, his bare shoulders crimsoned by the sun. Kiko's bearing a tray—my black lacquered yin-yang tea tray—on which a dozen crosses are displayed. And these are actually crosses, not exes. He tilts it so we can see. They are lined up, two rows of six. Each cross is symmetrical, composed of evenly affixed nails and wound tightly with colored wires, creating sharp right angles.

"Wow, Kiko! Did you do these?" I rise from the couch for a better look. The acrylic coating gives the crosses a polished sheen, but I wrinkle my nose at traces of that fruity chemical smell.

"Nah, me and Reggie never got the hang," Kiko admits. "These are the ones Bobby made."

I raise an eyebrow, nodding. It makes sense in a

perverse way that Carlotta's son would have talent for making crosses.

"Not bad," says Carlos, now standing beside me for a closer look. "The colors are really handsome." And he's right. The turquoise wire blends well with the brown on one cross. Another has a black-covered base that becomes deep purple, then red and orange, before the golden tip. "Do you take art classes?"

"No, they don't got art at my school," the kid croaks, his voice at that transitional stage where a single-syllable word can roll up and down the scales, like a long note on a slide guitar.

"Do you draw or paint?" Carlos asks.

"Yeah, I like to draw stuff, but my dad says…" Bobby trails off with a shrug. "It's just a waste of time."

Carlos scratches his chin, producing a raspy sound. "If you like it and you're good at it, then how can it be a waste of time?"

All this talk of wasting time makes me think of Reggie. "Where's your bud?" I ask Kiko. "He's not smoking out there."

"Nah, tía, no way. I told you we weren't doing that. He's just sitting out there. He didn't want to come in on account of…" Kiko shoots a glance at Xochi, who is also up now and crowding in to admire the crosses.

"What are you going to do with these?" she asks Bobby, who again shrugs his burnt shoulders, no doubt too tongue-tied by my sexy sister to speak.

"We're going to sell them," Kiko tells her.

"Really?" Xochi reaches for her purse. "How much?"

"Five dollars," Kiko says, and at the same time, I say, "*Ten*, at least ten."

Xochi stuns me by lifting a twenty out of her wallet. "I'll give you this—and you can keep the change—for the turquoise one...and a kiss." She waggles the bill at Bobby whose face, though sunburned, blanches in this moment. In fact, the kid looks ready to go into anaphylactic shock.

"It's supposed to go on a necklace," Kiko tells her. "We ain't got to that yet." He glances at poor, dumbstruck Bobby, grabs the bill, and stoops to offer a cheek for my kid sister to buss. "Go ahead and kiss me, tía. I don't mind."

"Forget the necklace part," Xochi says. "It's a gift for my date. He's some kind of minister or something, not a priest." She shoots me a sharp look. "And, Kiko, I can kiss you anytime. I want to kiss the kid." Xochi beams at Bobby. "You ever kissed a girl before?"

The kid's ears flame to match his shoulders, nearly the same shade as Xochi's lips. Carlos steps back, distancing himself from all this, and I quickly say, "No kissing underage people on these pre-mises." I snatch the twenty from Kiko, hand it back to Xochi. "Keep your money." I pull my sis-ter's elbow, draw her near, and lower my voice to say, "Haven't you embarrassed the kid enough?"

She laughs, balls up the bill, and tosses it at Bobby, who's slow to react, so it bounces off his tank top and plummets to the carpet. "Jesus, I'm just kidding." She glances at Carlos, for whose benefit she's likely staged this excruciating little scene. He's still hanging back, his face impassive yet plainly telegraphing distaste. "Can't anyone around here take a joke? Keep the twenty, kid. I still want the turquoise cross."

Kiko scoops up the bill. "They ain't been conse-crated," he tells Xochi, with a serious look on his face. "It says on the DVD that we're supposed to mail them to that pastor to get them consecrated first."

Xochi tips her head down, arches a well-shaped eyebrow, and gazes up at our nephew. "Do I look like I need consecration?"

Kiko mulls this over, but Bobby, big-eyed and mouth agape, shakes his head.

At the restaurant, a tortillería with sticky Formica tabletops and vinyl dinette chairs, we eat the most succulent green chili tamales I have tasted in my life. The place is filled with trabajadores—mostly short, swarthy men in grimy Levi's, long-sleeved flannel shirts, and dusty boots, but also a few women wearing stretch pants and oversized T-shirts or uniform dusters with hairnets. The pungent aroma of corn masa commingled with cumin and peppers wafts over us with bursts of a warm breeze issued by a rotating fan. Behind the counter, a trio of plump, shinyfaced women churns out heaping Styrofoam dishes for the middle-aged waitress to deliver. "How did you find this place?" I ask Carlos, stabbing another moist and tender morsel of masa threaded with sharply flavored green chili. Too many times, tamales I order in restaurants are dense, thick, and tasteless as paste, the chili no more than an afterthought. This masa tastes light, even springy. It nearly dissolves on the tongue, and yet the spicy center provides the point to the whole thing.

"My moms used to work here," he says.

"Really?"

"Yeah, she retired about five, six years ago." He scoops a forkful of beans onto a wedge of tortilla. "She still makes the best corn tortillas that I have ever tasted, bar none." He grins at me. "You cook?"

"Sure," I tell him. "Who doesn't? I mean I'm not Cordon Bleu material, but I can follow a recipe.

I like to grill things outside, like salmon and chicken. I try to make low-fat stuff—salads or steamed vegetables and grilled and broiled meats, nothing breaded or fried—because Kiko tends to put on weight."

"Kiko, he's your nephew, right? He lives with you?"

"That's right." I divide my last bite of tamale into two smaller portions, so it will last longer. At a table near ours, the waitress seats an elderly man with longish white hair straggling out from his cowboy hat and a thick, handlebar moustache. He has two toddlers—great-grandchildren?—both boys, with him.

"And that other kid, the artistic one?" Carlos asks.

"That's Bobby. He's just a neighbor. He doesn't live with us," I explain, watching the grandfather seat and reseat the toddlers, who keep climbing down from their chairs, trying to wander away from the table.

"Who all does live with you? I don't mean to be nosy," Carlos says. "I'm just curious."

"Well, there's Kiko and Reggie—"

"Reggie? Who's Reggie?"

I explain about Reggie being Kiko's friend and Xochi's ex-boyfriend, trying to get across how he came to live at my house. Even to me, it doesn't make a lot of sense, except that letting him stay has become a heck of a lot easier than kicking him out. Meanwhile, the old man at the next table rises so often to chase after one little boy or the other that it's like watching a game of Bop-the-Clown. No sooner is one child's culo planted in the seat, than the other swings his chubby legs over the side of his chair to slide down it. I catch the waitress's eye and tell her to bring the elderly man two highchairs for the children. When these arrive, I ask Carlos to excuse me so I can help her install the little kids in these seats with straps, from which they can't escape. The old man thanks us both, and I return to our table.

"Then there's Carlotta," I tell Carlos. "She's Bobby's mother, and she comes to stay with us when things get to be too much for her at home."

"Wow! It's like you're host to a whole realm of hungry spirits," he says.

"What?"

"No offense, but you've got a lot of people on your hands. I may be selfish, but I don't think I could do that." Carlos sips his iced tea and sets the glass neatly on the table in the ring of condensation it's made. "I need my solitude. I have to be completely alone at least an hour each day to chant."

"Chant?"

"Yeah," he says, "I chant to convert my negative

energy, my bad karma, into a positive force."

"There's a chant for that?"

"Sure, there is." He plucks a napkin from the dispenser on our table and pulls a ballpoint pen from his shirt pocket. He prints out a string of letters and turns the napkin around so I can see it. "It's Nam-Myōhō-Renge-Kyō, and it works, too."

"Wait, I think I've heard about this," I say, remembering something about Tina Turner, the rock star, and a movie I once saw on her life. "It's Buddhism, right?"

"Yeah, I'm a Buddhist," Carlos tells me, warily. "But I'm kind of eclectic. I chant, so that's Japanese Buddhism, but I also pick and choose what interests me from Hinduism and from Tibetan Buddhism."

"Wow, *you're* a Buddhist." I look him up and down, thinking, so Buddhists—like Miguel's cohorts, the cristianos—ride motorcycles...

"Anything wrong with that?"

"Of course not," I say. "In fact, it's great. You know I've been thinking about becoming a Buddhist myself." I explain about reading the Dalai Lama's work and my attempts to find a spiritual center, some kind of peace in my life, and how all I want is what others, including my mother and father, seem to find so easily in their lives. I explain how my mother ran off to join the Carmelite clois-

ter and about my father's involvement with Transcendental Meditation. "You'd think," I tell him,
"with parents like that, I'd have some kind of apti-
tude for spirituality, but it doesn't come easily for
me at all." I give him my music analogy, how I am
like a tone-deaf person at a symphony when it comes to spirituality, and my sense of loss or being
left out. I become conscious of talking too long
when the waitress places the bill on our table and
returns to place another before the old man with the
two youngsters.

"I wouldn't say that." Carlos takes up the check.
"Not many people even seek what you're looking
for."

"What was that thing about 'hungry spirits' you
mentioned?" I ask. "Is that a Buddhist thing?"

He nods. "It's called preta. You've heard of reincarnation, right?"

"Sure."

"Well, preta is the rebirth realm inhabited by hungry spirits that are constantly starved and thirsty, but
they can't satisfy these needs on their own. Visual-
ly, they're depicted as figures with large bellies and
long, narrow necks to symbolize the desires that torment them, the desires that they can't satisfy themselves." He glances at me, scans my expression. "I
may be making assumptions here, but doesn't that
sound a little like your household?"

I narrow my eyes at him. "My household or me?"

"I don't know you well enough to say," Carlos tells me, with a shrug. We both grow silent, as I picture this realm, those creatures, and he fiddles with the check. "Look, I didn't mean to offend you. I'm probably completely off base."

"It's not that," I tell him, shaking my head to free it of those strange big-bellied, long-necked creatures that I picture moving about my house like flesh-covered mandolins on spindly legs. "I'm just amazed that I've finally met a Buddhist, amazed and kind of impressed."

"There are lots of us," Carlos says. "I'm surprised you haven't met one before now. Have you been to Temple?"

"There's a temple?" I blurt out, before it strikes me how ignorant this must sound.

"Sure. If you're interested, I'll take you some time, but we also worship at home," he says. "I set up a shrine at my place for when I chant." He picks up the bill and leans to one side to pull his wallet out of a back pocket. Squinting at the tab as if wholly absorbed in the figures scribbled on it, he nevertheless says, "Would you like to see it? I don't live too far from here."

Here, that familiar old panic rises like acid at the back of my throat, a vestige from my first go-round in college when I was just eighteen. If I let a guy pick up the check, I always worried I would have to pay him back in some way. I remind myself that I'm not the same nervously vulnerable kid who believed she didn't have a choice in these matters. And besides, he invited me. Carlos is the kind of guy who'll be insulted if I offer to pay, so I try to make a joke to confront this panic. "Hmm," I say, "go to your place to see your shrine. That's new. Are you sure you don't also have some sketches to show me?"

"Oh, yeah," he says. "It goes without saying." He glances at me and grins. For the first time, I notice his dimples, like elongated parentheses carved into his cheeks.

The elderly fellow with the toddlers struggles to release the seatbelts strapping the boys in the highchairs. I remember how my father's hands grew thick and clumsy, the fingertips became bulbous and smooth, the sensation of touch diminished by illness and age. I push away from the table and rise to help the old guy again. "Con permiso," I say, showing him how to click the latch free. But in case his blunted fingertips can't manage the second toddler's seat, I reach over to free him, too.

He thanks me in Spanish, but switches to halting English to say, "You are good with the little boys, no?"

I smile at him and nod, wondering how the heck he's going to herd those rascals safely through the parking lot. When I turn to our table, Carlos is standing, ready to approach the cashier. He gestures at the old man and says, "He's right about that."

I shrug, knowing full well that the moment I take any kind of credit for anything, something horrible will happen to disprove the compliment, like the time I tumbled down a flight of stairs at my high school graduation right after someone remarked on how gracefully I moved. It's kind of a reverse karma, or really more like hubris, that I have to be careful about. "Let's don't talk about that."

"Well, okay." Carlos ambles to the cash register and pays while I stand by, staring at the menu printed above the counter, as if, though full to bursting, I am considering ordering yet another dish. When Carlos returns, he says, "What about it?"

"What about what?"

"Are you interested in seeing my shrine?"

I think about Letty and Miguel, even Rudy. Carlotta comes to mind, too, and I'm ready to turn him down because really there's too much going on for me right now, but then, what good is it to sit at home worrying? And do I really want to face that mess in my house, that lingering chemical stench, and those three stooges sitting around the hot living room staring at the television, or worse, pestering me to borrow my car? "Sure, and I want to see those sketches, too," I say, watching the old man, his eyes shut and pretending to be blind, as he is himself herded toward the register by the giggling toddlers, each tugging on his thick and blunt-fingered hands.

Chapter Eleven

The drive to Carlos's place goes smoothly, a pleasant contrast to that crazy trip navigated by Connie, on account of his sensible directions. Of course, when Carlos comments on how well I drive, I immediately yank a sharp right and roll over the curb, spooking a nearby homeless man in a wheelchair, who drops his begging sign to give me the finger. After that, I focus strictly on keeping all tires flat on the street and shut my ears to anything but where to go. All the while, I'm fretting about the "seeing his sketches" euphemism, my nervous joke, and remembering the disaster that was my one interlude—not counting last Sunday's transgression with Rudy himself, of course—in the whole five months since the Valentine's breakup.

Apparently, when word got out at school that I was no longer "involved," likely thanks to my loudmouth friend Pancha, the school counselor, I started getting visitations in my classroom by the woodshop teacher, Stuart Lindner. Stuart's this tall, lanky white guy who is not merely Caucasian, but literally white, from his blindingly new-looking gym shoes to his faded khakis to his bleached polo shirt to his papery, nearly translucent skin and to the top of his dandelion puff of silvery hair. At the start of recess and lunch and right after the final bell, he'd just materialize at my threshold, all glowing and ghostly against the backdrop of my dusty and disarrayed classroom. I had to wonder how he managed this, since the woodshop was by no means close to my bungalow. He had to have been letting his kids out early because he never seemed out of breath; instead he was calm and relaxed, luminous as a ghost, when he drifted through the door with some contrived reason or another for having to see me.

Despite the silvery hair, Stuart is probably just in his forties, married, but separated from his wife, who—from what I could gather—is a real estate agent, a smoker with a bad shopping habit. It turned out he had lots of regrets about marrying her, and he filled journals with these. He showed me one once. That leather-bound thing was heavy, filled with this tight, cramped script practically gouged into the pages, he bore down so hard on the pen. I ran my fingertips over the engraved print, slapped the thing shut, and thrust it back to him, saying, "Wow! That sure is something."

One thing led to another, and we both turned up at Pancha's misbegotten "wedding shower," which she held at the Wildlife Way Station up near Simi Valley. Instead of allowing guests, simply and conveniently, to trot over to Macy's to buy crystal pickle dishes or silver serving spoons, Pancha commanded us to volunteer our time at the Way Station for the afternoon. I was—let's face it—lonely and bored, having a pretty dull time "cleaning" the woods that comprised the Way Station's grounds. I mean, apart from removing litter, of which there was none, how does one tidy nature? Those of us who showed up had little idea what Pancha expected. We moved a few flat stones from one place to another, rearranged what twigs we could find, straightened out the fallen leaves, and searched vainly for debris to clear from the trail. So when Stuart invited me to his place afterward for dinner, I accepted. He prepared some kind of pasta thing with Alfredo sauce, *white* sauce for god's sake, served with steamed cauliflower and followed by vanilla ice cream. During the meal we shared two bottles of Chardonnay, and before long, I found myself nude and crawling between Stuart's snowy sheets, mildly curious what color his pubic hair would be.

But his entire torso, apertures, arms and legs were completely hairless, smooth as a Chihuahua's backside. He'd shaved off his body hair himself, he told me proudly, when I commented on this. I had to wonder how he managed the wrinkly testicle area; moreover, I could not figure out *why*. Apart from parasitic infestation or preparation for surgery, what reason is there for removing body hair? At the moment, I wondered if his wife kept journals of her own filled with complaints about him. This would make an excellent entry as would the sex, which was way too forceful. That hard angular body became insistent when aroused, and Stuart turned out to be the kind that likes to shove a pillow beneath a woman's buttocks for deeper penetration, which is not all that much fun when the man is rough and impatient and when the pillow is densely filled with feathers—all those sharp quills. Afterward, I wound up with a spectacular butt rash and a bladder infection that made me feel like I was squeezing out glass splinters whenever I peed. The next time Stuart manifested on my classroom doorstep, I lied to him, saying I had gotten back together with Rudy and we were thinking about getting married.

Now, as I pull into the driveway alongside the guesthouse that Carlos rents, my stomach knots up like I'm about to climb on a rickety roller coaster with hairpin twists, sheer drops, and those sickening anti-gravity loops. Just wondering if he has feather pillows makes my nalgas itch. I yank up the handbrake, stare through the windshield at a fat magnolia tree in the yard separating the guesthouse from the main residence. A breeze ruffles its green-black leaves, and I can almost hear their chilling rattle.

Carlos places a warm hand over mine, still on the brake. "I'm just going to show you the shrine, Marina," he says in a soft voice. "That's all. It's late for looking at sketches. You seem tired. And then we can drive back to your place so I can pick up my bike. Okay?"

I nod. We push the car doors open and climb out. The magnolia's thick, waxy blossoms emit the faint fragrance of burnt sugar that trails us into the small guesthouse like a sweetly scented veil.

The shrine turns out to be these three wooden shelves on which various brass containers are arrayed. The longest shelf is a base of sorts, and the next shelf is somewhat shorter than that. The topmost shelf or level is the shortest of these, so it's a pyramid setup with a terracotta statue of the Buddha at the center of the top shelf. The Buddha sits lotus-style. Propped against its knees is a photo of someone who looks similar to the Dalai, though clearly is not him, despite wearing the same saffron and dark orange robes. Near Buddha's right knee is a brass thing, maybe an incense burner, and next to the left knee is a small, satiny red sachet trimmed with gold thread. The next shelf contains several brass cups or bowls. This shelf is book-ended by a bottle of some bluish liquid on the left and a spray of peacock feathers fanned out in a cup on the right. A longish crocheted doily of sorts covers the bottom tier, and a series of even smaller cups are set on that with a bell, candle, and some unrecognizable brass pieces, one that has a spout and another, dead center, that looks like a jewelry case.

Carlos explains that Buddhists build a personal shrine to focus their faith and to inspire a deeper relationship with the Buddha. He tells me he has to maintain the shrine daily by changing the food and water in the containers. He explains about the offerings: water for the mouth to establish positive causes and conditions; water to cleanse the feet and purify or wash away ordinariness; flowers, or in this case peacock plumes, for beauty to please the eye and open the heart; incense for beauty to please the nose; butter lamp or candle to illuminate wisdom, compassion, and patience; scented water to cleanse the body; food or sweets to nourish the Samadhi, which Carlos says is the source of all miracles; and music, a small bell for wisdom and interdependence.

"Who's that in the picture?" I lilt my chin toward the photo as it seems impolite to point in this sacred space.

"He's my root-lama, kind of a personal teacher or life coach," Carlos says, a sheepish look on his face. "It's good to see his image every day. That's for confidence."

This reminds me of my father's TM mentor, the shifty old guy who pocketed my father's money to pull a mantra off a list for me. I look away from the photo. "Is this where you chant?" I point at a green-and-gold cushion embroidered with a pair of elephants. The plush pillowlike thing rests on a small stool, something like a kneeler set before the shrine.

Carlos nods. He leans down to smooth the fabric or brush off dust.

"What happens when you chant?"

"Well, the seed of Buddhahood planted deep inside kind of wakes up. Slowly, negativity washes away, and over time positive changes happen in everyday life, you know. Some people say sickness gets cured, family problems resolve themselves, and bad habits are overcome." Carlos tinkers with the containers on the lowest shelf, arranging and rearranging these before returning them to their original positions, and then he turns to me with a smile. "Of course, not all Buddhists are completely spiritual. I know some who chant for material things, like, say, a car or high-definition TV, and once some woman told me she was chanting for a new washing machine."

"A *washing* machine?" I say, disturbed by this idea. "Do you chant for what you want? I mean, is it like prayer?"

Carlos shrugs. "Sometimes."

"Does it work?"

"Well," he says, "you're here, so yeah, I guess it does."

I take a step or two back, thinking I should feel flattered, but instead I'm kind of bothered by this. In fact, it makes me feel somewhat like a washing machine.

Amazed as I am by the shrine and that some Buddhists will actually chant to get what they want, including household appliances, I am more astonished by Carlos's living quarters. The guesthouse is just a guesthouse, which is to say, there's not much of a kitchen really. It's more a galley kind of arrangement—no room for a dining set or even a counter with barstools in the place, so Carlos just has this drop-leaf table against one wall in the main room, where he probably eats. The front room also has bookshelves and a futon that no doubt folds out into his bed. Adjacent to this

room is a narrow hall—where he keeps the shrine—and this leads to a tiny bathroom.

What impresses me is the tidiness of the place.
At first I thought the windows were open; the glass
is so transparently clean. Books on the shelves
are nicely organized by genre and then author. He
seems to favor spiritual reading, and I spot a few
titles by our mutual friend the Dalai, including
Awakening the Mind, Lightening the Spirit, but
Carlos also has a good selection of paperback mysteries: the entire Henry Rios series, by Julian Nava;
and Lucha Corpi's great detective novels, along
with the obligatory Sonny Baca collection by Ru-
dolfo Anaya. When I turn from the books, I notice
the futon's wooden frame gleams, even its canvas
cushions are plump and smooth, wrinkle free. The
linoleum flooring gives off a wet-looking sheen,
and the windowsills, the molding, the corners and
crevices are dust free. Even the baseboards, the
true test of cleanliness in a home, are immaculate. 'Buela Lupita would have absolutely nowhere
to scrawl her insults in this casita limpia. I picture
her grim, toadlike face furrowed in frustration.

When Carlos excuses himself to use the bathroom, I nudge open a few cabinets in the kitchen.
These are also spotless: contents neatly arranged
atop fresh shelf paper. There are even hooks in a
long, narrow closet where Carlos has mounted a

few different sizes of brooms and dustpans, along with a fresh-looking mop. On narrow shelves that line the door he keeps kitchen matches and jars for variously sized nails, screws, nuts, bolts, and thumbtacks. When the toilet flushes, I hastily shut the closet, idly wondering where he would stow me if I came to stay in this tiny place.

"I guess you'd better drive me back to your house to pick up my bike," Carlos says when he reenters the kitchen. "You've got to teach in the morning, and I've got a social studies gig out near El Monte."

"Where is your art?" I ask, noticing for the first time an absence of wall hangings. "The sketches and printmaking work you do?"

"I keep my portfolios in some storage space that I have out in the landlord's garage, but when I signed the lease, I agreed not to drive any nails in the walls, so I can't hang anything," he says. "It's better this way. I don't like being held back by staring at stuff I've already done."

"Where do you do your artwork?"

"There's this nonprofit studio, a co-op out in East LA, where I'm a member, called Self-Help Graphics. I go there to paint, do silkscreen, and make prints. I'll show you sometime, if you're interested."

"Yes," I say. "I am."

"Also," he says, hesitating a bit, "I was thinking. I mean, um, if you're also interested, there's this film playing now at the Laemmle, that independent theater over on Fairfax. It's a film about Franz Kafka, his life and all that. It's a movie, you know, not a documentary, and I thought, well, because you're a language arts teacher and he was a writer...I guess...I just thought you might want to see it. Do you like Kafka?"

"I do, especially the story about waking up as a cockroach," I tell him. "I can really relate to that."

"Well, you want to go with me, then?" he asks, searching my face, no doubt, for the least trace of reluctance. "To the film? It's this Friday?"

"Sure," I say. "If nothing else falls apart, I would really like to go."

He sucks in this enormous breath that whooshes out, releasing his shoulders. "Great!" he says, and he reaches to squeeze my hand.

When we return to my house, Carlos walks me to my front door and kisses me in a brusque, nose-bumping way, and I'm relieved when he declines to come in. Who knows what lies on the other side of that (for-once shut) door? The only thing I can be sure of is that it won't be anything I especially want to find. I wave to Carlos and wait for the motorcycle to sputter off before opening the door.

Though it's not really late, only about nine, lazy-assed Reggie and Kiko are again sleeping soundly on the love seat and sofa with the whole house lit up like the Palace of Versailles, the television blasting some situation comedy with an obnoxious laugh track. I step forward to snap the thing off and nearly topple over a moving lump of blankets on the floor. It's Bobby rousing from sleep, sitting up just as I'm stepping over the mound. "You're still here?" I ask after I catch my balance and turn off the set.

He blinks several times and rubs his eyes. "I fell asleep," he says with a yawn. "Is it okay if I stay here tonight?"

"Does your mom know where you are?"

"Yeah, sure," he says, a little too quickly.

"Seriously, she better know." I glance around to assess the damage that took place while I was gone. A pair of socks that look like they've been thoroughly dredged in filth; grungy gym shoes; a few clouded glasses; empty water and beer bottles; magazines; loose sections of the Sunday paper; inexplicably, a laptop computer on the coffee table; the now sour-smelling cereal bowl still atop the television; assorted piles of clothing; and finally, the tray with the crosses, even more handsome than I remembered them. I glance at the kid. He's staring at me expectantly. "Another thing I'm serious about,

Bobby, is this," I tell him in a low, even voice. "I want to know why you hit your mother."

He looks away from me, his face dark, tight as a fist.

"Those crosses are really nice and all that, but I really want to know," I say. "I want to know why a person who can make such beautiful things would hit a woman, why *any* son would hit his mother."

Bobby draws his knees up, making a tent with the blankets, and buries his face in them. His shoulders quiver; his narrow back convulses. Without making a sound, the kid is weeping.

"You don't have to do it now, Bobby, but sooner or later you need to tell me why you did that to her." One by one, I flip off the light switches as I make my way to my bedroom, and despite the Dalai's insistence on compassion, I don't feel too bad about leaving that boy alone in the dark with his tears.

Again, I crawl into bed with the Dalai, but also with the latest novel in the Henry Rios series. It's been a while since I finished that one and seeing it on Carlos's bookshelf made me want to read it again. My sisters think it's stupid that I like to read books over and over—in fact, Xochi thinks it's an incredible waste of time reading a book in the first place—but really I find comfort in rereading novels, though I'm determined to finish *Awakening the Mind, Lightening the Heart.* To be wholly honest, Henry Rios, the gay Chicano lawyer who investigates crimes, has adventures that are way more riveting than the Dalai Lama's observations and insights. Before long, I'm twenty pages in and my eyes burn with fatigue. I settle the unopened Dalai on my bed table, but place a bookmark in my Henry Rios and nest that on the pillow next to mine, thinking about mysteries and still wondering why Bobby, who—unlike his father—seems like he might not be a total waste of human life, would strike his mother.

I twist off my bedside lamp and remember my own mother, the times I've been angry with her. Apart from frustration over her failure to react to things like 'Buela Lupita's insults or my father's bad behavior, I had next to nothing to flare up about. She was just there, all prayerful and serene, beginning and ending most statements with *gracias a Dios*, her large doelike eyes ever clear, even shining with conviction. I can still picture her long, slender form gliding through our house, silent but for the *tfft-tfft-tfft* of her moccasins scuffing against the wood floors and the muted music of rosary beads in her housecoat pocket. Once, when I was just twelve, I snuck out of the house to go to a concert with friends. I bundled clothes under my blankets to make it look like I was sleeping before climbing out the window. That night the smoke alarm over my bed malfunctioned, emitting ear-blasting shrieks around midnight. When my mother entered my room to investigate, she, of course, discovered my absence.

After I returned, I heard a multitude of *gracias a Dios*, but these were softly uttered. She pressed two pink baby aspirins into my palm and ran me a hot bubble bath. After my bath, she asked if I wanted to recite the Rosary with her. I declined and left her kneeling at her hallway shrine, mumbling the decades before a plaster statue of the Virgin of Guadalupe, her gentle face glowing in guttering candlelight. Getting pissed at my mother was like raging against the sky or the sea, becoming all infuriated by the indifferent vastness and impenetrable depth. Absurdly, I think of the brass cups arranged on Carlos's shrine, how they have no handles, and these somehow remind me of my mother, but I can't think how as I drift off to sleep.

I'm not even fully into my first dream when my bedroom door whooshes open, and I jerk awake, thinking, *burglars*, maybe armed, maybe homicidal. There was a home invasion a few blocks away not more than a month ago; the entire family, recent immigrants from El Salvador, shot execution style, even the baby. Maybe these intruders have already wiped out the boys in the front room, though I didn't hear the crack of gunfire. I hold my breath to keep still, pretend to be sleeping.

Footsteps followed by gentle tapping on my shoulder. "Marina, Marina?" It's Bobby whispering at my bedside.

I raise myself on my elbows. "What is it? Why are you waking me up?" Irritation rises in me. He's violating rule number one for my houseguests: Never disturb my sleep.

"I got to tell you something," he says.

"Tell me in the morning."

"I've got to tell you now. I want you to know why I hit my mom." His voice trembles, and he takes a deep breath. "You got to know I didn't want to. I really didn't."

I sit up, flick on the bedside lamp. "Then why did you do it?"

He squints at me, his face chalk-streaked with dried tears. "My dad, that day, he was in like a really bad mood. You know he got laid off?"

I nod. In La Chingada mode, Carlotta often explored this topic of conversation.

"Yeah, well, that kind of makes him all pissed off at everything pretty much of the time. But that day, he was even worse, like way more angry than usual, kept saying my mom is all useless, that she couldn't do nothing right. He told her to make him eggs for lunch and she fried him some, but he let them get cold while he watched baseball, and when he tasted them, he just flipped. He grabbed her by the hair and pushed her face into the plate, smearing the yolk and everything all over. She started screaming, calling him all kinds of names, and when she ran to the bathroom to clean up, he kept saying, 'Man, oh, man, this is it. Today's the day.' And he was doing this thing with his hands, flexing the fingers and then shaking them out, taking a few shadow punches, you know, like boxers do."

"So what did you do?"

"I went to the bathroom, stood outside it, and told my mom to get out, to come over here, to your place. She opened the door and got all, 'This is my house, too,' saying that he should be the one to leave, that she didn't do nothing wrong." Bobby's lips quirk, his chin crumples.

"And?" I pull the sheet over my shoulder. Though it's a balmy night, a chill traces up my spine.

"And I hit her, that's what," he says quietly. "The whole time my dad's in the front room, quiet while the game's on, but waiting, and I know as soon as there's a commercial, he'll stomp down the hall, break down the bathroom door if he has to, so I hauled back and I hit her. I hit her as hard as I could." Bobby bites his lower lip.

In a flash, I can see it, the whole nightmarish scene: the lunatic lying in wait in the living room, the television blaring, the boy and his mother whispering urgently in the hallway. I can almost smell Bobby's sweat, nearly feel the prickly hair on his neck, and hear his heart drumming in his throat on that terrible afternoon, the seconds tick-tick-ticking in his ears, growing louder and stronger, like a timer affixed to a detonator. "What happened when you hit her?"

"What I thought would happen. That's what happened. She got all shocked and scared, and she ran through the house to the front door to come over here. The old man was hot at first, but I told him, 'Good, the bitch is gone. We can watch the game in peace.' And after a while, he was okay with that. The game ended and my dad fell asleep on the couch. Then everything was quiet. I turned off the lights and looked out the window. I could see you bringing her a plate, and later, you, like, held her in your arms. I saw you hugging my mom, and I knew she would be okay."

"You hit her to make her leave?" I ask. "I mean, wasn't there another way?"

"No." Bobby shakes his head. "I couldn't think of any other way. I really couldn't. You know how my mom gets sometimes, all full of rage, and you can't make her listen to nothing, no matter what."

"You talk to anybody about this?"

"Yeah," he says, "just now—you."

"No, Bobby, you got to talk to somebody who knows what to tell you and how to help you. I can't do that."

He ignores me, stares off into space. "One thing, I didn't expect."

"What's that?"

"The look on her face after I hit her." His chin quivers again. "It's the worst thing I seen in my whole life. She looked at me like she didn't know me, like I was a stranger, some monster that really scared her. And I can't *never* forget that."

"Shush." I sit up fully and take his hand, squeeze it lightly. "Shush, it's late. You should get some rest. Listen, m'ijo, why don't you go and sleep in the other bedroom. That was where your mother slept when she stayed with me. You can stay there tonight."

The kid shakes his head.

"Why not? The bed in there is way more comfortable than the floor."

"Can't," he says. "My tía Connie's sleeping in there."

"*What the*—" I drop his hand, kick off the sheets, and vault from my bed. Bobby follows behind me into the hall. I swing open the door to the guest room, and sure enough, deep, swinish sounds resonate from the darkness. I snap on the light, and there she is, la borracha, wearing red brocade pajamas and a sleeping mask. She's splayed on her back, her mouth agape, snoring at top volume. A jumble of clothing looks to have erupted from this oversized rolling suitcase on the floor, and the dresser is littered with grubby tubes, jars, bottles, brush, and comb.

"What are you doing here?" I say loudly.

Bobby tugs my elbow. "She wears earplugs, and besides, I think she's passed out. You can kick her out in the morning unless you want to wake everyone up."

"*Why* is she here?"

Bobby, still clutching my elbow, guides me out of the room and he turns off the light. "I'm not real sure. I think my grandpa kicked her out or something like that. He brung her over to my house and *bam*—threw her suitcase in the street. He was pretty pissed off. And then, well, my dad wasn't, like, real glad to see her, nor my mom, so she came over here. That was around seven o'clock. She drunk all the beer in the fridge and then shut herself in here."

"Jesus Christ," I say, but quietly. The kid has a point about not waking those other chuckleheads up. I do not want to deal with them at the moment. "What is this? A halfway house for lunatics?"

Bobby's brown eyes grow round and he backs away, but I'm too steamed to care. Compassion and tolerance can be pretty capacious, even immeasurable, but I'm finding out the hard way that they are not limitless. Or maybe I'm not meant to be a Buddhist.

"That's it," I say, thinking, this *is* a home invasion. "No more people. Tomorrow, everyone goes. Everyone and I mean it." I wheel away from him and stalk out of the guest room.

I remember what Carlos said about the hungry spirits and once again picture those mandolin-shaped beings, big-gutted and narrow-necked creatures with tiny heads that wander through my house holding their bellies with thin arms, whining and puling for sustenance that never satisfies. Didn't he mention preta is a reincarnation realm? So will I have to *die* to be free? Irritation rises in my throat like bile. My thoughts churn darkly. But one crystalline and distinctly un-Buddhist insight penetrates this murk: I don't want to die for anyone, especially not this houseful of fools, until I have lived for myself. Once inside my room, I close the door, and back against it, still clutching the knob and pressing my spine against the hard wood, bearing into it with all my weight.

Chapter Twelve

In the morning, I find Kiko and Reggie huddled over a laptop, which they've set up on my kitchen table. Bobby stands nearby instructing them on finding websites, and Connie is nowhere in sight. I grist rich, dark beans to stoke the Coffeeville locomotive, pour in water, and all aboard, I press the switch, releasing that first noisy burst of steam before the engine clamors onto the tracks. Kiko glances up, grins at me. "Good morning, tía," he shouts over the commotion.

"You're moving out today," I tell him before reaching for my GOLEAN Crunch from the top of the refrigerator. It's suspiciously light, so I rattle the thing—empty, of course. And I'd rather munch on the cardboard box itself than eat Kiko's stale and tasteless Raisin Flakes.

"This thing is so cool," he says, eyes back on the computer screen. "We're finding out all kinds of stuff."

"Yeah," Reggie says. "Me and Kiko are thinking of starting a rap band."

"You're moving, too," I tell him. "You can't stay here anymore." Only Bobby seems to hear this over the coffee machine's clangor, and he glances at me, blushing.

"We're going to call the band 'Aztlan,' like the homeland in the north," Reggie continues. "Did you know we have a mystical or mythical or mysterious—something with an 'm'—homeland in the north?"

"It's mythical, a *mythical* homeland," Kiko says. "Later, we're getting on Craigslist to put an ad to find some musicians. 'Cause, like, we can sing. Anyone with a mouth can sing, but none of us knows how to play the other stuff, like bass and lead guitar and drums and keyboard."

"I can do maracas," Reggie tells him, then furrows his brow. "I think."

"All of you need to be out of here before I get back from school today. You got that?" In the refrigerator, I find a heel of bread and some margarine. I insert the bread in the toaster.

"If I could play an instrument," Kiko tells Reggie, "it would be the drums, man, and I would be all famous, like that chick in the White Stripes."

"Nah, dude," Reggie says. "I wouldn't. I'd play

lead guitar, and I'd be like a prodigy, and babes would be totally insane with lust for me."

"You'll need to pack," I say, staring at the glowing rods heating my bread. As with my purse and coffeemaker, I have a very dicey relationship with the toaster. I have to watch its every move.

"I'm going to call myself Tlaloc, tía," Kiko tells me, pronouncing the Aztec god's name *Stah-loke*.

"Estás loco," I say. "That's for sure."

"He was a cool god, all blue-skinned with fangs and bugged-out eyes." Kiko widens his own eyes and thrusts out his tongue, making a face that is far goofier looking than it is terrifying. "The Aztecs, like, they drowned all these little kids as sacrifices to him. Isn't that cool?"

"Not if you're one of those little kids," Reggie puts in.

"You guys, both of you, have to pack up all your stuff and move out today," I say again. "You can't stay here anymore."

Kiko, still staring at the computer screen, says, "They'd collect all their tears, the tears of the kids that they were going to drown, and put them in these bowls to offer up to Tlaloc, along with the drowned bodies. How badass is that?"

Reggie winces. "It might be kind of hard on the parents, too."

Bobby flashes a twenty-dollar bill, likely the

money Xochi gave him for the turquoise cross. "Come on, vatos. Let's bounce. We can get some doughnuts and coffee at that gas station down the street."

"Sounds good." Kiko rises from the table, scraping back the chair. "But I rather have hot cocoa instead of coffee."

"Should I turn this thing off?" Reggie asks.

"Nah, leave it on," Bobby says with another glance at me. "Maybe you can use it, if you want. Check your email or something."

"Where is she?" I ask him. "Where's Connie?"

He shrugs. "Still sleeping."

"I hope you guys realize this is moving day," I say, as the coffeemaker issues its final wheezing gasp.

"Later, tía," Kiko tosses this over his shoulder.

"Yeah, later," Reggie says.

The three of them tramp out of the kitchen into the living room, and in a few moments, the screen door slaps shut. My toast shoots out, predictably charred at the edges, but I catch it before it falls to the floor. "Hah!" I tell the toaster, "foiled again," and I open the margarine tub. Most of it is, of course, gone, but I grab a knife to gouge out what residue I can, planning to leave Connie a note, an eviction notice if you will. No way am I up to facing her chatter this early in the morning. I enjoy a few minutes of quiet and solitude while I sip my coffee. But before long, I find myself seated in front of the laptop, opening the email account provided by my school, entering my log-in name and password, and deleting the series of emails from all of the mail-order retailers that I have ever ordered anything from, my most loyal and regular daily correspondents. I scroll down, marking messages for trash. Yet another Ethiopian prince wants my help with a banking matter. Hmm...just when I thought I'd been bumped from that listserv. Then I delete a few pictures of cats wearing clothing and posing as humans doing human things, like talking on the telephone, pushing miniature shopping carts, and so forth, sent by my best friend from grade school, unfortunately another reliable correspondent. The danged attachments take up all the space in my mailbox, but I don't have the heart to tell her to stop sending the stuff.

But what's this? A message from *aortiz*. Before I notice the last two letters, I think it's one of those cutesy online names: aorta, as in the vessel to the heart, combined with the phonetic representation of *tease*. "Aorta tease," I mutter to myself, "how very clever." I'm just about to delete it, when I look again. Ortiz strikes me as familiar, though I can't think why. I open the thing, and it says:

Dear Marina,

   I looked you up through Olive Branch Middle School, the place of employment you listed on a hospital form. I hope you don't mind that I'm sending you an email message instead of calling, since the phone number you provided on that form seems not to work. On the school's website, I see that you are teaching summer classes. If you are not busy afterward, would you join me for lunch? There's a Jigglers not too far from the hospital. I can be there by 1:30.

   Arturo Ortiz

I'm puzzled for a minute or so before I remember the twitchy resident, or the bunny doc, as I have been thinking of him. Again, the likelihood of me getting asked out even once by one person is shamefully remote. Being asked out the same week by two different people has to occur with less frequency than a total eclipse of the sun. I consider those long months when I'd been sure that losing Rudy meant giving up all men. This burst of attention feels completely unfair. Why can't these people space themselves out? I toss the last wedge of toast, feathery with char, into my mouth and promptly bite my tongue hard enough to draw blood.

I type my answer quickly and hit send before I change my mind. Then I head to the bathroom for my shower. "Hi, there," I say to the Mahatma's photo on the wall. Gandhi seems a bit softer in the morning light, more cheerful and hopeful than he does at night. Though unsmiling, his wrinkled face looks like it's wreathed with lines etched from merriment, rather than chiseled by despair.

As I'm loading my purse and book bag into the car, I catch sight of Henry Fuentes across the street, watering his hibiscus and rose bushes. He sees me, waves, and then sets down the hose to cross over to my driveway. Cupping a gloved hand over his brow to shade his eyes, he says, "I guess you heard they let that asshole out." Henry juts his chin in the direction of Carlotta's house.

I nod. "Overcrowded jail."

"That's just stupid and dangerous. I wanted to make sure you knew because who knows what that joker might do. I'm on medical leave on account of my back, so I'm usually going to be home. Call me if he gives you any shit."

"I will." The morning sun warms my neck, drying tendrils of wet hair. Though the sky is clear, the air still smells of car exhaust and smoke blended with the fresh, loamy fragrance of mown grass and nectar-scented morning glories. I point at the house next door. "Carlotta's back over there, too. They let her out of the hospital yesterday."

"I know," Henry says, shaking his head. "The wife told me."

"She has a TRO," I tell him.

Henry rolls his eyes. "Hey, you missed all the excitement yesterday," he says. "That nutty sister of hers, the bigmouth, was hollering like crazy, stumbling around and cursing. It was hijo de puta this and pinche cabron that. Their father, I guess, threw her out. Skinny old guy, but strong. He lifted this huge suitcase over his head and threw the thing a good three yards, I'd say."

"I heard about it. In fact, she's at my house now."

Henry's mouth drops open. "Her, too? No offense there, Marina, but what are you *doing* with all those people? You can't keep letting everyone under the sun stay with you. Flojos like that, they just take advantage."

"This is true," I tell him, flashing again on those walking mandolins. A crashing sound emanates from the open window of his stucco duplex, followed by a rush of Spanish issued by many voices, and then children crying. "But you're a fine one to talk. How many people stay with you?"

"I know," he says, eyes wide, but he fails to give me an estimate. "That's why I'm warning you. At least I got family staying with me, but still, you shouldn't follow my example. I haven't had any peace since 1973, when me and Imelda was first married."

"After today, I'm not letting anyone stay. I told them this morning. It's moving day. They have to be out before I get back from school." I dust off my hands as if I have already physically removed them from my premises.

But Henry's unimpressed. "Good luck with that," he says, and turns to lumber back across the street to his hose and the flowers.

At school, the piñatas are not yet dry enough to affix the tissue paper with which students will decorate their creations, so we spend the time working on the progressive tenses, and inspired by Julian Nava, I make up an activity involving a detective story. For this, I cover my ruler with aluminum foil and wrap the base with masking tape. I tell the students it's a knife. "Un cuchillo," I say, when the students give me blank looks. They still seem confounded, and okay, I have to admit, a ruler, even disguised by aluminum foil and masking tape, doesn't look that much like a knife. Eventually, we work it out, and I hand the makeshift weapon to Elias, instructing him to step out of the bungalow and reenter it waving the "knife." The other students station themselves about the classroom engaging in activities with the various props I keep—dress-up clothes, play-store goods, toy cash register, plastic foods, and whatnot. Not brilliant, but the exercise entails the kids telling what they are doing when Elias enters. Maritza Saenz, a proficient English speaker, is the detective who then questions each classmate one by one.

"What were you doing when the murderer appeared?"

"I was shopping when the murderer appeared."

Or: "I was cooking the food when the murderer appeared."

A little formulaic, but I have the students write sentences using the continuous past tense to make a simple detective story. After they get into it, the kids find this activity hilarious, laughing uproariously each time Elias, wearing a fierce look, bursts through the door brandishing the fake knife, then giggling anew when reading their stories aloud, one by one from the podium at the front of the classroom.

Again, Felipe Ahuaul is absent. During the time we slog through the final chapters of *The Incredible Journey* in the advanced class, Armando, likewise, never shows his face. Like it or not, I trudge to the main office to phone Señor Gaspar Ahuaul about his sons, as no way do I want the man to have my cell number, even if it's just to the disposable phone I bought. He's unreachable, so I leave a message, asking him to meet with me the next morning before classes and to bring the boys. After I hang up, the school's administrative manager, Dee, catches my eye. "Marina," she calls from her desk at the heart of the reception area, "the principal would like a word with you."

I glance at my watch. "Uh, now?"

"Yes, if you have a moment." Dee's this lean and tough blonde in her fifties. Her leathery face suggests she's spent way too much time in the sun, but I can't picture this vigorous woman doing anything as relaxing as sunbathing. She more likely chops down trees or does construction work in her spare time. She never bothers with makeup to hide the fact of her age or to cover the sun's damage to her skin. Truth be told, she's scarier to me than the principal and certainly more powerful, especially to those of us who need school supplies, textbooks, and that monthly paycheck, so "if you have a moment" comes across like "you bet your ass I mean now." Without waiting for my answer, Dee lifts the interoffice phone and says, "She's on her way, Mrs. Jimenez."

As I make my way toward the inner office, I scroll through my memory for anything I might have done to get called into the principal's office, which I have discovered is far worse for teachers than students. Maybe, despite my most conscientious efforts, I have cursed audibly, or more likely, I've forgotten to complete some essential paperwork. Has Mr. Ahuaul complained that I denigrated his profession to his sons? There are so many mistakes to make that I'm not even sure I would know if I had made one. I tap lightly on the inner office door and it swings wide almost instantaneously, as if Mrs. Jimenez has been standing there waiting, her hand poised near the doorknob.

"Come in, Marina," she says with a smile. "Take a seat."

A thick cloud of a jasmine and musk, an expensivesmelling scent, rolls out and envelops me as I step into the principal's cool, dark office. With the heavy wooden furniture, leather-upholstered chairs, and the framed prints of classic cars on the walls, this always strikes me as a man's office, but Mrs. Jimenez is a short, dainty woman, not too much older than me. She's been "in education," as she likes to say, since she graduated from college, so at least twenty years or more. Soft curls frame her round face, and she sports a deceptively warm, deep-dimpled smile, but I've heard from the other teachers that she can be an absolute and heartless dictator, capable of exiling anyone who crosses her to teach in juvenile detention centers with a snap of her well-manicured fingers.

"Dee mentioned that you wanted to see me," I say.

"Yes," she says. She circles the desk to take her seat and indicates I should sit in the chair opposite hers. "I wanted to ask you about your experiences with a substitute teacher we had been considering for a long-term assignment." She rifles through a file sleeve on her desk. "His name is...Carlos Lozano, and I believe he covered for you yesterday."

"That's right," I say, shifting a nalga to get more comfortable in the rock-hard chair she offered me. "You see I had a family emergency—"

With a flick of her wrist, she waves this off. Not important. "How did he do? Any problems?"

"No, he was fine. He's an art teacher, and we happened to be doing a culminating project that involved craft, so—"

Another wrist flick. "The reason I ask is that he was hired by the vice principal to paint a mural in her guest room, and well, Ms. Myers had a questionable experience with him."

"Questionable?" My heart feels larger, heavier, throbbing thickly in my chest.

"Ms. Myers lives out in Saugus, you know, the

boonies, as we say, and she has a field in back of her house where she and her husband grow corn."

"Corn?" I say, as if inexplicably succumbing to echolalia. My stomach twists in expectation of disappointment and even disgust. And I'm also thinking, why corn? Isn't it enough to be an administrator? Does Myers have to be a farmer, too? Already, I resent her for her corn and whatever trouble it may have caused Carlos.

"Yes, corn. They grow corn." Mrs. Jimenez nods, an uncomprehending look on her face as if she, too, has no idea why anyone would deliberately choose to grow corn. "She says that Carlos did an exquisite job on the guest room. The mural is more than she and her husband expected. According to her, it's beautiful and tasteful and so forth, but after painting the thing, Carlos asked if he could look around outdoors. Ms. Myers agreed. How could she not after he'd done such a great job?"

I shake my head. No way could she have turned him down.

"Well, while Carlos was *taking a look around*"—that last phrase Mrs. Jimenez not only inflects, but she also applies air quotes—"Ms. Myers prepared some lemonade for him. It was a hot afternoon, humid, and so forth, so she thought it would make a nice treat. *But...*" Mrs. Jimenez leans forward on her elbows to study my face before she releases the next bit of information. "When Ms. Myers peered out the window to find Carlos, to call him in for the lemonade, she discovered, well, she happened to see—this is difficult to say . . ."

"What? What did she see? What?" I'm now perched on that cementlike cushion, leaning forward myself and straining to imagine what on earth the woman saw. A satanic ritual? No, it would have to be something to do with Buddhism? A bizarre lotus pose? *What?*

"She looked out the window and she caught Mr. Lozano running naked through her corn field."

"Running *naked*?" I nearly gasp, but my shock is more from the buildup of suspense and the absurdity of the thing.

"Precisely," Mrs. Jimenez settles back into her chair, a satisfied look on her pretty face. "He had taken off all his clothes to run through the cornstalks in the nude."

"Well, if it was a hot day . . ." I struggle to imagine the context for Carlos to shed his clothing and jog through the corn.

"It was hot." Mrs. Jimenez concedes this, nodding her head so vigorously that she seems to be rocking herself in her seat.

"I mean, is it illegal?"

Mrs. Jimenez shrugs, watching me intently. "Is he a friend of yours?"

Weirdly, I think of my neighbors' old rooster, who became soup. How he would crow three times each morning and then pause, waiting until I fell back asleep before starting in again. I can still almost hear those first three protracted shrieks before I speak. "I haven't known him long, so I wouldn't say he's a friend. He seems like a fine person, and he did a good job covering my class."

"I just wanted to be sure he isn't a friend of yours." Mrs. Jimenez lifts a pen from its stand and examines the tip. "You see, we can't possibly offer him a long-term position under these circumstances, and in fact, we really can't invite him back to substitute for any of our teachers. It's too much of a risk for us, for our students. I just wanted you to understand that."

I nod. But I wonder what she means by "risk." How is a man who takes off his clothes to run through a cornfield any kind of a risk to anyone but himself and maybe a few cornstalks, if he should trample any of these? And what business does Ms. Myers have growing corn when you can get it at the supermarket for practically nothing? There's something about growing corn in Southern California that's more suspicious than being nude outdoors. But I say, "Is she really *sure* that's what she saw? I mean, sometimes men take their shirts off, and if the corn is high…maybe he was wearing flesh-tone jogging shorts. Just how would she even know for sure?"

"She saw," Mrs. Jimenez says, "everything. She knows." Then the principal rises from her seat. "Thanks for taking the time to see me, Marina. I hope I haven't kept you from your lunch or any afternoon appointments."

I glance at my watch, scramble to gather up my book bag and purse, and stand on numb and buzzing legs. "I just don't get it. I mean it's so strange…"

"But we're not going to have a problem with this, are we, Marina?"

I shake my head and follow her to the door, which she opens to usher me out. "Good, and thanks again for meeting with me." With a cool and fragrant gust, she softly clicks the door shut behind me.

Chapter Thirteen

I scan the vast hospital cafeteria in search of the tall, jumpy resident, who's invited me to lunch, but tall people are not as easily recognized when seated, especially when likely wearing the same aqua scrubs everyone else in the place seems to have on. My stomach groans and I sniff the air. Curiously, there is no trace of food scenting about. In fact, I don't smell anything at all, though an array of cellophane-wrapped foods—from pudding cups to sandwiches and salads—is displayed beyond a transparent sneeze guard not far from where I'm standing. The cafeteria's white, well-windowed walls are lined with beige vinyl booths, and toward the center of this vast eatery, arranged on the also-white but glitter-speckled linoleum, are a series of tables for four with scoop chairs, the same hard, plastic jobs that are provided for visitors in patients' rooms upstairs. Most of the seats are occupied by tired-looking men and women in scrubs. They speak in low voices, barely audible over glasses chinking and flatware chiming. Then, I see him, *aortiz*, as I've begun to think of him since his email, alone at a booth, apparently spotting me at the same time and waving me over in a herky-jerky way.

I make my way to his booth, conscious of being late and relieved that he's at least ordered a cup of coffee while waiting for me. A manila file sleeve lies before him on the table. "Sorry," I say with a glance at my watch. "A problem came up with a friend of mine." The word "friend" nearly catches in my throat, after denying this relationship not forty minutes earlier during my session with the school principal.

He blinks several times, and I notice a smattering of freckles, a spray of chocolate-colored dots lightly peppering the bridge of his nose and his cheekbone area. These stand out in stark contrast to his pale complexion, a "fluorescent-light tan" achieved through spending most waking hours indoors. "One of the women who was here at the hospital?" he asks.

"No, someone else."

"Oh." He nods, and I can tell he's again thinking that I know too many people with problems.

"It's not medical," I say. "The problem."

He nods again.

"It's to do with corn. You see, he was hired to do some work for one of our school administrators…" And before I can stop myself, I've launched the abridged tale of Carlos and the Cornfield, leaving out the part about our dinner date last night, and placing Carlos firmly in the category of friend. This also feels like a betrayal or at least an omission. Still I can't seem to help myself. I wind it all up, saying, "It's probably something connected to Buddhism."

"Buddhism?" Dr. Ortiz says, drumming his fingertips on the tabletop. He clears his throat. "Well, do you want something to eat? A sandwich or soup? The food isn't great here. I should have mentioned that, but you seemed determined that we eat here."

In my email response to his invitation, I had written: *1:30. Hospital cafeteria. Not Jigglers!* "Maybe a salad or soup, and coffee." I point to his cup. "I can help myself while you get your lunch. I'll bet you don't have too long a break."

"Actually, I'm on a split shift," he tells me. "After lunch, I'm going home to sleep, so I'm drinking decaf. I have to be back here at eight."

We make our way to the food counter, where I select a small cello-wrapped Styrofoam bowl of shredded iceberg lettuce, whole cherry tomatoes, and cucumber slices. I snatch a packet of Caesar dressing from a basket on the counter. At the other end, Dr. Ortiz lifts a lid and stares into an industrial-sized vat, odorless steam clouding his glasses. "*Corn* chowder, I'm afraid."

"I'll have a sandwich."

"The tuna fish isn't bad," he says before grabbing a tray. He selects tuna on whole wheat, and I do the same, though I can see through the wrapping that the bread is soggy, the sandwich likely drippy with mayonnaise. We pour cups of coffee—more decaf for him and the real deal for me, pay the hair-netted woman at the cash register, and bear our trays back to the booth.

He peels the wrapping from his sandwich, saying, "Buddhism?"

"That's right, Dr. Ortiz. My friend Carlos practices Buddhism."

"Art," he says.

"Yeah, he's an artist, too." I'm puzzled as to how he knows this about Carlos. "That's actually why he was at the vice principal's place. He was painting a mural, but he's also a Buddhist."

"No, Art is my name. I'd like you to call me Art."

"Art? Oh, *Art. You're* Art. Of course, A. Ortiz. Arturo. Art. That's your name."

He lets me blather on like an idiot, grinning and blinking in a nonstop way the whole while.

"Art, yes, Carlos is a Buddhist, so maybe he was doing a Buddhist thing, some clothing-less ritual or what have you, and the vice principal no doubt saw that, misinterpreted it somehow."

"Do you know much about Buddhism?" he asks.

"Not as much as I'd like to know," I tell him. The salad dressing packet won't tear the way it's supposed to. I'll have to rip it open discreetly, somehow, with my teeth, but first I try stabbing it with the plastic fork. "Do you know much about it?" I ask. "Buddhism, I mean."

"May I?" He offers his hand, palm up, indicating the dressing packet, which I hand over. With precise movements, he tears a corner open and hands the thing back to me. His hands are long-fingered, deft, but trembly, always busy. After opening my salad dressing, the fingers on one hand zero in on the pepper shaker while those on the other lift a corner of his sandwich. "I don't know too much about Buddhism, aside from what I learned in an undergraduate seminar on comparative religion. I do know there are different kinds of Buddhists. There are Theravada, Mahayana, and Vajrayana Buddhists, and within these are various schools like Zen, Pure Land, and Nichiren. They practice in different ways, with different rituals, and sometimes they have disagreements, bitter arguments between schools, even within schools."

"Really?" Naïve, I know, but I have trouble imagining the plump and merry Buddha generating any kind of conflict.

"It's true," Art says. "My roommate in college was a Buddhist, and he married another Buddhist, but their lamas had some heated history with one another. This created a lot of problems in the marriage, many fights. In fact, they ended up divorcing."

"Couldn't they have worked it out? I mean, maybe, through chanting?" I say, feeling foolish about knowing so little about such things.

"That's Nichiren Buddhism, I believe, the chanting. It's Japanese in origin," he tells me. "My roommate and his wife were Mahayana Buddhists, you see."

I nod, not really seeing at all. "I mean, isn't spirituality supposed to bring you peace? That's what I'm looking for, and it seems like other people, like my mother and father, can so easily believe, just *believe*, with life-changing results." I tell him how the old man was a first-class asshole—a narcissistic, philandering misogynist whose spiritual conversion after a cancer diagnosis really changed him in a fundamental way. He became considerate and loving, even oddly optimistic once he knew he was dying. "He really achieved peace through spirituality, and that's kind of what I'm after."

"Well," Art says. "I don't know about that. I'm not too spiritual or religious. In fact, I'm an atheist, but I consider myself to be at peace." His nose twitches and he blinks at least another dozen times in rapid succession.

"O-*kay*," I say. "But don't you think that spirituality and faith are gifts, like artistic or musical talent; I mean, for those who possess them. Take my mother," I tell him, disturbed that this sounds like the opening to one of those corny vaudevillian jokes. *Take my mother. Really. Ha-ha.* "She is totally euphoric over Christ." I explain about the impact of her religion in her life and how she's now a nun in the Carmelite order.

"Ah, *Catholicism*," he says in a tone he might use for diagnosing tapeworm. "I was raised Roman Catholic and attended parochial schools all of my life until graduate school. I was even an altar boy." He compresses his lips in distaste. "I despised it."

"Well, not every faith is for every person," I say, surprising myself by not joining in to trash the faith I was raised in, seeing as I despise it, too, for the wholly stupid male hierarchy, the infallibility of the pope nonsense, the bad-behaving priests, and the nuns, especially the nuns who took my mother from me.

"Have you ever heard the theory of the bicameral brain?" he asks.

I shake my head, and for the first time since I met the guy, he looks purely delighted. He flexes his fingers, nearly rubs his hands together in his eagerness to impart what he knows.

As I pick at my damp sandwich and chilly salad, he tells me about some scientist who hypothesized that the two hemispheres of the human brain were once more distinctly halved, as in separated from one another. When the two sides of the brain communicated with each other, it created the impression that external voices were speaking to a person. He goes on to explain that this was in ancient times, when people were isolated from outsiders and limited as to what they could experience in their short lifetimes. So when someone like Moses claimed to be summoned by God to a mountaintop, it was likely a case of one side of the brain conversing with the other.

"Researchers have even performed experiments," Art says, "where lasers are used to simulate a separation between the two hemispheres of the brain, and afterward, subjects said they experienced a spiritual presence. Most commonly, they say they saw God or an angel, and that God or the angel spoke to them." He finally picks up one-half of his sandwich and devours it neatly in a series of rabbitty nibbles. "Over time, people encountered other cultures and experienced different

environments due to travel. Hardships and deprivation also stressed and stimulated the bicameral
brain, which wasn't well suited to dealing with
complexity, so adaptation occurred. The two hemispheres fused into the unicameral brain we now
have." He snatches up the second half of his sandwich and eats it rapidly.

"So are you saying that people like my mother,
who feel a godlike presence in their lives, that people like this are really *un-evolved*?" I never bought
into the visions and miracles bullshit—in fact it disturbed me pretty much when Mama claimed she
sometimes saw the Virgin Mary standing out on
the lawn in the mornings, wearing a spangled robe,
luminous with "estrellitas"—but hearing him dis-
miss this makes my face heat up. I used to think
I didn't believe *hard* enough to see what she saw,
but toward the end, just before she went into the
convent, I began to worry more about her than
about my lack of faith. True, I haven't seen her
in years, but a fierce feeling rises in me, the urge
to protect my long, slender mother, to shield her
gentle-featured face, those large, trusting brown
eyes.

Art shrugs. He blots his mouth with a napkin.
"Scientists have charted brain activity in schizo-
phrenics while they're hallucinating, hearing voices, and it's clear that the two hemispheres are ac-

ting independently, instead of cooperating or working in tandem with one another."

"So people with faith are crazy? Unevolved or crazy?" I gather sandwich wrappings, salad bowl, and napkins onto my tray, preparing to rise from the table.

"What are you doing?" he asks, his eyes widening and voice rising. "Look, I didn't mean to upset you. I just thought you'd be interested. There's a book called *The Origins of Consciousness*, by Julian Jaynes. Take a look at it sometime." He reaches for my forearm, clasps it with cool fingertips. "But don't leave now, okay?"

Aware of the sudden hush in the cafeteria and the eyes on us, I settle back into the booth, thinking it must be lonely to be a resident—the long shifts, the lack of sleep, disease and injury every day, all of it punctuated by the terrible sight of blood and gore, death and dying. "I do have to leave soon," I say.

"You have to be somewhere?"

"I'm cleaning house today, moving some junk out," I tell him, not wanting to go into things. There's probably some evolutionary or neurological reason for my condition, explaining exactly why my house is filled with lazy freeloaders. No doubt my brain isn't getting enough stimulation *and* I'm some throwback to Australopithecus, the left and right sides of my brain rattling independently in my thick skull like two halves of a hockey puck. With this absurd image, my anger fades altogether, and weariness settles over me, a heavy cloud that muffles my thinking. After Bobby's middle-of-the-night confession, I never did fall back to sleep. Instead I turned this way and that; twisting the sheets; mashing my pillow into one shape, then another; and dreaming in snatches of those longnecked, big-bellied creatures, their tiny heads tilted up toward me and hollowed mouths crying out. Around four in the morning, I gave up, flicked on my reading lamp, and cracked open the Dalai Lama's book, reading until it was time to shower for school. "I've got a lot to do," I say, swallowing back a yawn.

"Can't it wait? I have some information for you. I know you said it's too late, but I found out Leticia is an inpatient at a residential facility right now, and it's, well, not such a great place, really. I don't know if it will help her much, so here are some services she might want to look into when she's released—outpatient grief groups and counseling." He slides the manila file sleeve toward me. "And I want to ask you something, about this afternoon."

"This afternoon?"

"Yes, and, well, this will probably seem strange, but I wondered, if maybe, um, you might want to join me." He fixes me with his dark eyes, lips parted and an imploring look on his face.

But this feels like an incomplete sentence. I'm not exactly holding my breath, though I am waiting for the rest of it. Join him for what? A matinee? A walk in the park? Some shopping at Gelson's? I'm so tired none of that appeals to me, but still I wonder, *What?* When he adds nothing to this, I finally say, "Meaning?"

His face pinkens. "Will you come to my place and take a nap with me?"

I do a double take and then pause before speaking. "No offense, but are you, like, *really* bad at social things? I mean, do you ever *try* to go on dates or just talk to women, get to know them in some way before suggesting a hook-up? Do you even know how to do *any* of that?"

Eyes now on the tabletop, he remains motionless, though I can tell he's dying to blink, run those fidgety fingers through his hair, jerk his head one way and then the other. He is just burning to twitch.

"I ask because this is so not the right way. You don't even know me. That will-you-take-a-nap-with-me thing sounds like something you'd use to cold-call women. Know what I mean? You could go around asking strangers this, and sooner or later someone will say yes. Is that what you do?" I stand, holding my tray.

He shakes his head.

"I mean, I know you're going to be a doctor and that's probably worth a lot of attractiveness points, but you could, just for form's sake, finesse things a bit more." Since his eyes are downcast, I stare at him openly—that unruly black hair, those freckles, and the densely lashed dark eyes that *would* be attractive, if he didn't blink them all the time. "To be honest," I tell him, "I feel insulted that you even suggested that, like I'm some lowly non-doctor, which I am, some stupid public school teacher who will jump into your bed for the asking. That is *not* cool."

"It's just a nap," he says quietly. "Just to sleep."

I feel for the dude, this has to be colossally awkward for him, but what damn nerve, so I say, "How is that supposed to be a great time for me?"

"You could sleep, too," he tells me. "You seem tired."

My shoulders slump and I release a breath so deep it's close to a true suspiro. I nearly sink back into the booth's vinyl seat and bury my face in my hands. *I am tired.* My arms and legs are leaden, and my lower back burns. Even the thought of trudging to the elevator and making my way to the automatic exit door flattens me. How will I get to the parking lot? How will I drive myself home and once there, how—

He smacks his forehead lightly with the heel of his palm. "I'm sorry, Marina. I don't know what I was thinking. Call it sleep deprivation. Clearly, I'm judgment- impaired. Forget it, okay? Please forget it."

"Just to sleep," I say, "to really sleep?"

He looks at me, nods again, holding out a hand that is exquisitely shaped from the delicate knob of his wrist to his long-tapered fingers, his skin tone the same shade of ivory as a calla lily.

Driving myself home from Art's apartment, I feel restored in body, mind, and spirit, even ready to tackle that hefty helping of bullshit waiting for me at home. The nap in the doctor's disheveled but darkened bedroom was just what I needed after last night's interrupted sleep, and come to think of it, this entire horrible week. I thread my small car smoothly through the swift flow of traffic in all four lanes, hitting congestion—horns blare and brake lights flash—at the on-ramps and where the freeways merge. On the Pasadena Freeway, I let some hothead in a monster car cut in front of me, without even honking or throwing the finger, all the while wondering why my life has to be this way: long stretches of mundane nothingness inter- rupted by a succession of torturous days. It was like this even when I was a kid at home with my mother, father, and Della.

We were fine, stultifyingly bored maybe, but at least quiet for months on end, and then for one week or two, we weren't. Doors slammed, windows rattled, my father thundered, my mother wept silently, and Della curled herself up to hide in the cabinet under the kitchen sink. *It's like talking to a stone*, my father would tell my mother, asi se habla con una pared. Then he would disappear for days, and when he returned, he'd be wearing the same clothes, rumpled and reeking of perfume and whiskey. "Where were you?" I'd ask, wincing when his unshaven cheek rasped against mine. He'd wink at me and give me some nonsense answer about learning to breathe underwater or chasing tigers on the moon. Della and I were thrilled when he returned, but apart from saying that she had prayed for him while he was away, my mother never reacted much to these returns or the angry departures that precipitated them.

Once during a bad week, my father brought a gun home. To this day, I have no idea where he got it. He blasted a hole in the floor of the upstairs bedroom he shared with my mother, the bullet just missing Della, who was standing in the kitchen below. Another time, during what had to have been the worst week, he came home from work with a couple of buddies and they helped him load all his clothes, his shoes, his books, even his favorite chair and reading lamp, into a truck, and he moved out, returning a few days later for Della, who is my half-sister, my father's daughter from his first wife, who died of pneumonia when Della was three. He didn't come back again until it was time for him to collect me, when my mother decided to join the cloister—another bad week following a long stretch of quiet.

Despite those awful times, there's never been a succession of days as bad as these with the baby's death, Letty's overdose, and the business with Efrem and Carlotta. There must be a prolonged full moon or Santaanimosity to the tenth power. But apparently, for me, it's the perfect time for attracting men. I wish I'd known; I would have wrecked my life back in February when Rudy dumped me. No, come to think of it. I really wouldn't have. It's not worth it.

The nap, I can still feel it. It's helping me think in a level way. Maybe people don't need spirituality. Maybe they just need more sleep. And what a good sleep it was. Art played a compact disk that sounded like water flowing all around me. The womb, he said, a recording of the sounds a fetus hears in the womb, and I thought of little Rudy, glad he at least had that before he was born. Art also pulled blackout shades over the windows, and flicked on a rotating ceiling fan that stirred the cool air. We nestled under a silky comforter, and he threw one thin leg over mine. Though he stripped to his boxers and I was in my slip, bra, and panties, we did just sleep—a dense, dreamless and delicious nap.

Art turned out to be an ideal sleeping companion. He didn't stir, snore, gnash his teeth, or even mumble complaints in his sleep the way Rudy would when we spent nights together. Napping with Art was like sleeping next to a cozily warm corpse. I slept so soundly that when the alarm buzzed I not only had no idea where I was and why, but at the moment, I couldn't have said *who* I was. Maybe death is like this: complete erasure, a comforting blankness. This makes me feel better about little Rudy. Sure, we mourn him, but he is *done* with us and all our limping through boredom, our blind stumble punctuated by torment and suffering and interrupted only briefly by flashes of pleasure. "Life is unbelievably dull and painful," I once told a sociopathic tenth grader, a "recreational rapist" who'd caught me in the school parking lot one afternoon and pinned me down to lick my face with his sour-smelling tongue, back when I was student teaching in the alternative school. "I hope you live a very long time."

A dense knot of traffic slows me just before my exit, and my dark thoughts are weirdly lifting my spirits. I flip on the radio to an aggressively throbbing song about pimping 'ho's, and I think of Kiko and Reggie. For the first time I'm *glad* that they're thinking of starting a rap band that honors heritage. Who knows? Maybe they *can* sing. Much of the tune playing now seems more like shouting than crooning, and Kiko and Reggie have no trouble shouting. With these two, I really have to work at it to take an appreciative measure of their accomplishments, so I tell myself that at the very least, they are attempting cultural expression of some kind. In a small way, as if he were my son, I'm almost proud of Kiko for researching Aztlan and Tlaloc, for linking this spark of artistic ambition to Aztec mythology. Would he even have learned about Aztlan in college? Certainly not if he attended the two-year technical school Della was pushing on him, so he could qualify for certification in HVAC installation and repair.

Finally, I inch into the right lane and swoop for the off-ramp, thinking, Connie definitely has to go—no question about that—but Kiko and Reggie...it's not easy for struggling musicians, and I kind of like the idea of being a patroness of the arts. In no way am I looking forward to throwing them out on the street, and maybe, I'm thinking, just maybe, if they're engaged in this creative pursuit, I won't have to after all. By the time I pull into my driveway, I'm determined to make it clear there will be no band practice on the premises and they have to help out more in the house, but why shouldn't they stay, at least for the time being? Climbing out of the car with my purse and book bag, I half-expect to hear rap lyrics sounding through the screen door, but instead I'm greeted by growling noises interspersed with high-pitched barking.

I hurry up the walk and pull open the door to find Kiko at the center of the living room, sitting cross-legged on the floor with what has to be the most hideous-looking dog I have ever seen in my life. It's a short-haired mud-colored thing with slit eyes, a blunt muzzle, and a pink-and-brown splotched snout that's upturned like a pig's. The tail and ears have been cropped, but the latter in a haphazard way—one distinctly larger than the other. Reggie stands in the doorway separating the front room from the kitchen, examining a box of Milk-Bones. The entire house smells of dog hide, hair, and breath, mixed with the unmistakable stench of dog shit and a dash of Pine-Sol. The exact same mess I left in the morning remains, with the addition of a few slimy-looking dog toys and several water-darkened spots on the carpet. From the bathroom, water hisses from the showerhead, steam curling out from under the door. "What's going on?" I ask, needlessly, because it's pretty clear Kiko is using one of my throw pillows to play tug-of-war with the homely mutt.

Reggie glances away from the Milk-Bone box to nod at me. "We got a dog."

"Yeah, tía, isn't he cool?" Kiko gives me a big smile. "He's part pit bull, part Rhodesian ridgeback, and part Pekinese. We got him for cutting the weeds behind that house by the park." The dog releases the pillow, yips twice, and charges at it once more.

"*Stop!* Put that pillow down. You're going to tear it."

"I'm training him, tía," Kiko tells me, but he lifts the pillow over his head. The dog leaps and snaps for it.

"Training him to do what? Rip up pillows?"

Reggie, still poring over the Milk-Bone box, mutters, "I can't see how these things gave him the shits. They don't even got real milk in them."

"He's a fighting dog," Kiko says. "I'm going to call him Freddy Krueger, like the serial killer in those movies, the one that keeps coming back. He's just a puppy now, but——"

"Half-grown," Reggie puts in. "He's like six months old."

"Anyways, he's young, so I can still train him. He's a real badass, tía. Me and Reggie are going to enter him in dog fights and win tons of money."

"*Shut up!*" Every speck of calm from my nap vanishes, replaced by that familiar hot pounding in my temples. A vein in my neck throbs, and I snatch the pillow from Kiko and slap it on top of the bookcase. "*Just shut up!*"

"Tía, what's wrong with you?" Kiko's pebbly eyes bulge and his thick face grows taut with surprise and disbelief. "You and my mom are always on my case about doing something with my life, and now that I got a good plan, you're all pissed off."

"You can make big bucks at dog fights," Reggie tells me.

My ears buzz, my throat constricts as if I am choking, but I manage to breathe deeply, think of the Dalai Lama, Gandhi, and even the Buddha, before saying, "You are really, really idiots. Both of you. Don't you know that dog fighting is illegal? That it's cruel, inhumane, and just about as stupid as, as, as…you know what? I can't even come up with a comparison, it's so stupid."

The dog wanders around the front room sniffing, and Kiko turns to Reggie. "What did I tell you? I finally find something I really want to do with my life and—"

"This morning," I remind him, "you were ready to start a rap band. What happened to that idea?"

"Bobby's computer jammed," Reggie says. "We couldn't put the ad in Craigslist."

"Plus, we found out there's already a rap band named Aztlan with a bass player who calls himself Tlaloc." Kiko looks off, shaking his head.

"Can't you be, like, Aztlan Two?" I ask, unwilling to let go of my fantasy of these two as musicians. "Or maybe see if the original Aztlan needs extra singers?"

Reggie rolls his eyes, but Kiko keeps staring off and shaking his head. Meanwhile, the pup has squirmed into his lap. My nephew idly strokes his misshapen ears.

"Dude, you better cut that out!" Reggie tells him. "You're going to spoil the dog. You can't pet him. You got to taunt him and tease him, always keep him pissed off, or he ain't going to fight for shit." He steps over and nudges the pup's rump roughly with his foot. The dog turns to snap.

"Okay," I say, "*that* is it. You have got to go. Both of you get out of this house, and I don't mean just for the rest of the day. I mean *forever*." I lean to scoop up the dog. It's a hot, smelly thing. Its breath reeks of mildewed cookies, but I hold it close. "You get all your junk together, and you clear out of here. I don't care one whit where you go or what you do once you're there. Just get out of my house and do not come back."

"Man, that's cold, Marina," Reggie says.

"But, tía, what about Freddy? I got to have a crib now that I have a dog."

"The dog stays. You go." I clasp the dog more firmly. His tail nub thumps against my upper arm. The shower screeches off, the water trickling to a stop. "Who's in there?" I tip my chin toward the bathroom door.

"It's Connie," Kiko tells me.

"When she comes out, she's leaving, too." I glance at my wristwatch. "It's five o'clock now. You have half an hour to get out or I'm going to take all your stuff and throw it out in the street myself." I picture Connie's father as Henry described him, raising her jumbo-sized suitcase over his head to hurl it as far as he could.

Kiko sighs, but he lumbers to his feet. "I don't got nothing to put my stuff in."

"Me neither," says Reggie.

"Use trash bags. You know where they are, in that kitchen drawer under the coffeemaker."

"Cold," Reggie mutters, "*really* cold."

I wheel on him. "You want cold, smart guy? Keep griping and I'll throw your skinny ass under an iceberg."

"Just shut up, dude," Kiko tells him. "Let's get

our stuff and go. She don't want us around no more."

"Damn straight," I say, lugging that hot, stinky
mutt into the kitchen. He squirms in my arms, craning his neck to reach my chin with the tip of his
soft, wet tongue.

Chapter Fourteen

It doesn't take Kiko and Reggie long to snap open a few garbage can liners and shove in their extra clothes, shoes, stash box, and paraphernalia. In fact, they are almost ready and only waiting for Connie to emerge to collect their toiletries from the bathroom before they go. I let the ugly dog out in the backyard, where he's quiet for just a few moments before scratching at the door and whimpering to be let back inside. Reggie rattles around in the kitchen, no doubt scrounging food, and Kiko slouches on the couch with his trash bag of possessions on his lap as he waits. He gives me a long, sad look. "Tía, I'm sorry to be such a big disappointment."

I look away, force myself to count the fresh stains on the carpet: one by the front door, two near the television, and another by the bookcase that is long and droopy, shaped like the state of Florida.

I'll have to rent one of those industrial-strength, steam-snorting carpet shampooers from the supermarket. I do *not* glance at Kiko again. Because if I look even slightly concerned, if I say anything even halfway sympathetic to him, I'm a goner. I may as well add his name and Reggie's to my lease agreement.

"I know you want me to, like, succeed and all that. You and my mom, you just want the best for me. But it's *hard*, tía. You have no idea. It's super hard for someone like me. I don't read too good, you know, and let's face it, I'm kind of slow at things."

An idea strikes, and I step over to the bookshelf, scanning the titles. *Now, where is that thing?*

Kiko continues: "When I was a kid I used to think that girls were just like naturally smarter, know what I mean? Like Xochi and the girls at school could talk rings around me. I didn't even know what they were saying half the time. And then, Letty, when you started bringing her around, she could read all these books with words I couldn't even understand. I was already in high school, and she was just a little kid."

I find what I'm looking for and pull the well-worn paperback from the shelf. "Here," I say, handing it to Kiko.

"What's this?"

"It's a novel called *Rain of Gold*, by Victor Villaseñor. Dude wrote it and about half a dozen other books, and he's totally dyslexic. Just like you. You should read it, and if you can't read it, I'm sure it's available on tape through the library. They have headphones there, and you can listen to the story for free."

Kiko turns the book over to look at the author's picture in back. "Are you saying I should write books, tía?"

"No, I'm saying you shouldn't let excuses hold you back, m'ijo." I'm standing before him, my hands on my hips, which I drop to my sides when I realize how bullying this must look. "You need to find something to want that's worth wanting, pursue it, and stay with it, Kiko. You can't wake up one morning with the idea of becoming a rapper, and then by afternoon of the *same* day, you've chucked that because you want to train a dog to fight."

"But, tía—"

"And dog fights," I continue. "*Come on*. You were raised better than *that*. That's just savage. I don't even call that shit a sport."

Connie bursts out of the bathroom wearing my guest bath towel knotted at her scrawny cleavage. She stalks into the living room, shakes her pumpkin head, squints at me, and says, "Man, you got like zero water pressure and practically no hot. That was like having some old man piss on me."

"Connie," I say in a low voice, "listen up. You have to get dressed, get your crap together, and get out of my house. I am not even joking about this."

"Oh yeah," she says. "Well, where the hell am I supposed to go? The viejo kicked me out, Carlotta doesn't want me next door, and Raúl's wife made him get some kind of injunction. I can't be within a hundred yards of the dude."

"Yeah, tía, what about me, too? Where am I supposed to go?"

I glance at Connie, towel-clad but dripping on my carpet, and then at Kiko, his rounded shoulders and the plastic bag bundle like an extension of his soft belly in his lap. Reggie pokes his head in from the kitchen, a quizzical look on his dark, narrow face. "That is your problem," I tell them, "and not mine."

I pivot away from the lot of them, head for the kitchen to let the dog back in. Then I find a carton to line with an old sweater for his bed. I settle him in it in my bedroom. He raises his unattractive head, the slit eyes eager but apprehensive, and I stroke a mutilated ear. While the fur on his body is coarse, even greasy to the touch, his ears are chamois soft. "Feo," I whisper, "I'm going to call you Feo." Fea was one of 'Buela Lupita's favorite words to describe me when I played too long out-doors and came inside with sun-toasted skin or when my unmanageable hair freed itself from the tight braids she wove. Fea, fea, fea. I would repeat the word standing before a mirror and staring at my reflection, saying it again and again, until it didn't sting to be called ugly. Not that the dog understands language, but maybe if he hears this enough and understands that it summons him for food and water, companionship and caresses, this word—feo—will come to mean love.

Banging, footsteps, and rumbling noises resonate from the guest room. Connie, I *hope*, is packing up. The wheels of her suitcase shriek across the floor and the doorknob rattles. The front door slams, and those noisy wheels rumble on the sidewalk. I let out a long suspiro, rise, and make for the door. In the living room, Kiko and Reggie cast last looks around, to see what they might have missed. Their half-filled plastic trash bags slump by the front door. I find my purse where I dropped it beside my book bag, and rummage through my wallet, extracting all the cash from my billfold, at least four twenties and a few ones. I stuff these in the breast pocket of Kiko's T-shirt. "Here," I tell him. "I'm buying the dog."

"But, tía, I don't want to sell Freddy."

"You have to," I say. "And you can use that money to take a cab, get a room at the YMCA, or something."

"She's right," Reggie says, standing now beside us. "We'll need the dough."

Kiko scans my face for any sign of relenting, but I fix my gaze on the stained carpet. "Come on, Reggie," he says. "I guess we got to go now."

I give Reggie a quick peck on the cheek, and I pull Kiko close for a sweaty embrace. The familiar bulges of my nephew's body fold into mine. He nearly crushes me in a bear hug and pats my back in a comforting way. When he releases me, I swallow hard and hurry back to my room. No way do I want to watch him walk out that door.

While Feo sleeps, I pull gunky strands of Connie's hair out of the drain and scour the tub. Then I run a shower for myself, planning to pile the dog in the car for a trip to one of those pet supply places where animals are welcome. I need to pick up a collar and leash, food and water dishes, some kibble, a proper dog bed, and a few books on how to care for dogs. I have never kept a dog in my life, or any animal. 'Buela Lupita found animals disgusting; and even though she visited only on special occasions, she would not have tolerated one in our house. And when I got together with Rudy, I found out he is allergic to dogs. Now, it seems incredibly obvious to me that I have always wanted one.

When I was a girl, I filled notepad after notepad with sketches of poodles, bulldogs, cocker spaniels, and dachshunds. For Christmas one year, my best friend gave me a framed picture of a collie seated before its master's grave. The painting was titled "Man's Best Friend." I'd given her a poster of a cat clinging to a toilet seat that read "Hang in there, baby!" She was, and still is, nuts about cats—hence the email attachments—and I loved dogs. My favorite books were about dogs, and I wept inconsolably at the end of *Old Yeller* and *Where the Red Fern Grows* and all throughout *Beautiful Joe*. Come to think of it, this is why I ordered *The Incredible Journey*. Those dogs with the cat on the cover, they appealed to me.

In the shower, I keep myself from worrying about Kiko and Reggie by wondering how I have gone so many years without a dog, without even knowing I wanted one, really, until now. As I'm shaving my legs, a harsh pounding on the door nearly causes me to sever an artery. The razor slips from my hand, clatters into the tub. "Who's there?" I shout, but no one answers. "What do you want?" The knocking ensues, joined now with barking. I'm thinking, police raid? La migra? 'Buela Lupita, also given to officious knocking, is dead, so no way could it be her...

I rinse quickly, wind a towel around my body, and crack open the door to peer into Bobby's clear hazel eyes. I open the door a bit more, and Feo wriggles in to lap at my wet, half-shaven legs. "Why were you pounding like that on the door?"

Bobby shrugs. "I thought it was Kiko in there and sometimes he doesn't hear too good."

"He hears fine. He just doesn't listen," I say, pulling the towel about me more snugly. "What's up?"

"I was looking for Kiko and Reggie." Bobby glances over my shoulder into the bathroom as if he suspects them of playfully hiding from him behind the shower curtain. "I got my computer working, and I got all the stuff I need."

"Stuff?"

"Yeah, I found some two-by-fours and bought the plastic-coated wiring."

Mystified, I shake my head to clear it and raise a hand signaling him to stop. "Look, let me get dressed. Take the dog outside, will you? Into the backyard, okay? Make sure he pees, and I'll be right out."

Moments later, we're standing under my diseased grapefruit tree watching Feo sniff around the backyard, scoping out all sites in need of a quick leg lift. Near my table and chairs, Bobby has piled a stack of thick boards and several spools of brightly colored wiring. The late afternoon sun sinks into the tree line, and the sky blooms pink and gold. "What's all that for?" I point at the wood and wire.

"That's the stuff, the materials I got," Bobby says with a smile. He's wearing a striped soccer shirt, cut-off Levi shorts, and flip-flops. At the moment, he could be any kid in any backyard, excited about some nerdy plan. There's no trace of the wannabe cholo, not one smidgen of the screwed-up barrio boy with a lousy attitude in his open, grinning face.

"Materials?"

"Didn't Kiko and Reggie tell you?" he asks. "I'm going to build a sculpture." He smiles again, his teeth impossibly straight and lustrous.

"A sculpture of what?"

"It's going to be three crosses," he tells me. "A big, old cross in the middle and two smaller ones on the sides, just like those Calvary crosses, but bigger, much bigger." He spreads his hands, palms out, to indicate a spot along the cinder-block wall separating his parents' yard from mine. "The big cross is going to be like a color wheel, one color blending into another, like that first cross I made."

"Where?" I say.

"Top to bottom, I'm going to cover the thing with wire."

"No, I mean, where are you going to put this sculpture, these crosses?" I keep one eye on Feo. The pup snaps at a moth that easily evades him by lofting several inches over his head.

"Right there," Bobby says, pointing at the cinder-block wall. He paces six feet in front of it. "The first smaller cross will go here, the middle cross there, and the last one right beyond that. They'll be like four feet apart." His eyes shine and his voice rises eagerly. "It will be so cool, Marina, especially at different times of the day. You'll get all these great shadows and stuff, so sometimes it will look like six crosses."

"*Six* crosses," I say, wondering how in the hell to tell the kid that I do not even want one cross in my backyard. Over by the back fence, Feo sniffs something of interest and begins digging vigorously, clods of dirt flying this way and that. "Hmm..."

"Like, I'm surprised Kiko and Reggie didn't tell you nothing about this. They said it was a great idea. And you know what, Marina, I'm not going to charge you nothing to build it, not even for materials. I paid for those out of my own money." He searches my face. "It's like a gift for you, for your backyard." He grins at me. In the fiery streaks of sunlight, his dark hair is threaded with golden strands and his hazel eyes are tinged greenish blue. Why, he looks like Carlotta! How did I ever think he was just his father's son?

I force a smile. "Cool."

"Just think. If they come out the way I'm planning, then lots of people will want to see the crosses, like that cloth with the face of Jesus on it." Bobby stares off, a dreamy look on his painfully young face. He's likely imagining hordes of tourists tramping into my backyard to behold his Calvary creation. He turns to me with a rueful smile. "You could even sell tickets or rosaries, little crucifixes and bottles of holy water."

"Well," I say, "we'll have to see about—"

"Hey, where are Kiko and Reggie?" he asks. "I'm going to need help setting everything up."

"Kiko and Reggie? Um...they're actually not here right now. In fact, I kind of kicked them out," I tell him.

"Oh," Bobby says, pausing to consider this. "But you know they'll probably be back." He gives me a look and adds, "To visit and stuff?"

"Sure."

"That's okay. I got lots of things to do before then." He scurries up the cinder-block wall like a lizard. I'm amazed he can manage this in flip-flops. Even Feo barks in astonishment.

"What are you doing?" I ask as Bobby balances atop the wall.

"I got to get my dad's saw and some other

tools," he says before jumping off into his yard and landing with a dull clapping sound.

"Are you okay?" I call after him.

"Of course, I do this all the time!"

"When you come back," I tell him, "use the side gate. I got to go get some supplies for the dog, but I should be home in an hour or so."

"Okay, Marina," he says, but his voice sounds distant, as if he is already entering the tool shed.

"Come on, Feo," I tell the dog, who pants and wags his tail stump at me. I wonder if I will ever get used to those tiny eyes, the dung-colored fur, the hacked-off ears, and that swinish snout. I expect I will. Death, betrayal, loss, treachery, loneliness, people can get used to just about any heart-troubling thing, let alone an ugly-looking dog. I open the kitchen door and Feo rushes in, his toenails clattering on the linoleum. "Let's go get you some gear."

Two hundred dollars later, I'm nose deep in *No Bad Dogs* and highlighting techniques for training dogs through positive reinforcement. Bobby slams in the kitchen door now and again for water, but mostly he's outside hammering and sawing things. After eating a full bowl of a kibble mix developed by scientists, Feo has curled up around his taut belly in the sheepskin-lined bed I bought him for yet another nap. Apparently, young dogs need abundant sleep. I haven't gotten to that chapter yet. Or it could be he finds me boring, and sleep is a convenient escape. Who knows? I cap my highlighting marker, stretch, and yawn, thinking that tomorrow, after I see Letty, I will take Feo to a vet, one of those walk-in clinics, at least to get him checked out and see about shots and vitamins.

Despite that sick fluttery feeling in my stomach to remind me now and again that I've done something shameful whenever I think about Kiko and Reggie, I'm luxuriating in this solitude. The quiet, for one thing, is about as dense and sweet as pound cake, and I have the whole delicious thing to myself. Of course, Bobby's right out back, making a carpentry racket, and Feo's snoring his ass off nearby, but no blaring television, no stupid plans, and no pestering to use my car. A quiet like this magnifies my house's own gentle sounds: the refrigerator ticking, the fans whirring, and the floorboards gently groaning underfoot when I rise to brew a cup of chamomile tea. Just as I return to my seat with my steamy, apple-fragranced cup, Feo jerks his head up, those cockeyed ears perk, shifting this way and that like satellite disks. Then trembling with rage and barking like mad, he launches himself at the front door, which is, for once, shut.

"What is it, boy?" I step around him to peer through the peephole. One fearful eye and a metallic cup meet my gaze: *Carlotta!* I fumble to slide the double bolt and twist the latch in the knob. Finally, I pull the door wide, and she tumbles in, Efrem at her back, holding her by the shoulder and pushing in after her. I lunge at the door to shut him out once she has spilled onto the carpet. Feo snarls, baring his teeth. In the hot, chaotic tangle, Efrem forces himself inside, banging the door against my cheek and collarbone, nearly thrusting me off my feet, while Carlotta crawls away from him.

I catch my balance, stand before Efrem to block him from Carlotta, and shout over Feo's explosive barks, "Get out! You can't come in here." My voice sounds solid enough, but every other part of me rattles with terror. Truth is: Efrem, an ex-Marine turned laid-off construction worker, is fat but strong. The dude could kill us all with his bare hands without even breaking a sweat. Behind me, the door to the guest bedroom booms shut, the feeble knob lock clicks. Feo rears back and charges. Efrem boots him in the midsection, and he releases a high-pitched wheezing yelp, but rolls to his feet to renew his attack.

"Get that dog out of here," Efrem tells me in a low voice, "or I will kill the fucking thing."

I do not doubt this, so I grab Feo by his new red

collar and drag him—snorting, snarling, and squirming to get free—to the bathroom. After I shut the door behind him, he whines, scratching fiercely at the baseboard.

Surprised that Efrem has not gone after Carlotta, that he's instead collapsing into my love seat and burying his head in his thick, hairy-fingered hands, I find my voice again to say, "What do you want, Efrem? What are you doing here?"

Without raising his head, he quietly says, "I'm going away. I got to leave. I can't be around her like this."

"Then go." I tilt my head toward the open door. "Just go."

He ignores this. "There's something not right with me. I don't know what it is, but I get, like, *blind* with anger. I mean, I can't see, I can't think. I got to get some help," he says. "I need to get away."

"Then *go*."

He lifts his head, piercing me with his dull black eyes. "You think I'm a real shit, huh? You think I'm some hateful bastard that don't love his family?" His voice breaks and those lusterless eyes fill.

No credible way to deny this, so I say, "It doesn't matter what I think. If you need to go, you should go. That's all that matters." All the while, I'm chanting to myself, even praying: *Leave alrea-*

dy. Just get out of my house.

"I *love* them," he says. "I *love* Carlotta, and I *love* my sons. I love them so fucking much it rips me apart inside. It scares the shit out of me." He cups his face again with his hands, shielding his eyes, and he sobs.

I grab a box of tissues from the bookcase and set it beside him on the love seat.

He plucks a tissue, honks into it. "There's something that's not right with me. You don't think I know it, but I do. I never want to hurt Carlotta or the boys. *Never.* I want them to be happy, and when they're not, when they act all pissed off and like disappointed or let down, I can't stand it.

"These past few days with Carlotta have been so good, you know what I mean. It was like the way it was when we first met, and then tonight, she says to me that she's going to get a job, that they want to hire her part-time as a checker at Vallarta Market, and I swear, Marina, I could feel the blood pounding in my eyes. I wanted to break her fucking neck." He gazes at his hands, flexes the meaty fingers, and shakes them out. "Over that," he says, quietly. "A part-time job, I was ready to strangle my wife over that. I swear I couldn't think. I just grabbed her hard, and then I got scared. I scared my own fucking self, so I brung her here.

"You got no idea what it's doing to me, not having any work. Unemployment is *shit*, let me tell you. I'm about to lose the truck. And then what? How can I work without wheels?" He blows his nose again, snatches a fresh tissue, and blots his eyes. "You think I'm stupid? You think I don't know the things I done are all fucked up? You think that that doesn't kill me inside?"

Again, I tell him, "It doesn't matter what I think."

He shakes his head, stands, and shoots me a look, like he's about to ask a favor. "Give me like ten minutes to shower and change, a'ight? Then I want you to call the cops. Tell them I violated the terms of my release, okay? Just tell them that, and if they don't want to come for me, tell them I broke into your house, that I forced entry and terrorized my wife." He wipes his eyes with his forearm, gives me a tight smile. "You can even lie and tell them I terrorized you. Then they'll be sure to come."

He raises his arm and I flinch, but he just sets a thick hand on my shoulder. "You ain't bad," he says. "Even though you've pissed me off plenty of times, acting all uppity and shit, I know you don't really mean nothing by it. The kid likes you, Carlotta likes you. Take care of them, will you, while I'm gone? 'Cause I'm going to get better, and then, I'm coming back. They got treatments now, even therapy and drugs. The chaplain at the jail told me about this shit. I can get help when I'm inside."

"Okay," I say, thinking good luck getting mood-enhancers and learning nonviolent coping strategies while *in prison*, and wondering what the heck Carlotta and Bobby will live on once Efrem is locked up. I could be wrong, but I'm pretty sure his unemployment benefits will be discontinued while he's incarcerated. Maybe Carlotta can parlay the Vallarta gig into a full-time deal...

"Tell Carlotta that, will you? She don't have to wait for me, but tell her I'll be better when I get out. I got to be 'cause, seriously, I can't get no worse." He drops his hand and shuffles for the front door, no trace of swagger in his stride. "Ten minutes," he says over his shoulder and he winks at me from the threshold. He pauses there for a moment—his back bathed in lamplight and his face and chest obscured by shadow—before taking a deep breath like a diver, then plunging sideways through the screen door and disappearing into the night.

Chapter Fifteen

The next morning, the piñata pods are dry enough for the Beginning Reading students to affix tissue paper strips that they fold in half lengthwise and then snip part of the way across the fold, so these flare when turned inside out, the loops ruffling nicely. Those who are careful and precise, like Elias and Maritza, scissor the tissue so the incisions are close together for maximum ruffling before gluing the tissue strips close to one another on their piñatas for denser coverage. Less proficient students snip the folded tissue streamers haphazardly and stick them onto their piñatas carelessly, but they at least try to make up for this by using bright colors. Elias and Maritza use only black and white tissue paper. "Witch?" I ask them when I visit their desks to pour more glue into the Styrofoam bowl they share.

They shake their heads, look at one another, and

giggle. "No, maestra," Maritza tells me. "It is not a witch." She's actually been practicing her English for most of the project, while Elias lapses into Spanish now and again, especially in moments of high emotion, like now, when he fears spotting his new madras shirt with glue. "Dios mio," he warns Maritza, "cuidate con eso." Neither of them seems to miss their absent partner: Felipe Ahuaul.

At first, I had to work it to get into piñata-making mode, the encouraging voice and positive comments. All of it is such a strain after last night. Just as everything looked to be settling down, who shows up, wearing a sad look on her calabasa-face and dragging her gargantuan suitcase behind her? La Connie, of course. I managed to settle all of them next door in Carlotta's house, long after the police took Efrem away. In the end it was Bobby who called the cops on his father. He slammed in, after his father had loped off, completely unaware of what had happened. When I told Bobby and Carlotta, who held him in her arms, weeping while I spoke, the kid looked like he might start blubbering, too, but then he pulled away from his mother. He insisted that he would make the call. Bobby didn't want his brothers to find out that I had called the police on their father. He told me they can be like Efrem when pissed off, and he said that he didn't want to forget with time that I was only doing what his father asked. He didn't want to blame me for it later. Thinking of this now lofts my spirit, and I approach the next group bearing my super-sized glue jug and a smile that doesn't feel too much like it's painted on my face.

"That's a great pig," I tell the group, a trio of boys who have given up the snipping to glue whole swaths of pastel pink tissue paper over their papier-mâché boulder.

"Is no pig," Hernando Fontes tells me. "Is the girl at the ball, la Cenicienta."

"Cinderella? Is that right?" I stand back and squint at the thing, blurring my vision and still struggling to imagine this lumpy mass as the face that swept the prince off his feet. In places, the newsprint is still visible under the sheets of pink paper. "You might need a few more layers of tissue," I tell them.

Ignacio Huerta holds up a handful of grubby yellow yarn. "Is her hair."

And Jeremias Salas produces a rumpled ball of tinfoil, sprinkling crumbs on his desk; no doubt this was taken from his lunch. "La corona."

"Well, you'll have to shape it some," I say. "Maybe use some cardboard or wire to make that look like a crown."

"Si, si, si," they say, waving the glue bottle away. Using their method, they have plenty.

Gradually, the piñatas develop into recognizable shapes, except Cenicienta, the ballroom boulder, and Maritza and Elia's meticulous black-and-white creation, for which Elias is now fashioning a tidy black bow. I've just finished my rounds with the glue jug when Jovita Tomás tugs at my coverall apron. She's the youngest of the Beginning Readers, a political refugee from Venezuela who hasn't spoken once in class. Her hazel eyes are wide and she points a nail-bitten finger at the door. Señor Ahuaul stands at the entryway with the elderly paletero, his father, and the two boys, Felipe and Armando. The old man has his hands on the shoulders of one brother, while his son holds onto the other in the same way. The class goes silent. Students freeze in mid-action—scissors poised to snip, gluey streamers held aloft—and everyone gazes openmouthed at the family up front.

Felipe and Armando's lips and cheeks are unnaturally red, as if rouged and then scrubbed so forcefully that the flesh is abraded and irritated. Their eyes, though black smudged, are also red and puffy, as if they have been crying. Señor Ahuaul and his father thrust them into the classroom, releasing their grip, but blocking the doorway.

"Basura," Señor Ahuaul says, spitting on the classroom floor after the word leaves his mouth. The students and I stare in shock at the thick blob of spittle quivering on the dusty floor. The wiry old grandfather looks on, slackjawed. Now, I see it was no fluke that I warned the boys about their fate selling paletas. On a subconscious level, I surely must have recognized their pronounced resemblance in body type and posture to their white-haired grandfather, making the connection but unaware of the truth behind it, when I scolded them.

"Sit down, boys," I finally tell the twins. "Take seats near my desk in back. I'm going to step outside to have a word with your father." I figure I can get Elias or Maritza to escort Armando to his class once we get this sorted out. Heads down, the twins trudge through the classroom, trailing a lilac scent in their wake, and I turn to their father, indicating the door. "Con permiso, señor."

When we step outside, I shut the door, and Señor Ahuaul releases a tsunami of accusation, recrimination, and then flat-out damnation of his two sons. Apparently, tipped off by my phone call about their absence from school, he sent the boys off as usual that morning, and then he headed out to work. But he turned the paleta cart around after an hour or so. Returning to la casa, he found both boys deep in their mother's closet, he told me with uncomprehending horror in his jet-bead eyes. They were trying on her clothing—skirts, blouses, pantyhose and heels, even "los calzones y brassieres," and wearing her makeup on their faces. The old man remains silent, though he nods from time to time, as if to verify his son's incredible claims.

I chime in with de veras when appropriate, but mainly I have no idea what to say to the man or how to handle this "teaching moment," as one of my professors would call difficult situations we encounter in the profession. But nothing like transvestite twins ever came up in our seminars, not even as a hypothetical. When Señor Ahuaul finally runs out of steam, I recommend having the boys talk to Pancha, the school counselor, leaving out that she's a bigmouth who blabs anything she finds interesting all over the place. Still, I guess it's good to bring things out in the open. Who knows? Maybe that's her theory, part of her process.

I also explain that it's normal for adolescent boys to act out and defy authority, insisting that what is important is how we handle these transgressions so as to honor the spirit of independence that provokes them while establishing boundaries that are mutually respectful, and blah, blah, blah. Señor Ahuaul listens with his mouth open and the old fellow steps back, an amazed look on his withered face. I surprise myself with my own eloquence until eventually I, too, run out of words, so I tell Señor Ahuaul and his father that maybe the boys just miss their mother. I remember the time I found one of Rudy's Marlboros under the couch, weeks after we'd broken up. I lit it up in the backyard, smoked a few puffs, just to conjure his smell. Then I grew lightheaded, sick to my stomach, and I stubbed it out.

But Señor Ahuaul narrows his eyes at me. "Basura," he says again, and this time, I'm not sure if he's calling me or the boys' mother "trash." He's probably throwing this out as a blanket insult to all women. No way to defend more than half the population, so I merely ask him not to spit again on school grounds.

I send the two men off with promises to have the boys meet with Pancha and to speak to the twins myself about the truancy. I tell him that nothing is insurmountable if we work together. This last bit sounds like such caca, even to me, that it's no surprise both paleteros shoot me doubtful looks, but they finally shamble off for their pull-carts, the boys' father muttering bitterly about having missed a half-day of work.

Inside, the Ahuaul twins glance up at me, as if startled. Someone has cleaned up the babas. Just a wet smear, the shape of a small comet, remains. Of course, little progress has been made on the piñatas. Most students were likely straining to overhear the conversation on the front steps. Only Elias and Maritza must have worked despite the distraction.

Their piñata is at last becoming recognizable. It seems to be a penguin. "None of the fairy tales has a penguin," I say.

They again trade looks before dissolving into giggles. "The storyteller," Maritza says when she regains composure, "she is a penguin."

"The storyteller?" I ask, purely puzzled.

Elias produces his textbook and flips it to show me the back cover. "She tells the stories." Elias points to the imprint. "So we make the penguin." In an oval at the bottom is the publisher's trademark—an elegantly shaped penguin wearing a crisp bowtie.

At home that afternoon, I uncrate Feo for a quick pipi in the backyard, where I find Bobby winding plastic-coated wire onto the tallest of the three crosses he's fashioned. He nods at me without looking up from his work. The sun is high in the cloudless sky, blasting down on us like a blowtorch. What sickly plants I keep—begonia, hydrangea, hibiscus, and impatiens—in the overgrown backyard look desiccated, overwhelmed by the straw-colored foxtail and crabgrass, the leaves as shriveled as the crumpled tissue paper filling the wastebasket in my classroom. Even my diseased grapefruit tree seems to have shrunk in this heat, its branches nearly leafless, though still clutching a few lumpy hulls of fruit. "Why don't you come inside?" I ask Bobby. "You can work in the kitchen, where it's a little cooler, and keep Feo company while I'm out this afternoon."

"Where you going?"

"Long story," I say, "but to abbreviate, let's say I'm visiting a friend in the hospital." Feo shoots a limp arc of urine onto a scorched-looking patch of grass.

"Abbreviate," Bobby says with a smile. "You know lots of words. Is that why you became a teacher?"

"Well, it's kind of the other way around," I tell him. "I became a teacher and then I had to learn a lot of words. I'm still learning them."

He cups his eyes to gaze at me. "And you don't mind if I take all this inside to work?"

"Just don't bring in that smelly stuff, the finishing spray."

Feo trots over to claim a scrap of shade near the back fence and looks over at me, panting. A shadow crosses Bobby's face and he says, "My dad *really* told you to call the cops?"

Deep suspiro here. "Think about it. Remember how he left? He waved to us from the squad car, blew your mom a kiss. Do you think he'd do that if he didn't want to go?" I clap my hands for Feo, who bounds toward me, no doubt relieved to be called in from the heat. I crack open the kitchen door and Feo noses it fully ajar to squirm in. "But you ask him yourself," I tell Bobby. "You and your mom ought to go visit him and you should ask him about it yourself."

"I mean, why didn't he just call them himself?"

"Maybe he thought they wouldn't come. Cops aren't always eager to do their jobs. Some teachers are like that, too," I say, thinking of Stuart Lindner dismissing his students early for the purpose of flirting with me.

I step into the kitchen, pour myself dregs from the Coffeeville Express, and cover the kitchen table with newspaper from the recycling bin. Soon enough Bobby bangs in with the oversized cross, which he sets atop the work space I've prepared. While I play some Rubén Blades, Bobby winds the colored wire onto the wood, his head bobbing to the beat of the music.

Before Miguel arrives, I listen to the messages on my answering machine: A couple of hang-ups; one call from Della, hee-hawing something about the Calvary crosses, but I press the erase button before hearing the whole thing out; another from Xochi who wants me to meet her "smoking hot" minister date; next a call from Carlos to "check in about Friday night"; and lastly a message from Rudy, who mumbles something about Nestor's website. *Delete!* Nothing from *aortiz*, as I've begun to think of him again, aorta-tease, really. But just what are my claims on a man I have napped with once? What exactly is the etiquette? Should I call to thank him for the comfortable sleep? Or does he owe me gratitude for the pleasure of my slumberous company?

Instead of worrying about this, I should call Carlos back to confirm the date, but at the moment, I don't feel like it. Phoning him now would mean having to deal with the corn thing, and I'm just not up for that. I mean, what if there's an awful truth behind this, like kinkiness or exhibitionism? What if there's some school, a park, or even a daycare near Myers's cornfield, and he was flashing the kids? I'm not too anxious to find out anything like that, not this soon. I know I'm falling into that old trap—the willful blindness that bound me to someone as disappointing as Rudy for so many years when toward the end, apart from his eyes and those pheromones, all I really liked about him was Letty—but I can't seem to help myself when it comes to turning away what I don't really want to face, especially in a week like this.

Not a peep from Kiko and Reggie. I picture them bunking at the YMCA, waking early to take the bus to Human Resources in order to meet with a job placement counselor. Reality shuts that fantasy down pretty fast. More likely, they have crashed at some wastrel friend's place and are just now rousing themselves to light the first joint of the day. I glance at the large purple-and-white box on top of the refrigerator, wondering what Kiko will do without his cereal. The bowl of crispy flakes jeweled with sugar-spangled raisins that is depicted on the front panel of the package looks inviting, even if I know it is misleading, as false as Xochi's ruby fingernail tips. Even so, Kiko really should have taken his Raisin Flakes with him.

Miguel picks me up on time and we head out for visiting hours during the hottest part of the afternoon. The inpatient facility where Letty is staying is a flat sprawling building in La Crescenta, an arid suburb between Pasadena and Glendale. The developers seem to have seized on the only shaded oasis in the area to build the institution, or else immediately after breaking ground, they planted fast-growing seedlings. Sycamore, mimosa, and valley oaks spread great leafy branches overhead, shielding the building from the blistering sun. "It's kind of nice," I say, breathing in the woodsy smell.

"Yeah, out here," Miguel says. He's in his usual saggy jeans and a T-shirt. The hoodie left to bake in the car is his one concession to the heat. "Inside it's like a madhouse."

"Well, it kind of *is* one."

But I see what he means as soon as we step through the glass door. After the fresh outdoorsy smell, I gasp at the stinging odor of urine commingled with antiseptic. The front desk area is besieged by people in bathrobes and pajamas, many of these in wheelchairs. I'm surprised how many patients are elderly. Bent, wizened oldsters with hunched backs, pink scalps, and wispy white hair loiter about in walkers or wheelchairs, raising a din with their hoarse, insistent voices. Maybe I thought there'd be barred windows, shuffling aphasics, even padded rooms and straightjackets. I'm not sure exactly what I expected, but it certainly didn't involve the aged. I turn to Miguel to ask, "Are you sure we're in the right place?"

"Yeah," he says in a low voice. "They had some fire at the assisted-living place, also owned by the company, so a lot of the old people got placed here."

"It's so crowded…and depressing. That stench," I say into his ear. "How is any of this supposed to cheer Letty up?"

Miguel shrugs, and we part the crowd of old people to get to the harassed receptionist behind the front desk. As Miguel checks us in as visitors, an exceptionally twistedup vieja in a wheelchair tugs at my blouse. Though I'm no doctor, I would

diagnose her to be in the final stages of osteo-
porosis, the hump on her back as pronounced as
the papier-mâché Cenicienta's in my classroom. In
fact, she's strapped into a clear plastic back brace,
a yellowing torso-shaped shell, no doubt intended
to straighten her curved spine. "Can you help me?"
she says in a quavering voice, her long, sheeplike
face uplifted toward me. "I just need someone to
help me with this." She points at her back brace
and pulls at its grubby canvas straps. "I need to take this thing off."

I shake my head, but she crowds in closer. I
back into Miguel, who finally signs the sheet on a
clipboard with a flourish and passes it back to the
receptionist. He scopes out the knot of oldsters and
sidesteps the group by trailing along the desk. I follow after him, the wheelchair lady hot on my heels.
After we leave the reception area, the hallway is
free, except for the occasional distracted-looking
wheelchair- or walker-bound patient. We dash
through the corridor for Letty's room, but at my
back, the old woman's wheelchair whooshes after
us. "She's chasing us," I whisper to Miguel.

"I know," he says, taking impossibly long strides. "She was after me when I checked Letty in
here. You got to keep up. She's fast."

We race around a corner, and Miguel opens a
door marked with a sign that reads MAINTENANCE.

He shoves me in and follows behind, shutting it after him. "*Shh*," he says, and we stand in the darkness sniffing detergents, polishes, and more antiseptic smells. When the wheelchair whizzes past, I reach for the knob, but Miguel catches my wrist. "Wait," he whispers. "That vieja's real tricky. Last time she hid near the water fountain, just waiting for me to come out of the men's room."

After a minute or two, Miguel judges the coast to be clear. We emerge from the supply closet and double-back a few doors to find Letty's room, a twin bed setup with two chests of drawers and a vinyl chair near the window. The extra bed is vacant, but unmade—the blankets flung to one side and the sheets rumpled—as if the occupant just stepped out for a moment. Letty's reclining on the bed in her usual cornflower blue nightgown, staring at a soap opera on the television that is bolted to the ceiling. I rush over and throw my arms around her. "Honey, how are you?"

She hugs me back, tightly. "Why didn't you come sooner?"

"They wouldn't let us," Miguel tells her. "They got the visiting schedule, regulations, and all that. This was the first we could come."

I sit beside her on the bed, and she reaches for the remote control on the bed table and flicks off the television. "Did they tell you what I done, Marina?" Letty gazes at me, clear-eyed and without blinking. One finger traces circles, one looping into another, in the bedspread. For a split second, she looks like a twelve-year-old again, and I remember the time she admitted losing the expensive Rollerblades I bought her at the skating rink.

I nod.

"I wasn't thinking right," she says now in a clippedsounding way. "Now my thinking is much clearer. I feel ready to leave and resume my life without harming myself or others."

I pull back in doubt, and Miguel says, "Why are you talking like this, mi cielo? You sound like an answering machine or something."

Letty's large eyes well, and she draws a ragged breath. "I'm trying to figure out the right words, okay? I need to know what they are and how to say them. I hate it here. I got to get out. What the fuck do I have to say to get out of here? You tell me, huh? What do they want me to say? I'll say anything, any way they want." She collapses in my arms, warm and weepy.

Miguel perches on the other side of the bed, strokes her long hair. "Querida, querida, we'll figure things out, so you can come home."

Letty wrenches away from his touch. "Home? Who says I want to go home? I *never* want to go back there, never want to see that ugly, depressing shit-hole again!"

Miguel draws back, stunned.

Though I suspect I know the answer, I have to ask, "Where, honey, where do you want to go then?"

She peers at me through the dark strands of hair that have fallen into her face, her damp eyes—Rudy's tendercreature eyes—wide, hopeful as a child's. "I thought maybe...if it's okay...I thought I could stay with you, Marina, at your place."

Miguel rises from the bed, steps to the window and peers out. He clears his throat. "What about me?"

"We could *both* stay with Marina," Letty tells him. She brushes the hair from her face. "Can we, Marina? Can we stay with you?"

I glance at Miguel, still standing at the window. His back is to us, his shoulders tight, but his arms hang loosely at his sides. The many blue-green tattoos snaking from his wrists to his upper arms seem faded in the slatted sunlight streaming through the blinds, listless and anemic, instead of proud and fierce. But when Letty rolls into my arms once more, what can I do but smile hard and summon the most joyful damn voice there is to say, "Sure, of course, I was about to suggest that myself."

Chapter Sixteen

After saying our good-byes to Letty with promises to get her released as quickly as we can, Miguel tells me in the hallway that he needs me to help with the insurance and paperwork. We stride past the open doors to various rooms, television sounds emanating from these, and I try to avert my eyes, but one room is so silent, I have to glance in, thinking it must be empty. It isn't. A lone, elderly man sits—his posture upright but relaxed—in a chair near the window, staring in an unseeing way out the door. No mistaking that look, he's meditating. My heart squeezes with grief. My father's spiritual conversion had hinged on TM, as he called it. He would meditate for up to half an hour, silently concentrating on his mantra. I resented that he could zone out like that, still leave us while sitting at home, and he was disappointed that I couldn't master the technique. My many distractions, those yappy thoughts, prevented me from even being still enough to *pretend* I was meditating.

Here, I stop in my tracks, gaping at the meditating man and regretting my hard feelings about this practice that brought my wandering, womanizing father such peace.

"Marina," Miguel calls from a few feet ahead. "Aren't you coming?"

I hurry to catch up. "Sorry, I just saw someone—"

"I told the financial manager here that we'd stop by, and then I got to bounce. Got a meeting at five-thirty." Miguel pulls out his battered and bulging billfold to extract a plastic card that he hands me. "This here's my insurance card, my social's on that. I already showed it once, and they got Letty's information. I filled out a ton of forms. Still, there's stuff they need to know to see if we qualify for other benefits." He points to a door across the hall. "Can you go talk to the people? Figure out what's what?"

I take the card from him. "You're not coming with me?"

"Nah, I got to make some calls. Had to take the day off, so now I got to holler at my foreman, find out what I'm doing tomorrow. Then I need to talk to my sponsor. *Big time.* I'll wait for you up front after I make the calls." He avoids my eyes. "Look,

I don't know what the hell they're talking about in there, with the co-pay, deductible, and all kinds of shit I can't figure out. It's better if you talk to them, and tell me what's up. I mean, it's what you used to do—insurance, right?"

I nod, finally comprehending the underlying reason for my presence, why he was so eager to pick me up and bring me here: Once again, Miguel needs me to translate the insurance-ese. "Okay," I tell him. "I'll see what I can do."

He practically flies down the hall, he's so eager to escape. I open the door to the financial office, and who do I see inside but my wheelchair pursuer, the hunchbacked vieja herself! She's helping herself to a pair of industrial-purpose shears from a drawer in the unmanned desk. For a moment, I consider backing out, but she raises her wooly white head, baring overlong teeth and a good deal of gum, when she grins and says, "*There* you are." And another, much younger woman, with stylishly small dark-framed glasses and jet-black hair drawn into a bun, appears from an inner office. The vieja rolls forward, tries to hand me the scissors, jabbing them at me, blades first. "Here. Can you help me with this? I just need to get this thing *off.*"

"Have a seat. I see you've met Sister Mary Joseph," the younger woman says in a high-pitched and squeaky voice, a voice that calls to mind Minnie Mouse or Betty Boop. She turns to the old nun. "Now, Sister, I've told you only the doctor can remove your brace." But she doesn't even try to take those monster shears from the old lady.

When I hear the vieja is a nun, I nearly gasp. Dread, like a slowly melting ice cube, trails down my spine. I step back and shoot a glance at the door, which the wheelchair is now blocking.

"It itches like the devil," the nun whimpers before again thrusting the shears at me.

I shrink away from her, which only encourages her to approach, backing me into a corner of the small office.

"Go ahead and have a seat," the younger woman tells me with a smile. "I'm Nellie Muñoz, the financial manager. How can I help you?"

I'm not eager to sink into the chair, eye level with those shears, so I remain standing in my corner and reach to slide Miguel's card across the desk. I explain that I'm here to see about Letty's insurance coverage and to complete any paperwork.

The nun rolls even closer to me, shears in hand. "Just help me take this contraption off, will you? Oh, *why* won't you help me?"

"Um, Ms. Muñoz, do you think we could talk, like, privately? I mean…" I toss a glance at the shears-wielding hunchback in the wheelchair.

"Call me Nellie," she says before lifting a phone to summon help. "Now, Sister, Mr. Barber is on his way to take you to your room."

"That penis wrinkle," the old nun cries. "Why, he won't help me! He never does a thing for me!"

"In the meantime, I'll pull the patient's file." Nellie rises from her desk and disappears into the inner office. I'm tempted to ask if I can come along, but the old nun's wheelchair blocks my path in that direction, too.

"Just take these," she says, jabbing the air with the shears. "Go on, take them. You know you want to. *Take* them!"

Dry-mouthed and quaking, I shake my head, turn to look away at the nutritional pyramid chart on the wall with feigned fascination, as if I am amazed to find protein, grains, fruits, and vegetables are important in a healthy diet while she wheedles at me.

Finally, finally, a large black man in white arrives to wheel her away. "There you are, darling," he tells her in a voice as thick and smooth as rum syrup. "Why you run away from me? I thought we were sweethearts." He grabs the handles of her wheelchair and steers it for the door that he has propped open.

"*You*," she tells me as she's wheeled out of the

office, "are running out of time. And you know *exactly* what I mean."

When Nellie returns, I ask why the heck no one takes sharp implements from the patients, mentioning I don't like the idea of Letty staying in a place where elderly women in wheelchairs roll around armed with shears.

Nellie laughs. "Oh, Sister Mary Joseph wouldn't hurt a flea. Murder's a sin, you know, and that woman plans on shooting straight to heaven."

"I'm sure calling someone a 'penis wrinkle' is wrong, too, like bearing false witness, or some such thing, and she's all in for that," I point out. "And don't they have special homes for people in the religious orders?"

"That's what you'd expect," Nellie says, shaking her head. "But these days, when the old nuns go into retirement or pass away, there are fewer young women willing to enter the religious orders to take their places. Things fall apart. Basically, there was nowhere else for Sister Mary Joseph to go when her order disbanded, so she was placed here."

"The order disbanded?"

"Happens all the time," she says.

"What about the Carmelites?"

"I wouldn't know." Nellie passes a manila file sleeve across the desk, and for the next twenty minutes or so, I sort through the insurance information, completing forms as we go through Letty's papers. Though Miguel has done most of it, I find out that their benefits will fully cover no more than another forty-eight hours in this place, at which time—I predict—Letty's on-site therapist will determine that she has recovered enough to be released. Thank heavens for that! If she had fuller coverage, we'd have to battle to get her out, and two days will give me enough time to clean up, shampoo the carpet, and prepare the guest room for her and Miguel. As our session draws to a close, Nellie stuffs a few sheets into a large envelope; these are for Miguel to sign and return the next day.

We both stand, falsely claim to be pleased to meet one another, and exchange bogus expressions of gratitude. I open the door less than an inch to peer out. No wheelchair nun in sight, so I make a run for it, scooting down the hall until I hit the crowd at the entry, where I find Miguel. Tall, dark, and tattooed, he's pretty easy to spot in this group. And we tear through that main hall for the exit faster than a grease fire.

When Miguel drops me off at home, Bobby's nowhere in sight. I check my watch: dinner time. He's probably gone home to eat. It's too late for the walk-in vet clinic, even too late to call for an appointment at a regular animal hospital. Referencing one of the dog books I bought, I examine Feo myself. His small eyes are shiny, clear of mucous; his swinish snout soft, cool, and moist; and his nails and teeth seem strong, even if his breath now smells like sweaty socks. I palpate his stomach, checking for tenderness, something I did last night after Efrem kicked him. But Feo again reacts to this probing by rolling onto his back, his four paws waving in the air, so I can more fully stroke his soft, hairless belly. His coat, though shit colored, feels thick enough to me—no bald patches, flakiness, or abrasions. I sniff my hand after touching him. He definitely needs a bath, so I fill the tub and change into my housecleaning gym shorts and an oversized T-shirt. Sensing something up, Feo crawls under my bed to hide from me. I have to drag him out by one leg and then carry him like a baby into the bathroom.

Just as he's fully lathered with the flea shampoo I bought yesterday and I'm reaching for the spray nozzle affixed to the tap, my nalgas surely wide-angled in a spectacularly unappealing way, Xochi's voice bounces into the tiled bathroom from the doorway. "What on earth are you doing?" she asks.

"What does it look like I'm doing?" I toss this over my shoulder, catching a glimpse of my sister standing near some tall guy in black with a white clergyman's collar in the doorway. Feo barks belatedly at the intrusion. "I'm washing a dog. That's what I'm doing." I try lowering my behind, but the nozzle slips out of my hand, and I practically have to lunge into the tub after it.

"Why?" she asks.

"I *like* washing dogs, don't you know?" I tell her, making a lame joke, hoping to distract them from the view. "It's a little hobby of mine. I snatch them off the street, lather them up, rinse them off, and set them free." I twist the tap on to flush the foam out of Feo's coat. "Way too many dirty dogs in this city for me," I say, spraying Feo's back with warm water. "One dog at a time, that's my motto."

Over the rushing tap, I can't make out Xochi's response, but when I glance over my shoulder again, the doorway is empty. If I know my cheap and greedy sister, she's no doubt pulling a bottle of pinot noir from my "wine cellar," the plastic rack just above the washing machine in my kitchen, to uncork—a pre-dinner drink for her and her date, courtesy of big sis. I finish rinsing Feo, pull the plug, and kick the bathroom door shut to dry him before he slithers off to shake water all over the house. I really thought a bath would improve things, but a wet dog smells exactly like dog, only more pungent somehow, the odor intensified by wetness. Maybe I have to wait until he dries for the full effect. I towel him as best I can before plugging in the blow dryer. "This is going to seem scarier than it really is," I tell him before setting the thing as low as it will go and turning it on him. But Feo seems to dig the blow-drying. He turns this way and that, so I can reach all the wet spots, and he especially enjoys the blast of warm air on his backside. His stump tail wags as if to say, *More, Marina, please, more.*

But enough is enough, and I don't want to chap his skin, so I unplug the thing, wind the cord around it, Feo whimpering the whole time. "This will have to be a special treat," I explain, "a once-in-a-while thing." I remember the tabby my cat-crazy friend's family had when she was a kid; this cat enjoyed "being vacuumed," her loose fur and dander suctioned up by the upholstery nozzle attachment. I put away the blow dryer, thinking a person never knows what household appliance will appeal to the companion animal.

When I finish brushing him, Feo prances out of the bathroom and into the living room as if he knows he is spruced up and is eager to strut his stuff. I follow him to find Xochi and her date on the love seat, wine glasses in hand. Feo approaches them, sniffing warily, his tail stump still, but poised to wag once he makes up his mind about these newcomers.

"Whose dog is that?" Xochi asks, inclining her wine glass toward Feo.

"He's mine." I nod in greeting the preacher on my love seat. He's not so imposing now that he's seated. In fact, his eyes dart this way and that, meeting mine only fleetingly, as if he is aware of being judged. Or maybe he avoids my eyes so I can admire his looks—the gray eyes, the well-coiffed black hair, straight nose, high cheekbones, and cleft chin. Dude is fine, all right. Still, first impression: I don't like him much. Maybe it's his cologne, which is something corny like Old Spice, or his sweat, which I smell under the cologne, a cold clamminess that reeks to me of mistrust, fear, and defensiveness.

"You don't have a dog," Xochi says.

"Clearly, I do have a dog." I point to Feo, who has decided Xochi is okay but seems to share my opinion about her date. His tail wags as he snuffles at her shoes, but he stays clear of the clergyman at her side. "His name's Feo. I got him from Kiko." I turn to the guy, extend my hand. "I'm Marina, Xochi's older sister."

"Felix." He clasps my hand for a crushing handshake. "I'm Felix Léon."

"Felix is a minister with this non-*demon*-natio-nal church," Xochi tells me as I shake the pain from my fingers.

"*Nondenominational*," Felix says, but I like the way Xochi pronounced it better, the idea of a church that endorses a demon-free nation. I bet most people would go along with that—no problem.

"Interesting," I say.

"Yeah," Xochi says, "Felix is a minister, a chaplain for a semiprofessional baseball team, and he also works at the police station, the Rampart Division, as a DARE officer, *and*—get this—he's an MP in the military reserve."

"Military police," Felix explains, sitting up a bit straighter.

"Wow," I say, thinking: authority figure to the third power. None of these are selling points for me. I like this dude less and less. In fact, he strikes me as three dickheads in one. "You must be pretty busy."

"I manage my time well," he tells me, almost, but not quite cracking a smile. He takes in my living room: the mismatched furniture, the dog toys scattered about, the teacup left on the coffee table from last night, the stains on the carpet. "You live here?" he asks, meaning: *You live like this*?

So I say, "Why?"

"No reason. I'm just making conversation." This time he really smiles, but in a fuck-you way.

"Your church," I say, "tell me about your

church. You see, I'm very interested in spirituality and faith."

He draws a big, whopping breath and sits all the way back to give himself room to expound, but the phone rings, and I raise one finger. "Excuse me, please. I'll be right back." I snatch the receiver and retreat with it into my bedroom, Feo at my heels.

Once inside, I shut the door behind us. "Hello?"

"Marina." My older sister's voice is taut with urgency.

My heart lurches. "Della, what's wrong?"

"That's what I'm trying to find out. What happened? Where's Kiko?"

"Kiko?"

"Do you know where he is, Marina? Which hospital?"

"What?" My hands go slick with sweat. I'm holding my breath.

"Yeah, don't you know? He called me from an emergency room. He'd been there all night, something about a fight, and that's all he told me. He had to go. They called his name to see the doctor." Muttering in the background, and then a muffling sound fills my ear, as though she has cupped the phone. Even so, Della's voice penetrates this distinctly: *"Shut up, Duffy! For once, will you just shut up?"* When she speaks into the phone, she says, "I thought you'd know where he is. I thought he'd called you or maybe you were with him at the ER. Why don't you ever answer your cell?"

"I lost that phone," I tell her. "I swear I didn't know anything about this. I've been visiting Letty and I just got home." Feo looks up at me quizzically, narrowing his tiny eyes and tilting his head as if also trying to puzzle the phone call out. "Was it just a fistfight or was he shot or stabbed?"

"I don't *know*. I don't know anything!" she says. "I'm coming right over. He's got to be somewhere that's near your place or he'll probably call you. I'll have my cell in case he calls back and I'll be right there."

"Look, Della, if he's well enough to call, if he sounded okay on the phone—"

"But that's just it, Marina. He *didn't* sound okay," Della says, her voice harsh.

"How did he sound?" Here, I'm thinking labored breathing, moaning, even crying out in pain.

But Della says, "Scared. He sounded really, really scared." And she hangs up.

In the living room, I return to Xochi and her date talking together on my couch. My kid sister's lowered her eyes, and she's giving a deep-dimpled grin. The minister holds her hand, staring at her heart-shaped face and talking softly. I clear my throat. "That was Della. Kiko's been hurt."

Xochi pushes away from Felix, her eyes wide.

"*What?* What happened?"

I tell her as much as I know, and she says, "Where's Reggie?"

I shrug. "Good question." To be honest, Reggie hasn't crossed my mind, but he's always with Kiko, and that brings some comfort, unless something worse has happened to him. "I can't imagine what kind of fight Kiko would get in," I tell Xochi. "I mean, he's irritating for sure, but who would bother to fight him?"

She shrugs, shakes her head. And Felix straightens out his jacket, turning the cuffs so they are just right and aligning the seams of his slacks. He pats his gelled hair and adjusts his collar, behaving as if he's seated before a mirror and appreciative of what he sees in it.

"What is up with you?" I say.

He clears his throat again, emitting a deep baritone rumble. "I was just wondering something," he says. "You seem so tense and edgy. It makes me curious. That's all."

"Curious about what?"

He fixes me with a stern gaze. "Have you been saved?" I shoot Xochi a look. She refuses to meet my eyes, so I approach the love seat and stoop to pick up the half-full wine glasses they've set on the floor. "O-*kay*, well, thanks for coming by," I tell the self-righteous prig, this minister fanfarrón.

"Good luck with your ministry, the police work, baseball, and all that. Just be careful not to leave the door open on your way out." I stride into the kitchen, Feo trotting before me, his tail stump angled up in a haughty way.

"Xochi," I say over my shoulder, "if you're going now, too, I'll call you when I hear any news about Kiko."

As I'm rinsing the purplish dregs from the glasses, the slammed door resonates, and something tight loosens with a clicking sound in my neck. This is Kundalini, coiled energy, my *A.M. Yoga* instructor would say: The serpent rouses, shedding stiffness after sleep. I swing my head from the right to the left and back, and roll my shoulders.

But I start and fumble, nearly dropping the delicate stemmed glasses into the sink basin, when Xochi's voice, again, sounds at my back. "You know what, Marina? You need to take a fucking chill pill."

Chapter Seventeen

Before Della arrives, Xochi pours herself another glass of wine and convinces me to have one with her to calm my "fucking nerves," as she puts it. She's seated at my kitchen table, giving me an earful about how rude and intolerant I was to Felix, saying, "You go on and on about the Dalai what's-his-name and Gandhi, like you're some wise, all-accepting queen of the swamis, but you get just as bent out of shape with people who have different beliefs than you, just as bothered as I do when I, like, see someone wearing 'comfort' shoes out in public." I'm in no mood to argue, so I sip my pinot noir, knowing full well that I shouldn't, in case I need to drive somewhere to get Kiko. But, hey, I figure Della should be the one to do that, and after I empty the first one, I pour a second glass. By the time Della blows in from Pasadena, we've rinsed out the bottle, nested it in the recycling bin, and I am uncorking another.

Feo barks as our big sister bustles in without knocking and plops her heavy purse at the center of the dining table, like some especially hideous centerpiece. Xochi edges away from the thing, regarding the flaking black-and-tan faux-leather, the many bulging pockets and compartments, the grime in its creases and seams, with a look of revulsion on her face. My older sister is a large, sturdy woman, more statuesque than fat. Still, no one enjoys seeing her in a swimsuit. Her coarse black hair now sports a severe but stylish bob that somehow expands her face, elongating her sharp nose. Her face is already wide and long, like Kiko's, but her skin is more café than leche, while his complexion is strictly leche. Dark-skinned, raven-haired Della has always had a taste for blond men with milky complexions. Despite Kiko's last name, our last name, his father is some anonymous Nordic type I never met. Della scans my small kitchen with her intense, dark eyes, black as currants pressed into gingerbread. First thing, Della notices the empty wine glasses on the table, glances at me pulling the cork from a fresh bottle. She says, "I can't believe you're drinking at a time like this."

"What should we be doing?" I ask.

"Calling," she says, before stalking into the front room. Xochi holds up her empty glass. I fill it and mine before Della returns with the fat phone books, two volumes: A-L and M-Z. These she also smacks onto my soon-to-be-antique table.

"Take it easy," I tell her. "This table can only take so much abuse."

"We need to call the hospitals." Della steps out of the kitchen again, returning momentarily with my home phone and Xochi's compact, silvery handbag, crosshatched with intersecting lines of pearly beads. "Get your cell phone out, Xochi. You and Marina take M to Z."

"But don't they list hospitals in the front of the book?" I say. "Check it out."

She flips through the opening pages of the first volume, making such a page-rattling production of this that it riles Feo into barking. "Stop it!" she says, and Feo cuts off like Della's pulled his plug. "Whose dog is that?"

"He's mine."

"You don't have a dog," she tells me, still rifling pages. "Here it is: Hospitals, Clinics, and Emergency Care Facilities." She rips one page out and hands it to me. "You and Xochi call these places. I'll call the hospitals on the next page."

During the next half hour, we call and call, spending much time on hold and navigating tricky recorded message systems. Next round, I pour Della a glass of wine, and she drains it absently while waiting to reach a human voice. I refill her glass and pick up my phone to make another call—Manzanita Vista. No way do I expect *aortiz* to answer phones at that place, but my cheeks, already wine warm, burn as I press in that telephone number. Once I clear the first recorded hurdle and press another button for patient information, a burst of Muzak fills my ear, punctuated by the announcement that though my call is important, all lines are busy, and my patience is appreciated as I wait for the next available operator. This followed by more Muzak.

"Shit-heads!" Black eyes flashing, Della snaps her phone shut, tosses it on the table. "They hung up on me. I waited and waited, did everything they said, and then they fucking hung up." A coppery shade suffuses her dark skin and her eyes glimmer with anger and incomprehension. She grabs her glass, gulps the wine.

Xochi clicks her phone shut, too. "Maybe we should just wait for Kiko to call."

"What if he can't call? What if he's in surgery or needs a transfusion? What if he doesn't pull through?" Della says, her voice inflecting with each horrible possibility.

Finally, a female voice on my line, and I picture the white-haired volunteer at the information desk, though this woman sounds more harassed and impatient than that kind lady could ever be. Quickly I ask about Kiko, giving his full name—Francisco Lucero—and spelling it, then asking the woman to check new admissions. She inquires about my relationship to Kiko before she divulges any information, and because I'm afraid she won't tell me anything if I'm just an aunt, I say, "He's my son."

Della narrows her eyes, rises slowly from her seat, advancing on me as the operator checks. I cup the phone and say, "I had to say that. I didn't think they'd—"

The operator returns to tell me that there is no record of a patient with that name. I shake my head to let my sisters know, and I thank her before hanging up.

"You *wish*," Della says. "You wish he was your son."

"Come on, Della. Be real," Xochi tells her.

"I only said that to get them to see if he was there or not," I try to explain. "Some places don't consider aunts, uncles, and cousins immediate family."

"You could have said you were his sister," Della says, her face nearly purple now. "But *no*, you said you were his mother because that's what you've always wanted. Ever since he was born, you've been trying to take him away from me, reading to him, giving him toys, and taking him for ice cream. And *look*, look at you now. You have him all to yourself, living here with you like some prince who doesn't have to lift a fucking finger. Of course, he'd rather be here than with me."

"He only lives here because *you* kicked him out," I tell her, my voice louder than I like, and I realize that I'm standing, too. Tense as snakes coiled to strike, we're facing each other near my side of the table. Della, a good four inches taller than I am, looks down at my face and I'm staring up into hers, but aware that her arms are bent at the elbows, her hands clenched into fists.

"Okay, okay," Xochi says, an anxious look on her pretty face. "Be cool, will you? We still have lots of places to call." She picks up her cell phone, wags it at us.

"For your information," Della tells me, looming so close, spittle flies in my face, "I just wanted him to take responsibility for himself, to grow up, and be self-sufficient, which he would be right now if you hadn't interfered. He'd have a job. He'd be safe and sound, working somewhere, instead of lying in some hospital bed."

"That's not true," I say, "and you know it. Kiko's dyslexic. He has trouble making out street signs, and you've known it since he was in grade school, but you never got him any kind of help, never wanted to admit—"

"You think you know everything. You went to

college and you think you know just about all there is to know about everything and everyone. You have *all* the answers, don't you?"

"Cool it, Della," Xochi warns her.

"Nah, I'm not going to cool it. She needs to hear this. You're just as smart as can be and so spiritual and enlightened with your mother, the *saint*, tucked away in a Carmelite cloister." Here, she uses air quotes, like those Mrs. Jimenez applies, to offset her last phrase. "And our transcendental-bullshit father—you must think you're heir apparent to the mystical realm of omniscience, with your Dalai Lama and Buddhism and all that shit."

"Shut up, Della," Xochi says, looking at me, her smooth brow now pleated. "You better shut up."

"I'm just curious," Della says, weaving her head from side to side with her hands now on her hips. "Have you ever *looked up* that cloister? Have you ever bothered to *call* or *write* to your mother? I mean, Mother's Days, Christmases, birthdays, they come and go. Have you ever even sent a card to her?"

I lower my eyes, fixing my gaze on Della's big, hideous purse. A bundle of folded envelopes protrude from a side compartment. These look like bills, and tucked beside them, a white-capped orange vial from Sav-on Pharmacy.

"Well, if you had, you'd find out in a flash there

is *no* fucking cloister." Della closes in on me, her big face inches from mine. "Your mother's not a nun, stupid. She was a lunatic. Just like you. Dad had her admitted to a psychiatric hospital when she started calling him at all hours, talking about going to heaven and taking you with her."

"You're lying," I tell Della before turning to Xochi. "She's lying."

Xochi stares at the marred and battered tabletop, but she shakes her head.

"How would you even know?" I ask her. "You were just four when I came to live with you."

"I didn't know then, but my mother told me when I was in high school. She bragged that it was her idea, the cloister. I thought it was bullshit— you know how my mom is—so I asked Dad about it, and he got all pissed off. He made me promise never to tell you," Xochi says, still not looking at me. "He didn't want you to ever find out. He made us both swear never to tell you." She cuts Della a hard look.

"Where is she now? My mother?" I ask. My sisters glance at each other and cast their eyes down. The refrigerator whooshes, emitting its own suspiro before tick-tick-ticking to life. Outside a ball bounces, and high-pitched children's voices ring over the roar of a passing car. *Gimme that! I'm telling! No fair!* Feo whimpers, scratches at the back door to be let out, but I ignore this, removing my frail mother from the shadowy cloister I had imagined and installing her in a space like the facility Letty now inhabits. "Will somebody *please* tell me where she is?"

"She died," Xochi says in a quiet voice. Her eyes, large and moist, meet mine. "She had a blood clot in her leg, went straight to her heart. My mom says she was always praying, kneeling, just in that same position without moving for hours and hours. You get clots in the legs, you know, from lack of circulation. That was why my mom got the Exercycle."

"But your mom always had that-that-that *thing*," I sputter, unable to remember a time before the stationary bike was positioned before the television in the bonus room. Since it's easier to think of the gleaming chrome frame and vinyl cushioned seat than to take in what Xochi's just said, I focus on the Exercycle. My stepmother would mount it daily, pedaling vigorously while her favorite telenovelas were broadcast. And when Xochi was a teenager, they competed for turns riding the thing. I even tried it a few times, though churning pedals on a bike that never went anywhere held little appeal for me.

"Listen, Marina." Xochi approaches me, clutches my forearms and draws me close to look into my eyes. "Listen to me. My mom told me your mother died really soon after she went to that place," she says. "Dad maybe hoped she'd get better and they'd let her out, so she could come back to you. I don't know the whole story. Like you said, I was too young when it all went down. I just know that my mother told me."

"What about the burial? The Rosary? Why didn't I know about any of that? Why didn't I go to her funeral?" A numb, buzzing sensation overtakes me, that thick muffling blanket of unreality. I can't fathom this. It makes no sense.

"Dad handled all of it," Della tells me, her voice lower now. "Her family was in Mexico. No way could they come, so he had her body shipped over there. He took care of everything." She reaches to encircle my shoulders in an embrace. "Look, her- manita, I didn't mean to—"

"Don't touch me." I wrench free, shoving my sister's arm away with more force than I intend.

Xochi gasps.

"She's dead," I say in a voice that sounds disconnected from me, that seems to issue from someone else, as though I am a dybbuk channeling a flat-sounding spirit, or a ventriloquist's dummy. "She's *really* dead?"

Rubbing her upper arm, Della nods. "You should be glad. She was a pretty horrible mother."

"*You're* the horrible mother," I tell her, my voice my own again. "You let some low-life güero talk you into throwing your son out like garbage—"

Della's hand blurs in the periphery, a flash of palm, the sound of one hand clapping. My jaw burns, fire and ice at the same time. Feo explodes—barking, snarling, and lunging for Della. *She's slapped me.* I finger my face; the skin is smooth, rubbery, numb to my touch. Della draws back, her mouth and eyes wide open. "Marina, I..."

Feo bounces up and down, leaping and snapping as if to snatch a piece of Della's face in retaliation, and Xochi tells her, "Jesus, I can't even *believe* you did that."

I snag Feo's collar, yank him away from my sister. "I need some air, okay?" I hear myself say, but my words sound disconnected, even slightly off in the way that asynchronous television broadcasts show the actors' mouths moving seconds before their voices can be heard. I drag Feo toward the broom closet. There, with one hand, I fumble amid the clutter, feeling for the new leash I bought. Somehow, I grasp it right away and clip it to his collar.

"Listen, Marina, I didn't mean—"

"I'll be back," I tell my sisters in my strange, timedelayed voice. "I just need to clear my head."

I pull Feo to the front door, my sisters' hushed voices sounding in the background.

"What's *wrong* with you?"

"She should know—"

"But you *hit* her. How could you?"

I open the front door and shut it behind Feo and me. I don't want to hear anymore. Mercifully, the children with their bouncing ball have disappeared. I don't want to hear anything anymore, but there's a leaf blower now blasting across the street, nearly obliterating noise from an ice cream truck that rattles past, trailing a hot spume of exhaust and churning out the theme to "Popeye the Sailor Man." Feo and I cross over toward the Fuentes duplex, heading for the side street that winds up toward an unofficial entrance to Angeles National Forest. My mind roils with thoughts and memories, fragments of this and flashes of that—a kaleidoscopic tumble of sharp-edged pieces that won't snap together in a coherent way. Like my voice, my feet in their leather chanclas, and even my hands, seem separate from me, moving in predictable and practical ways that are completely independent of me.

Though it doesn't seem possible, the leaf blower roars louder, scraping even these tags of thought from my mind. I peer over the chain-link fence corralling dusty kid vehicles, gazing from the front to the Fuentes's side yard. There, Henry blasts away dirt, grass clippings, dried leaves, twigs, dust, and debris from his wife's santero garden. He's clearing off the base of Imelda's blue-and-white statue of the Virgin Mother. Henry's so close to the thing and working so intently that he can't see it rocking from the force of the blower.

"Henry," I call, and Feo barks. Unhearing, Henry persists with the blower, until the statue sways widely, tipping too far to one side and toppling onto the cement with an explosive crash. Ribbons of plaster dust rise from its chalky shards like smoky serpents. Henry switches off the blower and lowers himself unsteadily to sit on the statue's now vacant pedestal. His eyes on the broken pieces, he still hasn't noticed me, and I feel guilty, even intrusive, watching him settle his elbows on his knees. He removes his glasses to massage the bridge of his nose. I tug Feo's leash so we can get away unseen, but the dog barks, wagging his tail stump. Henry looks up.

"Sorry about the statue," I call out to him.

"Yeah, me, too." He stands, brushes off the seat of his pants, and crosses the front yard, approaching us. "The thing was hollow," he says, gesturing at the plaster fragments, "lightweight. I should have remembered."

"Where is everyone?" I point the leash handle at

his for-once silent house.

"Confession," he says.

"On a Wednesday night?"

He shrugs. "Special circumstances." And then he says, "So you got a dog now?" He tries a smile, but it looks more like a grimace.

I nod. A light breeze flutters through the leaves of his hibiscus bush, and lofting upward on a sudden current, it wafts over my face. With its cool fragrant touch, I realize my cheeks are damp and chilly, my eyes blurry.

"What's wrong?" Henry asks, his face a fibrous nest of wrinkles. He can't be sixty yet, but his skin is so shadowy and lined with fatigue that he looks like an anciano in this moment, one of those wizened viejos from the high desert.

"My mother died," I tell him.

"The nun?"

"She was never a nun." I take a deep shuddery breath. "It's a long story, way too long. I'm still trying to figure it out." And I do keep casting back in my memory to those early days when I first went to stay with my father and Xochi's mother. They told me she'd gone on a religious retreat, and when she didn't return, they said she had joined the Carmelite order, had taken a vow of silence. Why did I believe so easily, so unquestioningly? Why did *I* have such faith?

"Lo siento," Henry says, looking sad enough to weep, though he never met my mother, never even saw a photo of her.

A carload of teenagers speeds past, windows open, rap music thumping out, a blur of shiny laughing faces.

"How about you?" I ask. "What's the matter?"

"My fifteen-year-old, la Juanita...she's pregnant." Henry works at another smile, even less successful than his first attempt. He huffs on his glasses, wipes the lenses on his T-shirt, and puts them back on. "More diapers," he says. "I'll be changing diapers until *I* need diapers."

"So, felicitaciones," I say. "Another grandchild."

"I already got grandchildren, a bunch of them." He compresses his lips, shakes his head.

"No peace, then, I guess." I tighten my grip on the leash as Feo strains against it. He can't see the point in it, this standing on the sidewalk with Henry. To him, it's probably just mouths moving and random sounds, time wasted when there is much, much more to sniff and mark with his scent.

"Well," Henry says, "the way I see it, you can have people or you can have peace. And there'll be plenty of peace when I die, qué no?"

"I suppose so."

"Mira, isn't that your nephew down on the corner?" Henry points to a familiar lumpish form with a bandaged hand, bearing a bulky trash bag and loping toward us from the end of the block.

"Oh, my god, it *is* him!" I hand Henry the leash. "Hold this for me, will you? I'll be right back."

I race down the street, calling, "Kiko! *Kiko!*" The neighborhood of weary-looking houses and dried-out lawns spools past in my periphery, a rush of drab colors, while Feo barks uselessly in the background. Before I launch into my nephew's arms, I stop short to see how he is. Apart from the gauze-bundled hand, Kiko seems fine, maybe a bit thinner and more tired than he usually is, but upright and ambling along, even smiling at me. "Tía," he says. "I had to come back, just for a little bit. Is that okay?"

Gingerly, I embrace him, taking care not to bump his injured hand. "Oh, Kiko, of course you can come back. Do you have any idea how worried we've been?" I say in his ear. I pull away, staring at the gauzy mitt. "What happened? Your mom said you were in a fight. Are you okay?"

"Yeah, I'm okay. Sorry, tía," he says, after sniffing at his T-shirt. "I smell like an old fart." And, boy, he sure does, but I shake my head as though nothing could be further from the truth. Kiko squints at Henry still holding Feo's leash. "How's the dog?"

"Trust me, he's fine. Tell me what happened. But wait, your mom's at my house with Xochi. Let's go over there, so you can tell us all at once." We trudge back up the street to collect Feo from Henry before crossing over and heading home. As Henry hands me the leash, I glance over his shoulder at his duplex. Except for Sunday Mass and special circumstances like these, that two-storey stucco and wood structure is rarely vacant. I picture it now in the absence of its human inhabitants—the walls released of tension, the furniture easing out of compression from human weight, the very foundations loosening under the sheetrock while shadows pool in the beautiful silence. And I remember my house that night I was alone in it with Feo, before Efrem and Carlotta burst in, the quiet music of inanimate objects soothing me now as the remembered taste of a rare treat. I savor this briefly before Kiko and I let Feo lead us across the street where my sisters are waiting.

Chapter Eighteen

After all nature of ecstatic embraces and some weeping on Della's part, Kiko showers and changes into the clean clothes stowed in his bag, promising to tell us about his misadventures when he's cleaned up. While Kiko's showering, Bobby shows up, bearing a huge star-spangled navy blue pot, one of Carlotta's asopaos—a rich golden menudo, in fact, which we set on my stovetop to reheat. Since he's here, I ask the kid to stay and eat with us. Bobby gladly plants his bony culo in a chair at the dining table. No doubt he's already eaten, but he, too, is avid to hear The Story of Kiko's Fight.

When we're all seated before tall, sweating glasses of iced tea and steamy bowls of fragrant hominy, tripas, and flecks of red chili floating in rich amber broth, Kiko glances around the table, from face to face, and his lips quirk. "I don't ever want to go away again," he says. "I know I can't stay here forever, but I don't want to leave you guys no more. I don't know who I am out there. Bad shit happens." His eyes fill, and a fat tear leaks out, trails down his cheek. "I don't know how people do it, how they make it out there. I just can't figure it out."

"You *can* figure it out, son," Della tells him. "I know you can. Come back home, and I'll help you. That's my job."

"But Duffy says—"

"We'll deal with Duffy," Della says, a stern look on her bronze face. "He should be able to empathize more, now that he's out of work, too."

"No shit?" Xochi asks, and I say, "Wow," thinking, what is this new trend of men not working? After the nutty nature-trail clean-up and even before the wedding, Pancha's husband promptly quit his job to become a "producer," though what he produces apart from caca in the toilet is beyond me. And Efrem from next door has been collecting unemployment benefits for months. Even Henry Fuentes is on disability now, not to mention los dos bums—Kiko and Reggie.

"Yeah, he got laid off a couple of weeks ago," Della says. "And he's not looking all that hard for something new. I'm ready to try some 'tough love' on that huevón."

To be kind, I say, "I guess when the economy goes south, men feel it first."

"Well, that's one way to look at it," Della tells me, with a smile.

"So what happened?" Bobby says. "How'd you hurt your hand? Were you really in a fight?"

"Nah, man, I ain't never been in no fight with fists and shit," Kiko says.

Della shakes her head. "But you told me—"

"I told you I got in a fight, and I feel worse about that than the hand." Kiko slurps up a spoonful of soup.

"Where's Reggie?" Xochi asks.

"That's who I fought with, but it was just an argument," Kiko says. "He went off with these kids."

"My hand got hurt last night at some party out in Whittier." He turns to Della. "I know you don't want to hear this shit, Mom, but I was smoking mota and drinking beer, and I just kind of dozed off."

"More like passed out, I bet," Xochi says. "Where was Reggie?"

"He wasn't there. He was all pissed off at me, so he split with this bunch of teenagers. I think they were going to, like, Disneyland or someplace like that today. They had a bunch of passes."

"Disneyland?" I say, picturing gangly Reggie standing in line, towering over a gaggle of youngsters, waiting to shake hands with Mickey Mouse, or better yet, Goofy—a doppelgänger encounter of sorts.

"Yeah, it's kind of weird, huh?" Kiko spoons up more menudo. "So I'm at this party, sort of dozing, and all of a sudden my hand is like on *fire* with pain. I wake up and some crazy, bearded dude in a baseball cap is *biting* me." His eyes widen in disbelief. "Yeah, biting me as hard as he could. I swear I got no idea why. Maybe he was hungry and my hand looked tasty, or he was confused. Probably he was high. I seriously don't know. So I start screaming 'cause he won't let go, and there's blood, *my blood*, dripping onto the rug. Some other guy comes over and hits the dude that's chomping on me with this big old dictionary. Just hits him and hits him—*bam, bam, bam*, and that hurts, too—until the crazy dude loosens up his jaw and I get my hand out of his mouth. Hurt like hell, let me tell you."

"But that's insane," Della says.

"Tell me about it," Kiko says. "Some chick there was a nurse and she told me human bites are, like, really dangerous. She's the one who drove me to the ER at Whittier Hospital. I was in that waiting room all night. I thought they'd never get to me. Today, some guy let me use his cell phone to reach you, Mom, and that's when the nurse finally called my name."

"Wow," I say again.

"So you and Reggie broke up," Xochi says. "The great bro-mance of the century is over?"

Kiko tips his bowl to slurp up the dregs and sets it down. "I feel shitty about it," he says. "It's mostly my fault."

"What did you guys fight over?" Bobby wants to know.

"He found a job." Kiko gives a rueful smile. "First day, and the dude finds a job stocking groceries in the supermarket, supposed to start on Monday. You heard that Vallarta's is expanding, hiring all kinds of people?" He looks at Della whose ears perk at this news. "But they got this written test, so...oh, well. Anyways, I started making fun of Reggie, laughed at the job, called him a 'bag boy' too many times, and he said I was, like, holding him back." Kiko shakes his head, stares into his empty soup bowl. "I don't want to hold nobody back."

Later, after Bobby has gone home and Kiko is snoring softly on the couch, Della washes dishes and I dry them, while Xochi—unwilling to ruin her nails by helping out in any way—reclines on the love seat, Reggie's nest, watching television. She's all absorbed in some movie on the Lifetime channel, a tear-jerker I've seen before, involving sisters, a bone-marrow transplant, and self-sacrifice, so Della and I are amazed that it holds her attention. I've just stacked the bowls in my cabinet, when the phone blurts a half-ring. The receiver is still on the kitchen table. I snatch it up before the second ring, as if anything less than detonating a bomb could possibly disturb Kiko's deep sleep. "Hello?"

"Thank god you're home." Reggie's breathless voice rasps through the line, a cacophony of noises and Dixieland music blaring in the background. "You got to help me, Marina. I'm like freaking out in this place. My heart's beating way too fast and I can't get my breath. I'm about to pass out. Can you *please*, please come pick me up?"

"Where are you?"

A sheen of perspiration on her face, Della wheels from the steamy suds to stare at me, her lips parted and her inky eyes narrowed in curiosity.

"I'm at Disneyland. I was here with some people, but then we got separated. I was lost for the longest time in Fantasyland. Couldn't find the way out for nothing, and now, I think I'm like having an anxiety attack or something."

"An anxiety attack?" I have never heard Reggie like this. No question it's his voice, but altered in a tinny, desperate-sounding way.

Della raises her eyebrows, whispering, *"Who is it?"*

I cup the phone to tell her, "It's Reggie."

She clicks her tongue, turns back to the sink, and resumes dishwashing.

"Listen," Reggie says, "I'm by the first-aid place near the main entrance. They got some benches there where I can wait for you. Will you come get me, Marina? I'm begging you. *Please?*"

"Okay, okay, I'll be there as soon as I can," I say, thinking again of the Dalai Lama's directive to accomplish the highest welfare of all sentient beings and that it will take at least a danged hour and a half, if not two hours, for me to drive clear to Anaheim. And once I get to Disneyland, I'm pretty sure I'll have to shell out a twenty for parking, even to pick someone up. Plus, the place is a small city unto itself. Finding Reggie will be the real challenge. "Hey, Reggie, do you have a cell?"

"Nah, I'm at a pay phone."

"Then stay put at first aid, okay? Don't go anywhere 'til I get there."

"I will, I swear. I won't move an inch. Thank you, Marina. Already I feel a little better." He hangs up.

I turn to Della and Xochi, who's stepped into the kitchen to pour herself another glass of tea. "That was Reggie. He's at Disneyland, having some kind of anxiety attack." Energized, even relieved by the prospect of this new mission, I glance around for

my purse, the car keys. If I am busy collecting
Reggie from the amusement park, providing for
his welfare, I don't have to think too much about
mine. "I've got to go pick him up at the first-aid
center near the main entrance."

Xochi shakes her head. "Disneyland? That's a
longassed haul. Why couldn't he have his stupid
breakdown somewhere in San Fernando or even
Van Nuys? Just about anywhere in the Valley
would be better than way the hell out in Orange
County."

I shrug, and Della says, "What a pain in the ass."

Maybe influenced by the sister flick, Xochi snatches up her stylish bag. "I'll do it," she says in a
grudging way. "I'll pick up the mother-fucking idiot,"

Both Della and I say, "*Really?*"

"Dumb-ass with his stupid anxiety attack," she
mutters as she heads out of the kitchen.

"Hey," I call, following after her, struggling to
make sense of this strangely generous offer from
her, "you're not going to be mean to him, are
you?"

"No more than he deserves," she says.

I catch her elbow. "Look, Xochi, if you're going
to drive out there and torment the poor fool, forget
it. I'll pick him up. I don't mind," I say. "An anxiety attack is pretty serious. He doesn't need to feel

worse about things right now."

"Okay, okay," she says, rolling her emerald eyes. "I'll be nice. I swear I will. But don't get me wrong. I'm not doing this for that crybaby. I'm doing it for you guys." She tilts her chin at Della, who is rinsing out Carlotta's pot. Xochi lowers her voice. "So you can get things right." From her designer bag, she extracts a compact mirror and a tube of lipstick, *my* Hawaiian Dusk. "A sister is like a forever friend," she says, and I *know* she got that straight from the sappy movie. She applies a few deft strokes of lipstick, smoothes it with her pinkie. "Think about it. Plus, for you, it's like your mother just died. You barely found out. You don't need to be driving to Anaheim right now." She snaps her compact shut and heads for the front door.

When the house is quiet, except for snoring from Kiko and Feo, I brew some peppermint tea and set out two bright yellow mugs, a Christmas gift from a student who was clearly more accomplished in his ceramics class than he was at learning English. Della and I settle again at the dining table, this time with the steamy, menthol-scented mugs. It's hard for her, but she manages to choke out something like an apology that's only part accusation, and I accept, telling her that I'm sorry, too, for calling her a horrible mother. And then we talk about my mother, those long years ago. Della asks what I remember, so she can fill in the rest.

"I remember my mother would go on those religious retreats at some convent, even when you and Dad lived with us. She would pack that beige suitcase with blue trim. You remember that? She'd fold her nightgown, housecoat, her sweaters, blouses, and skirts. She dressed like a nun. Remember?" When she went out, my mother wore gray cardigans, white blouses, navy or black skirts that hung just past her knees, white socks and ugly flat shoes with rubber soles, "comfort shoes," as Xochi would say. "Did she really go?" I ask Della now. "Did she really go on retreats or did she like check in for treatment somewhere? Electroshock therapy or something like that?"

"She really went, I think," Della says, crossing her arms over her big bosom and then nodding. She squints, frowning as she strains to remember. "Remember she would come back with those pamphlets and holy cards." She goes on to tell me that our father really loved my mother, but she loved Jesus more and made no secret about it. "I mean," Della says, "she was kind to me, always kind, but I never felt like she was *there* with me. Here, I was, this little kid who just lost her own mother, and this nice lady marries my father, but when she'd talk to me or play with me, she always seemed to be looking off in the distance, thinking about something else. It's like she wasn't part of this world, the world of people."

I think of what my neighbor Henry said about people and peace, how these are incompatible, even mutually exclusive, and I nod.

"And then you were born, and she was okay for a while, still distant, but okay. When I was in junior high and you were around seven or eight, that's when things got strange. Do you remember?" Della asks, fixing me with her gaze. Her dark eyes now telegraph gentle encouragement, and her broad face seems softer in the golden glow from the overhead kitchen light.

"I remember the visions, the voices," I say, thinking of the Virgin Mary's appearances on our front lawn. Once, right after Della and my father moved out, my mother roused me from sleep early one morning, and led me, groggy and yawning, outside where she pointed at our battered aluminum trash cans, saying, *Can't you see her, m'ija? There she is, there. Our Lady.* She crossed herself, knelt to pray, and I slipped back inside the house to watch from the front window, hoping with all my heart that none of our neighbors would see her like that, praying before the garbage. "The mirrors in the house—do you remember how she would cover the mirrors with pillowcases and dishtowels?"

"She didn't always hear good voices nor have such great visions." My sister unfolds her arms and leans across the dining table to thread my chilly fingers in her warm ones. "Do you remember her hands?" she asks, staring into my eyes, "the palms of her hands?"

"Sores," I say, flashing on an image of those nearly forgotten wounds, coin-sized rubies, one in each hand. "She had sores, and on her feet, too." When I was old enough to wash clothes, I would soak the rust-colored stains from her socks in cold water before laundering them.

Still looking deep into my eyes, Della raises one eyebrow.

"Why didn't anyone tell me anything? And why didn't Dad take me with him when he left?" Toward the end, I was cooking meals my mother would barely touch and trying to keep the house clean. I guess my father paid the bills. There was always money in the bank. At twelve, I was writing checks for the groceries at a neighborhood market and lugging them home in a long wire basket on wheels, my first rolling cart. I haven't thought of it in years—so sturdy, so useful. It was one of my favorite things. "Why did he leave me with her like that?"

"Don't you remember, Marina?" Della says, her brow furrowed in skepticism. "You refused to go.

You threw a fit! Quiet little kid like you—no one saw it coming—but you raved like a freaking maniac, threatening to kill us all, and yourself, if we took you away from your mother. Dad tried and tried, and then he gave up, probably figured you'd keep her from going off the deep end."

"But I couldn't."

"No one could have."

"I wanted to believe what she believed," I say, recalling her soft-featured face, the gentle music of her voice. "I wanted the peace she had through her faith, through spirituality. I've always wanted that faith, that belief in something larger than me that would snap everything in place, make all the connections, or weave all the threads together, so my life would unfold in some kind of sensible, even meaningful way."

"But you did have faith, mensa," Della tells me, a knowing look on her large brown face. "You had faith in your mother. Even when you couldn't see the visions she saw or hear the voices she heard, you still believed in her. Without the smallest shred of evidence, in fact mostly with information to contradict this, you believed in her. All this time, you *believed* in her, and that's what Dad didn't want us to take from you—your belief in your mother. And maybe you know the truth now, but you still have faith. You have abundant faith in even the most hopeless people, like that goof Reggie, like Letty and Miguel, your nutty neighbor, those kids you teach, even in people who don't deserve it, like that shit-head Rudy. You even have more faith in my son than I could muster."

"That kind of faith can look an awful lot like stupidity."

Della shakes her big head. "You are a woman of great faith," she says. She lifts her cup, blows softly to cool the tea before sipping it. "And you make really good tea."

I wrap stiff fingers around my brightly glazed mug, the mint tea radiating warmth through the skin to my bones. It's like cupping a ball of sunlight in my palms.

Chapter Nineteen

Following a heated phone conversation with Duffy conducted in my bathroom, behind the closed door for privacy, Della emerges, eyes averted and tight lipped, but she wakes Kiko gently to take him home with her, and Xochi never returns to my place with Reggie, so Feo and I have a quiet night together. My rarely empty house eases perceptibly, the way I imagined Henry's duplex doing that afternoon, with gentle sighs and groans, like a woman kicking off high heels and peeling off her tight clothing. In the morning—after the Coffeeville Express wheezes into the station—I phone Xochi, worried she might not have found Reggie at Disneyland or that she changed her mind, deciding it was way too much trouble after all to pick him up in Anaheim. "What happened last night," I ask her when she answers with a sleepy moan. "Where's Reggie?"

"He's here," she says, before yawning. "It was superlate by the time we got back to the Valley, so I let him stay here. We didn't want to wake you."

"You're not messing around with that boy, are you?" I need to know because I'm the one who will wind up cleaning the mess when she breaks his foolish heart. I think of his chipped eyetooth, the hideous engagement ring she tried to shove down his throat, idly wondering where it is now, that gross, garish ring.

"No one's messing with anyone. We're both consenting adults, you know," she says, and I have no doubt he's in bed beside her, a besotted grin on his ferrety face. "I'm keeping him here a few days," Xochi tells me. "He's going to help me clean up the apartment, and I'm letting him use the car for work on Monday."

"Why, that's mighty nice of you," I tell her as I drizzle water over my cacti on the window ledge. And really, it's the least she can do since he bought the car in the first place. "What happened with Father Smoking Hot, your boyfriend of the cloth?"

"I found out he's divorced," she says.

"So?"

"He has *children*." She shudders audibly. "That's why he's got all the damn jobs—child support, alimony, tuition, braces, and all kinds of shit like that. Just like those pendejos at the cable company, most of the jackasses in that professionals club are divorced with kids. Face it—I am *not* stepmother material."

"You've got that right."

"Dude told me yesterday when you were in the kitchen, said it was interesting to meet my family and that he wanted me to meet his *five* kids, so I said, '*bye-bye.*'" Her voice climbs an octave to affect the cheery, impersonal tone of her farewell.

"Wise of you," I say.

"No shit. I don't want to date anybody's father. I don't want some guy who has a lot of expenses, and kids are fucking expensive these days. I want someone who'll help pay my bills, someone to help me keep this place up."

"Good luck with that," I tell her. "Seriously, Xochi, about Reggie, an anxiety attack is no joke. And you remember how messed up he was when you broke off that so-called engagement?"

"Huh?" Xochi says, before yawning again.

"Don't take his feelings lightly," I tell her. "That's all I'm saying."

She promises that she won't, that she will be kind to him. I have my doubts about this, but what can I do? As she's pointed out, they *are* consenting adults, so I have to let it go, and we hang up.

After walking Feo, I straighten the love seat and fold the flannel throw. I should maybe send the cushions out to be dry-cleaned now that Reggie is gone. Unfurling my mat for *A.M. Yoga*, I again appreciate this small slice of solitude, wondering why on earth I dreaded being alone when Rudy broke up with me. Feo cocks his head this way and that, watching as I mirror the poses portrayed on the television screen, comfortably and without interruption. How could I have worried about loneliness when every solitary moment now is such a luxury to me?

I shower and then load my materials into the car for the penultimate day of summer session classes. This is when we culminate the culminating projects, and make preparations for *Café con Leche*, a little program I've planned for the parents who can attend on Friday. It's no big deal. The students will simply act out the skits we've been practicing all along, scenes from the summer's reading, and display their storyboards and piñatas. I provide coffee with nondairy creamer, herbal tea, and pan dulces for the parents who show up. Afterward, everyone goes home feeling like something has been accomplished, though it's doubtful any of us will be able to say exactly what.

The school day passes in a busy blur of students rehearsing their skits, setting up their storyboards, and putting finishing touches on the piñatas. In the advanced class, all we have are the storyboards and a couple of skits from the beginning and the end of the novel, where the human characters appear, so there's time to view the second half of *The Incredible Journey*, an early Disney film that depicts strictly white folks in the human roles, wearing corny fifties-style clothing—lots of red plaid and boxy brown corduroy pants—and like most early Disney productions, this one seems far too infatuated with Technicolor, especially where red is concerned.

Throughout the final scene, students keep swiveling their heads, turning to check on me at the back of the darkened classroom. Reading the last chapter of the book aloud to them earlier in the week, I wept shamelessly when the old dog, an English bulldog, is reunited with the family. (Another thing stressed in teacher training: Never cry in front of the class. But I would modify that some: Never cry in front of the class out of self-pity, anger, or frustration. It's really okay to blubber over an aged bulldog who finally limps home. Half the class cried with me, and those that didn't offered tissues and words of comfort.) But this film doesn't even cause my throat to clot, though the elderly dog looks a bit like an albino Feo. The background colors are too disturbingly bright, making the film seem much less real than the book did to me.

The Ahuaul brothers show up on time for their

respective classes, and again both are subdued and well behaved. Surely the word is out about their dressing up, but at least in my classes, no one dares tease them about this or even bring it up. In fact, the other students treat the twins tenderly, catching them up on what they've missed and speaking to them in soft tones, as if the boys have just been released from the hospital after major surgery. In the beginning class, Elias and Maritza warmly welcome Felipe back into their group, allowing him to construct a pink tissue paper bouquet for their penguin narrator that they paste to one black flipper. For the first skit, Felipe wants to play Cenicienta's stepmother. In case his father attends, I encourage him instead to take the role of the prince's "foot" man, the one who tries our imaginary glass slipper on each stepsister's, and finally on Cinderella's, foot. The kids have great fun with the makebelieve footwear. After I make a few lame jokes about taking care not to lose it, they keep pretending to misplace the nonexistent thing, blaming one another for sitting on it or stealing it. The boys accuse each other, though not Felipe, of wearing it.

Back home, I uncrate Feo to walk him, and honestly, I have never excited so much enthusiasm in any living creature by my presence as I do when I return to Feo. You'd think we'd been separated for years under traumatic conditions. His entire torpedo-shaped body courses with ecstasy when he emerges from the crate. He doesn't so much leap with joy as he *boings* with it, like there are tightly coiled springs attached to the pads of his paws. Though I enjoy it, this effusion of pleasure at the sight of me is a bit unnerving. I'm just a middle-school teacher, but he acts as if I'm some kind of divine being, a passionately missed food-, water-, and affection-dispensing deity.

After our walk, just as I'm opening the front door, the phone rings, and I race in to answer, thinking, *Oh my god, Letty.* I've planned to fix up the guest room for her and Miguel later this afternoon, idly wondering what would become of their apartment and thinking of tactful ways to suggest Miguel maintain it for that future time when they want to be on their own again. I grab the receiver, gasp out a breathless "*Hello.*"

And it's Rudy, saying, "Listen, mujer, I been trying to reach you."

"How's Letty? What's going on?"

"I guess she's fine," he says. "I ain't talked to her in a while."

"Have you been to visit her at that place?" I carry the phone into my bedroom while Feo slurps water from his bowl in the kitchen. It's stuffy in here, so I lift the window to Bobby's rustling and scraping—cross construction noises—in my backyard. "They had visiting day on Wednesday," I tell Rudy. "Did you even go?"

"Nah, man," he says. "Places like that—they just ain't my thing."

I glance at the Dalai Lama's book on my bed table, and swallow back some pretty harsh words of judgment. "I see."

"No, look, I'm calling on account of Nestor's website. Didn't you get my message?"

A dull booming sound reverberates from the backyard as though Bobby has dropped something as heavy as a safe or an anvil on the ground. "I didn't listen to all of it," I tell him. "There's a lot going on. I don't have time for—"

"Listen, Marina. There's a problem with the website and you got to deal with it."

"I can barely check email and look up things on Google," I say. "How would I be able to fix some problem with Nestor's website? Plus, *why* would I want to help that baboso in the first place?" I step to my chest of drawers, the restored earring tree sparkles satisfyingly, but a fine sifting of dust powders the near-antique wood. I huff on it lightly. Glittery motes tumble in the sunlight pouring through the open window.

"Nah, you don't get it," Rudy tells me. "It's *your* problem, not his. He's posted your name, your picture, even your email address on his website, see, as an enemy of Santería. When the website gets a hit, he's like encouraging people to take, like, a *real* hit at you. He's asking them to blog curses—and there's already a few of these—or to email the shit to you directly. It's like virtual voodoo."

Bile churns up from my stomach, scorching the back of my throat. I click my tongue against the roof of my mouth. "You've got to be kidding. Blogging curses? That's just ridiculous."

"No, Marina, this is serious," Rudy says in his deepvoiced, mock sabio tone. "You got to deal with it before worse things happen, and not just to you. Think of Letty. There's still time. Nestor's willing to work with you, to give you another chance."

"What is that fool still doing here? Doesn't he have to get back to his practice or ministry or whatever it is back in Miami?"

"The novia wants to do Disneyland, Universal Studios, and stuff like that while they're here."

"Don't they have exactly the same amusement parks in Florida?"

"Yeah, but they're kind of far from where they live." Rudy clears his throat. "So, here's the thing: Nestor's inviting that lawyer out for happy hour drinks at this place near the law office, and you and me could just kind of show up—"

"Forget it," I say.

"No, listen, hear me out, okay? So we show up like by coincidence, and you can tell the dude you were threatened or something like that. You say you testified under 'duress.' That means—"

"I know what *duress* means."

"Okay, so then the abogado can set up another hearing thing, and everything can get all straightened out. Nestor'll remove you from the website. No more virtual voodoo, *and,* get this, *and* he's going to do you the limpieza—no charge!" Rudy's voice swells with triumph, as if he's just negotiated a workable peace agreement in the Middle East.

My left eyelid jumps and that vein in my neck throbs—involuntary twitches I've come to associate with Rudy but had nearly forgotten during our separation, the way a person gradually suppresses memory of an impacted molar long after the tooth has been pulled. I remember Miguel's insight about Rudy's limitations and blindness and his advice about not hating him for this. Now I understand what Miguel was trying to get across: Resentment and hatred mean succumbing to the same ignorance I deplore. In the calmest voice I can muster, I tell Rudy, "No, I really don't want any part of this."

"Maybe I didn't explain it too good," Rudy says before drawing an audible breath, no doubt regrouping to renew his plea.

"I said no. Now, please stop calling me." I press the button to disconnect, wondering what the phone company charges to block calls from certain numbers. I'm half-tempted to holler out the window at Bobby, to ask him to bring his laptop over so I can check out that website. But then I decide that this is just bullshit. Or it isn't. If I look up the website, then—for me—it's no longer bullshit. It becomes something I will have to deal with. As to the emails I may or may not receive, there's the ever-handy delete key for handling those. If it comes to it, I can get the school to change my email address like they did for the typing teacher who started getting harassing messages from a parent whose kid she failed.

I roll my clenched shoulders, knead the back of my neck, wishing I had learned from Carlos how the chanting thing works or that I'd paid more attention when my father tried to teach me TM. But when the phone chimes yet again, a white-hot surge of anger replaces these thoughts. I snatch it up. "Why can't you leave me alone?"

"Marina?" It's Carlos's voice, sounding a bit shocked. "I'm sorry. I didn't know I was bothering you. I only called one other time."

"No, no," I tell him, thinking I also need to ask about caller identification for my home line when I call the phone company to block Rudy's calls. "*I'm* sorry. I didn't mean you. I thought it was...oh, never mind—another long and ridiculous story."

"I just wanted to know if we're still on for tomorrow night. I phoned a few days ago, but you never called me back, so I wasn't sure."

My mind goes blank, and I'm momentarily confused about the days of the week, but outside, a low-rider rumbles down the street, tooting a horn that plays "La Cucaracha." Of course, Kafka! "Yes, yes," I say quickly to make up for the delay. "I'm looking forward to it."

"Okay," he says. "I'll pick you up at seven-fifteen. The movie's at eight."

"Um, we should take my car," I suggest, peering out the window at the cloudless, nearly crystalline sky, "in case it rains."

"Not quite ready for the bike, are we?"

"No," I say, "not yet. And why don't you come by around six? I can fix supper for us at my house before the movie."

"Sounds good."

"Great!" I say with more enthusiasm than I really feel. Truth is: I offer the meal to make amends for betraying him in my conversation with Mrs. Jimenez. Now I'm wondering if this is the right time to broach the topic of naked cornfield jogging. I could say something like, *So you said you were a Buddhist, perhaps you also mentioned being a nudist...* or open more generally with, *Nudism and Buddhism, the words sound so similar....* Maybe, *Tell me about some of your recent experiences in cornfields....* Ultimately, there is no reasonable way to bring up the subject, so I let it go, lamely repeating, "That's great."

After we hang up, I steel myself to clear out that guest bedroom for Letty and Miguel, especially the closet, which has become my junk storage place. But just the thought of that jumble—those board games with missing pieces; winter coats and sweaters; shoeboxes containing greeting cards and letters; 'Buela Lupita's stern-looking portrait; mysterious vacuum cleaner attachments; the blender that just needs a new cord; and assorted regiftables: scented candles, soaps, cups with sayings like Teachers Always Have Class; and all the useless things I have forgotten that I own—just contemplating that mess creates more pressure on my shoulders, compressing my vertebrae, and straining my neck as if I have hefted the closet itself and all of its contents onto my back. What was it the Buddha said about possessions possessing us, freighting and anchoring us to the physical world, diminishing any hope of ascension into the spiritual plane?

Yawning, I sink into my bed and then clap my hands for Feo, who's dozing nearby. He springs up and trots to my side, his tail stump and ears quizzically erect. I lift him onto the bed, saying, "This is not an everyday thing, okay?" And I settle him so his head rests on the pillow next to mine, and throw an arm around his thick compact body. I know he's a dog and not my child, no substitute at all, but still I kiss his smooth head anyway and whisper, "*Sleep well, querido*," stroking the velvety fur covering his ears, gently fingering the smooth scar tissue where they were cropped until his rapid breathing slows, thickens into snoring.

Chapter Twenty

Feo yaps at the closed bedroom door and scratches at its base. Over this racket, voices resonate from the living room—*male* voices. Kiko and Reggie? Back so soon? I roll out of bed and stumble for the door.

I follow Feo, who's barking nonstop, to find Rudy on my couch and Nestor seated beside Loída on the love seat. Nestor has settled a black briefcase at his feet. The strangeness of such a thing in Nestor's possession arrests my gaze. Though the room is hot and smells of sweat, late afternoon sunshine filters feebly through the drawn curtains, imbuing the place with an orangey haze. Or maybe my eyes are sleep-blurred. I rub them with my fists and shake my head to dispel the grogginess. In case this is a dream, I squeeze my eyes shut and snap them open, but there they are. All three remain perched on my furniture, hushed now and looking at me in an ex-pectant way. When Feo cuts off the barking to snuffle shoes, Rudy says, "We just came by to see about that thing."

"What thing?" I ask, still not sure this isn't a dream. "How'd you get in here?"

Rudy sneezes. "Some kid—said his name was Robby or Bobby—he let us in. He's out in the back, working in your yard." He sneezes again and again. "What's that dog doing here? You know I'm allergic."

I stare without blinking. It's a full-sized, wingless Rudy on my couch this time, the tender-creature eyes narrowed in disbelief and accusation.

"Yeah, so," Nestor says before reaching down to flip the briefcase open, "Rudy told you about the website." He pulls out a small leather pouch that looks like a digital camera case. "I didn't want to have to do that. But you really didn't give me no choice." He sighs and unzips the pouch. "I can't lose my girls. And you have any idea what kind of child support they're asking?"

La novia, still wearing her prized brown jeans, beams at me as if we are old friends. "Buenas tardes." She gazes about my living room with an eager, even acquisitive look on her childlike face, though I can't imagine what she finds so compel-ling about the mismatched and lumpy furniture, the stained carpet, and coffee-table clutter. "¿Vive usted aqui?" she asks me. "¿Sola?"

"Más o menos," I say with a nod.

Flashing dimples, she sighs with longing. She glances at Nestor, who is occupied with the leather case. Slyly, Loída places a hand on her neck, curling her pinkie to rake its fingernail over and over the red patch of skin at the base of her throat. Nestor extracts a small machine from the pouch. It's a miniature tape recorder. From a compartment in the leather case, he plucks a teensy cassette that he inserts into the recorder. "You can just talk into this," he says. "Rudy told you about duress and all that, right?"

"Where's the lawyer?" I glance at the doorway to the kitchen, half-expecting the bald, red-eyed man to emerge, bearing bottled water from my fridge.

"Pinché puto wouldn't come with us," Nestor tells me bitterly, "wouldn't even have a drink with us. That pelón just laughed when I asked him to come out here."

"Uppity son of a bitch," Rudy adds, "won't lift a finger to help a brother out. Talk about a sellout." He throws a possessive arm over the top of my sofa and stretches his legs out before him, until Feo sidles over for another whiff. Then Rudy recoils, drawing his feet away from the dog.

"But I figure," Nestor says, "we can make the tape and enter it into evidence at the hearing in Miami. Don't need no fucking lawyer for that. Plus he charges three hundred dollars every time he opens his mouth to talk to me."

Now I know I must be awake. Granted, my dreams don't always make sense, but they're never *this* stupid. Part of me wants to kick them out, but another part identifies with Feo, whose swinish rooting seeks out every olfactory clue attached to their footwear, and I am curious, even fascinated, to see how this nuttiness will play out.

"Get that dog out of here!" Rudy plucks several tissues from the box on the bookcase, blows his nose into a handful of these.

Mouth open and still staring, I shake my head.

Nestor rewinds the cassette with a squeaky sound. "Just go ahead and give your name, say that you're a teacher, and tell about being under duress. Then you can say why the girls should live with me." The recorder clicks, and he presses a couple buttons, holding it a few inches from his mouth. "Testing—one, two, three. Testing." He reverses the tape and pushes in the play button: *Testing— one, two, three. Testing.*

At the sound of Nestor's recorded voice, Loída draws her hand from her neck to clap like a delighted child.

Satisfied, Nestor rewinds the tape. "Just press the buttons labeled play and record." He stands and then steps forward to hand me the thing. "You can say Daisy threatened you or something like that."

Shaking off sleepiness, I raise my hands, palms out, warding off the proffered tape recorder. "What on earth makes you think I'd be willing to do that for *you*?" I ask Nestor. "You've acted like a jerk to me ever since you got back to LA. You've harassed and harassed me, and now you've slandered me on your stupid website. You've even taken advantage of your so-called friend here by trying to use his family tragedy to get what you want. Just because he's foolish enough to believe you doesn't mean that I do."

Rudy wipes his streaming eyes, blows his nose again, edging away from Feo, who licks the toe of Rudy's gym shoe. "Marina, listen—"

"Maybe you don't understand," Nestor says, "You don't want the kind of trouble I can bring. You don't even *know* what I can do." He spreads his arms, gesturing at my untidy living room as if it represents the earthly goods that can be taken from me with a snap of his fingers. "The website's just the beginning."

"I don't *care* what you can do. What makes you think I don't have a conscience?" I ask, genuinely puzzled about this. "Why on earth would I perjure myself? To tear two little girls from their mother, so they can be raised by someone like *you*?"

"At first you said you would do it," he tells me. "That time I called, you said you would. You said you knew the deal."

I shake my head. "You took advantage, Nestor, and you know it. You show up when Letty's baby is *dying*, and you can't see what everyone else sees—a horrible, heartbreaking tragedy. No, what you see is an opportunity. You called when I was desperate, when I would have tried anything to help the baby. You talk about duress. *That* was duress. I didn't mean what I said then. You pressured me into saying it." I reach for the compact recorder. "Give me the thing. I'll gladly record *that* for you, if you want something about *duress*."

Nestor jerks the tape machine out of my grasp so forcefully that it flies out of his hand, a projectile launched smack into the wall where it cracks apart, the pieces bouncing to the floor. Excited, Feo leaps up and down, barking and snapping. The novia's huge brown eyes grow even huger and browner. With that once-discreet hand, she now claws openly at her neck. Rudy rises from the couch, approaches Nestor, who is blanched beneath his Miami tan and trembling now with rage. "Okay, man." Rudy draws an arm around Nestor's shoulder. "We tried. A'ight. We tried."

"*You.*" Nestor chokes this word out, pointing a long finger at me. "*You.*"

Loída is up now, too, smoothing the creases in her brown jeans. "¿Vamonos?"

"Claro," I say. "All of you go. Get out of my house." I crouch to get hold of Feo's collar. His thick, hot body struggles, writhing to get free, but I grip him firmly as they file out my front door, Rudy leading Nestor and murmuring into his ear. Loída is the last one out. She pivots to smile and wave to me, singing out a friendly "¡Adios!" from the doorstep. "¡Hasta luego!"

I wave back, echoing her words, though I'm pretty sure they won't be back. I shove the door shut, thinking, if we're all super-lucky, that luego won't ever come to pass.

That evening Bobby stays to share an egg-white spinach omelet and orange slices with me for supper. He tells me he's nearly done with the crosses. He plans to call Kiko and Reggie to help him set them upright in wet cement which he'll pour into holes near the cinder-block wall. Bobby asks me for phone numbers where he can reach them. After we eat, I print their phone numbers on a Post-it for him, and he invites me to take a look at the work. His face is so open and eager that there's no way I can refuse, though right now, it is not my deepest desire to see crosses in my backyard, or anywhere else for that matter. Feo and I trail him outside, and there they are, fully covered with colorful plastic-coated wire and leaning against the cinder-block wall. These are just as meticulously erected and exquisitely designed as the smaller versions he constructed with the kit, but even more astonishing for their size. I ask Bobby how tall they will stand.

"They're about six feet," he says, "so probably not as tall as the actual ones were supposed to have been at Calvary, but pretty tall, don't you think?"

"They're tall enough," I say. Though I had admired the design of the smaller crosses, I'm amazed by the patterning of colors on these large ones, especially on the central cross. The ebony wire gives way to deep sienna which becomes navy blue and then deep purple which yields to a dark magenta before flaming into crimson and gold at the tip. The side crosses mix colors, creating a marbled effect with black, white, and gray on one cross and a psychedelic mix-and-match of neon bright hues on the other. Never in my life have I seen *anything* like this trio of crosses. "But these are so beautiful," I tell Bobby. "I had no idea…"

Feo approaches one of the three crosses, sniffing appreciatively before hoisting a back leg. I clap my hands. "Hey, you! Get away from there!" He scoots off in surprise. I remember that supermarket shelf arrayed with Doggy-No at the grocery store, making a mental note to buy a can of the stuff. Then I glance about the backyard, assessing the mess Bobby's made during this project: leftover cans of that acrylic, bolts of wire, a pile of tarps on the table along with some tools and a few jars of nails, screws, and bolts.

Bobby, watching me, says, "Don't worry. I'll clean everything up before the unveiling."

"The unveiling?"

"Yeah, didn't I tell you? My mom's making carne asada, beans, and a ton of tortillas. My tía Connie's helping her. If you want, you can make the salad."

"I can make the salad?"

"Or bring ice cream, if you don't feel like fixing salad." He smiles at me. "I'm flexible."

"When is this unveiling?" I ask, dreading his answer.

"Tomorrow night. I thought I told you," he says. "It's going to be so cool. I'm going to ask Kiko and Reggie to rap and—"

"*Where* is it going to be?" Again, I brace myself for the obvious reply.

"Here, of course, that's where the sculpture is." Bobby looks at me as if I must be an ignoramus. "Here and at my mom's house. We're breaking the lock off that side gate, so people can come and go between the two yards."

"But I have a date tomorrow night," I tell him. "I've invited someone over for supper."

Bobby shrugs. "That's cool. There's going to be tons of food. My mom's already marinating like a whole side of beef."

"Are you sure you told me about all this?"

"I *think* I did." He squints, no doubt casting about in his memory. "Anyways, it's going to be really great. You'll get to see my girlfriend."

"You have a girlfriend?"

"Well, technically, not yet. It's, you know, the kind of thing where I like her, but she hasn't really noticed me too much. She's a little older than me." His cheeks flush, but his eyes shine; a smile tugs at the corners of his mouth. "Maybe you know her—Juanita Fuentes, from across the street."

I nearly do a double take when he names Henry's daughter, the pregnant fifteen-year-old. Instead, I smile hard, the Dalai's words practically ringing in my ears: *Do not think only of your own joy, but vow to save all beings from suffering.* Though incomprehensible when I first read this edict, now in the face of Bobby's openness and anticipation, nothing could possibly make more sense. My joy, or really, my comfort, is trivial compared to the change he has undergone in this handful of days, a transformation that every single one of us should be invested in preserving. How can I even consider adding to the disappointment about to confront him? I tell Bobby, "I can make a *huge* salad, and I'll pick up some ice cream on my way home from school." I call Feo and trudge back into the house, sidestepping a few dog turds and wondering when I will have time to clean up this overgrown, stinky patch before tomorrow night's pachanga.

"Strawberry," Bobby calls after me. "Make sure to get strawberry ice cream. That's my favorite!"

As soon as Feo and I step into the kitchen, the phone rings. I race to find the receiver in my bedroom, hoping it will be Carlos to postpone our date. But it's Miguel, calling to tell me Letty is being released tomorrow afternoon. He says he's packing their stuff and he plans to bring her directly to my place from the facility. After we hang up, I stick my head out the window. "Hey, Bobby! Can you come inside and help me with something?" If the two of us can clear out that closet and straighten up the guest room tonight, it will be one less rollo to deal with in the morning. I bang the window shut and yank the curtains closed, shutting out the heat and that unholy mess in my backyard.

In the morning, I swing by a Goodwill bin in a

nearby supermarket parking lot to part ways with that broken blender, unneeded winter apparel, and assorted gifts I will never re-give, except the candles, which I can use tonight for the unveiling. And I stop at a panaderia to buy pastries before heading to Starbucks for a carton of dark roast to go with my nondairy creamer and the industrialsized thermos of herbal tea I brewed at home for *Café con Leche*. As I roll my handy collapsible cart toward my classroom, I half expect to find Señor Gaspar Ahuaul with his twin sons awaiting me again, so evocative is the crunch of gravel under those hard plastic wheels. But, blessedly, there is no one in sight, and I set up the refreshment table, peacefully and privately.

The old paletero, the twins' grandfather, shows up late for the first round of *Café con Leche* during the Beginning Reading class. He shuffles into the classroom as the first skit, *La Cenicienta*, narrated by Maritza, is nearly over. Felipe Ahuaul crouches before Jovita Tómas in the role of stepsister number two, an elective mute in this rendition of the story, futilely trying to cram her foot into the imaginary glass slipper. Quietly, the white-haired man slips into a seat next to Elias's mother, who wears a bright red Chanel suit and enough perfume to sting my eyes. Maritza's mother and father, both active in the PTA and regular volunteers for field trips, sit in front-row desks. They were the first to arrive, and they contributed a bowl of fresh cherries and a homemade flan to the refreshment table. Behind them, Jeremias's father, a cholo in baggy khakis and flannel Pendleton shirt, leans forward in another desk, beholding the performance with rapt attention (or dozing—who can tell?) behind dark sunglasses. Another three or four parents I've never met file in after the aged paletero. One woman, in a blue-jean miniskirt and lacy black leggings, looks young enough to be a student herself. She could be an older sister, but sadly, she is more likely someone's mother.

When the skits are over, I make a short speech thanking our guests for coming and praising the students for their progress in the class. Then I invite everyone to enjoy the refreshments and socialize in the time that remains. Since it's a summer course, I merely assign a pass or fail grade to students, so I'm not too worried about being bombarded with questions about report cards, but I steel myself for the inevitable Cómo se porta mi hijo/hija en su clase inquiries. Usually, I answer these as pleasantly as possible, especially now at the end of the session. What good does it do to complain about a kid that I won't have to deal with for another month or so, if ever again? Besides, many of these parents avoid having much of a public presence due to residency status, so I figure they should be rewarded for taking this risk. "Bien, bien," I say, "se porta muy bien," and I rack my brain to find some reason for the parent to be proud of the kid in question. Sometimes that's the hard part.

With Maritza's parents, it's no problem complimenting her skill at language acquisition, her proficiency in reading. Her mother and father approach me first, and the three of us stand near my desk—at a strategic distance from the refreshment table—extolling her many virtues, while Maritza listens nearby, grinning and blushing. Elias's mother glances at her stylish wristwatch as she awaits an audience, so I wrap things up with Maritza's parents, who beeline for the refreshment table. Elias's mother nods, a stern look on her powdered and painted face, when she hears that her son behaves well. Elias, at her side, releases an exaggerated whoosh of relief, pretending to wipe sweat from his brow. She doesn't smile, though, until I praise the boy's beautiful shirts, and here we have a lively conversation about the importance of dressing well. Except for the mini-skirted young woman who rushes out after gobbling a wedge of flan, the other parents take their turns conferring with me, and Felipe's grandfather is the last of these.

He begins by apologizing for his son's absence, explaining that the boys' father had to work, but he goes on to say that things have been difficult at home. His son, he admits, is a hard man, still very young himself, and he can be unforgiving.

I'm surprised by his quiet eloquence that is at odds with the slack-jawed, vacant expression on his weatherworn face. "Lo siento," I say, with a sympathetic smile.

He bares gapped and stained teeth in a grin, and he assures me that his son will get over his anger and disappointment. Sooner or later, he will forgive the boys. "*Porque no tenemos nada mas.*" What else do we have, he then asks me, emphatically. *What else do we have in our lives but each other?*

Felipe trots over to join us, bearing a large pan dulce, its sugary crust scored like a turtle's shell, on a paper plate and a cup of coffee for his grandfather.

"¿Vale?" the old man asks his grandson, as though Felipe has been privy to our conversation, instead of retrieving refreshments.

The boy nods, saying, "My grandfather is right. He knows."

The old man raises a bony hand, ropy with thick veins, to ruffle the boy's straight black hair.

Chapter Twenty-One

After the second class's *Café con Leche*, I gather up the used paper plates, cups, and napkins, stowing these in a trash bag I brought from home. I lug this to the bins beyond the gymnasium, so Mr. Gustafson, the custodian, won't have to pick up after us. The paletero, who stayed for Armando's program in Advanced Reading, offered to help me with the mess, but I refused, thanking him. No doubt he had already sacrificed valuable paleta-selling time just by coming to both performances, so he didn't insist. I wrap up the leftover pan dulces and cherries to add to the refreshments I will buy for the unveiling pachanga.

At home, Bobby helps me put away the ice cream and salad ingredients, arguing that the time to clean house is *after*, not *before* guests arrive, and though he has a point, I'm not about to have people traipse through my pigsty of a house to the weedy, dog-shit jungle in my backyard without making at least some stab at order and cleanliness. When I return from walking Feo, I put him out back with Bobby so I can tidy up. I collect teacups, newspapers, and dog toys from the front room. I plump the furniture cushions and shake dust from the curtains. I'm just about to haul out my dust rags, wood polish, and the vacuum cleaner when footsteps sound on the front walk. Based on what he told me yesterday, it's early yet for Miguel to be bringing Letty over, but maybe due to the overcrowding, they released her sooner than he expected. I swing the door wide, poised to catch her in an embrace, all traces of hesitancy and reluctance wiped from my face.

My big smile fades fast. It's the unwanted trinity: Rudy, Nestor, and Loída—again! In loose shorts and mesh shirts, as though they are collecting funds for some ragtag soccer team, Rudy and Nestor stand, side by side, at the front door, flanked by Loída, still in her brown jeans and wearing a long-sleeved white turtleneck sweater with these as if it were the dead of winter, instead of late July. "What are you doing here?" I fold my arms over my chest and step into the doorway, planting myself to block any advance.

Rudy, looking foolishly tentative, even bashful despite his sharp-guy sunglasses, says, "Listen, Marina. We got a problem." He turns to Nestor, maybe expecting him to take over from there, but Nestor, his dark skin tinged greenish gray, clamps his jaw tightly, so Rudy continues, "Es qué, Nestor had a call."

"Hola," Loída chirps over Nestor's shoulder.

I nod, give her a curt smile. "He had a call. So what? Why do I care?"

"It's my oluwo," Nestor says at last. "He's the one who called. He saw the website, and he got all worked up with the stuff I put there about you."

"The virtual voodoo?" I say.

Rudy nods. "It's a mentoring thing."

"See," Nestor explains, "my oluwo is consecrated to Ifa after the asiento ceremony. He's at the second level. Dude's a real holy guy."

"Nestor's just a babalawo," Rudy says before peering over the top of his sunglasses at Nestor. "What level is that?"

"Fourth. I'm a babalawo at the fourth level." Nestor shows four fingers on his right hand. "I been consecrated to Ifa, but I ain't had the asiento ceremony yet. I was planning to have it this fall, but the dude got all pissed off with the website. Now he says he won't do the asiento, says the stuff on the website shows, well, that I'm not ready."

"Take it off the website, then," I tell him, conscious of the heat flooding into the house as I stand at the threshold with the door wide open. Already, my armpits prickle with perspiration. "I haven't even looked at the thing. You can tell him that." I step back to shut the door.

Rudy grabs the knob, jams his gym shoe in the space between the door and frame to hold it open. "It ain't that easy, Marina. Listen." He turns to Nestor again. "Go on, man. Tell her."

"So anyways my oluwo says, like, I done you a wrong, and I got to make up for it to restore balance." Nestor frowns in distaste, his thick moustache quivering, at the prospect of making things up to me. "You know what I mean, restitution, that kind of thing."

Loída fans her face with one hand and tugs at her turtleneck for some intermittent scratching. Sweat beads on her smooth brow. Wearing shorts, Nestor and Rudy have their hairy calves exposed to the occasional cool breeze; la pobrecita has got to be broiling in that turtleneck and those skintight brown jeans. "You've done Daisy more harm," I tell Nestor. "Make it up to her, and we'll be square."

"He's already got to do that," Rudy says in an eager tone. Clearly, he's anticipated this question and feels proud of himself for having an answer ready. "The dude busted him on that when he heard the whole story."

Nestor shakes his head, gives a wan smile. "You

can't lie to your oluwo."

"Exactly what are you doing to make things up to her?" This I want to know.

"I ain't going to fight her in court. I'm going to pay the child support like the judge says, and I'll visit the girls every chance I get. My oluwo says I got to show respect for my daughters by respecting their mother in my words and in my actions." Nestor recites this as if he's learned it by rote. No doubt he's had to repeat it a few times in order to meet his oluwo's satisfaction.

"Just tell the guy we're square, okay?" I pull at the knob, in spite of Rudy's foot. "Move your foot."

"No, wait, Marina," he says. "For once, just wait and listen."

"It's like this," Nestor tells me. "I got to actually make this restitution. I can't just *say* I did—that's a lie, see. I got to really do it."

I squint at this new repentant version of Nestor, taking in his pallid skin and sickly grimace. "This isn't some joke, is it?"

Nestor removes his sunglasses. His brown eyes, softened by contrition, gaze into mine. "It's not a joke. No way. Look, Marina, somehow I came off the path I was on. My life went all patas arriba, out of balance, and—shit, I don't know how else to say this—I just screwed up. Even the orishas make

mistakes, okay? The important thing is to correct
these. I need to get on the right path, so I can earn
asiento."

"What do you want from me?" I ask him.

"Let me do you some act of restitution. Let me
make this up to you. How about I do the limpieza
for you, no charge?"

"No offense, Nestor," I say, "to you or your
faith, but I don't really want any animals sacrificed
on the property. I'm pretty sure there's something
in the lease agreement forbidding this, so that's
out."

"Okay, forget the limpieza. I can do something
else. What do you need?"

"Well," I say, thinking of my neglected
backyard: a two-man job really with all those
brambles and weeds, that tormenting push-mower
provided by my landlord. "Does Rudy owe me restitution, too? Because I need the backyard cleaned
up this afternoon."

"We'll all help, even her." Rudy juts a thumb at
Loída.

I shake my head. "No way," I say. "She doesn't
owe me a thing. I do need some help in the house,
but I'll *pay* her." I speak to Loída in Spanish, offering her fifty dollars to help me get the house ready
for the party. But I make her agree to one condition: She cannot spend a penny of it on anyone but

herself. Grinning, she claps her hands again, readily agreeing to my terms.

I reach past Rudy and Nestor to clasp her elbow and reel her inside with me. "You two don't need to come indoors. Bobby's out back. He'll get you whatever tools you need, and he knows where the mower is. If you get thirsty, tell him. If you need the bathroom, go next door to his house. You have to be done with everything and out of my sight by five-thirty."

Nestor breathes deeply and smiles. "Thank you, Marina."

"Didn't I tell you? I told you she'd be cool," Rudy tells him, moving his foot away and releasing his hold on the door to pull off his sunglasses. He looks at me, those woodland-creature eyes more cartoonish than compelling, especially with his thick eyebrows waggling over them suggestively. "Marina, trust me. I ain't never going to forget this. I can make even *more* restitutions afterward. ¿Me entiendes?"

I kick the door, shutting out his foolish face, that insipid wink.

When Letty arrives before five, my little house nearly dazzles, it's so clean. After we changed into gym shorts and raggedy T-shirts, I offered Loída some calamine lotion for her neck. As we dusted,

polished, and vacuumed the front room and be-
drooms, not once did she disturb the chalky pink
blotches of the stuff she swabbed on her neck. In
the bathroom and kitchen, we mopped the floors;
scoured sinks, tub, and toilet; and squeaked water
spots and film from the mirrors and windows with
wadded newspaper and vinegar water. We flipped
over the mattress in the guest room and put laun-
dered sheets on the double bed. With soft rags and
orange oil, we even swiped the baseboards clean. I
arranged candles strategically throughout the house and lit joss sticks for that fresh sandalwood
scent in each room. All the while, Loída peppered
me with questions about living on my own in this
house, sometimes stroking the furniture and appliances, especially the television set, murmuring,
"Que suave." We've just finished with the house
and are ready to start in on the super-sized salad,
when Letty and Miguel bustle through the front
door with bundles of their stuff.

Letty thunks her duffel bag and backpack on the
floor. She rushes to embrace me, her eyes glistening. "You cleaned up for *me*."

"Well...," I say, glancing at Loída in the threshold to the kitchen, an avid but uncertain smile on
her face, "actually, there'll be some people coming
over."

Letty draws away, turns to Miguel. "I told you

she wouldn't forget. Look, Miguel, candles and everything." She flings her arms around me again. "I saw my dad's truck outside, too," she says, her voice warm on my hair. "You even got him to come. I knew you wouldn't forget the two-week anniversary of my baby's funeral."

Startled, I shoot Miguel a look, and he shrugs. "Of course not, m'ija," I say, "how could anyone forget. We're going to have a big supper, a memorial kind of thing..." I scramble to come up with more. "We're even having a blessing and some music—a real...celebration of his life," I say, wishing I could communicate all this telepathically and immediately to Bobby, Rudy, and Nestor, not to mention all the invited guests before Letty encounters a one of them. Luckily, Loída has no idea what's going on. She'll be the easiest to bring up to speed. "Why don't you rest in the guest room? You have time for a short nap before people start arriving." With a pang, I notice Letty's face is sallow and drawn. Dark smudges underscore her large eyes.

"You know what? That sounds really good. I *am* tired. I couldn't sleep at all in that place. Want to lie down with me?" she asks Miguel.

But I say, "No, m'ija, Miguel needs to help with the preparations."

Once she's ensconced in the guest room with

their belongings, I snatch Miguel's shirt front, pull him into the kitchen, and hand him the telephone. "Call up your mother, your friends, and Letty's friends," I whisper at him. "Tell them to get over here for this pachanga and fast." I glance at the clock over the refrigerator. "They've only got an hour." I turn to Loída, tearing lettuce into an enormous wooden bowl in the sink, and I tell her to make an even bigger salad. Better yet, she should make two, and I haul out a huge ceramic bowl from under the sink. Then I dash outside to explain the situation to Bobby and the others.

Feo crawls out from the shade under the table to greet me, squirming with glee. I pat him obligingly and summon the guys over to the cinder-block wall to clue them in without Letty hearing us from the guest room. Bobby, puzzled at first, comes to like the idea of a memorial for Letty's baby. He even offers to dedicate the crosses to little Rudy. And Nestor and Rudy, sweaty and dusty, have no choice but to consent to clean up and stay for the memorial. "They can shower at your house," I tell Bobby. "Right?" He nods, and I ask Nestor to perform some Santería memorial blessing that does not involve animal sacrifice. By the time everything is all clear, Kiko and Reggie emerge through the kitchen door into the yard. Apparently they've reconciled. They're laughing and talking together as they approach. Of course, I have to go through the explanation all over again. Then I say, "Bobby, don't forget to go next door and tell your mom and Connie what's up. I've got to go in and call Della and Xochi, make sure they come."

"They're already here," Kiko tells me. "Reggie came by the house after work. My moms drove us over and we stopped to pick up Xochi at the cable company on the way here."

Sure enough my two sisters are in the kitchen, Della slicing yellow bell peppers while Xochi, in a tight Lycra glove of a red dress, crouches, rooting around in the pots and pans cupboard. Loída's chopping celery while Miguel sits at the table making hushed phone calls to numbers in the tiny spiral-bound tablet he uses as a phone-book. Xochi pulls out my Dutch oven, saying, "Somebody better make some rice, just in case there's not enough food."

"Go for it," I say, knowing full well that by "somebody," my kid sister means somebody other than herself, but before she can clarify this, I head for the bathroom to shower and get ready for the unveiling pachanga and my date.

It's just before six o'clock, and a few people have already arrived. The first is Rosaura, who steps into my living room wearing a zebra-print shift for the occasion, instead of the fake leopard coat, and curling her upper lip in distaste as she glances about. Next to arrive is Miguel's sponsor, a portly middle-aged white guy in a short-sleeved sport shirt, complete with pocket protector and pens, and a tie. A few cristianos show up next, their big-haired women bearing six-packs of canned soda and king-sized bags of potato chips and pretzels. Then Letty steps out of the guest room, her hair brushed and glossy, but her face still wan, pinched looking. Xochi intercepts her and leads her to the bathroom, and when Letty reappears again, her lips are ablaze with tropical incandescence, and she looks, if not exactly happy, at least more vivid.

At six exactly, two somber thumps sound on the front door. From the peephole, I spy Carlos, removing his helmet and then patting down his hair. He's wearing a crisp turquoise guayabera under his windbreaker with black slacks. Though distorted by the small curved circle of glass, his dark face looks tentative, even a little wary. He leans to see his reflection in the curtained side window, practices a smile, and scrapes at a tooth with his fingernail. I wait a few seconds and then open the door to slip outside, shutting it behind me. "Here's the thing," I say, before I launch into yet another explanation of the situation with Letty, the memorial celebration, and the unveiling pachanga.

"Wow," he says, eyebrows raised toward his widow's peak. "You've got a lot going on. You sure you still want to go to the movie?"

I shrug. "Let's see how it goes. You're going to stay, right?" I ask, worried he will leave if he thinks the date is off. "You'll eat with us, won't you, and see the unveiling?"

"Sure," he says. "I wouldn't miss it. And I understand if we can't work in Kafka, too. It's playing again tomorrow night. We can do a rain check."

On impulse, I throw my arms around him and kiss him wetly on the mouth. A thrill sparks in my stomach, coursing up into a ticklish feeling at the base of my throat when we embrace. The heat of his body, the scent of hair oil combined with exhaust from his bike and his own slightly salty smell wash over me in a powerful wave. I almost stagger with the force of it.

"Nice," he says when my head clears and I pull away to rub at the lipstick smearing his mouth.

"Don't mention it." I cup his warm hand in mine to lead him inside. "Ready?"

Nestor and Rudy had cleared the weeds, bumpy grapefruits, and dog shit completely out of the backyard. They'd mowed the crabgrass and foxtails, before raking away the mess. I'd about forgotten how pleasant and cool this shady dell can be when it's been tended. Now, as I whiff the aroma of mown grass and citric fragrance, I remember that this pretty yard was the main reason I decided to lease the house. The sun dissolves into the tree line, pinkening the sky, and my small backyard fills with people—cristianos, neighbors, family, and friends. Their voices combine in a cacophony of English and Spanish from which I can only catch an occasional phrase here and there.

Bobby, Kiko, and Reggie have lugged out every chair from both Carlotta's house and mine to seat the guests, including a stack of folding chairs from Carlotta's garage. Henry Fuentes and his family make up a good number of the guests. Bobby and Juanita, her long, auburn braid snaking down her plump back, sit cross-legged on an army blanket under my diseased grapefruit tree, deep in a whispered conversation that makes them oblivious to the others. After a few hard looks at Carlos, Rudy manages to get over himself, and now he talks quietly with Letty, both seated on folding chairs with paper plates balanced on their knees. Miguel and his sponsor chat with Connie, whose pumpkin face is frozen with tension, she is so excruciatingly sober. All of them sip iced tea from red Solo Cups.

When Bobby asked me earlier about beverages, and overhearing this, Kiko offered to buy a keg of beer (with my money, of course), I said, "Absolutely not!" A party to unveil crosses constructed by a thirteen-year-old boy and attended by his friends, plus a whole load of recovering cristiano addicts, is no place for beer. I could just imagine the trouble that would create, and then the headlines when things go awry: *Minors Served Beer at Middle-School Teacher's House.* No doubt that Reggie and Kiko are slipping out to the tool shed next door to smoke mota every chance they get, but no one is drinking beer or firing up as much as a Marlboro Light on these premises.

Carlotta, her bruises faded dull brown and wearing aviator-style sunglasses to cover her damaged eye, smiles at me and nods, as if to say, *Isn't this something?* Earlier she'd told me that Connie, too, had been hired at Vallarta, and she's agreed to let her sister stay with her as long as she doesn't drink. Carlotta and Loída now chatter like a pair of chipmunks in Spanish, with Rosaura nearby, contributing the occasional hilarious remark that sends all three into fits of laughter. Who knew that Rosaura is funny in Spanish? Kiko and Reggie practice their rap in the side yard, and from what I can hear, it is beyond awful. Xochi turns her vamping smile on Henry Fuentes while Imelda glowers at his side. Carlos sits with me on the doorstep, Feo at my feet, his loose, moist jowls nesting on my toes. Carrying an empty pitcher, Della goes for more iced tea. When we move apart so she can pass us to get into the kitchen, I ask about Duffy, and my sister shakes her head, puts a finger to her lips.

"Oh, I've been meaning to mention this," Carlos says when the screen door slaps shut behind my sister. He lifts a plastic fork, pointing with it for emphasis. "Had you heard the news about your friend?"

"What news?" I ask. "What friend?"

"The Dalai Lama," he says. "Did you hear he's given up?"

"*What?*" I picture the smiling, bespectacled monk shedding his saffron-colored robes to don cargo shorts and a polo shirt. Then I imagine him leaving Tibet, hopping on a plane for... Rio, maybe, or Las Vegas...

"Yeah, it happened like a month ago, but I just found out. I looked him up online, and there's a bunch of articles. You should check it out. Apparently, he's given up trying to get autonomy for Tibet from China."

"Oh, *that*," I say, remembering an article I read about this in the *Los Angeles Times*. In my mind's eye, I redress the Dalai in his robes, swiftly reinstall him in Tibet. "I did read about that. But it's just to get the Tibetan people to do more, to shoulder their part of negotiations. How did he put it?

'It's up to them to take the dialogue further.' One person can't do everything for everyone."

"Oh, *really*?" Carlos says, looking at me in a pointed way. When he faces me directly, the openness of his expression and the intelligence in his dark eyes strike me as compelling, even irresistible in a way. Why, he's attractive when he looks at me like this. I glance at Rudy, deep in conversation with Letty, and I lean toward Carlos as if drawn again by his body heat. I close my eyes and—

Della bangs open the back door, shouting, "Marina, you got a phone call."

"Excuse me," I tell Carlos, before rising to step into the kitchen, where Della hands me the receiver. "It's some guy," she says in an exaggerated stage whisper.

Covering the mouthpiece, I take the phone into my bedroom and shut the door before saying, "Hello?"

"Hi, Marina. It's Art, Art Ortiz, and I was just wondering if you might be free to have dinner with me tomorrow night."

"Tomorrow night?" My heart squeezes and then drums in my ears. My face grows hot, and I lower myself to sit on the bed. "But that's not even twenty-four hours away. You're supposed to ask people out at least a few days ahead of time."

"I just, well, I'm really busy."

"I'm kind of busy, too," I tell him, thinking about the postponed date with Kafka. "I have plans for tomorrow night."

"Okay," he says. "I see. Fair enough. Sorry to have bothered you."

I grip the phone with both hands and quickly say, "*Next week*, though, I'm pretty free. We could have lunch again on your afternoon off."

"It's Wednesday," he says. "My free afternoon is Wednesday. I'd love to have lunch with you."

The sound of his voice conjures the memory his long warm body, curved against mine, silent and still as we napped together. Had I ever slept so well before or after that afternoon? "Lunch...and maybe we could go to your place afterward for a nap?"

"That would really be great, Marina, but let's not eat at the cafeteria. I know a better place, a Thai restaurant near my apartment." He gives me directions, and we agree on a time. I tell him that I have some guests over, so we say good-bye.

After hanging up, I step to the window, lift it open, and lean out. Voices and laughter spill in with the cool evening air. Rudy's calling for everyone to gather around for Nestor's blessing and the unveiling of the crosses. Earlier Nestor explained to me that since he didn't have his sacred objects with him, all he would be able to do is issue something like a spiritual toastmaster speech.

I should hurry back out to be present for his words memorializing baby Rudy and to witness the unveiling of Bobby's crosses. Someone is sure to wander in to find me. But for now, I linger at the window. A soft, damp breeze buffets my face like a diaphanous veil spun of mist. People or peace, Henry Fuentes said, suggesting that we have to choose. In this moment, I make up my mind to try for both, but if that's not possible, for me, this is not much of a choice at all. There's really only one option, and I will choose it every time. Rustling sounds and then voices hush. In the lull, Nestor's blessing rings out. Using his deep and resonant babalawo voice, he names the orishas, praising each one before beseeching them to fill our lives always with strong spirits and with hope.

Reading Group Guide Questions

1. The epigraph, a quote from Yiyun Li, asserts that the weak-minded choose to hate as it is the least painful thing to do, and Miguel urges Marina to avoid hatred because it is a corrosive emotion that will destroy her from within. How does Marina resist hatred of others and what does this cost or benefit her?

2. In the beginning of the novel, Marina assumes the role of a mediator, translating between Letty and Miguel and the medical establishment they must deal with during their infant son's illness. She also translates the high level of diction in the novel her middle-school students are reading. How else does Marina perform the task of mediating or translating between parties who do not understand one another?

3. Over the course of the novel, Marina invokes and attempts to adhere to the words and teachings of the Buddha, the Dalai Lama, Mahatma Gandhi, and Nelson Mandela. How does reliance on male spiritual guidance complicate Marina's journey to discover and improve her-

self as an independent and self-sufficient woman?

4. Though skeptical of mantras, Marina adopts the
phrase "by force of generosity" to remind herself to act compassionately toward others, even
those who betray her. How does this benevo-
lence complicate her interactions with others
and compromise the generosity and compassion
which she might bestow upon herself?

5. In the novel, Marina, Connie, and Loída are portrayed as single women who have become involved with married men with potentially harmful
consequences to themselves and to the wives of
their lovers. Since Rudy's wife has died and Marina is detaching herself from him, she is best positioned to understand such consequences. As such,
what is her responsibility in mitigating these for
the other two women? And how does this responsibility inform her actions in the novel?

6. When Marina goes out to eat with Carlos, an elderly man tells her, "You are good with the little
boys," and Carlos, after hearing of her living
arrangements, agrees with this. But Della sees
her sister's help to Kiko as enabling behavior.
How is this gift for nurturing young males also a
curse that prevents Kiko, Reggie, and even Rudy from taking responsibility and maturing into
self-reliant men?

7. The novel depicts two sets of close male friendships—or "bromances," as Xochi would say—between Kiko and Reggie and Rudy and Nestor. What do these relationships offer these men? How are they both nurturing and stultifying to these characters?

8. The teachings of the Dalai Lama encourage Marina to regard those who mistreat her as spiritual guides. In what ways are characters like Rudy, Nestor, Connie, and even Rosaura illuminating to Marina as she struggles to find spirituality?

9. Clearly, Marina will soon be confronted with a choice between Carlos, an artist and Buddhist, and Arturo Ortiz, a doctor and atheist. Given what is known about these characters and about Marina, who is she likely to choose and why will she choose him? Which of the two men is more likely to make a satisfying partner for Marina and why?

10. Marina's neighbor Henry Fuentes says that a person can have people or peace, suggesting these are mutually exclusive, and the elderly paletero asks, "What else do we have but each other?" Marina determines to have both people and peace in her life. What are her chances for finding the balance in life that will enable her to enjoy involvement with others and peace of mind? And how can she manage that?

Acknowledgments

This book could not have been written without the spark of idea and pragmatic advice given to me by my colleague, mentor, and friend, Mark Jarman. I also owe profound thanks to my trusty peer readers: Beth Bachmann, Joy Castro, Lauren Cobb, Teresa Dovalpage, Kathryn Locey, Meredith Grener-Gray, Lynn Pruett, Justin Quarry, and the resplendent Heather Sellers. These astute readers and generous writers gave their time to read, in some cases, many drafts, and their insights enabled me to see the work with greater clarity than I ever could have managed on my own. And I am deeply grateful for the unflagging support and practical help from my mentor and great friend, Judith Ortiz Cofer. Gracias también to my colleagues and friends: Bryn Chancellor, Sara Corbitt, Kate Daniels, Tony Earley, Blas Falconer, Teresa Goddu, Peter Guralnick, Janis May, William Luis, Karen McElmurray, Alex Moody, Margaret Quigley, Nancy Reisman, Sandy Solomon, and Wade Ostrowski. Thanks, too, to my agent Lauren Abramo and to Selina McLemore, a remarkable editor who has invested herself personally and professionally in this work.

The author Harry Crews says this about writers: "If you have a family, someone will have a problem with what you do." Of course, he is right, but I am fortunate in belonging to the kind of family that sees such problems as opportunities to communicate, clarify, and redefine ourselves in relationship to one another. Plus, my family has been patient beyond belief with my astonishingly slow learning curve in figuring out which stories are mine to tell and which are not. For that, I am ever indebted to my sisters, Debra, Frances, and Sylvia; my brother, Kenneth López; my father, Espiridion López; as well as to my children, Marie and Nick, and my grandchildren, Jasmine, Nick, and Anthony. By association, my husband's family also has reason to have a problem with what I do, but these contrary folks—Jane, Mindy, Andy, Lynne, Becky, Larry, Priscilla, Bob, and all their children—number among my most appreciated supporters, and I am immensely grateful to them for their goodwill.

And for my husband, Louis Siegel, simply this: *What would I do without you?*

About the Author

edited a collection of essays titled *An Angle of Vision: Women Writers on their Poor and Working-Class Roots* (University of Michigan Press, 2009). Currently, she lives in Nashville, Tennessee, with her husband, Louis Siegel.

Prior to returning to graduate school for a doctoral degree, Lorraine López taught middle school in Pacoima, California, where she instructed ESOL classes with an emphasis on piñata-making, story-boards, and skits. She now teaches in the Masters of Fine Arts Program at Vanderbilt University in Nashville, and she is an associate editor of the *Afro-Hispanic Review*. Her fiction has appeared in *Prairie Schooner, Voices of Mexico, CrazyHorse, Image, Cimarron Review, Alaska Quarterly Review, StoryQuarterly/Narrative Magazine*, and *Latino Boom*. Her short-story collection *Soy la Avon Lady and Other Stories* (Curbstone Press, 2002) won the inaugural Miguel Marmól prize for ficti-on. Her second book, *Call Me Henri* (Curbstone Press, 2006), was awarded the Paterson Prize for Young Adult Literature, and her novel *The Gifted Gabaldón Sisters* (Grand Central Press, 2008) was a Borders/Las Comadres Selection for the month of November. López's short-story collection *Homicide Survivors Picnic and Other Stories* (BkMk Press, 2009) was a Finalist for the PEN/Faulkner Prize in Fiction in 2010. Most recently, she has edited a collection of essays titled *An Angle of Vision: Women Writers on Their Poor or Working-Class Roots* (University of Michigan Press, 2009). Currently, she lives in Nashville, Tennessee, with her husband, Louis Siegel.

Also by Lorraine López

"Enchanting debut." —*Good Housekeeping*

"Reminiscent of the novels of Cristina Garcia and Sandra Cisneros, López's book presents a lively, loving Latino family...Highly recommended for public library collections." —*Library Journal*

"López's engaging novel chronicles how four sisters' lives are shaped by the loss of their mother and their belief that they were granted magical abilities." —*Publishers Weekly*

"*The Gifted Gabaldón Sisters* is a laugh-aloud funny and lay-your-head-down-and-cry lyrical tour of melded cultures and traditions, of blended tongues, and the sites of the inevitable clashes between worlds; it is a window into the strange conjunctions that exist as parallel universes in today's multicultural America. The result is wisdom and delight, delight and wisdom."

—Judith Ortiz Cofer, author of *Call Me Maria*

If you enjoyed *The Realm of Hungry Spirits*, then you're sure to love these emotional family dramas as well—

Now available from Grand Central Publishing

"Lyrical, poignant, and smart, as compassionate and hopeful as it is heartbreaking...a novel you will never forget."

—*New York Times* bestselling author Jenna Blum

"*Tell Me Something True* is a bittersweet journey about coming to understand and forgive the indiscretions of one's parents through the simple act of living one's life."

—*Miami Herald*

Look for future books from Leila Cobo.

"An intricately woven tale of love and memory from a deeply talented writer."

—*Booklist*